THE WEDDING DUEL

THE WEDDING DUEL

KAREN L. KING

ZEBRA BOOKS
Kensington Publishing Corp.

To my husband, Mike, who always believed in the dream.

ZEBRA BOOKS are published by

Kensington Publishing Corp.
850 Third Avenue
New York, NY 10022

ISBN: 0-7394-2725-3

Printed in the United States of America

ONE

London, December 1814

The carriage rattled along the cobblestones. The steady clop-clop of the horses and the sway of the vehicle made sleep impossible. Keene Whitmore Davies lifted the shade and a shard of sharply angled morning sunlight pierced the dark interior.

This pure light should have been reserved for saints. He dropped the shade. A saint he was not.

" 'Tis a bright morning," said his companion John.

Keene smiled grimly. "Good morning for killing fools."

John shifted nervously.

Poor boy, he happened to be in the wrong place at the wrong time, and out of misguided nobleness had offered to stand second. "Were you able to find pistols for me?"

"Yes, yes. Look at these. The workmanship is very fine." John opened the walnut box and held it out for Keene to inspect the contents.

Keene gave the matched set of pearl-inlaid pistols resting in a red velvet nest a cursory glance. "They'll do."

John ran a finger over the guns. "Perhaps you should not continue this."

Keene arched an eyebrow.

"I mean for your father's sake. He has just lost your brother.

He should be heartbroken to lose both his sons in so short a space."

Keene didn't bother to correct John. His father would suffer his loss gladly. His younger brother's death had devastated both of them.

John shifted in his seat. "I'm sure Lord Wedmont will extend his apologies for the insult."

"I shall not accept his apologies."

"P-perhaps your brother's loss has shaken your normal good civility."

"I assure you, I'm not often accused of good civility."

"As you are well aware of your humors, you do not often find offense in others' comments."

"Give over, John. I know your duty is to talk me out of my intentions, but don't waste your breath."

"You are not known to demand satisfaction, sir. You are more known to laugh and find truth in others' insults."

Keene folded his arms across his chest and gazed at his nervous companion. "Dawn is too ungodly an hour to be about. I daresay I often refrain from demanding settlement for want of rising so early in the morning."

John squirmed in his seat.

He didn't understand that the insult offered by Victor Wedmont had happened many months ago. Approximately nine to be exact. There was no way to repair the ruin of their best friend George's marriage with a simple apology.

Victor and George had both been part of a group of friends that had ties back to Keene's school days at Eton. They had all been close to each other. Only now was it obvious how much in each other's pockets they had been.

"Are you afraid of blood?" asked Keene.

John threw back his shoulders. "Of course not."

"Good, because I expect there shall be some."

An odd expression crossed John's face. "Perhaps." He looked down at the box that held the matched set of dueling pistols.

Keene watched his companion. "Are they Mantons?" Weapons made by the London gun maker were renowned for their accuracy.

"No. They are not. Legend has it they are from Spain."

Keene frowned.

John opened the box again. "They are quite beautiful. See the Spanish tooling on the grip? Quite a bargain. Only forty guineas for the pair."

"Quite," echoed Keene dryly. "Let us hope that a pistol worth twenty guineas is as capable of wounding as one worth twice as much."

Again that odd look flitted across John's face. Keene made a mental note to have his other second, the one in charge of fetching the surgeon, pack the pistols in case John had any ideas of using too little powder.

John cracked his knuckles and shifted in his seat. The case slid on his lap, and he grabbed it. Keene flicked his gaze over his second. Odd that John was so nervous, when Keene was the one on the way to fight.

"They are really quite beautiful, are they not?"

Keene closed his eyes. He didn't want John's nervousness to soften the icy rage that propelled him toward this meeting.

"Bewitched, they say."

Keene cracked one eye open.

"I say, there is a legend that goes with them."

"Yes, they are from Spain."

John twitched. "There is a legend that, regardless who stands or falls, the real winner shall be married to a fine woman and enjoy marital bliss."

Keene closed his eye. "A rare state."

John mumbled, "I know you have maintained these many years that you shall never take a wife as you wanted Richard to be your heir."

"Richard is dead."

"Yes, I know."

Keene grimaced. He knew John knew. The two had been

fast friends. John had been his brother's friend more than his own. Sometimes Keene needed to remind himself that his lighthearted fair brother was gone, snatched away in the prime of his life by a fever. His brother had epitomized all that was good in their mother, and like her had found his way far too early into the arms of an eternal Morpheus.

The carriage drew to a halt. Keene swung the door open. The rare sunny morning cast long shadows through the lines of trees. Three other carriages were drawn up beside the lane. His opponent stood apart from a cluster of men.

Rage sifted through Keene. He stared at Victor. The man raised his arm in a half salute, his exposed linens showing that he was prepared to go through with the duel. Keene unbuttoned his coat and waistcoat. The cluster of men approached him.

"Sir, Lord Wedmont extends his most gracious apology. He withdraws any insult he may have spoken and claims he meant not the words as they sounded, but begs your leave to explain his true meaning."

Keene stared through the man acting as Victor's second.

Another held up a slip of paper and began reading, "Lord Wedmont also extends his apologies for any past action of his that might have brought offense to you, sir. He swears that his actions were never intended to offer any harm to anyone, least of all you, a man he greatly respects. He swears his behavior has been directed by a foolish heart." The speaker frowned.

To be sure, it was an odd apology for an insult.

The four seconds clustered around him waiting for his acceptance of the apology, to declare that he was satisfied. He wasn't.

He peeled back his jacket and waistcoat. The cool December air blew through the fine linen of his shirt.

Oddly, the wording of the written apology fueled his icy rage. Victor gave him a wry smile as his seconds shook their heads. Keene crossed the lawn in long strides.

"Should you wish to settle this with fists, sir?" asked Victor.

"I shall not draw enough blood with my fist."

Victor blanched.

Keene glanced back to make sure the others remained out of hearing range. "How could you have done it? You've ruined her life. George is ready to blow his brains out."

"If I could have, I should have married her, rather than let George have her."

Rage pulsed through Keene's system. "Why didn't you?"

Victor's voice was low. "Why didn't *you?*"

Keene wanted to walk away, return home and pretend it was all a bad dream. "I had no plans for marriage."

Victor's face paled. He looked haunted. "I would have married her. I thought I loved her—"

"Everyone loves her." Keene struggled against the surge of compassion that threatened to dampen his rage. If Victor had truly loved her, he would have married her.

"I thought I loved her before I knew she would fall into my bed with so little persuasion." Victor eyed him speculatively. "Is that why you challenged me?"

"I fight for George's honor." Keene stumbled over the words he intended to deliver with his usual aplomb.

"It is not my blood you want," said Victor softly.

Keene watched the man run a shaky hand through his artfully disordered brown locks. It wouldn't be a fair fight if Victor couldn't hold his hand steady to fire the pistol. Honor tore Keene in a thousand ways. What loyalty did he owe Victor? George? George's wife, Amelia?

"I should do it again. If George has no care for his wife, I shall be pleased to take her into my keeping. She should be happy in a cottage as long as she had my service."

Cold fury poured through Keene. "You, sir, are no gentleman. She is a lady."

"That, she is not. I have reason to know. Besides, 'tis not so uncommon a situation. At least the child is a girl; she shall not be George's heir."

In that moment Keene hated Victor. There was no dealing with the man. Keene heeled about and crossed the field to the cluster of men where he could make sure the pistols were properly loaded and primed.

"A shame you fight this battle with me, Davies. You should have picked an opponent less willing to shed your blood."

Keene watched the pistols being loaded; a single shot would have to be enough to quench his thirst. Amelia didn't deserve to be belittled for her weakness or the failure of her chaperons. George didn't deserve the unhappiness of a wife unfaithful to him before marriage. Life would not be so hellish for the offspring if men did not ruin good women and then leave them to make the best of it in a world that did not look kindly on impure gentlewomen and their by-blows.

They paced out their ten steps and turned.

"Stand and deliver."

Keene raised his gun, taking careful aim. He did not wish to miss. At the same time, his finger refused to tighten on the trigger. Victor's gun pointed straight at his heart. The burst came from Victor's pistol, and Keene held his involuntary flinch to a mere flicker of his eyelids. He waited for the burn of a bullet . . . and waited.

"Deliver, sir," said one of the seconds.

Victor stood his ground as he lowered his gun. How was it the bullet missed? Victor was nearly as good a shot as he was. Keene cursed his patient aim. He couldn't kill him. Victor's words echoed in his head. *It is not my blood you want.* He lowered the nose of the pistol to aim at his opponent's left thigh. He would draw blood and let it fill Victor's top boot.

The shot rang out in the cool bright morning. Smoke wafted away from the barrel of his pistol as Victor fell to the ground, his hand clasped on his right shoulder over the blossoming red stain.

"I daresay you have ruined my linens, sir," Victor said.

"The yellow offends me. You need new."

"I won't stay away from her."

Keene strode toward the fallen man. All his precautions

would be in vain if Victor spoke Amelia's name out loud when the other men could hear. "Shut your mouth."

"I won't. A moment of her pleasure is worth a thousand wounds."

"Next time I shall see you to hell."

"You cannot. You cannot shoot a man who has missed you. Damn, Davies, I had every intention of hitting you."

Keene whirled around to face his seconds. "Load the pistols again."

John stumbled out to him, bearing powder and balls. "You do not mean to fight again?"

"Load them."

John complied, while Victor lay bleeding on the ground.

"I must regretfully inform you that I cannot give you satisfaction at the present," said Victor.

"Quiet." Keene took the first pistol.

"Dear God, Keene, no," whispered Victor. "Please no."

Standing above Victor, Keene raised the gun.

The report sounded loud to his ears. Victor whimpered. Keene took as much satisfaction from that as anything. Perhaps Victor should feel enough humiliation from that sound as George felt upon learning his wife bore another's man's child.

The shot was high and to the left. A spray of leaves fell from the tree he wounded. He took the second pistol from John's hand and aimed once again for the trunk. The shot didn't hit the trunk, nor did any leaves pepper down.

"These are the most untrue weapons I have ever fired."

"Are they?" replied John.

Keene faced the young man. "Did you know?"

John replaced the pistols in their case. "Know what?"

"Know that the pistols are inaccurate?"

"How should I know that?"

It had been Keene's experience that John evaded questions more than he answered them. "I ought to call you out."

John bit his lip, but managed to meet his gaze squarely.

Keene stalked toward his carriage. "Tell the damn surgeon

to attend him." He paused before ascending the step. "John, return those defective weapons to the place you bought them. I have no wish to keep them."

John bowed.

Keene allowed the grin that threatened to overtake him to break only when he had shut the carriage door. The little milksop John had bested him. Legends of a winner's wedded bliss, indeed. The only curse of those guns was that a man couldn't hit an elephant at six paces. Unless of course he aimed to miss, which was why a shot intended for Victor's thigh had hit him in the opposite shoulder.

Keene's grin died as he directed his coachman to George's house and the enormity of what he'd just done and why hit him.

Three weeks later he received a summons from his father. The trip home took a day and a half. After an impassive greeting, the butler led Keene to his father's library.

The old man sat by the fire, his face half in shadows. Keene crossed the room, splashed a healthy dose of brandy in a glass and sat down in the Morocco leather chair opposite Lord Whitley, the seventh baron in a straight line to hold the title.

Keene took a sip of his brandy and told himself to remain civil, no matter the provocation. The silence did not bode well for a prodigal son welcome. But then, he had never been the favored son. Keene realized he'd clenched his empty hand into a fist. He splayed his fingers out and forced himself to relax. "You wished to see me?"

"Word has reached me that you tried to kill a man."

No point in mentioning that his opponent had also tried to kill him. "I did not succeed."

"Ever you are a wild profligate. Now you are shooting men."

"Only one. I was provoked." Keene took a healthy swallow of his brandy. What would it be now? Would the old man demand he move out of the town house now that Richard was no longer there?

"I could have you thrown in jail for less."

"I'm sure many would find throwing your eldest son and heir into prison an interesting move."

Lord Whitley leaned forward. The firelight caught his florid complexion. His light eyebrows furrowed together. He shook a sausagelike finger at Keene. "You are a disgrace to my name, with your gaming and whores."

"Only one, and I let her go." He'd had to. With only his winnings from the gambling tables to support him, he couldn't afford to keep his high-flier in the style she deserved. But then, he preferred discreet liaisons with married women. In the long run they cost less.

"I cannot break the entail, but only the old manor house and ten acres are assigned to it. The rest I have willed to your cousin Sophie Farthing."

The house in London, the farms that supported the estate, still wouldn't be his. Keene gulped a drink of his brandy. Damn, now the glass was dry. It wasn't that he wanted the money. He was content with very little. Maintaining appearances was another thing. When one was the presumed heir to a rich baronial estate, others expected more.

As a gentleman, trade was not an option, not that he would know how to make a living working. The only thing he cared a fig about was his father's right to sit in the House of Lords, an honor Lord Whitley didn't bother to exercise, but Keene would be a sitting member of Parliament when his time came.

That and the house in London, which had been his home these last ten years, were the only important things. Otherwise he should have left to seek his destiny far away from here.

"Not much has changed then," commented Keene mildly. Lord Whitley had intended the bulk of his estate to go to Richard.

"Everything has changed. I spoke with my solicitor. He says if you are exiled I might be able to break the entail."

As far as Keene knew there were no male relatives in line to inherit. "But then the barony should pass into oblivion. Or had you a mind to sell the title?" Or it could revert to the crown to be bestowed on whoever the prince regent fancied. A scary thought at best.

"I had in mind that Sophie carries my blood, albeit through my father's sister."

"Are you hoping she whelps a boy before your demise? That still will not get you around the rules of primogeniture." Keene had spoken with solicitors, too. His father's title had to pass through him. There was no way for him to renounce his right to the title before it was his. Now, there was no need.

Keene raised his glass to his lips and remembered with frustration it was empty.

"I have decided you shall marry your cousin, or I will have you charged with attempted murder."

Keene stared into the empty glass. The last time he had seen Sophie she had been sitting in a tree spitting cherry pits. She hadn't been that young, either. At least fourteen or fifteen. She was a hoyden. She ran through her father's house. She laughed too loud. Once he even heard her swearing at an uncooperative fence gate. He shuddered and swallowed hard.

A year ago he would have laughed. He would have stuck to his guns that he would never marry. Certainly not that awful, unruly girl. Not marrying had been the one sure way he could give his father what he wanted. "If that would please you, sir."

His father guffawed.

Not the expected response.

"What happened to your pledges of eternal autonomy? Were you not the one who said fifty horses could not drag you to an altar?" asked the old man.

Had his father hoped he would choose exile? "That was when Richard was *my* heir."

Lord Whitley's eyes sparkled with a dewy glitter.

Keene stood and crossed to the brandy decanter. He poured a glass full and downed it in practically one swallow. "I am standing here in my dirt." He pulled the bellpull. "I shall attend you at dinner, where you may inform me of particulars. I assume, as I am willing to do your bidding, that you will see fit to allow me the wherewithal for a wife."

"That's it, you sniveling cur. You would marry that girl for the money."

Keene brushed his sleeve. No, that wasn't it. "I am sure that I could find a much more suitable and demure heiress who would accept my suit. Sophie is your choice, is she not?"

Keene moved to the door; fortunately, the butler arrived to show him to rooms he hoped had been prepared for him.

He dreaded the coming evening. Without Richard, who had loved them both, to buffer them, it would be an ugly business.

The next day he eagerly climbed into his carriage to travel to the Farthings. As he drew out into the lane, he laughed, realizing he was so glad to be free of his father he actually anticipated seeing Sophie again. He could hope that someone had taught her the meaning of the word demure in the last few years.

Sophie hitched up her skirts and skittered down the hall. She would have run, but she feared her footfalls would be overheard. Her thin slippers made little sound against the thick carpet. She ducked into her room, pulling the door shut ever so gently.

"Oh, miss—"

Sophie jumped and hit her head on the door.

"—you are wanted in the drawing room."

Sophie rubbed her forehead. "Lord, Letty, you gave me a fright. I didn't know you were in here."

"I was sent to fetch you."

"I'm not going. I saw Squire Ponsby's carriage. He'll just ask me to marry him again, and I'll have to say no. Then there will be nothing but unpleasantness for the rest of the day."

"Please, miss." Letty wrung her hands.

Who was foolish enough to send her maid to fetch her? Letty wouldn't have any more success than if one of the carp from the fountain had come calling. Sophie kicked off her slippers. She reached for a pair of shoes and sat on the bed to put them on. "Just tell them that I have gone out and you don't know where."

"Please, miss. Your mother said I had two minutes before she would come herself."

That was why they had sent Letty. She was to stall Sophie long enough so her mother could find her. Sophie dropped her shoes and sprang off the bed. "Oh, Ludcakes."

"There is another visitor coming to see you."

"Dash it all. Is it the vicar? Because I tell you, if he proposes and I refuse, I shall be damned to hell."

"Miss, please."

Sophie hardly knew if Letty was protesting her language or her sentiments. She was too busy pacing the room, looking for a hiding place. Her mother would check the wardrobes, and Letty wouldn't be able to contain herself if Sophie hid under the bed. Sophie's gaze fastened on the windows.

"I just can't take another proposal, Letty. Papa is so sure that I am about to wither and die on the vine at the grand age of one and twenty that he encourages any remotely eligible man to propose. Do you remember the widower from Cornwall, Sir Gresham? Papa led the poor man to believe I should be glad to entertain an offer."

Sophie threw the casement back.

"What are you doing, miss?"

"I'm going out."

Letty wrung her hands. "It's three stories down."

"I won't fall. Don't give me away."

Sophie hoisted a stockinged foot up to the sill. There was a ledge of sorts running between the windows.

"They'll see you."

"I daresay neither the squire nor the vicar would look up.

The squire might get a crick in his back, and the vicar's collar is so stiff it should saw a hole in his head. I shall be fine."

Sophie suffered a moment's qualm as she stared down at the half-circle drive in front of the house. Better to not look down at all.

"Sophie, darling, you must come to the drawing room," called her mother from the hallway. "If you hurry you might change to the peach dress."

Uh-oh. Sophie nearly hated that gown. Almost every time she wore it, her parents would plunk some poor besotted fool down in front of her. She turned and backed out through the window, her stockinged foot searching for the ledge. Her skirts and petticoats hampered her hasty departure. She pulled them up far enough to get her knees on the sill and made a lunge for the ledge beside the window.

The door clicked open. With desperate fingers, she clutched the mellow brick and inched sideways. Oh, Lord, what if she fell and broke her neck? Why, then she wouldn't have to fend off suitors. She closed her eyes, resisting the temptation to peek.

"Sophie, where are you? Letty, isn't she here? The footman downstairs thought he saw her heading toward her bedroom."

Sophie could just picture Letty's slow shake of the head.

"Have you checked the wardrobe? I know she was in the house."

"I believe she went outside, ma'am."

Good girl, Letty.

Heavens, why have you opened the window?" said Sophie's mother. "Shut and latch it now."

"Yes, ma'am," mumbled Letty.

Sophie watched in horror as her maid shut the window and lowered the catch.

TWO

Keene paused his horse in the driveway. The pale brick of the Farthing house was a soothing sight, until he caught sight of the upturned petticoats and drawers on a young woman backing out a window three stories up.

Sophie.

He heaved a deep sigh. Before he expelled it fully, his breath snagged in his throat.

Surely the news of his impending arrival and proposal hadn't prompted her to leap to her death. When he had her alone, he would explain that she could refuse his suit. A small hope surged through him. Certainly his father could find no fault with him if Sophie rejected him. He trotted his horse toward the house, hoping she didn't fall in front of him. He hesitated to call up to her for fear he would startle her.

The wind whipped her petticoats and long blonde curls. From what he could see, she had a rather nice form, not that he liked the idea of his future wife displaying her backside to the whole countryside. She straightened on the decorative ledge. Her full skirts settled around her ankles where they belonged. She inched away from the window.

Whatever she had in mind, leaping wouldn't have required a move away from the casement. Walking along ledges was probably her preferred method of traveling between rooms.

Keene shook his head and walked his horse around back to the stables. A waiting groom took his reins. Earlier in the day, he had sent his carriage ahead to inform them of his arrival. His father had also included a letter, which Keene presumed contained news of his suit. Upon entering the house, he was led to the drawing room.

His father's cousin Jane Farthing quickly embraced him with a happy greeting. "I'd like you to meet our neighbor, Mr. Ponsby."

Keene bowed slightly to the robust man sitting on one of Jane's delicate chairs. The chair looked like it might disintegrate into matchwood at any moment. Jane gestured for Keene to sit.

"Mr. Ponsby is the local squire."

"How d' you do?" The squire shifted thick legs stuffed like sausages in his broadcloth knee breeches. "Pray tell, have you located Miss Sophie yet?"

"I am sure she is just taking a constitutional. I've sent her maid to search the orchards. She will be sad if she misses you." Jane perched on the edge of one of the delicate chairs.

"The gel needs a couple of children to occupy her so she hasn't the time to gad about the country at whim," said the squire peevishly.

Keene drew up stiff. Who was this unmannerly man to comment on Sophie's behavior? Not that he was terribly wrong, but criticism should be reserved for family.

Keene brushed his sleeve and said negligently, "I daresay children should not require a great deal of Sophie's time. I'm sure she might discharge her daily duties to their nanny in the space of a quarter hour. Although I am told one can be done in less time."

"Quite right, sir, quite right," blustered the squire, taking the not-so-subtle reminder of their difference in stations with ingratiating grace. "I have missed her these last few times I have come calling."

"We are looking for her. I have sent my maid upstairs to search. I haven't even had a chance to inform her that Keene is to join us."

So it wasn't on his account that Sophie was impersonating ivy on the house.

The squire ran a work-calloused finger under his cravat. Keene flicked his gaze over the brocade embroidered waistcoat and tight tailed jacket the squire wore. Although his clothes were clearly of the country, he was very well dressed for an afternoon social call, but he looked uncomfortable, as if the clothing sat ill on him.

"Mr. Farthing assured me he would speak with her," mumbled the squire.

Jane's eyes widened. "I'll just check again." She reached for the bellpull.

Keene settled on the sofa.

The squire had the ruddy complexion of a man often outside. He looked as out of place as a rusty plow would among the myriad polished rosewood tables scattered around the room, ready to trip up a man of the squire's stature.

"Do you hunt, sir?" asked Keene.

The squire looked uncertain, as if a trap lay ready to spring on him. "Why, yes."

Keene relaxed. "Farthing finds such amusements trivial." Jane's husband found most entertainment frivolous. The man should have been a minister rather than a country gentleman. Although many might have found his sermons on life too dour. "Perhaps you might indulge me in a day of grousing during my stay."

"Shall you be here long, sir?"

The conversation digressed into a discussion of hunting, while Jane made several inquiries of her servants as to Sophie's whereabouts, all to no avail.

Keene doubted she still hovered on the ledge of the house. Although the cherries weren't in season, he had no doubt she was somewhere she shouldn't be and wouldn't be found until she was ready.

He suffered a momentary qualm as he remembered once pulling her out of the river behind the orchard and another time freeing her dress from a fence that had her feet dangling uselessly above the ground.

Disappointment covered the squire's face when he finally took his leave.

"Oh, dear." Jane sank back into her chair with a sigh. "I have no idea where she's hiding."

Keene resumed his seat on the sofa. "Is she hiding?" Or was she still clinging to the side of the house?

"I presume. She and Mr. Ponsby were great friends. They often rode together. Of late she avoids him like the plague."

Had all the upstairs rooms been checked? "What happened?"

"Mr. Ponsby proposed. Sophie should be married. Of course, you know that. And, well, Mr. Farthing and I thought . . . they seemed to enjoy each other's company. Mr. Farthing has been seeking her settlement for several years. She never likes any of the men he has set before her."

So the girl was not without prospects. Although Keene could imagine the dour men Sophie's father would choose as potential husband material. He suspected they would be grossly offended by the notion that she displayed her drawers to the countryside, not that he cared for such behavior.

"I don't recall her being brought out."

"Oh, no! Mr. Farthing objects to the London season. He thinks all that indulging in gaiety, the balls and such, should be quite bad for her. Sophie is far too frivolous as it is."

Frankly, Keene didn't understand his cousin-in-law's Quakerish bent. Most girls of Sophie's station were settled with a London season. He supposed even a hoyden like Sophie would be satisfactorily engaged if she had done the rounds at Almack's and been presented at court. He shifted in his seat. What if Sophie still clung to the ledge?

Jane leaned forward and patted his hand. "I am so glad your father and you have offered a solution to our problem. I know that Sophie was ever fond of your visits as a child. And of course, we all will miss Richard dearly."

"We all will miss Richard."

Richard's death was still too raw and new. Keene turned his head and tried to ignore the tangled lash of emotions. He forced himself to think of Sophie, while Jane squeezed his hand.

Sophie had probably enjoyed Richard's company more than his own. They were nearer in age and played together during their yearly summer stays. Keene had done his best to shake off her presence. Although a strong urge to find her and make sure she was still of sound body and not a stain on the cobblestones of the drive was making it difficult for him to sit still.

"So has Sophie refused Mr. Ponsby?"

"At first when the squire approached Mr. Farthing, we thought—well, that it would be a misalliance, but she is . . ." Jane smiled brightly. "I am so glad you have come. I do wish one of the servants would locate her."

So did he. He dimly registered Jane's concerns. On some level he knew that if Sophie's parents were so anxious to be rid of her, it must be worse than he thought. Keene stood. "I daresay I shall see her soon enough at dinner."

"Oh, dear, I'm sure you wish to rest from your journey."

He had no need to rest as he'd spent a leisurely morning at a nearby inn allowing his carriage and servants time to announce his arrival and give Jane enough time to be ready for his visit. But he did need to assure himself that his future bride was not plunging to her death due to some negligence of his own.

Sophie clung to the bricks as the cool wind whipped her skirts and hair. Cold seeped through her toes until she wasn't sure they were agile enough to see her back along the ledge. She couldn't stay outside forever. She inched along the ledge to the next room to see if the windows were unlocked. All the while she cursed her foolhardy way of avoiding Mr. Ponsby.

Trouble was, she was fond of him, but not nearly fond

enough to want him as a husband. But Ponsby was like a dog with a bone. Once he got the idea in his head that they should marry, short of her marriage to another, he couldn't see any objection to it. Especially since her father encouraged his fixation. As if her female mind was fluid and it only required catching her at the right tide.

Sophie had no real opposition to marriage. She had pleaded and begged for a season, promising to bring a gentleman up to scratch. What she really wanted was a chance to see London, to dance, to dine in state, to live the life she was born to. Of course, her father detested all manner of indulgences and even the local subscription balls were off-limits.

As the rough surface of the bricks tore at her hands, Sophie swore to herself she would marry the first man who offered her the opportunity to go to London. Trouble was, her father, while he meant the best, sought perfect upright men, the sort of men who made Sophie want to scream in vexation.

She might need to start screaming soon. The windows of the next room were locked.

Where was Letty?

"Might I be of assistance?"

Sophie whipped her head around and suffered a momentary lurch of her stomach as she contemplated the long drop from the ledge. Slipping now, when help stood at hand, was a real possibility.

Leaning out a window several rooms down, her cousin Keene watched her.

She stared as if he were an apparition. Maybe he was. He hadn't visited in an eternity. Only, if she was seeing ghosts, his brother Richard would be the one to appear.

"Don't fall," he said in his usual calm, almost bored, tone. While his warning confronted her greatest fear of the moment, his smooth deep voice soothed her.

He appeared at her window so fast she would have thought he ran, except she had never known Keene to run to her rescue. Instead, he would fold his arms across his chest and wait until she begged for his assistance and he'd sufficiently scolded her for needing help.

He opened the casement and reached out, tucking his arms around her and pulling her inside where her toes could curl against the thick Aubusson carpet. She wanted to hold on and sob against his chest. "Oh, thank God you are come. You are ever my rescuer."

He put her away from him. "What were you thinking?" He folded his arms across his chest.

That posture she recognized. Somehow she didn't think Keene would react with compassion to a fit of the vapors. "I don't expect I thought my maid would lock me out."

"Have you been out there the whole time?"

How long had he known she was hanging on to the ledge? "You knew I was out there?"

"I never thought you'd still be on the wall. It's a good thing I decided to check."

"Yes, it is, and I'm ever so grateful. I should return to my room. Even if you are my cousin, it's quite improper for me to be alone with you in a bedroom."

"I daresay it shouldn't matter." His dark eyes flicked around the room and returned to her with a wry assessing look that made her want to cringe. "Whose room is this?"

"It's just one of the guest rooms." Sophie backed toward the door. She wanted to run to her room, throw herself across her bed and indulge in tears for a half-hour or two minutes. Pride kept her from indulging in front of Keene.

"Wait," said Keene.

She stopped backing away.

He closed the casement, then turned around. His dark eyes finished his assessment of her.

Sophie wanted to run, but displaying weakness to Keene was like inviting a bird of prey to swoop down and pluck out your eyeballs. He already thought so little of her she didn't want to add to that impression by opening her mouth in her own defense. Besides, what could she say? Crawling out on the ledge was one of her more stupid tricks. Even she knew that, now.

In the meantime, she knew he would find her dress hopelessly provincial. She wasn't allowed to wear the newer Grecian style dresses, because her father found them too revealing. Her hair was tangled, not to mention down. In general, she was a mess, but then that should fit with Keene's expectations.

He shifted.

For a second he looked uncertain.

Sophie blinked. The man she knew was always certain of himself, wry, self-contained, assured. "What's wrong?"

The uncertainty was gone. Perhaps she imagined it.

"Isn't it time you gave up climbing trees and such?"

"I haven't climbed a tree in"—she started to say years, but a recent rescue of a stranded kitten made that a gross exaggeration—"ages."

"You could have fallen, Sophie."

"I know. It was foolish. Please, Keene, do not lecture me. I was quite cold and scared. I should never climb out a window like that again. I just . . ."

She didn't know how to explain she just didn't want to deal with another proposal from Mr. Ponsby. Of course, it was rather presumptuous of her to say that he would propose again. And she quite feared she would have to sever all relationship with him if he kept pursuing her, and she should never find another riding companion who didn't mind indulging in a wild gallop. That is, if he ever got over this notion that they should marry.

She liked the squire well enough, although he was such a big man. But she knew his wife should never be allowed to indulge in a book or a party. Unlike her father he didn't think of them as bad for her character, but simply a waste of time.

Keene stood tall and slender, although his shoulders were broad enough to leave no doubt that he was manly enough to satisfy a woman. From what she knew, he satisfied a good number of women. Her mother and father whispered about his awful reputation as a rake.

Her father, of course, blamed it on his residence in London, that den of iniquities. Her mother said it was more that he was devilishly good-looking. After all, Richard had lived with him the last few years and did not share his reputation, although they were known to follow the same pursuits.

Sophie agreed with her mother. In their mostly blond, blue-eyed family, Keene was an anomaly. His dark, almost black, hair, his deep brown eyes and his startling, pale aristocratic skin contrasted with the fair hair and the ruddy complexions that his brother and his father had shared. She'd often wondered if there was a swarthy pirate in their shared ancestry. Her mother had disabused her of that notion.

"Are you to spend Candlemas with us?"

An odd look passed over his face. "No. I won't be staying that long."

How had the holiday season passed for him with Richard's loss so recent? In addition, Keene and his father never seemed to get along. Had he spent any time with family? "Where did you spend Christmas?"

"I've been in London," he said quickly.

She sat on the bed. "You could stay with us. I am sure Mama and Papa should be glad to have you join us. Not that we do a lot, because Papa finds excessive celebration, well, excessive."

His eyes moved over her in a way that had her stockinged toes curling. Her mother was wrong. It was the looks he cast, not the way he looked. Not that she would be lucky enough to be the focus of his attention when she didn't need rescuing from hanging on the side of a house. Already his gaze had moved away.

"I thought you said it was improper for you to stay here talking to me."

That was when she wanted to run away and cry. She was quite past that as long as she didn't think about the ledge. Now she was concerned that he might need to be with family for the remainder of the holiday season. "I am sure I am quite safe with you. You are my cousin, after all."

"The relationship is rather distant."

"Second cousins to be sure—what are you doing?"

He'd flicked the door shut with a nudge of his toe and moved to the bed, where he leaned over her.

"You take your safety far too much for granted. Never assume that a situation is harmless."

She leaned back from his closeness. "I could scream."

"Perhaps you should."

She didn't want to scream. At least not yet. Not that he wasn't surprising her. She never thought Keene was terribly aware she was alive. This new twist on his rescue was unexpected, but it was welcome.

"I've been kissed before."

He grinned. His white, even teeth fascinated her. Even though up close like this she could see there was a tiny chip in one of them. His mouth drew her.

"Like this?"

Not even close. "I don't know. You haven't kissed me yet." Her words came out strangely breathy. She felt odd, lightheaded, melting on the inside. She forced her gaze up.

"Are you scared now, Sophie?"

His body pressed against hers, his length hard and solid. She felt something similar to fear, but she wasn't quite sure what it was. "Should I be?"

Keene abruptly moved away. "You better go."

He moved to the window, staring outside. Sophie tried to catch her breath. He leaned his palms against the windowsill. Disappointment flooded through her. Her one chance to be kissed by a rake and he put paid to it.

At the last minute he must have found her too messy, or inexperienced or . . . she was too naive to know what gentlemen might find distasteful about a woman. She fled the room and encountered a tearful Letty in the hall.

"I'm so sorry, miss. Your mother made me lock up the window and then sent me to the orchard to look for you. I was ever fearful you'd be mad."

"I'm not mad, Letty. I was able to come in another window."

"Oh, no, miss." Letty clutched Sophie's arm. "Mrs. Waite makes us keep all the windows latched on account they rattle in the wind if we don't."

"Be that as it may, I'm fine."

Letty looked toward the room where Sophie had left Keene. "I'd best check to make sure the window is latched proper."

"Not now. I need you to comb out my hair." Sophie grabbed her maid's arm and propelled her into her room.

She didn't see Keene again until dinner, where the conversation, much to her dismay, turned to politics. Sophie stirred her fork around her plate. She stopped listening. Instead, her mind turned to the moment in the guest room when she thought Keene would kiss her. She didn't dare look at him directly, but every now and again she would peek out from under her lashes at him.

Feeling a momentary lull in the conversation, she glanced up and found Keene's dark eyes trained on her. Had she missed something?

"What do you think, Sophie?" Keene asked.

"About what?"

"Napoleon's exile to Elba."

"It's good that we shan't be at war, isn't it?"

"No use in asking Sophie's opinion. She cares not a whit for what happens with our government as long as she is comfortable," said her father.

"I'm sure she would prefer to pick your brain about the latest news of London," added her mother.

Sophie wished they would stop talking about her as if she had as much sense as a hedgerow. Although, with the conversation centering on politics she felt about as animated as a shrub. She set her fork down.

"Then I daresay we shall bore her even more. In London

the talk of the day is of the redistribution of lands, and how Parliament can turn to our own problems now the emperor is deposed and exiled."

"Surely that is not all that is discussed. There must be talk of books and plays and . . ."

"There is that, too. But there is much talk of politics."

"I do remember that, too. In my day the political talk was always quite animated," said Jane.

She might as well sprout leaves. If there was one thing Sophie knew it was that her mother had found London squalid and wretched and cried herself to sleep every night of her season. Of course, her mother was much more content with her own company than with others.

Keene smiled. "I daresay it seems a might more interesting when you are talking to those who have charge of Parliament and your opinions might influence their decisions."

Sophie couldn't imagine anything less exciting. Somehow she'd thought a rake wouldn't concern himself with more than his own entertainment.

Her mother rose from her chair. "Sophie, we should leave the men to their port, as I'm sure they have much to discuss."

Keene's smile disappeared. His gaze moved away from her.

Sophie wondered how much more politics they could discuss. They certainly had nothing else in common. And why did Keene look so gloomy all the sudden?

She hoped they didn't take too long before joining her mother and her for tea. She had to believe her father and Keene would get on better for the extra company.

The women moved into the drawing room. Her mother patted the sofa beside her. Sophie sat down.

"Are you fond of Keene?"

The question seemed odd. "Of course. You don't suppose Papa is giving him a homily about his behavior in London, do you?"

"He might do that."

"Do you think it well that we left them alone together?

Remember how Keene would be in a bad humor every time his father would lecture him. I'm quite sure he hates strictures on his behavior. Papa is so very fond of moralizing."

"It is well that you are concerned for Keene. We should talk about your future."

"Oh, Mama, please do not spoil my evening. I know I missed Mr. Ponsby when he came calling. I just cannot see that we should make a good match. My silliness should drive him insane inside a twelvemonth. We do well enough when we can ride and talk of horses, but beyond that . . ." Sophie shrugged and looked for her knitting basket. Not that she wanted to knit, but her father would want to see her occupied in an acceptable pursuit when he entered the room.

"Not Mr. Ponsby, dear. But—"

"I swear I shall marry the first man to propose to me who is not over fifty, not a widower with an odd lot of children to raise and who will take me to London." Sophie jumped up and paced the length of the drawing room. "Just so long as he is pleasant in appearance and agreeable in manner."

She expected her mother's usual soft dissent that she expected too much. Instead, Jane nodded. "I shall hold you to that."

Sophie wondered if there was another hapless suitor on the way at this very moment. Had she lowered her standards too far? At first she'd insisted that she wanted a dashing, handsome gentleman under thirty who of course would be madly, deeply in love with her. "Perhaps Keene has a friend in need of a wife," she said in a small voice.

Maybe that was why Keene was here. He hadn't visited in a half dozen years. Had her father's thinly veiled hints turned to outright pleas for help in his letters? Who would be better to turn to for help than family? Had her pending spinsterhood thrust Keene into the role of matchmaker? Was he even now wondering what single gentleman of his acquaintance was so in need of a fortune that he would find her modest inheritance appealing enough to overshadow her wild streak?

She knew Keene had no good opinion of her. With his arrival coinciding with her daring escape, she had no hope of convincing him she was not always such a sad romp.

Sophie plunked down on the sofa. "I should hope that my frivolity shall not be a burden."

Jane patted her hand. "Oh, Sophie, you have been such a good daughter. I do not think your life will always be so quiet, but that is what appeals to Mr. Farthing and me. When you marry, you will be allowed more freedom in your dress, and if your husband has no objection to balls, I am sure you will be able to dance your fill."

"Is that why Keene has come? To see me settled?"

"Why, that is exactly it. His father has sent us the solution to our dilemma." Her mother smiled brightly.

No hope now for a season. "Did you dislike London so much?"

"I always felt awkward and on display. I daresay it should be different for you."

The tea cart arrived. Shortly afterward Keene entered the room. "Mr. Farthing asks you to attend him in the library."

Sophie stood and prepared herself for a lecture. Perhaps Keene had ratted her out.

"Not you, dear, me." Her mother tugged on her arm.

Sophie glanced at Keene and his grim nod confirmed her mother's assumption.

A peculiar summons, to be sure. Had Keene's reputation overcome her father's desire to get along with family? Would Papa request that Keene leave?

"Pour your cousin some tea, and I shall be back directly," instructed Jane.

"How would you like it?" Sophie watched her mother's skirts disappear through the door.

"I do not need any tea, thank you."

Sophie replaced the cup and saucer on the cart. Keene walked across the room and stood in front of the fireplace.

She wanted to say something witty and entertaining, but

the only thing she could think of was to ask why he hadn't kissed her earlier. On no account would she ask that. She took a sip of her tea. Her cup rattled loudly as she set it down.

Keene turned so he was in profile to her. His hands were clasped behind his back. Silence stretched out as he studied her. She started to feel like a curiosity, as if she were some two-headed freak of nature that astounded the eyes.

"It has been brought to my attention that you are in want of a husband."

She would have preferred being two-headed rather than being thought of as unmarriageable. Sophie wished more than ever for her knitting basket so she might spread work upon her lap and have an occupation for her nervous fingers and darting eyes. "I expect my parents feel quite desperate about my situation."

Keene frowned.

Sophie dropped her gaze to her lap. She clasped her hands together. "I have assured my mother I shall not refuse any reasonable offer."

"Just Mr. Ponsby?"

"Mr. Ponsby would find me a disagreeable wife, even if he does not believe so." She felt the need to defend herself. "I have only refused him once. The rest of the times I managed to avoid him."

"An ace card up your sleeve?"

Sophie jerked her head up.

Keene moved from the fireplace toward her. The scowl on his face alarmed her.

"So . . . so have my parents appealed to you to find a solution to my predicament?"

"What predicament, Sophie?"

She blinked at the tightness in his voice. "Why, that I am one and twenty and unmarried."

Keene stopped.

"I assure you that you needn't concern yourself. I am not without prospects, you see. There was a gentleman from Cornwall . . ." her voice trailed off. She had no more desire to marry Sir Gresham than she wanted to spend another afternoon clinging to the side of the house. She just didn't like the idea that the job of finding her a husband was being foisted on Keene, and he seemed none too happy about it.

"Tell me about this gentleman from Cornwall."

"There is nothing to tell. He was here a fortnight ago, and I liked him well enough. I was just not sure I wanted to become a mother so soon."

Keene looked almost ill.

"Are you all right?" She stood and moved to stand in front of him. "He had three children already, you see. Perhaps you should have some tea, Keene. The traveling has done you in."

He shook his head and glanced at the closed door. "Sophie, I have come to ask you to do me the honor of becoming my wife."

THREE

Sophie looked stunned.

He had expected any one of a number of responses to his proposal, but thunderstruck was not one of them. Her blue eyes took on a skeptical glint. "Do not tease me, Keene. It is very unhandsome of you. Richard told me you never intend to marry."

A raw pain struck him. "I never intended for Richard to die before me."

"Oh, Keene, I am so sorry." She put her hand on his shoulder. Heat smoothed down from her touch, the same way it had in the bedroom upstairs.

Oddly enough, for a man that prided himself on staying calm and collected, his thoughts were in such a reel as to make a whirling dervish dizzy.

He hadn't expected half-baked explanations of a man from Cornwall or her oddly prideful way of telling him he needn't concern himself with her plight. Nor was her plight particularly clear to him. There seemed a lot of fuss for a girl who was getting a little long in the tooth, but not so very old as to be cast aside for want of freshness. In fact, she seemed incredibly fresh to a man used to the town polish and world-weariness of young ton matrons ready to don the horns of cuckoldry on their husbands.

Upstairs he had thought her too naive to be subjected to the urges he felt. Naive, but not resistant. He'd wanted her to be aware that she couldn't trust a man to control himself. For once, he wondered if he'd have trouble reining himself in without a protest from her. It had occurred to him that he should not be trying to scare her with his passion, not if he didn't want her afraid of him when they shared a marriage bed.

The strength of his carnal cravings surprised him. He blamed it on the fact that he'd let his little opera singer go free, and he'd been too long without release.

All the while he was aware the clock was ticking. Farthing had promised him fifteen minutes alone with Sophie and not a second more. It had seemed like enough time when he was under the impression she expected his proposal.

He wanted to press her hand against him, draw her into his arms and kiss her until she hadn't a thought in her head. From what he knew of Sophie, that shouldn't take long. But her wording about her unmarried state brought concerns he hadn't expected. In all the swirl of his thoughts was the concern that Sophie needed to know he would understand a refusal and the equally troubling realization that she had not answered him.

"Sophie, I will understand if you refuse. I will not hold you to any promise your parents have solicited. If you say you cannot like marriage with me, I will explain it is all my fault."

"Are you sincere?"

"Yes, I am serious about this."

"You don't even like me."

True, there were many things he disliked about her. Namely, her lack of modesty and restraint. "I'm told it is not necessary for a successful marriage."

Her eyes grew wider and then dropped. Her face was crestfallen. He cursed himself for being callous with her. She wasn't used to his sarcasm, and she had always been too open. He reached for her chin and tilted her head up. "I daresay I like you well enough in the ways that are important."

He would have to kiss her.

He reached for her waist, curling his hand around her side. Her slender suppleness beneath the layers of material pleased him. With his other hand he traced the delicate edge of her chin. Her lips parted before him. He leaned toward the meeting of their mouths.

"Mama and Papa should never believe a failure to agree on marriage was your fault."

He paused, his gaze shifting from the beckoning petals of her mouth to the bottomless blue of her eyes. Her sweet breath blew across his chin, and he wanted to taste her.

Yet, the content of her words suggested she was thinking of a refusal. On one hand he absolutely wanted her release from his obligations. On the other hand he just wanted to use the remainder of his fifteen minutes to persuade her to become his wife, or at least share his bed.

A small voice of reason crafted his words. "I should convince them my reputation has offended your sensibilities."

She giggled.

The sound touched off a welter of thoughts. Women he was about to kiss didn't usually find it a laughing matter, not that her laughter didn't touch a part of him that was amused. But the very form of her laughter reminded him of her relative youth and inexperience—at least he hoped she was inexperienced. The news of a man from Cornwall concerned him.

All the while he was aware of the brush of skirts against his thighs. He smoothed his hand over the curve of her hip, involuntarily pulling her closer to his hardness.

"My parents know that I have no sensibilities."

He dropped his hand from her chin, trailing his fingertips down the column of her neck. Her pulse leaped under his touch. "I daresay it is time you found some."

Her head dipped.

How would he kiss her if she stared at her feet?

He would be walking a fine line convincing his father that the refusal was solely Sophie's while preserving her reputation and good graces with her parents. That and a small voice in the back of his head pointed out there was really no reason to kiss her if she intended to turn him down. He would seduce a lot of women, but his cousin and unmarried gentlewomen weren't his usual prey.

"Sophie?"

"Yes."

"Do you think you might give me an answer before your parents decide our tête-à-tête has gone on long enough?"

"I just did."

Her yes was the answer to the proposal? He placed both hands along the sides of her face. "Look at me, then."

She looked up. Then her wide blue eyes darted away.

"You will marry me?"

She gave a short jerky nod.

Her uncertainty tugged at him. His own ambivalence was bad enough. Somehow he expected Sophie to be more sure of her choice. She never did anything in half measures. He hadn't realized how much he was counting on her certainty.

Perhaps his duty as a future husband was to reassure her. One aspect of their marriage was likely to be satisfactory to him at least. He wanted to believe that the quickened cadence of her breathing and the rapid leap of her pulse was proof that the physical side of their marriage would be pleasing to her. He also knew these symptoms could be nerves, as well.

Not that he was used to seeing Sophie scared, but earlier when he'd pulled her in from the ledge her expression had the same fearful edge to it. Which had nothing on the pounding of his own heart.

He smoothed the pad of his thumb across her lower lip. He knew he should gentle her into his touch, but a quarter hour was such an awkwardly short time. Her eyes fluttered shut and back open. He leaned down to brush his mouth across hers.

The full softness of her lips clinging to his shot fire through his veins.

The door opened and frustration burst through Keene.

"That's quite enough," said Farthing.

Sophie sprang away from him.

Concealing the growing hardness of his response was impossible given the knit pantaloons he wore. Keene found himself wishing for a book as he would have used in Eton days, not that there was anything particularly wrong with a man desiring his future wife. He just wasn't sure he wanted to display the evidence in polite company, especially in the company of such a morally staunch man as Sophie's father.

Did Sophie have any idea that he would like to be hiding behind her skirts at the moment? He couldn't even sit down until the ladies took their seats. Keene turned to the fire, not that he needed the extra heat.

Sensing three pairs of eyes crawling all over him, he held his hands out to the fire. The onyx signet ring on his pinkie reminded him he had not given any thought to a ring for Sophie. The practical thought slid away as he mulled over the kiss that had ended far too soon. He cleared his throat.

"Well," said Jane.

"Sophie has done me the honor of agreeing to be my wife." That they had really gotten no farther than that astounded him. They had not made it to a discussion of when or where the marriage should take place. "But that is all we have settled."

"We shall have the banns posted this Sunday," said Sophie's father. "There is no point in waiting. After the first of February, when the banns have been read three times, we can have the ceremony."

Keene glanced at Sophie to see if she objected to the speed with which they galloped toward the altar. "Will that allow you enough time to assemble your trousseau?"

Sophie blanched. She cast a desperate glance in her mother's direction.

Jane leaned forward and poured tea for her husband. "We shall be able to make accommodations for what Sophie needs. Would you like some tea?"

He needed a brandy. Keene looked between the three of them and felt on the outside of an inside joke without the humor. Farthing gestured toward him. "Would you care to accompany me to the library? We'll pick out a book to read aloud."

That Keene's input on a choice of a book was superfluous quickly became apparent as Farthing beelined to a Hannah More treatise. Instead, Keene was treated to a homily about his disgusting display with Sophie and informed that he should not be allowed to be alone with her before the knot was tied.

Keene felt bound to protest. How was he to fix Sophie's affections if he was not allowed access to her and a modicum of privacy? "I daresay it is not so uncommon to seal an engagement with a kiss."

"That is well and good, but that is quite as far as it needs to go. You have no further need to be alone with Sophie. As her protector I must protest your familiarity with her person."

"If I might speak frankly, with all due respect, with our marriage in less than a month perhaps I should allow her to grow accustomed to my person so she is comfortable with me."

Farthing turned pale. "She is a gently bred young woman. I am sure she will understand and submit to her duty, but there is no reason to expose her to any unpleasantness before necessary."

Keene leaned against a bookshelf. He was not asking permission to seduce the man's daughter, although with the engagement agreed upon it was not such a horrible crime. But Farthing was putting the worst possible spin on his words, like only an extreme moralist would. "I assure you she would not find my company unpleasant. As we have not spoken much in these last few years, I think it would do well for us to reacquaint ourselves with each other. I am thinking of her comfort."

Certainly not his own; he wasn't particularly looking forward to getting reacquainted with Sophie. Although getting to know her in the biblical sense did have a certain appeal, he could wait three weeks.

"I have not spoken of it as you are my wife's cousin, but

your reputation precedes you. I shall only rest easy when she is tied by the church to you. Until then, I will not allow you to be alone in her company."

Might as well throttle the cat with the bell. "My word as a gentleman, I shall not tempt her into my bed before I have the right."

Farthing looked positively sick. "I wish your word as a gentleman that you will not assault her person."

"Sir, I would never assault any woman's person."

Farthing looked like he might have an apoplexy. Detailing that no woman found his kisses an assault might take too much time, thought Keene. If approaching the claws dead on didn't help, perhaps he should try milksop and toast. "I give you my word as a gentleman that I will attempt no familiarity beyond holding her hand."

Farthing drew up stiff. "That, sir, will be entirely too much. Your influence upon her is not the sort I would wish for her in her unmarried state. It will be best if you leave after the paperwork is settled. I shall notify my solicitor at once so we might have the agreement worked out quickly."

"As soon as the marriage contract is signed, I shall be on my way."

Farthing nodded.

"Please make my excuses to the ladies, I think I shall retire." Keene didn't want to sit through an evening of Holy Hannah. Especially not since he expected certain passages might be illuminated for his edification. Why would Farthing accept his marriage proposal for his daughter if he found Keene's lifestyle so aberrant? How would his influence after marriage be more acceptable?

Keene shook his head as he read the spines of the books on the shelves.

Later, he decided he'd had enough of the expurgated version of Shakespeare he'd chosen from the limited selection in the library. Reading the bard's work in a sanitized form was sort of like deciding if a man had an attractive beard after all his facial hairs had been shaved.

He shed his coat and pulled his untied linen cravat away from his throat. He debated whether or not to ring for his valet. As he was reaching for the bellpull a tap on his door sounded. He didn't think his valet capable of clairvoyant communication, but he called out, "Enter."

Sophie darted around the door and shut it with a stealthy gentleness.

He wasn't sure if he was shocked or it was the sort of behavior he expected from her. "Come to put me to bed?"

She had the grace to blush. "Of course not. I hope Papa did not upset you earlier. He told Mama he thought he might have offended you, but he thought it was necessary."

"Perhaps it was. Sophie, you don't belong in here."

"I know. They told me I am not allowed to be alone with you. Which is silly. When your room is just down the hall and as none of the doors have locks, I should not know how they propose to prevent us from sneaking together if we have a mind to."

Keene's pulse took a little leap. "Have you a mind to?"

"Of course not. I just don't understand why you have offered for me. If you felt we were too familiar earlier when you helped me in the window, I am sure there is no need for you to make reparation. No one would know my reputation has been sullied with me buried in the country like I am."

Keene cursed the promise he had given earlier. Even though Farthing had not found his pledge to pass on seducing Sophie sufficient reassurance, he could not ignore his word. "Sophie, I came here with the intention of asking for your hand. Your parents knew that. I had thought they would have told you."

She plunked down on the chair he had just vacated. "They applied to you for aid." Her words were between a question and a stoic recitation of a casualty list.

"I believe they applied to my father."

She watched him with a furrow between her delicate eyebrows. "And your father asked you to help?"

"Something like that."

"You don't always do as your father wishes."

How did a woman who so often ran around like a trooper still manage to look so feminine? "I often do the opposite."

"I am confused, because I thought you didn't like me."

He knelt beside her chair and took her hands in his. He rubbed his thumbs over her knuckles. "If you don't wish to be my wife, all you have to do is say so."

"I fear you would take a refusal with too much glee."

She had grabbed the tiger, wrestled him right to the ground and belled him, but then, with her penchant for unladylike pursuits, he shouldn't have been surprised.

He doubted an explanation of why he consented to his father's plan would aid the situation. His reasons were more complicated than he understood. Not only Richard's death, but George's trials in the past year affected his decision to go along with his father's command. "Sophie, if you should be content, I shall consider myself lucky. And I promised your father I should not be overly familiar with you, so you should go back to your room."

She winced. "Papa is excessively worried about your reputation."

"My reputation is overdone."

"I don't think so. With Richard by your side following your pursuits, no one called him a rake."

Richard fell in love too easily. He never had the reserve to be seen as a rake, not that Keene was sure he deserved the appellation. "And how do you feel about the rumors about me?"

"I should be relieved you do not think of yourself as a shining example of perfection."

He grinned. "Oh, but I am."

"You are not. Papa is nearer to perfection than any man, and it is a sore trial to live with when one is so very imperfect.

Mama says my high spirits are the problem, but I am often in a pickle. Papa thinks it is the impurity of my character. I should think that since you often indulge in your own pleasures, you should be more understanding of my weaknesses."

"What weaknesses?"

She pulled her hands away and stood. "That I often indulge in frivolous pursuits for my own pleasure." She shrugged. "Like I would read novels instead of Hannah More—a great sin according to Papa. I prefer galloping across the fields to sitting with my embroidery." She took a step away from the chair, clasped and raised her hands. "I should very much just like to dance, but Papa considers all those things precursors to more indecent behavior. He feels my morals are sorely lacking."

"Yes, I am aware he is a very moral man." So much so that he found normal pursuits objectionable. "I daresay he thinks I am doomed to hell."

"Papa is just not sure you are to be trusted."

A sinner in one regard apparently made one suspect in all other matters. Keene wondered if his restraint with Sophie in his bedroom would be seen as honorable or if he should fail for not ushering her out immediately. "Is that why he would rush us through the banns and ceremony?"

Sophie shifted her gaze to the door. "He might fear if you know me too well you would cry off."

He smoothed his hand down her arm. "If I knew you too well, I should be obliged to make an honest woman of you."

A slight shudder moved down from her shoulders.

"Sophie, go now or spend the night in my bed."

Her eyes widened. "Should you like that?" she whispered.

"I daresay I shall be gravely disappointed in myself for not honoring my word to your father."

She turned away from him and clasped her upper arm with her other hand. "And if I should disappoint you?"

She needed reassurance. Trouble was, he wasn't sure he should use any more persuasion than he already had. "I daresay you shall disappoint me sooner or later, although I doubt that it will be in bed."

He gave up on restraint and wrapped his arms around her, pulling her against him with her back to his chest.

She trembled against him. Although he doubted she would regret it if he persuaded her to stay, he didn't want to callously trample her innocence. His approach had less finesse than usual and that was reason enough to send her on her way. He couldn't ever remember demanding a woman share his bed or leave. "Sophie, you are not ready for this, and there is no reason to rush."

"I should like to get it over with."

He steered her toward the door. "I think not. A rake like me has a reputation to protect." His women were always willing.

When he had the door open, he propelled her through it. He slid his palm down her spine to the small of her back where he rubbed his thumb in a light circle. "Sleep well."

He backed away before he slung her over his shoulder and tossed her on his bed without regard for her sensibilities or the sensibilities of his host, who seemed much more likely to take offense. He shut the door and leaned his head against it. If she knocked and asked for readmittance, he wouldn't be able to exercise any restraint. His total lack of control overwhelmed him.

He couldn't even take pride in that he had ultimately done the right thing, because he wanted so badly to fling open his door and march boldly into her room and exercise rights he didn't own yet.

Sophie stared at the shut door with a mixture of emotions; relief and disappointment, exhilaration and anguish. She thought perhaps Keene desired her. She wondered when this fine turn of events had happened. Perhaps a rake desired all women and that was what made them successful in their pursuits. She was none too sure he truly wanted her as his wife, but she had no reason to question his purpose. Still, she was uneasy that all was not as well as it seemed.

That thought was echoed the next morning when she learned that Keene had chosen to spend the entire day in Mr. Ponsby's company. Her mother patted her hand and said, "He is a gentleman much used to following his own pursuits. If you want a husband who is not like Mr. Farthing, then you shall have to be content when he is about his amusements."

"Truly, Mama, I shall not mind, if he offers me the same license to amuse myself."

"Sophie, I know you do not understand the ways of the ton. And like your father I think they are unsavory, but you shall be expected to deliver an heir and a spare before you are free to seek your own . . ." Her mother blushed. "Not that I approve of such goings on, but Keene is not known to be content with one woman's company. It should be unlikely he shall change after marriage."

"And I am not to notice?"

"No, you may notice, but you are not to object. You shall make yourself miserable if you do. I can tell you, it shall only make unpleasantness if you insist on loyalty from a man who does not feel it in his heart."

Her mother stole a peek at the doorway. "Mr. Farthing should have an apoplexy if he heard me speak to you of such things. But I had a dear friend who married a libertine and she was quite miserable. You see, he was interested in her for a short while, but then he moved on, as his sort are wont to do."

"I see," said Sophie, but she didn't. In fact, the waters seemed much more murky than before.

Keene tugged on his jacket sleeve before entering the salon where the family met before dinner. He'd spent the day hunting with Mr. Ponsby. A toiling event to be sure. The local squire regarded hunting as purely a food-gathering operation, whereas Keene preferred the finer aspects of marksmanship and sport.

He was glad he had waited until the end of the day to inform Ponsby of the engagement as it was possible the squire's accuracy with his shot could have noticeably declined. Accidental shootings were always a possibility while grousing. Or perhaps his accuracy could have much improved, depending on one's perspective and Ponsby's wishes.

Instead, Ponsby had turned to him with a solemn look out of place on his chubby-cheeked cherubic face and said, "You had better take good care of her."

Ponsby had turned away with a bent head, which left Keene wondering about the vagaries of human nature. Why would Sophie turn down a man who thought so much of her? Not that he was normally given to noble thoughts, but perhaps he should withdraw his offer and allow Sophie to marry someone she inspired to devotion not just desire.

Keene could have waited until just before dinner was served before making his appearance, but he didn't want his future in-laws to feel neglected even if his presence wasn't entirely welcome.

Jane's voice drifted out of the salon. "Are you very sure that is the right path to follow? I mean, to request him to leave so soon?"

"Of course it is the right way. You can't mean that you want him to make love to our Sophie?"

Keene paused, caught between moving forward or retreating. He feared in backing away he would alert the Farthings to his presence in the shadow of the open doorway.

Keene strained to hear Jane's soft reply. "He is to be her husband. I cannot think it should be so very terrible if we gave them a little time together."

"I cannot allow it. If he learns what he is getting into, he might cry off."

"I know you don't approve of his lifestyle, but he is a gentleman. He will honor his commitment."

"Not if he learns Sophie is not as seemly as she should be, he won't."

"You are too harsh on her. She is just high-spirited."

"The consequences of her *high spirits* make me shudder, madam."

What consequences?

FOUR

Jane's voice was very low. "Which is why you should permit more interaction between the pair. Keene is a smart boy, he will . . . Is someone there?"

Keene cursed his hesitation. He walked forward confidently as if he hadn't hidden in the shadows indulging in an unmannerly exhibition of eavesdropping. "Good evening, Cousin Jane, Farthing."

Jane's posture was overly stiff, and Farthing's face looked as inviting as a mud puddle. Keene did his best to be oblivious to the obvious signs of discord. "Is Sophie down yet?"

"Not yet. I shall see what is keeping her." Jane ducked out of the room in a flurry of swishing skirts.

Was Farthing worried that Keene would find out how unrestrained Sophie's behavior could be? Or was there a deeper concern? Some other problem Farthing wanted to conceal? Keene couldn't ask without admitting he'd been listening at the door. Nor could he reassure Farthing that he had a pretty good idea of Sophie's faults. He couldn't share details of the event he'd witnessed on his arrival or her late-night visit without getting her into trouble.

In three weeks, Sophie's behavior would no longer be Farthing's problem.

No, it would be Keene's. That thought was enough to give the hardiest of souls pause.

Keene dropped down in a chair, thinking how very ostracized Sophie would be if her antics were publicized to the wrong people. How would his hopes for a future political career fare with a wife whose behavior could prove a huge embarrassment? Not that his behavior was above reproach, but society allowed a man much more license.

"I trust you had a pleasant day," said Farthing.

"Well enough. The weather was very fine, much milder than this time last year." Keene rolled his eyes. He had digressed to having so little to say to his future father-in-law that he had begun to speak of the weather, much like his relationship with his own father. Only, Lord Whitley would have found some fault with Keene's description of the conditions.

Keene rubbed his temples.

"My solicitor shall attend us tomorrow, so we might conclude the marriage settlement."

Keene nodded. Did Farthing know that Sophie was heir to the bulk of his father's property? If that information became common knowledge, she would be considered quite a catch. She might garner even more offers than his, the squire's and the gentleman from Cornwall. Was it fair to withhold that detail?

Sophie and her mother entered the salon. He rose to his feet. Sophie's gaze assessed him with a grave inquiry out of place in her normally blithe attack on life.

What now?

She moved to the far side of the room and sat.

Jane inquired after his day while Sophie stared at him without a smile. How long would she be able to sit still?

Not long. She popped up and moved to a window where she pulled back the edge of a curtain. She didn't participate in the desultory conversation.

Keene assessed her form under the yards of peach material. The dress was hopelessly outdated, although he could see some effort to modernize the capped sleeves. He supposed Farthing objected to the latest fashions as frivolous and too revealing. Sophie wore her dress with a careless disregard. Her shawl was draped negligently over her arms in what she probably didn't know was a most fashionable display.

Finally, dinner was announced and Keene offered her his arm. She tucked a bare hand into the crook of his elbow. Had she forgotten her gloves?

He lagged behind, glancing around to see if she had laid them down in the sitting room.

"What are you doing, Keene? My parents are already ahead."

"Where are your gloves?"

"I didn't wear any." She tugged on his arm as if to pull him forward.

He stopped completely. "What's wrong, Sophie?"

"Mama and I had a long conversation this morning. It has been on my mind since."

"What was the talk about?"

Sophie tilted her head. "Marriage." Her blue eyes narrowed and then dropped away. A hint of color appeared on her cheeks.

What had Jane told her? Keene stared at the backs of Sophie's parents and wondered if with their prudishness, the Farthings had conveyed to Sophie that the intimacies of marriage were a repulsive business. In this instance he should prefer his bride be totally innocent rather than have misconceptions tainting her spirit.

What exactly did Sophie know of relationships between men and women? For that matter, what of her parents' marriage? There had been no more children. He couldn't recall ever witnessing Farthing touch Jane other than when formalities required it. Even now as they walked down the hallway, Jane's hand on Farthing's arm, a considerable distance gaped between her skirts and Farthing's legs. "I daresay our marriage should be quite different than your parents'."

"Yes, Mama said it would be."

Keene pulled his arm close to his body and smoothed his hand over Sophie's. He didn't want her fretting over *her duties* or however Jane had explained the intimacies of marriage to her.

She tugged at him.

Yesterday she had exhibited no desire at all to pull away from him. "Did this talk of your mother's frighten you?"

She stopped tugging and lifted her face to stare him directly in the face. "I daresay it did."

Until this visit he hadn't thought she could be frightened. Even now she met his gaze squarely. He moved his hand to her face. "I promise you, I shall see to your pleasure. There is no need to be afraid of my touch."

"Your touch?" She blinked.

"Of making love." He should have said the hell with proprieties and promises and pulled her into his bed last night. "That is what your mother spoke to you about, isn't it?"

"No, not exactly. I'm not afraid of the intimacies of marriage, per se," she said with exasperation. Color flooded her cheeks. "Is that what you think we are speaking about?"

Keene felt a twinge of uncertainty. "What are you afraid of?"

She looked away. "Well not of *that* precisely. Come along, Papa shall be furious if we are too far behind."

Not being allowed to talk to his bride was annoying. Not having a clue what she was talking about was worse. And her claim of not being afraid didn't match with the trembling she'd done last night in his arms.

But then, he knew from his occasional rescues over the years, Sophie did not admit fear when she had to be in the throes of terror. Instead, she'd always spit fire. She'd reminded him of a dunked cat the time he'd pulled her out of the river, all fury and raised wet fur. She'd screamed at him for removing his shoes before going in after her.

He'd yelled back at her for being so damn foolish as to nearly drown herself. She'd turned and stomped away. He'd stalked after her, both of them slopping water across the lawn as he told her how foolhardy she'd been. She finally picked up her sodden skirts, the weight of which had nearly drowned her, and ran to the house.

Later, Richard had told him she'd had tears on her face. Could it be that her fury was a cover for fear?

She tugged on his arm, and he reluctantly started forward. The workings of her mind were a mystery.

Any mistake he made now could haunt him for the rest of his life. Even his attempt at reassurance had fallen off the mark. And tomorrow after the marriage settlement was concluded, he would be leaving. With the marriage to take place in less than a month he had business of his own to attend. He hadn't expected everything to happen so fast.

In the natural course of events, the engagement would be settled and her parents would bring her to London for the season where he would court her, and the marriage would follow next summer. Instead, everyone seemed in a rush, even him. Of course, *his* rush was more about wanting the rights of the marriage bed, before he remembered how very off-putting her behavior could be.

Something had happened when he watched her climb out the window and seen parts of her anatomy he shouldn't have.

Actually, something had happened years earlier when he pulled her from the river, and her wet bodice had plastered against her barely formed breasts. At the time, he'd had no business thinking that way of his cousin. She was far too young for the lascivious thoughts of a twenty-year-old. He'd stayed away after that. Now, with her window escapade, it didn't appear her behavior had changed in the intervening years.

Out here in the country who was to know how badly she behaved? He didn't have to face his friends and explain that she wasn't aware of the impropriety of displaying her drawers to the masses. Not that there had been any masses, but in London, even in his quiet square, if she backed out of a window in the middle of the day, more than blades of grass would witness her antics.

He looked down on Sophie's blonde head. Her hair was

neatly pulled up and twisted into a complicated arrangement. He knew by the end of the evening, little strands would escape from their confinement as if her hair mirrored her personality, unable to remain restrained and dignified for long.

What was going on in that head of hers? What did she think of this rush to wed? Of his not-so-subtle reminders that she would be his to bed soon?

Surely she deserved a chance to be wooed. What woman wanted a hurry-scurry to the altar—well, other than a woman in trouble? A woman like George's wife, who had not hurried fast enough to cover the problem and delivered a baby girl weighing seven pounds six months after her marriage. Of course, a compromised woman's best-laid plans could be thwarted by a child who refused to look like his mother's husband. Keene pressed his hand to his temple.

"Are you feeling well?"

He glanced down. Sophie looked up at him, her blue eyes searching his face.

"I'm fine." It was just that his life had decided to hurtle like a fallen log down a steep hill. A year ago everything had been normal, if a little boring. Now, his brother was dead. Keene was on the verge of marriage to a woman he could only imagine being tied to in his nightmares. He'd nearly killed a man who had been his friend since childhood, and his best friend George might off himself at any moment.

With Sophie in the mix, it was bound to boil over.

"If your head aches, you could have a dinner tray sent to your room."

"I'm fine."

She eyed him skeptically. "I've made you upset." Her voice was the epitome of quiet acceptance of her negative effect on people. "I give my papa many headaches."

It wasn't her at all. Or only a part. "It is not my head that hurts."

She flushed and looked away.

He smiled. Perhaps she was not as naive as he feared.

She turned back to him, her gaze boldly on his face. "We shouldn't have you in pain. What would ease your discomfort?"

He let his eyes drop to her lips, pink as rose petals.

"A hot compress? Have you perhaps strained yourself following Mr. Ponsby? He is quite vigorous in his activities although you should not know it to look at him."

Oh, well, maybe she was innocent. "I assure you I met with no injury in Ponsby's company."

"Are you very sure you do not have a headache? You were rubbing your temples when Mama and I came in earlier."

Was her solemn look concern? For him? He gave one of his more engaging smiles. "Do not give it a thought. I assure you I am in excellent health."

"Good, then." She tugged on his arm and half pulled him down the hallway.

"Sophie, *I* am to lead *you*."

"Well, all that is well and good, but I should not like to have bread and water for supper. I like to eat." She continued forward half ahead of him instead of by his side.

Farthing returned to the dining room doorway and watched them with a scowl on his face.

Why he thought anything untoward could happen between the sitting room and dining room, Keene didn't know. And why would Sophie be the one sent to bed without supper? Not that Farthing had much ability to punish him.

Keene allowed her to tow him into the room. He would definitely have to curtail that behavior. Not that he would withhold meals from his wife.

A cold sweat broke out over his body. Damn. How would he curb her waywardness when her father's repeated attempts to temper her conduct met with no success?

Later, Sophie sat at her dressing table as Letty ran the brush through her hair.

"Forty-eight, forty-nine," counted Letty under her breath.

Sophie's head nodded with each stroke. Waiting out the hundred strokes Letty insisted was proper attention tried Sophie's patience. But if she stopped the brushing before it was done, Letty would burst into tears.

Sophie had escaped the drawing room as soon as she could. Not that she wanted to be away from Keene, except that the conversation had turned to politics again. It was likely the only thing her father could think of to talk about with Keene. Sophie listened for a time, but all the different names meant nothing to her, and she had ended up more confused than interested.

A tap sounded at her door, and Sophie leaped up, disregarding the way the brush snagged in her hair. She pulled it out and threw back the door. Sophie expected her mother and a secondhand lecture about her delay in making it into the dining room.

Keene leaned one palm against the door frame, his stance relaxed as a tiger watching prey before deciding to spring. He didn't say anything for a long time.

His lids lowered over his dark eyes. He gave her one of *those* looks, a hint of amusement hovering around his unsmiling mouth. His voice low and vibrant, he said, "Brushing your hair?"

Sophie nodded, clutching the brush to her chest.

"Oh, miss, shut the door. You mustn't speak with him. You're not decent."

Keene's expression changed, tightening and closing off. He stepped back from the doorway.

"It's okay, Letty." Disappointment surged through Sophie. Letty would no more be able to keep quiet about this late-night visit than a trapped pig could keep from squealing.

"Oh, no, miss, you mustn't."

"Go on and go to bed, Letty."

"Oh, no, miss. I can't leave you with him here. I knows my duty."

Keene assessed Sophie. His head tilted slightly in inquiry.

Without moving his gaze from Sophie he said, "Letty, if you wish to stay with your mistress, you might remember that you shall be in my employ in a few weeks."

"Oh, Lord." Letty twisted her gown in her hands, her gaze darting between them. "I haven't finished your hair, miss."

"It's enough for tonight."

"You cannot do this, miss. You know you should not."

"Wish my future husband a good night? He does not mean to come in. Do you, Keene?"

"I am here because I leave tomorrow after your father and I conclude our business. I am not sure that I shall be allowed to bid you farewell without him standing between us."

He was leaving? Disappointment settled in her stomach like an unpleasant meal. She swallowed. "What business?"

"The marriage settlement."

"I hope you are pleased with it."

An odd expression flitted across his face. "I am well satisfied."

Letty crossed the floor and tried to pull Sophie from the doorway and shut the door.

Sophie knew she couldn't ignore her high-strung maid for long or she would have hysterics and that would bring the whole house down on them.

Keene brushed inside the room and shut the door. "Stay, then, but don't make a sound."

He might as well ask for the moon.

Letty released her. Her whisper was strained. "Miss Sophie, you are in your *nightgown.*"

"She needn't stay in it on my account." Keene's gaze flicked over the long flannel gown.

He reached for the sides of the gown and Sophie's heart pounded. She wasn't quite sure what he meant to do.

He fanned the folds of material out. "Quite a modest gown. You have enough material here to house half of Wellington's army."

"I shouldn't think you'd care to find any soldiers using my nightgown as a tent."

His eyes flicked to hers. "I daresay not. I should have to shoot any man I found under your nightgown."

The words were delivered with a mild, amused tone, but there was a hint of steel in his eyes.

Letty gave a choked sob.

"Not a sound." He didn't even bother to turn his head toward the maid.

Letty stuffed her fist in her mouth.

"You do not care for my nightclothes, sir?"

"Perhaps you have something a little less concealing in your trousseau?"

Sophie shook her head, mesmerized by his presence. The dim light from the single lamp on her dressing table caused his face to move in and out of shadow. "It's warm."

His grin caught at her heartstrings. Tingles danced over her skin. He dropped the sides of her gown and reached for her hand. "I should imagine it is." He lifted the lace-edged knuckle-length sleeve and raised her hand.

The warmth and pressure of his lips against her skin made her heart pound in an erratic tattoo.

"Must you leave tomorrow?"

"Yes, I must. Did your father tell you?"

Sophie shook her head.

Keene pressed his lips together and looked at her maid. "You can leave. I shall take no further advantage of your mistress."

"Miss, please, you'll be on bread and water again."

Keene rolled his eyes.

Knowing her papa, Sophie suspected the decision to leave wasn't entirely Keene's. "I want to hear why you're leaving. Did Papa say you must?"

"They don't tell you much, do they?"

No, they thought quite a bit should be kept from her. Unfortunately, they didn't reckon with her natural curiosity and inquisitiveness. Sophie was sure she knew much more than either of her parents suspected. She knew they thought Keene was a rake of the worst sort, and while her mother had discussed that with her, Sophie knew they would never in a million years discuss things like her marriage portion with her. Would Keene insist on keeping her in the dark, too?

"What disposition was made for me?"

"You will inherit your father's estate. For now, you have a dowry of three thousand pounds, or rather, I shall receive it."

"Thank you."

Keene blinked. "You didn't know that, either?"

Sophie shook her head.

"I gave my assurances that your mother shall continue to live here as long as she wishes if your father predeceases her. I thought that is as you would want it. Of course, if you wish to stay here, you may."

Did he mean alone with her parents? After their marriage? She wanted to live in London with Keene. "I should wish to stay in your home."

Keene looked away.

"After we're married, of course."

What was he thinking? Did he wish Letty would go? Sophie wished he would kiss her. She thought she would die if he didn't kiss more than her hand. His thumb rubbed slowly across her knuckles where he held her.

"Your father tells me you do the accounts."

"Well, yes, the household and some of the rents."

"Ah, I see."

"So you have come to wish me good-bye?" She heard the breathiness in her voice.

Keene's attention returned to her, his dark eyes traveling over the voluminous gown, landing on her face and holding her eyes. He lifted a strand of her hair and let the curl wrap around his finger.

She was tired of waiting. "Would you kiss me farewell?"

"No."

Her heart landed at her knees and punched a hole in her stomach on the way down. She felt wobbly and sick. Had her boldness repulsed him? The silence in the room was deafening. And to make it worse, Letty witnessed Sophie's humiliation.

He tugged on her hand, pulling her closer. "I shall not kiss you, but you might kiss me."

A flash of anger threaded through her and entwined with desire, forming into a knotty tangle in her stomach.

He waited, a sensual half smile inviting her liquid response.

She sidled up to him like she had observed a prostitute do to a man in the nearby town of Shrewsbury. She slowly draped her arms over his shoulders, pressing her body against him. His dark eyes lit with an anticipation. She reached up with her mouth, and realized she had no idea what to do next. But then, she was a creature of impulses, and it came to her.

Keene waited to see if Victor would receive him. His manservant had taken his calling card with a skeptical look. A year ago they would have ignored the formality. Keene rubbed the sore spot on his lower lip and grinned. The little minx had nearly drawn blood when she bit him. One thing was sure, Sophie would never bore him.

"Lord Wedmont will see you."

Keene nodded and followed the valet back to the bedroom at the rear of Victor's rented London rooms.

Victor sat propped in his bed. The bandage over his right shoulder made a large lump under his open shirt. Keene paused at the foot of the bed.

"Well, sit down, man. You can write this damn letter for me as you inflicted the injury that makes my writing illegible."

"I aimed for your thigh."

"I know." Victor leaned back against the pillows and closed his eyes. His skin looked pasty and grooves bracketed his mouth.

Remorse trickled through Keene. "What do the doctors say?"

"They say I shall have limited use of my arm. God help me if I cannot write. I shall never manage my estate."

Victor's estate was a crumbling old, fortified house on a small patch of land in the north country. His father and grandfather had sold off all the adjoining farms and pasturelands to raise funds, leaving only a forest good for hunting.

Now, Victor had to make regular arrangements for food and livestock to be brought in. Even the toll road his family had once owned was now a regular drain on his pockets because of the frequent trips he made home to straighten out problems.

Keene was glad he'd avoid such a thankless situation, assuming his father did not change his will again.

"Here." Victor handed Keene a piece of paper and pointed to the ink and pen on the side table. Blotchy, smeared chicken scratches covered the top of the paper. Victor handed over the book on his lap that doubled as a writing surface. "The worst part of using my left hand is that it drags through the wet ink. Look at this." He raised his blackened left hand. "It'll be a fortnight before these ink stains wear off."

Keene wrote the letter as Victor dictated it. He handed it to Victor, who read it and set it on the table beside his bed. "Good, now, if you mean to take offense at anything I say, you may leave."

Keene leaned forward in his chair and raked his hands through his hair. "I should not have challenged you. I am sorry."

Victor held his silence.

Keene didn't know if his explanation of what happened would help. Either way, he felt he had to account for his behavior. "I went to congratulate or console George on the early arrival of his child. The servants told me he was closeted in the library and no one will disturb him. Amelia was quite distraught. I thought maybe the baby was born too soon and was in trouble, but no. The baby is healthy and full size. I had no thought other than George had been a little before in his duties. I opened the library door and found him with his pistol in his mouth."

Nothing could explain the sheer terror that had iced his spine at that sight. George had put the gun down before Keene could approach him to wrestle it away. Put the gun down and told Keene to go away. Instead, Keene had taken the gun away and held George as he sobbed like a baby over Amelia's betrayal and learned it was with a friend they both considered as a brother.

"She never told me," said Victor.

Keene stared at Victor as another piece of the puzzle clicked into place. "I promised George to punish you. I would have slit my own wrists if I had thought it should stop him from killing himself."

"So you would kill one of us to save him."

"I was not thinking straight. Richard was not in his grave above two weeks."

Victor waved off his explanation. "Have you seen George?"

"This morning. He is drunk."

Victor reached behind him and grabbed the headboard. "So early? It is barely noon."

"They tell me this is normal. It is better than blowing his brains out, isn't it?"

"How is she?"

"Amelia is despondent. George will not speak to her."

"Not her."

Keene looked at Victor's pinched face and the dark brown locks that normally would be brushed into a disordered study of windswept waves. His hair was simply brushed back, although its natural tendency to curl meant his hair swooped down and brushed over, his temples.

"My daughter."

Keene felt a wellspring of despair. Why did everyone persist in making this situation worse? "She's not your daughter; she's George's."

"Is she well?"

"The baby is healthy."

"Do they care for her? Or will she be an outcast in her family?"

"George will do what is right. He will raise her as he should." Keene would see to it.

"But will he love her?"

The question plagued Keene. George was one of the most honorable men he knew. Surely he would come around. "Give him time."

Victor's brown eyes narrowed. "Her lifetime?"

Keene shifted uneasily.

"Perhaps we should join George in his cups so all these confidences seem less painful."

"You do not look healthy enough to indulge."

"These concerns for my health overwhelm me." Sarcasm laced Victor's voice.

None of Keene's apologies and explanations would mend the wound in Victor's shoulder. Remorse sat heavily on Keene. He stood. "I should leave. Your servant, sir."

"Sit down. I have no company. George has disowned me and everyone else is out of town. I am heartily bored with myself."

"Would you care for a game of whist?" offered Keene.

"I should. I see you have announced your engagement in the paper."

"Yes."

"Shall you care to introduce me to your bride?"

"After she is my wife."

Victor grinned. "This is quite sudden. Where did you meet her?"

"I have known her all my life. She is my cousin."

"So when shall you marry her?"

"Three weeks from yesterday."

"So fast? Is there a rush?"

Keene frowned as he dealt the cards he'd retrieved from the cluttered dresser. "No. She is as pure as I found her."

"You disappoint me."

"I promised her father."

"So why the hurry? It's rather fast upon Richard's passing."

Keene shrugged. It was indecently fast considering his brother had only been dead three months.

"Amelia's parents tried to convince George to marry sooner, right after he proposed."

Keene hadn't heard that before. He looked up at Victor.

"Said they wished to have her settled before they traveled to Europe."

Keene vaguely remembered George complaining that his in-laws hadn't taken a trip they had said they would take, but then shortly afterward Amelia's father had passed away and their intention to travel was irrelevant.

"Perhaps if he'd allowed himself to be persuaded sooner or been less honorable in his behavior toward Amelia we should not have this mess on our hands."

Keene closed his eyes. George had wanted to believe the child was his. He'd even commented during Amelia's pregnancy that he thought there might be twins, she was growing so large so soon. George had believed the child was his long after the rest of them grew suspicious. In fact, his complete confidence that the child—or children—was his convinced Keene that Amelia's pregnancy was of George's making.

"And if you should find your bride had need of a timely wedding, what will you do?"

Keene tugged at his lip.

Victor watched with a mixture of wary trepidation and curiosity.

"I should not do anything."

"Would you want to know? Personally, I should prefer to leave the matter in question. I should have liked to think the baby might be George's." Victor shifted and pain lanced down from his torn shoulder. "Go away, man. I need to rest."

"Are you sure?"

Victor wanted to throw something at him. At the same time, his rage toward Keene was sliding away. He wanted to hang on to it, yet he didn't want to throw away the friendship that had bound them since they were children. It was just his luck that a man he considered one of his closest friends would try to kill him over a woman. Or, not just a woman, but a woman whose situation tore at the illusions that held them all sane.

Now there was a baby. His baby, yet not his. Why hadn't Amelia told him?

And as Victor stared at the ceiling in his room he wondered if it would have made any difference to him then. He honestly didn't know.

FIVE

Sophie ran through the frost-tipped grass to the stables. "Where is she?" she demanded of the first groom she saw.

"Which one, miss?"

"The one that is to be mine."

"I don't rightly know. They's in the last two stalls past Thunder and Lightning."

Sophie lifted the skirts of her morning gown as she stepped around the rakings. She should have changed into her riding habit and boots. She would as soon as she got a look at the horse her papa had bought as her marriage gift.

When she learned the news from her mother, she'd been too impatient to wait. Actually, she'd hoped to catch her father before he left on his morning ride, but she didn't see him in the dim light of the stables.

She found the two horses toward the end of the row. Both gleamed in brown glory, but one was older than the other. Sophie moved to the younger of the two horses. Surely this was to be hers. The young mare raised her sleek velvety nose and nudged Sophie, looking for a treat. "I'm sorry, love. I shall bring you an apple next time."

The mare's large brown eyes appeared to accept her as Sophie reached to stroke the nose of the horse.

A commotion at the far end of the stable caused the horse to shy back violently only to start and roll its eyes.

Sophie shushed the horse. "I know, my pretty, it is all strange and new. I bet you need to get out and run free."

The other horse cast a disinterested glance in their direction. The young mare allowed Sophie to stroke her nose and soothe her. One of the grooms swept by her, and the horse shied away again. "What's her name?"

" 'Ey tell me her's Salamanca and that one is Daisy."

Daisy, the other new horse, looked like a Daisy, placid and tame. "What kind of a name is Salamanca?"

The boy shrugged. "I guess her's named after the battle."

"It's a silly name for a horse."

"I'm going to have to lead her outside to the paddock so I can muck out her stall."

"I'll take her out for a quick ride. She needs the exercise to gentle her. Go get me a saddle, please."

"I'm not sure you should do that, miss," said the groom skeptically.

"Sure I should. She is to be mine, after all. Poor thing is confused and frightened in a whole new place. She shall be better for being ridden. Besides, she likes me, see."

The horse edged forward, allowing Sophie access to her flank. Sophie rewarded the mare with long soothing strokes. The groom shook his head.

"Go on and fetch me a saddle. I should hate to have to tell Quigsby I had to do it myself." Sophie smiled at the boy, but she knew he would do her bidding when she threatened to report him to the head groom.

He grumbled as he put on the saddle. "If you please, miss, I'll be just a minute to fetch me a 'orse."

"No need. I shall just trot her up the drive and back. We shall be gone no longer than it takes you to sweep her stall. I'm not really dressed for riding."

Sophie led the young mare outside into the yard. The horse shied and twitched, tossing its head.

"Come, love, I bet you haven't been ridden in a week." Sophie led the mare to the mounting block, stroking the sleek brown coat. "You are such a pretty thing." The horse was all smooth muscle and bundled energy. "I do not like the name Salamanca. I shall call you Grace."

Sophie shifted into the saddle, and Grace took off without waiting for her rider to settle. Sophie managed to get her foot in the stirrup as the horse ran forward. Grace was not of a mind to follow the drive so Sophie let her have her head as they took off across a field toward the woods. Once Grace burned off some energy, Sophie would steer her onto a bridle path.

Only, directing Grace proved harder than expected. Sophie gave a solid jerk on the reins, trying to wrest control from the headstrong horse. Grace reared.

Sophie pitched forward and held on for dear life. She considered herself too good a horsewoman to be thrown. Grace came back on all fours and careened through the trees.

"Dear God, why are you riding that unbroken horse?"

Sophie whipped her head around to see Mr. Ponsby galloping his horse behind her.

"Hello, to you," she yelled back. "She's just a little nervous with the new surroundings."

"Sophie, I was with your father when he bought her. She is not broken yet. I was coming over to speak with your father about her training."

Sophie tried again to steer the horse toward the path. Between her efforts at redirecting the horse and Ponsby's approach, Grace took exception.

"Stop that horse!" shouted Ponsby.

Grace bucked.

Sophie had the bizarre thought as she tumbled forward that if she had not been braced for Grace to rear, she should not be watching her skirts fly over her head and about to have an intimate meeting with the ground.

She seemed to be in the air an extraordinarily long time. Ponsby cried out her name. Then the ground jarred every part of her from her head down.

Grace gave an hysterical neigh and then there was silence. Images swam before Sophie's eyes, and she shut them rather than allowing the motion to make her sick.

When she opened them again Ponsby was over her, or rather, two Ponsbys leaned over her as if one were not enough. At first she heard his pleas as if he were far away.

"Sophie, please say something. Sophie!"

"I'm all right."

Ponsby moaned.

Sophie wasn't sure the words had come out as she thought them. Ponsby didn't seem too reassured. She raised an arm and put her hand on his shoulder. He pulled her hand between his own and kissed it.

He stroked her hair. "Talk to me, Sophie."

"Everything is fuzzy."

"Oh, dear Lord," muttered the squire. "I need to get you home. You landed on your head."

Why should she move when everything around her was moving? "I should like to lie here a moment, please. I shall be fine in a trice."

"Are you sure?"

She nodded, which hurt, so she closed her eyes.

As senses and sensations returned, Sophie was aware that her legs were quite cold. She shivered. Her teeth rattled painfully in her head.

Ponsby tore off his coat and draped it over her. Sophie tried to sit. The movement made her dizzy. She clutched at Ponsby's shirt as she lay back down, uncertain the ground would be there. Everything swung around at an alarming rate.

Ponsby ran his large hands first over her head and then over her body. She should stop him, but Sophie was more concerned with simple things like getting the world to stop tilting.

"I do not think you have broken anything. Where does it hurt?"

The question didn't make sense to her although she knew it should, but everything seemed fuzzy, even her thoughts.

"Sophie, look at me."

She tried to obey as his large beefy hands framed her face. At least only one image of him remained. "I landed on my head?"

"I shouldn't have shouted at you."

"It's my fault. I do not blame you. I thought that . . ." Sophie forgot what she had meant to say.

"Yes?"

She frowned. Something about, "Marriage?"

"Why are you marrying him?"

"Keene?"

"Your father doesn't like him."

Sophie felt bad that her refusal had wounded the squire, but not so bad that she wanted to comfort him when her head was pounding like a regimental drum. And that reminded her of her punishment when she'd refused Sir Gresham's suit. She didn't want to spend the next week on bread and water. Lately, she'd spent far too much time confined in her room for all sorts of unclear transgressions.

"We can't ever tell Papa about this." Sophie grabbed the squire's shoulders. "Just like that first time I drove out with you to the old abbey. Please, swear to me you'll never tell."

The squire looked confused. Sophie's head swam.

"Please, Papa should be so upset with me if he ever learns of my fall from Grace."

"If it doesn't work out with your cousin, my offer still stands. I know that you are so very high above me, but I should wish for nothing more than the honor of being your husband."

Sophie hugged the burly man. What else could she do?

Daniel Farthing gripped the reins so tightly he could feel the bite of leather through his gloves. Tears sprang to his eyes as he recoiled at the sight of Sophie and Ponsby on the ground. Where had he gone wrong?

He'd tried so very hard to raise his daughter right, but Sophie had shown an alarming tendency to indulge in pleasures of the flesh from the earliest moment when she would rub her fluffy crib blanket against her cheek. He remembered her tiny hands as she sat on his lap and tugged on his ear or hair. Always so busy, always touching and feeling things as if seeing wasn't enough.

He should have married her off sooner. Thank God he had not let her go to London for a season where her tendencies could have drawn her into worse trouble. A month ago when he had watched her sneak stealthily from Sir Gresham's room, terror had struck his heart. His daughter in a man's bedroom in the middle of the night!

He had heard the baronet's low moans, ending some time before she crept out. The noise had woken him from a sound sleep.

The thought of Sophie with a man made him sick. But what could he do? The damage was done at that point.

But then she had refused Sir Gresham's offer. Daniel'd put her on bread and water for the rest of the week. He had been far too indulgent with his daughter.

When the squire had made his offer and haltingly suggested that although their stations were not equal he had reason to believe Sophie held some affection for him, it had seemed like a Godsend. Then, she refused the squire's offer, too.

In desperation Daniel had written to his wife's cousin, Lord Whitley. He'd always thought that as a second son, Richard might have made a good match for Sophie, but by the time his letter arrived Richard was dead, and Keene was sent instead.

That Keene, the eternal rake who rarely associated with any woman more than a fortnight was willing to marry Sophie surprised him. That Sophie accepted without a fight surprised him even more, but perhaps the two of them with their penchants for indulging in pleasures of the flesh were best suited for each other. Daniel only hoped that when Keene learned of his bride's wicked ways he should not turn her out on her ear.

His hand shaking, he led his horse away from where Sophie and the squire lay on the ground. Her skirts were tumbled around her waist and he'd seen Ponsby's hands on her limbs, cupping her face. Sophie had reached for the squire, pulled him down by his shirt when he moved away. He'd heard his own daughter speak of her fall from grace.

When Daniel was far enough away to not overhear or be overheard he dismounted and leaned his forehead against a tree. The bark bit into his skin, and he fought the sickness and tears that threatened to overwhelm him.

Although at the moment he wanted to shoot Ponsby, he couldn't fault him. He'd offered again to make an honest woman of her. And damn her wicked flesh, she must have set her ambitions on a title and a path to that den of iniquities. London.

If he could do anything to save her from herself, he should make sure she never set foot in that place. For a young woman who had no control over her morals that city would be the death of her.

Keene cradled the infant against his shoulder, feeling a tight bond with the unwelcome child.

"Ah, there you are."

Keene turned to the doorway of the third-floor nursery where Amelia stood.

"Yes."

"George is in the library."

"Has he seen his daughter?"

Amelia shook her head. Keene studied her. She had the soft lines of a woman who had recently given birth and a deep sadness that made Beowulf seem like a lighthearted romp. She carried it all with an inborn grace, her shoulders straight and her neck arched like a swan's.

Little Regina already showed hints of her mother's elegance in the delicate way she stretched out her hand and her little fingers curled around his lapel.

"Shall we go see your papa?"

Amelia gave a start and reached out a hand, which fell to her side. "Perhaps she should stay here in the nursery."

"Hiding her will not make his anger go away. If he sees she is just an innocent little child who needs his care and protection he may snap out of his depression."

Doubt tainted Amelia's porcelain features. "I wish for him to be happy. I have thought the baby and I should go to the country."

"You made him happy once."

"Before he learned of—" She broke off and bit her lip.

Keene hesitated to call it a betrayal. From what he knew, Amelia had been loyal once the ring was on her finger. "Your indiscretion."

Amelia dabbed at the corner of her eye with a lace handkerchief. "He will never forgive me."

Since they were speaking of it. . . . "Why didn't you tell him sooner?"

She gave a smile that looked more like a grimace. A tear leaked out and dripped down her cheek. "I thought he was being so very noble and understanding by pretending to believe the baby was his. I thought he knew. It would have been obvious to you or any other man. I loved him all the more for that."

She turned away. Keene was torn. On one hand he thought she had brought her troubles on herself. On the other hand, last year they had all been so free and easy. Never in a month of Sundays would he have thought life would have spun them into such an uncomfortable weave.

"I hear you are to be married."

"Yes."

She watched him out of the corner of her eye. She balled up her handkerchief. Huge signs of distress from a woman who was always perfectly demure and ladylike.

"I was given to understand that you would not marry."

"Things change. I wanted Richard as my heir."

"Oh, Keene, I am so very sorry." She glided toward him. "I hope your wife will not be a burden like me. I wanted so very much to make George happy, and all I have done is make him miserable. Please, Keene, you are his dearest friend." She touched his arm ever so lightly. "Tell me if I should go away. If you could learn what I should do to ease his mind, I will do it. I hate that this has come to pass. I have told him how very sorry I am, that I would do anything to put things right. We were so very happy."

She patted the baby's back.

"I'll talk to him. I want you both to attend my wedding." Perhaps it would serve as a reminder of how much in love they had been on their own wedding day.

"He will not wish for me to go, but perhaps it shall be good for him to do something. Please do convince him."

Keene could smell her soft fragrance, hear the whisper of silk as she moved. At one time he would have wanted to touch her, to have her gentle smile turned in his direction. Now, he only wondered why she had chosen to stand so close to him. Shifting her baby into one arm he reached out and smoothed his hand down her back.

Amelia shuddered. The expression on her face turned from serenely distant to something between horror and fascination. She took a half step back. "Please, Keene, your betrayal should kill him," she whispered.

No point in mincing words. "And yours, madam?"

She stared off at a corner of the room. Her elbows were bent in the perfect pose of composure, her spine straight and her features once again in that bland expression that hid her passionate nature. "He expects no less of me."

Only George's drunken confessions of his pleasure in

his wife's bed made him know that Amelia was not the cool goddess in every respect. That and her transgression with Victor.

Keene's blood ran cold. "Would you have married any one of us?"

"George is the only one who asked."

She turned to him, her gaze clear and direct.

He couldn't bring himself to ask if she would have slept with any of them. Obviously she had slept with Victor and hadn't told him that she conceived.

"I loved all of you, but I loved George best. I never thought he would . . ."

"Propose?"

"I never thought he would love me."

Why hadn't Victor proposed? Why hadn't she told Victor about the baby? Why hadn't she told any of them?

Amelia crossed the room and straightened the baby's bedclothes. He could see her shaking as she performed the domestic task. He wanted to wrap her in his arms and comfort her. He hated the urge. Amelia was too complicated. She tucked her yearnings under like a dove, the momentary attraction discreetly hidden, until he wondered if he'd imagined it. Only, he didn't think so. He had good instincts around women, and they rarely proved wrong.

Thank God, Sophie was straightforward and honest as the day was long. Sophie wore her emotions like a peacock wore his feathers, bright, bold and baleful.

He stared at the woman across the room, wondering what he could do to set the situation to rights. George did love his wife. Otherwise he should not be so desperate now. "Tell him Victor attacked you."

She clutched the crib sheet she had just straightened, pulling it off the bed as she turned. "I cannot lie."

"George needs to believe in your honor. If you tell him Victor forced you he will . . ." be martyr enough to welcome her back into his heart, "feel you did him no dishonor."

"I already told him the truth," Amelia whispered, as if the truth was too awful to be acknowledged in normal tones. "I would not ever speak of it to you if I did not think you could help George. But upon my word, Victor did not force himself upon me."

"Amelia, tell George you lied because you didn't wish to damage his friendship. Give him back his dignity."

"So he can shoot Victor, too? No, Keene, I will not lie. There would be no honor in that, and it should all be false." Her voice broke. "He is such a good and honorable man. I know that I aspire too high to expect his esteem, but I would not have it on false pretexts."

"Yes, he is so good and honorable as to be drunk insensible by noon each day." Keene moved restlessly across the floor. Regina whimpered. He bounced her, hoping to soothe both their agitations.

"I have wounded him beyond measure."

"And he would continue to plunge the knife in the breast of those who are innocent because he is in pain." Damn him, and damn her for showing dignity when he least expected it. "Either you will do anything or nothing at all."

Amelia stood with the sunlight filtering in on her hands clasped before her. "I will not lie. I should not have withheld the truth before."

"Well there is honor in that, I suppose."

Sophie passed the next few days in a fog. Sometimes she was fine, while other times her ability to concentrate on what was being said disappeared totally. She was pretty sure the odd sensation of fading in and out of reality and occasional dizzy spells were due to the fall and the hard knock on her head.

Her mother attributed Sophie's unusual behavior to prewedding excitement. Her father—well Sophie wasn't quite sure what to think of her father. He became grim and solemn, as if not at all happy with her. Sophie couldn't quite figure out why.

She didn't think her father knew she had taken the horse out for a ride. After Mr. Ponsby helped her to a side door of the house, he'd tracked down the riderless mare and led her back to the stables.

The big day approached rapidly. Other than a formal letter from Keene informing her parents that he meant to arrive the day before the ceremony, they hadn't heard from him. Her attempts at letters had ended up balled up or shredded. She couldn't find the right tone with which to address him.

Nerves and excitement kept her awake long into the nights. Fear propelled her out of bed in the mornings. Fatigue made her fall asleep in the sitting room after dinner, only to have her mother wake her with a gentle shake. Did Keene even give her a thought?

By God, what must he think of her? She had bit him like a rabid dog when she had last seen him. He had thrust her away and looked like he had every intention of throttling her, except for a wicked—amused?—gleam in his eye. But she wasn't sure the gleam wasn't a trick of the flickering lamplight. The slow deliberate look he'd given her meant something. He'd stepped toward Sophie, and her maid gave a squeak. His glance at Letty had prompted some change in his plan.

She'd pressed her fingers to his lower lip, regretting her impulsive action, all the while her heart had threatened to leap out of her chest and dance on the floor in front of him. Heat had flooded her body, making her damp and weak. All he'd done was turn slightly and press his lips against her fingertips, and she was ready to swoon. He'd bowed and left.

Letty had given her a wide-eyed stare and said, "Oh, miss, he'll make you so happy."

Sophie thought it was a rather odd statement, given that

he'd just made her quite cross by refusing to kiss her and suggesting she, who had rather limited knowledge of such things, take the lead. Rather like letting Grace have her head. It only led to trouble.

Although Sophie admired the sleek perfection of the horse, she was relieved to hear she was not to be hers, Daisy was. Her mother explained it was because she might soon need a more gentle horse if she became enceinte. Frankly, Sophie didn't think she wanted to be thrown again. She could hardly walk straight for the two days following and had endured her father's fierce frown when she waddled through the hall.

"Her head's in the clouds again," said the seamstress, pinning and tucking the wedding gown around her.

"Are you very sure this gown is in the latest fashion? I shouldn't wish to embarrass Keene in front of his London friends."

"I am quite sure your father shall disapprove," answered her mother.

Sophie nodded and wiped a hand across her sweat-beaded forehead.

"Although in a way this style of gown is revealing, I think it should be quite handy for concealing one's condition. I do remember finding most of my clothes so very uncomfortable when I was expecting you." Her mother twitched the high-waisted skirt of the gown around.

"Do you think Keene is quite eager to get an heir?"

The seamstress and her mother exchanged glances. Sophie felt momentarily excluded from a private sisterhood of women.

"Most men are eager to do their part," said the seamstress.

Her mother hushed the woman. "He doesn't have Richard as a reserve heir any longer. He needs to think about the future."

Was that the only reason he had proposed? Now that Richard was dead he needed a son, therefore a wife, and her parents had applied for aid at the exact right time. What better choice than a country bumpkin cousin who'd followed him around like a lovesick loon when they were children? He could be assured of her devotion and count on her lacking the sophistication of a lady exposed to society.

Her stomach rolled, and as so often had happened since her fall, the room tilted at a sickening angle.

Hands caught her. The seamstress and her mother led her toward the sofa and guided her down.

They were talking, and she couldn't understand. Slowly, the sound came back as a cold compress was pressed against her head, and a straight pin poked her in the ribs.

"Did you eat this morning, Sophie?" asked her mother.

"I ate, but it didn't agree with me." Should she tell her mother about the fall from the horse? Perhaps she needed a doctor.

Her mother dismissed the seamstress. "How long have you been feeling like this?"

"Just a couple of weeks. I should have told you, I suppose."

Her mother patted her hand. "Now you see why you need a gentle horse."

Sophie nodded, wondering when her mother had learned of the fall from the unbroken mare. "I did not mean to fall from Grace."

"I'm sure you didn't. I don't know when you had the opportunity. Your father tried to keep such a close eye on you. I suppose Keene slipped into your bedroom when we were all abed."

What did that have to do with falling from the horse? "Well yes, but—"

"It's quite all right, Sophie. No point in worrying about spilled milk. I shan't tell your father of this. Although he has his suspicions already."

"But what is wrong with me that I am so dizzy all the sudden?"

"It's quite normal. It shall pass in time."

"Do I need to see the doctor?"

"It's unnecessary. Perhaps later when you are settled you should have Keene arrange for your care. I am having a tray brought in. I want you to try to eat a little."

"Oh, Mama, I couldn't."

"Yes, you must keep up your strength. We shan't speak of this anymore. I daresay Keene is very persuasive, although I had thought . . . well never mind."

"He has a way of looking at me." Sophie blushed and realized she didn't want to discuss her rampant fascination with her future husband with her mother.

"Sophie, darling, that is all well and good, but you must think of behaving with more seemliness. In my day a young woman who was a little wild was looked upon with indulgence, but I'm afraid in today's society there is much less tolerance for untoward behavior."

"Should Keene dislike it?"

"You will be his wife and of course he will inform you of what he wants, but you must not speak of these things in the drawing room."

Sophie wasn't any more clear than a moment before, but sometimes her mother's explanations could get all tangled like a kitten's play yarn. Perhaps Keene would explain it to her better. She would ask him. "Yes, ma'am."

A servant knocked and entered the room with the tea cart.

Keene moved through the doorway and down the stairs to the library where, if he were lucky, he would find George in something less than a drunken stupor. He heard the rustle of Amelia's skirts as she followed him.

He flung back the door of the library and crossed the room. "Look who I have brought to see her papa."

George didn't look at him or the baby. "I'll ring for her nursemaid."

"Come, George, she is a pretty little thing. I daresay we

should plan for her marriage. Perhaps I'll have a son, and we can pledge them to each other in the cradle."

"If that would please you."

George's dull response frustrated him. "And if my son is a no-good rascal, how should you feel then?"

George waved his hand as if dismissing the notion.

"Have you held her even once?" asked Keene softly.

"What care have you for the baby? Why are you always toting her around? Is there a chance she could be your brat?"

Amelia's stiff intake of breath brought both men to heel. She pressed her lips together as she crossed the room. "I'll just take her back to the nursery."

Keene reluctantly gave over the little bundle. "There is not a chance."

Amelia shut the door behind her, the fading sound of baby wails left the men in silence.

"That child did not choose her parents. She will know nothing of her lineage if you don't want it mentioned. I won't speak of it. Amelia only speaks of it when forced to, and Victor won't speak of it even if I have to shoot him again to keep his silence. You are the only father she will ever know."

George stared down at his desk.

Keene sank into one of the leather chairs by the window. "You disappoint me, sir. I thought you had more honor."

"I have so much honor, my friends trample over it gladly and laugh in their sleeves when I am too much the fool to realize."

"No one is laughing."

"I cannot look at that child without thinking of her conception."

"So Amelia was not virtuous. How many of us are?"

"I was." George's blue eyes met him sincerely.

"Well, then it is good that at least one of you knew what to do."

"You bastard."

"Yes. Well we all have our failings, George. Amelia has hers, but she loves you, and you were happy when you didn't realize that the child wasn't yours. She thought you knew and were just being kind in allowing her to keep her dignity."

"Did you know?"

"I knew the baby had been conceived before the marriage. All of us knew that when she began to show less than a month after your wedding."

"How you must have laughed at me."

"No one was laughing. I thought it was yours. Victor thought that the child could have been yours. It is only by your reaction and mine that he knows differently."

"I cannot look at her the same."

"Then look at her differently, but look at them both. The child who will know you as her father and the wife that is devoted to you now." Keene squirmed as he said the words. Was Amelia devoted enough?

George rubbed his hands over his face.

Would it ever be enough? "Think, man. She is your wife. You cannot turn your back on her, and the child doesn't deserve to be punished no matter who fathered her."

"What would you do? What if this little cousin of yours comes to you with another man's seed filling her belly?"

"I should make the most of it. I should not fault my future wife for a sin that I have repeatedly indulged in, and a child, any child, should never feel the lack of my affection."

"Then you do not love her, for you do not understand the pain of this."

"That I cannot, sir." Keene shifted in his chair. "I would wish that you and your wife would accompany me to my wedding."

"I am not going anywhere with her."

"Then come alone."

"I won't leave her in London with that man here too."

"Then I shall insist Victor come along, too."

"You just shot him. I heartily doubt he will dance at your wedding."

"If he agrees to accompany me, are you pledged to attend?"

George gave an abrupt laugh. "By all means."

SIX

So it was with the unfair advantage of knowing that Victor and he were on speaking terms that Keene pressed the bargain with George. Only the unfortunate circumstance of a rainstorm and a broken axle on the second coach resulted in the three of them pinned together in the confines of his carriage on the road to the Farthings' house.

Until now, Victor was the only one who required the use of the carriage, his shoulder not healed enough to ride a horse.

George pulled a flask from inside his coat. "I cannot conceive of how you thought this was a good idea."

From his corner, Victor quirked an eyebrow at Keene as if he wondered the same thing.

"George, do contrive to make sure you can stand through the ceremony."

"We should have stayed at the inn." George raised the flask.

"Just like old times," commented Victor facetiously.

Keene suspected it would never be like old times. Richard was dead. Amelia had slept with Victor and married George. He supposed if they followed their normal patterns, his turn with Amelia would be next, although they hadn't always shared women. Certainly, now that he thought about it, he couldn't recall George ever participating in the skirt-chasing they had done.

"We couldn't have stayed at the inn if I am to make my wedding."

"You do not seem terribly enthusiastic, else you should have planned to arrive a few days in advance."

Keene rubbed his forehead. "I am honoring my promise to her father. Besides, if we had not lost a day because of the problems with the other carriage we should not be so late."

Victor watched him. "I've never known you to be so concerned with a young woman's virtue."

"I am so. I never seduce unmarried gentlewomen."

"Now, where is the harm in seducing your future wife?" asked Victor.

"Perhaps we should talk of something else," suggested Keene.

Victor kicked the seat across from him. "Share the flask, George."

"I shall not share anything with you, sir."

"You already have. Give Keene some. He is in sore need of some Dutch courage."

"I am not," protested Keene.

"Was he always so stingy?" Victor asked of no one in particular.

George handed the flask to Keene. He took a swallow and absently passed it to Victor.

"I think I shall send her away."

"For heaven's sake, George. You cannot do that. You will ruin Amelia."

"She came to me ruined."

"Seemed in rather fine shape to me," commented Victor.

George lunged across the carriage, reaching for Victor's throat. For two days of traveling they had been spoiling for a fight. Keene was inclined to let them go at it. In the limited confines of the carriage a boot caught him in the shin. He grabbed the forgotten flask and stopped the spreading stain on the seat. He opened the carriage door and planted his boot in the nearest rear end and pushed.

The coach drew to a quick halt.

"Fine way to arrive at one's wedding," he muttered.

The two men rolled in the mud for a few seconds, until a completely sodden and soiled Victor broke away and climbed the steps of the carriage. "Damn, man, I was dry until now."

George stood outside in the streaming rain, his hands on his hips, his chest heaving. His lip bled.

"Is it necessary to keep needling him?"

Victor put his hand on his shoulder as he sat back down in the carriage. "He needs to get it out of his system instead of wallowing in his misery."

Victor kicked Keene in the other shin. "That is for fighting his fights for him. We all should have been better had you left well enough alone."

Keene took a long drink from the flask and handed it over. "Your servant, sir."

His bedraggled friends dripped mud over the seats of the carriage. The carriage he had meant to transport his new wife in tomorrow. Victor winced and clutched his shoulder. A black eye was forming above a scratch on his cheek. George's light brown hair was plastered to his head on one side, his cravat was askew and a button on his jacket hung by a thread.

"Tell the coachman to stop at the next inn that looks as if it might supply a bath, and get in the carriage, George."

He prayed he would make it to his wedding in time.

Sophie paced back and forth in her wedding gown. "Where is he?"

"He'll be here. He has probably been held up by the rain," her mother reassured her.

"What if he doesn't come?"

"He'll be here. His father is here, is he not?"

"What if he changed his mind?" What if she had so totally alienated him by biting him, he not only meant to call off the wedding, but to humiliate her by waiting until she stood at the altar?

"Oh, miss, you know he'll be here," whispered Letty.

Sophie checked the window for about the thousandth time that morning. The door shut behind her, and she glanced around to see her father. "I suppose if he does not show up for the ceremony, Mr. Ponsby would step forward."

"If you wished to marry Ponsby, you should have accepted his offer." Her father's face appeared pinched and strained.

He must be worried, too. "Oh, Papa." She moved forward to hug her father. "I was teasing. I so very dislike waiting, and it is quite disagreeable of Keene to bring about a delay."

Her father absently patted her back. "I suppose we might have the ceremony tomorrow if necessary, but I don't know what we'll do with all the food Cook has prepared."

"We simply will have the wedding breakfast first and explain to the guests that the bridegroom has been unavoidably detained by the weather. Keene is a gentleman. He will be here as soon as he's able," Mrs. Farthing said with an air of confidence Sophie didn't trust.

She wasn't sure if she should inform her mother that she had bitten Keene, and that might very well have changed his attitude about whether or not she deserved to be treated as a lady.

"You don't understand," Mr. Farthing spoke in a low undertone. "I have it on good authority that Sir Gresham is now in London. Keene might have encountered him."

"Oh, pish," said Mrs. Farthing. "There is no shame in that he made Sophie an offer and was turned down. What of it?"

"Ma'am, he might have spoken of other carryings on."

Her parents were having the sort of conversation where she as their child was not privy to all the underlying meanings. Except her father watched her as if he expected her to understand. She felt obligated to comment. There was nothing that the baronet from Cornwall could say that would be a surprise to her bridegroom, who had, after all, seen her at her worst. "I daresay Keene knows me as well or better than Sir Gresham."

Her father blanched, and her mother grabbed his arm and hauled him out of the room.

She presumed her mother had saved her from a lecture or worse. Perhaps a bride deserved better than to be put on bread and water on her wedding day—perhaps her wedding day, if the groom showed up.

Sophie paced back to the window feeling every bit like a caged animal. She longed for a ride or a long walk.

Jane tugged her husband into their suite. "Please, do contrive to avoid upsetting Sophie." She turned her head and lowered her voice. "I hadn't wished to speak of it, but in her delicate condition she shouldn't be made anxious. She is worried enough that her groom is late."

"Oh, no." Daniel sat down with a hard thump. "You are sure of it?"

"Well, yes, she told me, but I beg you, don't speak of it to her. She would not have said anything, but she was afraid she needed a doctor. I assured her she is just going through the normal symptoms of her condition. Remember how I, too, would fall asleep in the evening."

Daniel wouldn't have felt more unsettled if a hole to China opened below his feet. "No."

"I told her she should wait and then speak to Keene about a doctor after she is settled with him. Although it is early yet. She will have plenty of time."

"I feared this," Daniel said with finality.

"Well, yes, but nothing can be done, and she is to be married, so I cannot see any need to speak of it. She is an impulsive, impatient creature, and I suppose Keene is the same."

Desperation clawed at Daniel's innards. What would Keene do if he knew his future wife was not only impure, but carrying another man's child? Cry off? Expect a larger dowry? It was bad enough to know that Sophie was not as she should be, but this was worse. He hadn't wanted to know. "In all honor, I should speak with him about this."

"We could warn him to have a care of her condition. But it can wait until tomorrow."

"I should speak with him before the ceremony."

"Oh, for heaven's sake, Mr. Farthing, adding any further delays should be silly. I know it is a shock that we shall become grandparents so soon, but it is a good sign. As Keene is his father's only heir they will wish to know that the line will continue unbroken. Obviously Sophie will not have the difficulty conceiving that I had."

"Madam, a man should know his future wife is breeding."

"If you insist, but do wait until after the ceremony. We should have no further delays to the service."

Daniel supposed after the ceremony an annulment was possible, although he could offer Keene more money to keep Sophie as his wife. Other than that, he should insist his daughter marry the squire—if he would still have her. The whole affair made him sick, and he dreaded his talk with his future son-in-law. He wondered if he should make some reference to Joseph's trials with Mary, but since Sophie was in no wise carrying the savior, that idea seemed rather blasphemous.

Keene checked his watch as they turned into the Farthings' drive. He would have to remember to give John Coachman a hearty vail for his diligent work in driving the coach through the sheets of rain. Although time was short, he wanted to make sure his servant was treated to a warm mug of ale and a dry spot in front of the fire, before he proceeded to marry Sophie.

His friends were a different story. He was half tempted to toss them out of the carriage and leave them to flounder in the mud and muck. "Do endeavor to make sure you shall not pass out at my wedding, George."

At the inn where they had all changed and Keene had donned the clothes he had set aside for his wedding, George had given up on the flask and purchased three bottles of good French brandy. He and Victor were drinking as if they had a bet to see who could swallow an ocean first.

"Right-o. Are you sure you wish to do this? Nothing short of misery, marriage is." Well, the drink had improved George's mood. The tone was at least jovial if the message was not.

"You wouldn't have said that six months ago."

"I should have, if I had known then what I know now." George's words were slightly slurred. He looked puzzled, as if he wasn't quite sure what he had just said made complete sense.

Since he was coherent, whether or not he was conscious of it, Keene supposed he was presentable enough.

There was no hope for Victor's shiner. He had retreated to a corner and said little since the scuffle in the mud.

The Farthings' butler greeted the carriage with an umbrella. George slipped as he stepped off the carriage steps. Keene caught his arm to keep him from falling. It was only then that he realized the rain had turned to ice on the cobblestones of the drive. Lord, what a day for a wedding. An occasional sting told him the rain had begun to mix with sleet.

Huddling together under the umbrella, he steered George to the front door.

Victor trailed along behind them, his head turned down against the biting barrage of precipitation. He hugged his shoulders as if the cold were too much.

"The family and guests are assembled in the drawing room, sir. If you would follow me."

"My good man, please be sure my coachman is treated to a warm drink and a place in front of a fire."

He'd left two footmen at the inn with the instruction that he would pick them up the following day, weather permitting.

The butler paused outside the drawing room door, patiently looking at Keene. Belatedly Keene gave his friends' names and titles so they could be properly announced.

His father and an elderly aunt were there. A dozen people

he did not know milled around the room with another dozen that looked vaguely familiar, people he had undoubtedly met in his myriad childhood stays at this house. Sophie's father frowned in his direction, while Cousin Jane gave a welcoming smile. His glance around the room did not turn up Sophie. Disappointment curled through him. Until he failed to find her, he wasn't aware he was looking for her. Of course she wouldn't be here.

Victor collapsed onto the nearest chair. Keene gave him a preoccupied glance. Victor looked pale, which made his shiner stand out all the more. George wobbled beside him.

"Where have you been, boy?" asked his father.

"On my way here." Keene thought of the broken axle, the rain and ice, his friends' fight. He turned from his father and headed toward Sophie's parents.

"My apologies for my late arrival."

"It's quite all right, Keene." Jane patted his sleeve. "We assumed the weather had delayed you. We've decided to serve the breakfast before we leave for the church."

"Perhaps we should postpone the service." The sheer terror on his future father-in-law's face distracted him. He'd meant to speak of the weather conditions. Instead, he said, "We should have waited until summer."

"Well, everyone is here now, so we shall proceed, shan't we?" said Cousin Jane.

Keene shook off his reaction to Daniel Farthing's expression. "The weather is turning ugly. The drive is icy. George nearly took a nasty spill. I am not sure we should risk the horses, let alone the company."

If anything, his father-in-law looked even more upset. "You cannot delay."

"Why don't we send for the vicar?" suggested Jane. "Surely we can use the chapel here in the house. I know that it hasn't been used in many years and is tiny, but we are a small gathering and Keene has not brought so many friends that it will create a problem. We will just invite the vicar to spend the night."

"Some of our neighbors might be waiting at the church."

"The vicar could announce the change in plans and post a notice on the door." Jane patted her husband's arm.

"I would send my coach to pick him up, but I fear I have already exposed my coachman to too much of the weather." Not to mention there were muddy spots on the seats. To be sure, they had acquired sheets at the inn in order to protect their clean clothes, but Keene would rather not explain. Not to mention that George's spilled flask and discarded brandy bottle had left the interior smelling like a den of iniquity.

In less than an hour the vicar arrived at the house and opened the chapel. The paneled walls gleamed with the dark patina of age. The three short pews were crowded with the guests. There was only a narrow side aisle, which would make the bride's march a difficult proposition. The room was much taller than wide or long, giving Keene an odd feeling of foreboding. The family chapel had been designed in a time when religion was often a life or death matter, and it showed.

Victor slid into a seat. George tottered up to the front with Keene, hitting the edge of the last pew as he rounded the corner toward the altar.

The finality made Keene feel like weaving, too. Instead, he held himself still. A sense of being watched made him look up at the rear section of the chapel. He couldn't see her, but she was there. Heat rivaled the pall of the chapel. George bumped his shoulder and when Keene turned back, he knew she was gone. He only hoped she had not had to scale a wall in order to see down into the chapel.

The ceremony went smoothly, until it was time to kiss his bride. Out of the corner of his eye, Keene caught sight of Victor slumped over, his right shoulder clutched in his hand. Keene brushed a kiss across Sophie's cheek and turned back to George and in a quiet whisper said, "See to him."

"I shink not," answered George rather loudly, in an attempt at precision that fell short of the mark.

Sophie chewed her lip and cast Keene a sidelong look. He wrapped his arm around her waist.

His father-in-law frowned at him. He moved her toward the narrow aisle. George stumbled and fell into him.

Keene reluctantly let go of Sophie. He needed to take care of his friends. He didn't want to call any more attention to them than he already had. The only good thing about bringing the both of them was that they now seemed to be on speaking terms, even if it was only to hurl insults at each other.

Sophie turned away to receive the hug of her mother. With only the narrow aisle, Keene didn't want to get trapped. He scooted around his bride and her mother. His wife and his mother-in-law. Somehow, it didn't seem real yet. He supposed later tonight the reality would set in.

He managed to get Victor to his feet and lead him out of the chapel. He walked him down the hallway away from the spill of guests from the open chapel doors. "My God, man, what is wrong?"

"I think I reopened the wound." Victor pushed him away. "It's your wedding. I shall be fine."

Keene cast around for an upper servant. Hearing rapid footfalls behind him, he turned just before Sophie drew to an abrupt stop. She dropped fistfuls of her skirt. "Keene, the vicar says we must sign the certificate."

He swallowed hard, thinking of the delicate turn of her ankles, now hidden below her dress. "I'll be there in a moment. I need to see that Victor is settled."

Sophie thrust out her hand. "I am Sophie."

Victor gave a small bow. "Charmed." He didn't reach for her hand, though.

Sophie cast a puzzled look in Keene's direction. She should have waited for him to introduce them, but since he had delayed, his mind on her legs, he supposed he couldn't fault her.

"Sophie, could you find a footman or a maid to take Lord Wedmont to his room?"

"Go on. Don't neglect your bride. I shall find my own way."

Keene was torn. Sophie frowned and then darted down the hall. She opened a door and called to a servant.

She returned in a trot. "Someone will be with you directly." She grabbed Keene's arm and tugged him back toward the chapel.

Victor watched with interest. Keene's new wife was a pretty thing, but vastly different from the sophisticated women who usually drew his attention. There was more here than Keene's sudden need for an heir.

As Keene pulled his wife back to lead her, Victor's knees buckled. He reached for the nearest door and found an office. Leaning all his weight on the doorknob he stumbled into the room, swinging with the opening door. When it hit the wall, he let go, only to watch the door slowly shut. He sank down against the wall, pressing hard against his shoulder. As he stared at the back of a chair he thought, it should be just his luck that a wound not initially fatal would prove so after a fistfight.

Sophie was disappointed that Keene was back to treating her as if he hardly noticed she was there. There had been a couple of times during the ceremony that he had turned his dark gaze on her, and she found his look enigmatic. Later, when they were alone, no doubt she would have his full attention.

She wanted to tell him that he could have kissed her properly, she wouldn't bite him. At least not in front of witnesses.

As soon as he signed the certificate, he had pulled away to lead his friend George to the dining room. Of course, during the breakfast, sitting next to her and receiving the toasts, he couldn't help but speak to her, but he didn't comment on her gown, or really do anything more than would be required of a polite meal companion. Afterward, they milled separately about the drawing room and received good wishes from relatives and neighbors.

Lord Whitley grabbed his son's arm and hauled him to a corner of the room. Keene did his best to appear as if he were simply walking alongside his father, although his mouth tightened. Sophie pushed around Keene's friend, Mr. Keeting. The other gentleman she assumed had retired to his room. The pathways through the room were clogged, so she scrambled over a footstool to reach Keene.

"I have done as you asked, sir," said Keene as she approached.

"But what you were you thinking to bring your drunken, brawling friends? I cannot believe you dishonor my cousin with such obnoxious personages."

"Lord Whitley, did I tell you how glad I am that Keene brought his friends to meet me? I shall be glad of a friendly face or two when I actually go to London." Sophie looped her arm in Keene's as she sidled up to him. "They have been ever so kind. Why, Mr. Keeting has been giving me pointers on piquet and has promised me a game later. I shall be so grateful to learn how to play. Oh, I should call you Papa, now, should I not?" She pasted a big smile on her mouth.

Lord Whitley appeared startled by the notion. "Why, yes. You may."

Keene watched her with such complete reserve she had no idea what he was thinking.

Her father crossed the room head down as if he was bent on a mission or searching for dropped pennies. He stopped in front of Keene. "I should like to speak with you, sir."

Sophie grabbed her father's arm. "And you should call Keene, son."

"I . . . I should like to do that," said her father distractedly. "If you would attend me in my office, sir."

Keene leaned over and whispered in her ear, "Don't ever

do that again." He disengaged her arm from his without so much as a squeeze or pat.

Sophie kept her smile big and nodded, although her eyes stung. She only wanted to spare him one of his father's lectures. She knew how very unpleasant Keene could be afterward. Well, perhaps not exactly unpleasant, but so withdrawn as to seem not to be there.

She hardly thought as she spoke with Keene's father. She was too busy watching her husband follow her father out of the room.

"Well, you look very happy," said her new father-in-law.

"Oh, I am."

"I believe your eyes are sparkling. I do hope my scoundrel son will not dampen that sparkle."

Since Sophie suspected the shine was partly due to unshed tears, partly nerves, she replied, "Why, I'm sure your son put the sparkle there." And she smiled some more, and her face started to hurt, and she longed ever so much for a wild gallop—with a horse or without.

Keene followed his new father-in-law down the same corridor that led to the chapel. He wondered if he had neglected to sign some other paperwork, a family bible, a receipt for Sophie's dowry, a pledge of his soul to the devil.

He might as well pledge his afterlife to hell. After all, he had just married Sophie, a woman who only appealed to him in one way. The way she had intruded on his conversation with his father irritated him. As if he needed to hide behind a woman's skirts at his age. He'd been dealing with his father for years, since his mother died when he was twelve. He didn't need protecting, least of all from his wife, who couldn't possibly understand the basis of the animosity his father held for him.

Daniel ushered Keene into his office and walked forward to his desk.

"Sir?" asked Keene, impatient to be done and look in on Victor. As their valets had been left behind with the carriage with the broken axle, Keene didn't know if anyone had attended Victor.

Daniel didn't sit and kept his back to Keene. "I fear I have some grave news to impart."

What? He couldn't come up with the entire dowry? "I'm sure it won't be a problem," said Keene. After all, he was quite used to a life without regular funds, and his father had promised to keep him solvent.

"I hope not. You see, I would quite understand if you wished to seek an annulment."

That was taking things a little too melodramatically. "I'm sure that won't be necessary."

"I certainly hope not. You know Sophie is so frivolous, and I had meant to speak of how London should be so very bad for a girl of her disposition. She should be exposed to all sorts of temptations, and I very much hope that you consider her nature before you take her to that place. In fact, I advise you to keep her in the country."

So did his father-in-law think Sophie would spend money they didn't have? No, Farthing had insisted Sophie handled his accounts well. Perhaps he was having a hard time letting go of his daughter. "Sir, I shall take good care of Sophie. She shall not want for anything she needs."

"I do hope that you will take into consideration her weak character and not fault her too much for her condition."

A chill ran down his spine. Farthing continued to look away from him. Although the noon hour rapidly approached, the rain-snow mix continued, allowing little light through the streaming windows. Keene had the odd sense of being underwater.

Daniel lifted a paperweight from his desk and set it back down. "I have been far too indulgent with her. I fear her weakness can be laid at my door."

Keene didn't comment.

"This, sir, is one of the hardest conversations I've ever had."

Keene just wished they'd have it.

"You see, I've feared for some time that there was a problem."

No, Keene didn't see. Perhaps it really was the money. No one liked to admit to being insolvent, and last year had been a difficult year with crop failures across the country. "Is it about the money, sir?"

"Well, I have thought I could offer you an annual income of five hundred pounds if you are willing to stay married to her."

Keene almost laughed. He had to stay married to her to gain his inheritance. Besides, his father wanted *her* sons to inherit and guarantee the bloodline. "That is not necessary."

Daniel reached across his desk and picked up a bank draft and handed it to Keene.

Keene stared at the numbers. The full three thousand pounds of Sophie's settlement. Dread trickled down his spine. If it wasn't the dowry, what was it?

"This is drawn on my account in Shrewsbury. I am assured you will have no trouble cashing it in London." Daniel moved to the window and stared outside. "It is starting to snow."

Keene wanted to shout at him to finish telling him what he wanted to say. "What was it you wished to say about Sophie?"

Daniel grabbed the curtain and bunched it in his fist. "I should have married her off sooner. I should have insisted, but she is my only child and perhaps in my own weakness I did not think of what was best for her with her weak character."

If Sophie had a weak character, Keene hated to think how his own character was classified. She might have a penchant for inappropriate behavior, but was she so headstrong as to defy all attempts to temper her faults? "To what weakness are you referring?"

"Why, her lack of innocence. I did wish to speak of it before the marriage was consummated. I wish before God to do the right thing. As much as I am tempted to conceal the truth of her condition, I cannot in good conscience allow this to go forward without informing you that . . ."

Keene wanted to scream, *What?* On the other hand, he preferred not to know.

"I do not pretend to understand my daughter. In many ways she is a foreign creature to me." Daniel's voice trembled as he spoke. "If you wish an annulment we will announce it directly."

Why would he want an annulment? "Sir?"

"I felt you must know. But in any case she has begun to exhibit symptoms of a delicate condition."

SEVEN

The silence in the room stretched thin. Victor feared the room's two other occupants would hear him breathe. He could see Keene's shoulders above the chair he sat in, and every now and again Sophie's father would enter the narrow line of vision between the chairs.

Victor had not meant to eavesdrop, and now that he had heard the worst—that the new bride was in a family way—he might be trapped in here forever. Certainly he couldn't intrude on such a private conversation. Such a thing was bad enough without witnesses.

Yet, how would Keene respond to his father-in-law's offer of more money to stand behind a wife bearing another man's child? If *he* were offered more, Victor would certainly take the money. Keene might take the other route offered and denounce the union.

But, Keene was his own man and his words proved it. "That won't be necessary. We shall speak no more of it."

"The pension?"

Take the money, Keene.

"Not necessary, sir."

"Thank you. I am so very relieved. I shall thank God that you have saved her from disgrace."

Keene was an idiot. His new father-in-law was worse, and Victor had no nice words for Sophie. The whole sordid affair made alerting anyone to his deteriorating condition a nightmare. Victor wished they would leave.

His head was awhirl. Holding his breath was about to make his lungs explode. His shoulder burned. They were so achingly polite to each other he wanted to shout for them. And Victor couldn't quite figure out why his concern over their pride ranked higher than *his* possible death. That rankled perhaps worse than that he had the luck to be neglected and forgotten for several hours.

Keene said, "I shall rejoin the company shortly."

No doubt a discreet request for time alone. Perhaps Keene had not expected this pretty turn. Victor exhaled with relief. While he couldn't intrude on both men, he *could* interrupt Keene's solitude. After all, Keene had been the one to insist upon his presence. He could damn well put up with the consequences of it.

"Yes, I should check with my wife to see how the accommodations for our unanticipated guests are going. N-not your friends, the vicar and our neighbors that will stay as the weather is so bad," said Sophie's father.

Keene's voice took on an edge as he asked, "Have you spoken with Sophie about this?"

"No. I had no idea what to say. I saw . . . her leave his bedroom and . . . well, I knew she must be married as soon as possible. I swear, sir, if I had known that this complication had come to pass, I would have insisted she marry the man she . . . allowed . . . such . . . liberties with her person." Mr. Farthing shook his head and moved rapidly toward the door. "I shall pray for her soul."

Tears dripped down the older man's face. If Mr. Farthing had bothered to notice anything beyond himself, surely he would have seen Victor.

Victor grabbed the chair back in front of him. He wanted to see Keene before he spoke. He would have preferred to sneak out quietly and pretend he hadn't overheard, but he needed help. Keene sat motionless in his chair, his head bent forward and his forehead resting on his interlaced fingers, thumbs at his temples.

"As pure as you found her?"

Keene jerked. "What are you doing here?"

Which, now that Victor thought about it, Keene's statement had told him nothing. If she had not been a virgin when Keene proposed to her, and according to her father she wasn't, then certainly Keene's statement meant little other than he had not trespassed on unexplored territory.

"I came in here to avoid falling down in front of the company. I think I passed out. I promise I have never met your wife before this day." He'd meant it as a joke, but something in Keene's face made his words fade. "Are you all right?"

"Of course." Keene reached for Victor's good arm and hauled him to his feet. Sweat beaded Victor's upper lip, and he felt woozy.

"Good God, man, you're bleeding."

Victor looked down at the growing red stain on his jacket, which had undoubtedly ruined another shirt, as well. "You didn't think one bottle of brandy could put me under, did you?"

"Damned if I know."

Victor leaned heavily against Keene. "You don't suppose it is contagious, is it?"

Keene opened the door. "What?"

"This thing with the pregnant wives. First George, now you."

Keene guided him down the empty hallway to a back staircase. "Her father is inclined to presume the worst."

"You see, because I believe I shall be tying the knot soon myself, and I wonder if I shall be bearing the same burden."

"She's not carrying a child."

"With the quickness of the wedding, I daresay you shall never know for certain it is not yours." Victor cast a sidelong look at his friend as they slowly ascended the steps.

Keene pressed his lips together in a resolute line, but a hopeless look shadowed his eyes.

Victor regretted his needling, but he couldn't stop. Anger fed him like mother's milk. "I do hope you will not demand satisfaction, sir. For I won't be able to give you a good fight."

"I should not ask it of you."

God, the man was always so perfectly polite and poised. Victor envied him his composure as much as he wanted to rattle him out of it. "What will you do?"

"Nothing. You will not speak of it, either."

"You are such a cold fish."

The glare Keene gave him was anything but cold.

"I swear on my father's grave, I shall not speak of your wife's condition or how she came to that pass. To anyone else, at least. It's quite understandable, though. She is a pretty thing, very lively."

Keene's glare intensified. "Stay away from her."

Victor knew he had pressed enough. "I am in no condition to pursue your wife, sir."

"I'll kill any man who so much as touches her."

Did Keene actually love his wife? "You could have chosen annulment."

Keene's lips twisted. "No, I could not."

There was more here than met the eye, but Victor no longer had the energy to ferret out the truth. The exertion of climbing the stairs wore on him. Sweat streamed down his sides and back although a winter chill permeated the house. Keene deposited him on a bench while he sought out an upper servant to inform him where his friend would sleep. Victor supposed if he died here in the main hallway someone would find him eventually.

In the end, Keene had to seek out his Cousin Jane to learn where to deposit his friend and request aid in getting him to bed.

"I hope your friends shall not mind, but I have put them

together as we have more guests than we anticipated. You, of course, will be in Sophie's room. You know where that is. Your friends shall be two rooms down on the same side of the hall." Jane patted his arm and moved on to another guest, who was asking where she might retire for the afternoon.

Keene didn't know how well sharing a room would go between Victor and George. He supposed if they refrained from killing each other it would be well enough. Keene searched the drawing room for Sophie, wondering if he should ask for her assistance in getting Victor care. He didn't see her among the guests. He wasn't sure he was ready to see her after the news her father had shared.

The information hadn't settled in his stomach yet. The haste of the marriage surprised him, so there was reason to be suspicious. Yet, he hadn't reconciled what he thought was Sophie's innocence with the notion that her father had seen her with a man. Although the language had been couched enough that he couldn't quite be certain how much Farthing had seen.

Very likely Keene could have asked him to be more specific, but as the words fell from his father-in-law's mouth he wanted to scoop them up and shove them back in. Not that it would have made any difference if he had known in advance of his proposal. His father wanted Sophie's bloodline. He felt the fool, playing to what he thought was her innocence.

After a passing glance at George, who was imbibing rather freely of the champagne offered in the drawing room, Keene left to return upstairs. But as he passed the main hall he saw the front door shut. He moved to a window and saw his wife slipping and sliding through the newly fallen snow.

Sophie kicked through the snow. A layer of ice below the thin coating of white prevented running. The late winter snow resembled little pellets more than the fine mist of dreams, but then, snow was rare around her home. She'd needed to get out of the crowded drawing room, where her new husband was missing and everyone politely refrained from mentioning his absence while their eyes circled the room.

Only his friend's attendance let her know that Keene was even in the house. His other friend, the one who had looked ill, had been missing since the ceremony. Sophie supposed Keene found his friend more entertaining than her. Although he rarely noticed her when she didn't need rescue. Which was all a pack of feeling sorry for herself, and she needed to quit this instant.

Sophie threw her arms wide, embracing the chill of the winter storm. Her boots slid out from beneath her, and she met the ground with a jarring thump. She giggled, releasing pent-up energy. She couldn't be too mad at Keene when she had spent hours before the wedding wondering if he would even show up. He had done that, and, God willing, she would have years with him.

Tonight he would join her in her bedroom and would kiss her and do all the other things that made a woman a wife. No doubt Keene would be good at that.

She supposed it was odd to be looking forward to such things. Certainly no one had encouraged her to anticipate her wedding night with pleasure.

Maybe if it was anyone other than Keene she would have been more frightened. Sir Gresham had been so serious that she feared a misplaced nervous giggle would bring his wrath down upon her head. Ponsby was so big that the thought of him sharing a bed and possibly rolling over her in his sleep was frightening.

Her heart thumped madly when she thought of Keene kissing her, as if she were in the throes of terror. She rather liked the feeling of it, the way her bones melted like wax, her stomach danced like dragonflies on a pond surface, the warm heat that flooded through her. Each brush of his body, each touch of his hand, every press of his lips made her tingle from head to toe. And if he invited her to take the lead, she promised herself no more biting.

She leaned back, indulging in her speculations about the coming night. Her father would have her on bread and water for a week if he knew the wicked nature of her thoughts.

Cold seeped from the ground up through her body. She welcomed the sensation. The wind whipped, whistling around her, and the sting of ice pellets bit her cheeks. Settling the hood of her cloak more firmly around her head, she sat up.

The crunch of thin ice shattered her thoughts. She scrambled to her feet. Who had joined her outside? She swiveled around. The wind whipped her hood against her face, blocking her vision.

"Sophie?"

"Keene," she breathed his name on a sigh. She managed to get her hood adjusted so she could see.

He looked mad as thunderclouds. "You should not be outside."

Her smile froze on her face. The last thing she wanted on her wedding day was a lecture from her new spouse. She turned around, sucking down her disappointment. "Why not?"

"You could fall and hurt yourself. You should not take risks with your condi—you should not be out here."

"I wouldn't get hurt if I fell, I'm very near to the ground." It was not as if she was on horseback or racing a dogcart.

"Sophie, come along. I want you back inside."

Would he be just like her father? "Have I made you angry? For I did not mean to."

He came closer. "I am concerned for you. I should not wish to see you endangering your health or your . . ." His voice trailed off.

Sophie faced him. He looked both angry and distracted. "My what?"

He looked off toward the horizon. Sophie frowned. He

turned back toward her. His eyes searched her face. The wind tugged at her hood and made her cheeks sting with cold as she waited for him to speak.

"You are my wife now, and mine alone."

She hadn't expected him to say anything like that, but the words poured through her like heated honey.

"Whatever has gone before is done. Do you understand?"

No, but Sophie decided to nod. She wasn't about to protest anything when he had claimed her as his.

"Certainly I have been with many women before, but what's past is past."

Sophie stared at him. Was he saying he would be loyal? After what her mother said about making herself crazy for expecting too much, she hadn't thought he'd promise fidelity.

She stepped toward him. "You will be true to me?"

He blinked.

Sophie had the awful sinking feeling she had assumed too much. In her effort to back away, she slid, probably on the same patch of ice that had done her in before. Whenever she was around Keene, her normal grace—or at least normal ability to avoid predicaments—deserted her. Both feet went in opposite directions, and she fought to plant them on the layer of snow-covered ice.

Keene caught her around the waist and jerked her against him. For a second they both wavered as her face plowed into his midsection. Then he raised her upright. She wasn't sure why she did it, perhaps to reassure herself that he was really here, but she brushed her fingers across his cheek. His hand closed over hers, his skin warm where hers was cold.

The moment hung in the air like the white puffs that marked their expelled breath. His dark eyes searched her face and dropped to her lips. He pressed against her, and found her mouth with his.

There was a second of the gentle pressure she expected, but then the kiss changed. His breath mingled with hers. His flavor invaded her mouth. The wet swirl of the kiss was like nothing she had ever experienced. This was no namby-pamby kiss, it was wild. It was scorching. And she loved it.

He pulled her tight against his frame. The cold wind assaulted her as her hood fell back, but his hold fired her blood. She clung to him, her arms around his neck. He bent her backward as if he meant to devour her. He moved his hands under her cloak, pulling her closer and stroking over her in the same motion. His mouth never leaving hers, he lowered her to the ground.

Sophie couldn't think beyond feeling his weight against her, the demand of his lower body, the magic he created with his mouth. The wind whipped around them while he kneed her legs apart. His hips settled in the cradle of her split legs. The heaviness against her woman's core was strange and hard and made her breath come in short snatches.

Her breasts ached. She grabbed his roaming hand and placed it over her chest. He flicked his thumb over the tightened tip of her breast. A shooting burst of sensation traveled down her body, centering low in her, where his body met hers. Instinct took over and her hips twisted, both seeking and escaping the pressure of his body. Her legs drew up involuntarily, rubbing against his. She wanted this to go on and on. At the same time, the powerful sensations brewed like a storm within her. She whimpered, wanting the fury and fearing she would fall apart within it.

His mouth moved away from hers. She couldn't tell what he was doing, but she suspected he was tugging their clothing aside. Panic rushed through her. *Here? Now? In the snow?* "Keene?"

He stopped moving, closed his eyes and turned away slightly. For a second the only sound was the rasp of their breathing. Then he settled his lips against her neck, his kiss gentle but nonetheless evocative. His hand lay against her thigh, his fingers rubbed in a circle. He shifted his hand up, his thumb settled just inside the jut of her hipbone.

Keene brushed his lips over her forehead. What was he doing? Her hands were like ice. Seducing his wife on the ground outside her home in full view of the windows hadn't been in his mind when he'd approached her. Seducing her? Hell, he was all but forcing her, except she hadn't uttered a protest and had thrown herself into his kiss with enthusiasm, with every inch of her body. But she sounded alarmed when she whispered his name. Confusion swirled through him. He never lost control.

He found her hands and brought them under his coat, tucking them under his arms to warm her nearly frozen fingers. He pulled her up to a sitting position and resettled her hood over her tangled blonde curls. He had never meant to handle her so roughly, treating her no better than a ha'penny whore. Her hands were so cold, they chilled him through his clothes. "We should go inside."

She looked at him, her blue eyes large, her lips swollen. She whispered as if unsure of him. "What just happened?"

God, she seemed so innocent, so uncertain of her response, which didn't seem a likely reaction for an experienced woman bearing another man's child.

He pulled her into his lap and bent his head, touching their foreheads. He had come out here with a plan to guide her back inside, and a half-baked idea that it would be a good time for a confession. That is, if there was anything to confess. She was so ready and willing, yet managed to project an air`of inexperience. His head swirled with confusion.

"I daresay I got carried away. Forgive me?"

"If you forgive me for biting you." Her gaze slid away from his, and she leaned into the crook of his neck.

He grinned. "I'd forgive you anything that is past, so long as you confess."

He waited with baited breath, but she didn't say anything. They couldn't sit out here in the ice and snow while he waited for an admission that might or might not come.

Perhaps there wasn't anything to tell. She was a physical

girl. She liked running, jumping, swimming and climbing on window ledges. Perhaps the one saving grace of her enjoying athletic pursuits was that she should enjoy bedroom antics in an enthusiastic, whole-body way.

Her lack of reserve shouldn't matter. The saints forgive him, he should not be making love to his wife outside in February, whether or not she encouraged him.

The real question was, why would he get so carried away with her that he tried to lie with her on the cold ground? Any woman deserved the comfort of a bed, at least the first time. Even if it was only the first time with him, not the first time ever. "Come inside, Sophie, before we both catch our death of cold."

Christ, he had completely forgotten about Victor.

Keene found Victor slumped on the bench where he had left him. It had been nearly a month and a half since the duel. "Why is your wound still bleeding?"

"The surgeon has lanced it twice. He says it keeps growing putrid with infection. I daresay George managed to reopen it during our scuffle."

Keene tucked his arm around Victor's ribs, helping him rise to his feet. "Perhaps you need a new surgeon."

Victor leaned heavily on Keene. "Perhaps I need new friends."

They moved down the empty hallway. "Likely you do, but I daresay they will not punish you enough."

Victor laughed. It was a weak, coughing sound. "For heaven's sake, Keene. Go beat your wife if you feel the need to punish someone. I have done taking abuse from you."

Keene reached for the doorknob of the room assigned to his friend. He wouldn't punish Sophie. He hadn't a right to expect better of her. Spending one day in her father's house and her company in the last six years hardly made a reasonable foundation for a marriage. Damn Victor for overhearing everything, anyway. "But you are not done taking abuse from George?"

"The man is raising my child. I prophesy I shall take more cruelty from him."

Keene took note of his friends' traveling bags deposited near the door. "No doubt, for Mrs. Farthing has assigned you to the same room."

"Dear Lord. Shouldn't you have said something?"

Keene kicked the door shut. They hobbled toward the bed. At least it was rather large. "What should I have said? No, they cannot room together as Victor ruined George's wife, and they cannot stomach each other's company."

"Does George know?"

"No. He may be completely insensible by the time he is brought to bed, anyway."

"Ah, he is not the man we have known and loved."

Keene turned toward Victor as he helped him sit on the bed. Victor's observation rang with reality. George's reactions were not what either of them would have expected. In all their carousing over the past few years, George had been the one to temper their wildest urges, to remind them they were gentlemen and that everyone from the lowest violet seller to the tiniest chimney sweep deserved kindness and consideration. He had been the one to preach moderation in food and drink, reminding them that overindulgence would lead to headaches and hangovers. "It only goes to show how deeply hurt he has been."

Victor shrugged out of his jacket. "Amelia loves his restraint."

Pulling the jacket down Victor's arms, Keene was caught off guard by the sincerity and regret in Victor's tone.

The words could have easily been facetious given the latest turn of events, but they weren't. There was both longing and resignation in Victor's tone, as if he both wanted her and yet knew she wasn't for him, and had perhaps known all along. But why hadn't Victor married her? Why bed her and not offer the shelter of his name? He obviously cared for her in spite of his protests that she was too easily seduced.

Victor had also spoken of marriage for himself. While Keene couldn't bring himself to ask the complicated questions about Victor's feelings toward George's wife, he could needle him about his single state. "Are you so jealous of George's and my deep wedded bliss that you intend to emulate our state?"

"Something like that. You know those pistols we used in the duel have a curse."

"Yes, they are about as true as a sailor's wife."

"Truer than the sailor, no doubt." Victor smiled weakly. "You should be thankful for that, for I did not mean to miss. No, there is the legend that the true winner of the duel shall find happiness in marriage, and the loser shall be doomed to a wife from hell. Since you so obviously have been the loser in the parson's mousetrap, I must, of course, seek a wife."

"Now, there is a good reason to marry."

"Well as it is, I need a wife."

"Do you have someone in mind?"

"Perhaps a cit. You should have taken the five hundred pounds a year. Do you think I could find a girl in trouble whose father would pay me large sums to save her honor?"

Keene paused in pulling the shirt away from Victor's wound. He yanked it hard, feeling the tug of dried blood as the shirt ripped free.

"Damn, man!"

Victor covered the oozing wound with a folded handkerchief. Fresh blood soaked the cloth. A drop crept out from underneath the pad and trickled down his bare chest.

The sight tempered Keene's anger. He couldn't lambaste a man who was bleeding all over the place, and he would have to help him bandage the wound as it was his broken carriage that had forced all their valets to stay behind. He had to ask himself, was he truly angry at Victor or did

Victor's willingness to probe at his wounds make him a useful target?

"I would ask you, sir, to not speak despairingly of my wife."

"You love her, don't you?"

The assumption floored Keene. "I daresay not. My father loves her pedigree." Which was information he had not intended to divulge. "Good God, Victor, do not ever repeat that or I shall have to find a better set of pistols."

Victor's brown eyes studied him as he spoke gently. "You know, Keene, killing me will not assassinate your troubles."

"Yes, but no one else would dare speak of them."

"So it is the reminders that are a problem, rather than the problems themselves." This time Victor's tone held sarcasm.

"No, it is that you are so deep in my concerns, it makes me deuced uncomfortable."

"I am deep in George's concerns. Ow!" Victor winced as Keene rubbed a wet flannel over the freshly exposed wound. "You have no need to cause me pain to ease yourself."

"I'm cleaning you. Do you have another jacket?"

"Not in that bag. I have a fresh shirt and some linen for a new bandage."

"I daresay I must loan you one of my own. Do contrive not to bleed upon it."

"Deuce take it. I should not bleed upon anything if you had not shot me."

The initial wound was a puckered round hole that was half healed, but two fresh slashes across it and the angry red flesh around it showed the questionable aid of the surgeon. Keene deeply regretted the duel, but what could he do about it now? Perhaps if Victor found a good woman to wed, Keene could assuage his guilt by believing in the curse and reminding his friend that he'd played a small part in the deed.

But to seek a wife among the cits? Victor had a title, he could look as high as he wanted. It could only mean one thing. "You have decided money shall bring you happiness."

"It shall keep my home in repair. It's not a choice, Keene. I go deeper into the cent-percenters each day. I must find an heiress who will tolerate me."

Keene knew his friend had inherited an estate in disrepair. Several years ago Victor had made him feel ashamed by implying that Keene had no knowledge of responsibility. Ashamed and misjudged, because Keene had more knowledge of fending for himself than most young gentlemen. But he'd always kept his circumstances to himself—but then, so had Victor.

Keene turned away. Nothing he could do would help. He couldn't offer Victor a loan or bail him out with moneylenders. In part, Victor's application for aid had begun a rift between them many years before.

"For heaven's sake, what are you brooding about now?"

"Forgive me, I have nothing to concern me, of course."

"I already know the worst, so you might as well tell me your thoughts. What do you mean to do about Sophie?"

At one time Keene would have told Victor anything, had told him much more than most, but a lot of things had happened since that time. He moved across the room to retrieve Victor's bag. "I mean to do nothing."

"And live as your father did, with the constant reminder? Or do you hope that her child resembles her?"

Keene felt the floor under his knees. He dimly registered surprise. He had only meant to bend over to pick up the bag. But since he was kneeling on the ground, he fumbled for the catch. He couldn't see the bag's contents. He wanted to talk of anything but Sophie, but he couldn't form another question to save his life. He finally accepted the inevitable. "I should not fault a child."

"For you will have much in common with it."

"But she is not with child."

Keene had led her into the house, brushing snow off her cloak before opening the door for her. He instructed the footman to send Letty to her room. He'd brushed his lips across her forehead and said, "I need to check on Victor. You should tidy up and return to the drawing room. I daresay we have both been absent far too long."

Disappointment wafted through her. Sophie couldn't even have said why. She climbed the stairs to her room. She could feel Keene watching her as if he would redirect her if she strayed from the prescribed path.

On one hand she was glad he was concerned about her welfare, concerned enough to follow her into the cold. And she was glad he'd finally decided to give her a real kiss. She rubbed her lips absently as if she could recapture the feel of his mouth on hers. On the other hand, she wished he was following her to her room. She was impatient to learn where his kisses and caresses would have led if she hadn't whispered his name, if she hadn't panicked.

Although the truth be known, she was inclined to panic around him, like the time she had fallen in the river. She'd been about to remove the sodden heavy skirts weighing her down, but Keene had been there on the bank. She'd tried to tell him to leave, but water filled her mouth, and the current, rain swollen and much swifter than normal, tugged her under.

She'd resurfaced sputtering, and the thought of exiting the water minus her clothes had been almost as frightening as drowning. Although after he'd pulled her from the river, she couldn't pinpoint why she had been so frightened of losing her skirts in Keene's view. Except there had been something more powerful at work, something in the way he'd looked at her sopping-wet bodice.

All of it had been terribly confusing at the time. She'd been furious with herself for getting in such a predicament. If she had emerged from the water half naked back then, would there have been a similar episode to the one that had just happened outside in the snow?

In her room, Keene's valise rested near the door. The sight

of it sent an odd shiver through her. He would be sleeping with her this very night, and whatever had started outside would be finished. She grabbed the bedpost, suddenly feeling lightheaded and weak in the knees.

No! She did not want the odd sensations residual from her fall from the horse to interfere with this day. That was her last thought as the floor rushed up to meet her.

EIGHT

Victor stared at Keene's back. Now that he had broken the man's composure, he regretted it. He shifted on the bed. He felt lightheaded and weak. He wasn't sure his legs would support him, but he slid from the bolster anyway. Pressing his hand hard against the washcloth he held over his wound, he took shaky steps across the floor. He wanted to sink down and lie on the carpet beside Keene, but then he would have to stay there, because there would be no way he could find the strength to stand again.

"No chance at all she could be bearing your brat?"

Keene shook his head and rummaged in the valise. Victor put his hand on his shoulder.

Keene stiffened.

"You are angry with her."

"I cannot be angry with her." The tightness of his voice belied Keene's feelings.

Victor awkwardly dropped to a knee. "You can and should, but do not allow it to fester. Trust me, I know. A festering wound is worse than a bleeding wound. Except that if I bleed to death, I should wish for you to blame that butcher of a surgeon."

"God forgive me, I thought George was the only one among us with honor."

"We all have honor, Keene. What we do not have is compassion. Although I think you have exhibited more than

George or I. Now, tell me what you mean to do about Sophie. For you would not wish to give her the treatment your father gave your mother. Or do as George is doing to Amelia."

"My father loved my mother, as George loves Amelia more than life. I have only the blow to my dignity to consider."

Victor disagreed. He doubted a blow to Keene's dignity could bring him to his knees, but as he spoke, Keene regained his composure by perpetuating one of the illusions that kept him sane. If Keene wanted to believe he didn't care about his wife, Victor wouldn't challenge him on it. "So what shall you do with her?"

"I cannot take her to London. I will not have the whispers and speculation. If she is very far along, everyone would know that I could not have fathered her child."

"Why not?"

"It's two days of travel here. My name is entered into the betting book at Waiter's nearly every day since the little season started."

"No doubt you were uncommon lucky."

" 'Tis not luck. I doubt my finances are much better than yours."

Victor pulled back. Keene's father was rumored to be quite wealthy. But then, the baron had in many ways cut his son off. Or the man who was not his son.

Victor shook off his surprise at Keene's admission. He didn't have the energy to do more than concentrate on the problem at hand. He knew better than most that Keene feeling powerless was tantamount to loosing a starving lion among a herd of gazelles. He'd snap off a head before he thought. "But how shall you treat her? What will you expect of her?"

"I have always known her to be honest. I expect that she will not attempt to foist off this child as mine. In return I shall never mention, nor show by word or deed, that the baby is not mine. She almost told me. She spoke of her parents' desperation about her situation and that she promised to accept any reasonable offer."

"Well, then, you must tell her that."

"How should it be honest if I tell her beforehand I know the child is not mine? She should behave as she will and let her true colors fly."

"If she pretends the child is an early arrival, what then?"

Keene shook his head. "I won't allow it." He stood and pulled Victor to his feet. "You need to be abed."

"Amelia should have told George."

"She assumed he knew."

"But then, she doesn't speak out."

"Why didn't you marry her?"

Victor closed his eyes. "She knew I could not."

Keene halted. Victor saw a mirror of his own emotions in the pain and yearning on Keene's face. "Where is Sophie?"

Keene shook his head, as if warding off deeper emotions. "I sent her to her room. She was wandering about in the snow."

"You had better go to her."

Keene pushed him toward the bed. "I need to rebandage your shoulder."

"Go on, I shall yank on the bellpull."

Keene looked torn. He pressed the fresh bandage material against Victor's shoulder and quickly wrapped it around, tying the ends. Victor pressed his palm over the wad of material, while Keene heaped all the pillows against the headboard.

"I can't go to her. I very nearly took her in the snow. If she hadn't . . ."

Victor studied Keene's wild-eyed look. The man needed to realize there was a reason his control was slipping.

"She didn't know that you would ask her to be your wife, did she?"

"No, she had no idea."

"Then whatever she did, she did not know it would affect you."

"Are you my wife's advocate?"

"Treat her kindly, for I do not think she meant to wound

you." In fact, he suspected Sophie adored her husband. But then, what woman didn't?

Victor was tempted to ignore the scream. But it turned to hysterical pleas for help. Even he could not sit back. Reluctantly, he opened his door and moved down the hallway.

He didn't think Keene would mistreat his wife, but then, Victor had joked about beating her. Perhaps Keene had taken him seriously.

A maid ran to him. "Oh, my lord, she is dead. My Sophie is on the floor, cold as ice. Saints preserve us." The maid's voice rose and fell in an unstable cadence.

Victor rather hoped not. In any case, it wouldn't do to create a stir. If Keene had killed his pregnant wife, Victor would prefer to have enough time to alert George so they might have a fighting chance of getting him to the coast. Not tolerating it took on a whole new meaning.

"Calm down. Take me to her."

Letty led him to the room. Victor crossed the floor to the crumpled form. He took her hand in his. Sophie did feel like ice, but she had just returned from outside. He also saw the soft rise and fall of her chest, the flair of her delicate nostrils as she breathed.

The maid was rocking in the doorway. "I have to go tell them. Oh, Lord, on her wedding day, no less."

"She's not dead." The immediate problem was preventing the maid from alerting everyone to Sophie's condition. Whether or not she had been knocked out by an irate husband or fainted due to her pregnancy made little difference.

"She's cold as death, she is. Oh, Lord, how shall I tell her mother?"

"Do not tell her mother. Sit down and regain your composure."

He rubbed Sophie's hand. He would have lifted her into the bed, but with his shoulder he could not. He didn't see any evidence that Keene had followed his wife to the room. The cover on the bed was pristinely smooth. Of course, if he only intended to beat her, he might not have availed himself of her charms.

"Sophie, wake up."

The maid clasped her hands in front of her mouth. "Lord Almighty, sir."

"I assure you, she is just fainted."

Victor heard footsteps in the hallway. The last thing Keene needed was the rumors of another man in his wife's bedroom within hours of the ceremony. "Shut the door, and be quick about it, miss."

The maid did his bidding, and she also slipped out in a few minutes when he sent her to fetch Keene. Sophie began to stir.

"Are you all right?" asked Victor.

Sophie blinked. "What happened?"

"You tell me. Did Keene strike you?"

Sophie shifted, sat up and leaned her shoulders against the bed. She frowned. "Keene would never hit me. I think I fainted."

"Do not be so sure. A twelvemonth ago I shouldn't have thought he would shoot me."

"He shot you?" Sophie's eyes grew wide as saucers. "Why?"

"You shall have to ask him. Come, can you stand?"

Sophie blinked. "Why would he shoot anyone?"

"Let me help you stand."

Sophie shook her head and looked at him. "Did he blacken your eye, too?"

"No, George did that."

She allowed him to help her to her feet. Victor kept his arm about her waist as he led her to a chair. He wondered if he should have sent for her mother instead of Keene. He knelt by the chair.

"You three have a very strange friendship."

"It has been under much strain lately." Victor wondered at the loyalty he felt even now.

"I do hope that none of this is because of me. I should not wish to create any problems."

The only problem Victor knew of with her was the very private one he had overheard. If he could urge her to be honest, perhaps Keene's marriage would not end in a state like George's. The trouble was, he only had a few minutes of privacy before Keene showed up, and he would not appreciate the interference.

Victor wasn't about to rest on a noble precept such as whether or not Sophie did the right thing without being told. "Madam." How strange it felt to address her in that fashion. "I would implore you to confide in your husband."

Sophie looked confused.

"I know it is quite bold of me to offer advice, but I know Keene. He will forgive you anything if you just tell him of it. You should tell him the reason you fainted."

"I should?"

"Do not attempt to deceive him. He will not have it."

"I would not."

"Then you have already told him?"

"Told him what?"

Victor shook his head. He hated to be so blunt about it. "Do not speak of this to anyone, but George's wife was with child when he married her."

Sophie's forehead crinkled. "But what does that have to do with me?"

He finished in an urgent whisper, "Not his child."

She covered her mouth with her hand. "Oh, my."

"Yes, so you see."

"Is that why Mr. Keeting drinks so much?"

"Well, yes, for he did not before." They were getting off the topic and Victor was anxious to convince her to follow a different path than Amelia had chosen. "But Keene . . ." Victor searched for a delicate way of saying it. "She did not tell him."

Sophie whitened. She blinked, her large blue eyes filling with tears.

Ah, so he was getting through to her. "So you must be totally honest with Keene. You must tell him why you fainted. Do not deceive him. The accident should not trouble him so much as the attempt to hide it, for he would never forgive the lie."

"But—"

"Do not tell him I said anything."

Sophie swallowed hard and squeezed the hand he still held. "Thank you."

The door opened and Victor hoped they did not look as guilty as he felt.

Something sinister in Keene's expression did not bode well for that hope. "Come to fetch that jacket?"

Victor dropped Sophie's hand and stood. "Your wife fainted, sir. I heard her maid call for help."

Keene's gaze lighted on every detail, from Victor's posture on his knees to his open shirt. But once Keene's gaze landed on his wife, his face softened. "Are you all right, Sophie?"

She nodded and gave a hesitant glance at Victor before she said, "I have had some dizzy spells of late. You see, I—"

"I will leave you in your husband's hands," interrupted Victor.

Sophie blushed and looked away.

He backed to the door. Had they forgotten his presence in their midst? Either way, Keene deserved to hear his wife's confession in private.

The door clicked shut after Victor left the room.

Alone together, Keene wasn't sure he wanted to hear. His heart pounded in his throat and unlike earlier in the snow when he had been caught in desire, this time dread and yearning churned into lumps inside him. He turned around the chair at her dressing table and sat in it, facing his bride. "Go on."

"I should not have done it I suppose, but I thought Papa had bought the horse as my marriage gift."

This was not where he expected the conversation to lead. He heaved a sigh of relief.

"But it was really the other horse, and I did not know."

"Know what?"

"That she wasn't broken. I've fallen from a horse before. But this time I've had these dizzy spells." Sophie stared at him earnestly.

Keene felt the world slide. "Are you saying you fainted because of a fall from a horse?"

She nodded.

Keene took a stab in the dark. "I suppose the inability to keep your breakfast down is attributable to the fall, too."

"No, that was nerves. You were not here yet, and I didn't know that I hadn't angered you beyond reason. I feared you no longer wanted to marry me." She looked down.

Keene stood and pushed the chair out of his way. He took a step toward her.

She flinched.

He wheeled about, feeling sick to his stomach. How was it she flinched when he moved toward her? He wouldn't hurt her. He had never raised his hand against any woman. His father had at least taught him that much honor.

"How did you know that I was sick this morning?"

"Only this morning, Sophie? Come, you must do better than that." She meant to deceive him. She meant to pretend that the child she bore was his. He wanted to throw something.

He wanted to grant her the fuel to perpetuate her little deception, yet he respected himself too much to be a willing participant in her trickery.

Keene spun back around.

Sophie wasn't sure what he wanted. His brow lowered over narrowed eyes. She wanted to plunge through to the end of this discussion and let it die. The underlying tension ate at her.

She pleated the skirt of her gown in her hand. "Well, I have been ill often of late, but I'm sure it is nothing."

"Nothing that another seven to eight months won't cure."

Why should seven to eight months make a difference? Perhaps he had experience with concussions and knew that was how long it took one to be over it. "Do you think so?"

He silently watched her. What did he expect of her?

"Perhaps it is because of the fall, too."

An ugly look crossed his face. Sophie blinked. It was almost as if he hated her. A helpless confusion wafted through her. She wanted so badly to please him, even though Victor had just told her—well almost told her—that George's wife had borne Keene's child. Or at least, Sophie thought that was what Victor had implied.

It was all so unsettling. He'd also told her to be honest with Keene and tell him why she had fainted.

She had, and Keene looked at her as if she were an unsavory offering left by a cat. But then, Keene was never fond of her impulsive behavior. Had Victor misled her? Perhaps Keene wanted to lay the past to rest. Outside he had said it was over and done. He'd also held her tight and led her to the door, enfolded her in his embrace as if he could hardly stand to let her go.

Sophie realized she had underestimated the complications of marriage. But then, she had always been a fool rushing into situations where angels feared to tread. Why should her marriage be any different?

"I am sorry," she said.

"Whatever for, Sophie? You have not told me anything you should be sorry for."

"For being ill?" she offered tentatively.

"Illness is hardly something for which an apology is required."

His tone was so crisp she suspected his words conveyed more than one meaning. She smoothed out the pleats she'd mangled into her skirt. "You seem angry."

Angry enough that she had flinched earlier. Partly that was because Victor had put the idea in her head that Keene might actually strike her—not that she believed that he would. "Did you really shoot Lord Wedmont?" she blurted out.

She regretted the question as soon as it left her lips.

"Do you mean to distract me?"

She shook her head.

"I'll send your maid in to attend you. If you feel well enough, you should join the company in the drawing room."

"Shall you be there?"

He flicked a glance at the window. "I daresay."

There was a hint of bitter resignation in his voice. She wanted to chase after him and pound on his back. Why had he married her? Or was his attitude only frustration at needing to politely wait until bedtime to bed her? As much as she wanted to think that, it didn't feel like a complete answer, but then, he had seemed angry outside before he kissed her.

Were these yearnings as unsettling to him as they were to her? If so, surely all would be well in a few hours.

After he shut the door, Keene leaned against it. How had his marriage to a girl he disliked descended into this viper pit of deception? Why did he care? If the choice had been his alone, Sophie wouldn't have entered his head as a possible wife.

He realized he had forgotten to get the jacket he promised Victor.

A motion down the hallway caught his eye. Letty, the maid, hovered near the servants' stairs. "Come here, miss. Please take my bag to Lord Wedmont's room."

Letty bobbed a curtsy.

Keene felt his stomach clench. A fall from a horse. He had seen Sophie ride. She was perhaps the best horsewoman he knew. He doubted she had taken a spill from a horse in the last ten years.

Keene put his face in his hands. What had he been thinking when he subjected her to conditions such as ice and snow? He hadn't behaved so badly with any woman ever before. Especially not with a woman in a delicate state; but with Sophie, all constraints were off. The stars only knew why.

Keene knew he had let loose the reins on his desire. A protest, a push, or anything less than her welcome participation would have stopped him cold, but she had been with him every step of the way. She'd even moved his hand to her breast. Now that he thought about it, not the likely move of a virgin bride. What had happened to his normal world when he married her?

Supper was a tedious affair. Sophie preferred to eat and be done, but an elaborate meal complete with course upon course had been prepared. Keene said little, but watched her in a way that made her want to squirm in her seat.

She understood only half of the jokes. She would have asked Keene to explain, but he projected an air of impenetrability. His cool demeanor after the episode outside unsettled her. She half wondered if she had dreamed those hot kisses in the cold. She shivered and flushed all in the same motion, as if the heat and chill had left an odd mixed reaction to the extremes.

The ladies withdrew after supper and the gentlemen were slow to follow. Keene came in, only to depart with his friend Victor.

When Keene reentered the room, she felt his presence with every fiber in her being. She looked up to meet his dark gaze. As if drawn to him by a will more powerful than her own, she moved across the room. He stepped to the side of the doorway. "Going to bed, Sophie?"

Was he suggesting she should? She stammered a response. "W-why, yes. I suppose I should retire." Would he follow her?

He watched her silently, his eyes slightly narrowed.

"It has been a most exhausting day." Then, concerned she had given the wrong impression, she added, "I am looking forward to bed." Which seemed like an even worse admission and had done everything or nothing to counteract the notion that she might be too tired for him to exercise his husbandly rights; neither meaning was at all what she meant to imply. "Shall you come with me?" she whispered.

He was silent so long, Sophie thought she must scream in vexation. She had no patience. Only the way his eyes had taken on a strange glint held her still. He belatedly raised his fingers to her cheek. His stroke was feather soft, and her breath came spilling out in a shuddering rush.

"Should you wish that?"

Her response was all air. "Y-yes."

"You are feeling well now?"

She swallowed hard, trying to regain her composure. "I am sure I am fine." A little weak in the knees, but not dizzy.

He leaned forward and brushed his lips across hers. "Go on to bed, my pet. I must needs see to George and Victor."

She nodded and tore out of the room. Not bothering with a candle, she raced toward the stairs, her skirts hitched to her knees. She plowed straight into his friend George, who rounded the corner just as she reached the bottom of the staircase.

"Excuse me. I'm so sorry." She didn't stop to see how her apology went over.

Her running wasn't entirely due to eagerness. Nervous anticipation curled through her in ribbons of energy that required action.

Sitting still as Letty brushed out her hair was trying, but she managed because she wanted it to look good for Keene. Her nightgown on, she climbed into bed and waited.

She tossed and turned and waited some more.

The candle burning on her dressing table became a stub, then a pool of melted wax and finally flickered out. The fire of anticipation in her faltered and ebbed until it became a chunk of ice sliding down her spine.

Where was he? Her eager admission that she wanted him to join her burned as the ultimate humiliation. Tears stung her eyes. She blinked them away.

Didn't he want her? Or only when she was handy?

The memory of Letty retrieving Keene's bag popped into her head, making her quake and stew in anger. Why would he demean her by making her state she was looking forward to his presence if he had no intention of joining her? Was he being deliberately cruel? Was he installed in another room even now?

She turned over his words, his actions, and could find no promise that he would join her. Perhaps she should climb out the window or run out and dive into the river. If she needed rescue, he would remember he had a wife.

She searched her impressions of the day and kept coming back to the conclusion that he wanted something from her, but she had no idea what. Perhaps if she had been more worldly she would have known. She turned her face into her pillow and willed herself into a fitful sleep.

The first light of dawn peeped over the horizon when Keene silently slid into the room. He slipped off his shoes and stood waiting to see if the form in the bed moved.

She remained still. A sliver of disappointment lodged under his skin. He tiptoed across the room until he could see her face under the tangled strands of blonde curls. Sleeping with the covers pulled up to her chin, she looked angelic and sweet.

He sank into the chair wanting her, yet knowing he couldn't have her. Rubbing his hand across his face he willed down the ache in his body. In a few months, perhaps after the season, when her pregnancy couldn't be concealed, he could make her his wife. Until then, he wouldn't give her the ammunition to foster a pretense that the child was his.

He'd stayed away from the bedroom, knowing from that little tête-à-tête at the door of the drawing room, he wanted to throw caution and self-preservation to the wind. He didn't care that he wouldn't be the first. Her enchanting eagerness more than made up for any virtue he cared little about. But he would be her last. Any other children she bore would be his. As it was, he didn't trust himself to crawl under the sheets next to her and keep his hands to himself.

Part of him yearned to slip in with her, wrap himself around her sleeping body and hold her as he drifted to sleep. Yet, he knew that once his body felt the soft curves of hers, his nose filled with her fragrance, he would have no more chance of falling asleep than a dray horse had of running at Newcastle.

He leaned forward and deposited his shoes on the floor. He stripped off his jacket and cravat, and draped them over her dressing table chair. The armchair would make for cold and awkward sleeping, but he would manage.

He woke to find Sophie staring at him. He blinked groggily. She pulled the dressing table chair near his armchair and sat in it.

"Are you awake?"

"No."

She tugged on her lower lip. He wanted to push her hand away and give her mouth a different sort of attention. He didn't want to wake up, but part of him was springing to rigid attention.

"Then you should come to bed."

He groaned.

"It is still warm where I slept. I promise I shall leave you to your rest."

Keene opened his eyes fully, studying his wife. Delicate, violet half moons shadowed the brilliant blue of her eyes. Her concern for his welfare made him feel like a heel. She was the one who needed extra concern about her well-being. "You have not slept enough. You should return to bed."

"I cannot sleep. Really, Keene, there is no need for you to stay in the chair."

He sat up and floundered for an explanation. He hadn't thought what reason he could give for failing to join her in bed. He wouldn't be party to a pretense that her pregnancy was the result of his bedding her, but he didn't want to tell her that. "You were asleep. I didn't wish to disturb you."

"You must have been very late."

"I had trouble with George." His explanation felt weak and transparent.

Sophie sat rigid in the chair, her hair all a tangle and her prudish nightgown concealing nearly every inch of her flesh. He wanted her.

A part of him said just confront her with the knowledge of her pregnancy. What could she do, then? If she confessed, he could have her this morning. But a sick dread kept his tongue still. What if she still denied it? He would want to believe her. He would make love to her anyway. He would become a willing dupe.

She pinched her bottom lip between her thumb and forefinger.

He reached out and pulled her hand away.

She looked at her hand, then up at him. He leaned forward and brushed his lips lightly across hers. She closed her eyes, and then pressed them tightly shut. She drew back before opening her eyes. Her withdrawal wasn't what he expected. He studied her silently. If she was eager to foist another man's child on him, then she should be pursuing any chance of getting him to act accordingly.

"Did you wait up long, love?"

She turned her head and stared out the window. "I fear I have disappointed you in some manner."

Keene didn't know how to answer. She looked miserable and confused. His heart softened. He could give her time to realize her plans wouldn't bear fruit. "No, I had thought I should go gently with you."

She turned to him again and studied him a moment before her eyes dropped down. In a soft voice she said, "I assure you there is no need to delay. I do not require gentleness."

He stood and moved toward her. She recoiled.

"See, you do need time to know me. Don't be scared of me, Sophie. I should never hurt you no matter the provocation."

"I'm sorry. I just cannot fathom that you could have shot your friend."

"It was a duel."

"Oh!" Her eyes rounded, and she seemed so very innocent.

No, not innocent. Countrified, he reminded himself. Even those down on the farm were inclined to that universal sin, fornication. He took her hands in his and pulled her to her feet. "You see, I had thought that when I asked for your hand in marriage, we should have some time, an engagement of some months, to become better acquainted with each other."

"I have known you all my life."

"Yes, but you were little more than a child the last time I spent any length of time here."

Her expression was earnest. "So you did not expect to find yourself married this soon?"

"No, I did not. And I should not like to go overfast. I do not like that you sometimes flinch when I come near."

"I shall endeavor to stop."

"I should imagine that in time you will come to trust me better."

She frowned and looked torn. "I do trust you. I simply am on edge, for I should not wish to displease you."

He took a deep breath, knowing he would test his control to the limit, and led her toward her bed. "Go back to sleep, you need your rest."

She cast a nervous glance over her shoulder. "Is that what you wish?"

"Yes. For I am tired, and you are tired."

She slid under the sheets at his urging. He closed his eyes at the sight of her bare ankle. Wondering if he was making the biggest mistake of his life, he pulled the covers over her. He sat on the bedspread next to her and leaned back against the headboard.

Keene stroked Sophie's blonde curls and inhaled the light fragrance of her hair. She smelled clean and soft and . . . pure. The image of the frightfully honest girl he'd known growing up was at odds with the deception she would have to perpetuate. She tended to be trusting. She had always trusted him, even when she shouldn't. She never even suspected that he had forced her fall into the river.

She seemed frightfully naive at times. He would bet she never guessed that he was in truth not a blood relative of hers, since his father had not sired him.

Perhaps he should just ask her if she was breeding. Would she be able to lie directly to his face?

He bit back the agony of desire and concentrated on the warm comfort of touching her. She felt so right, yet he had to remind himself he shouldn't have to wait long. A few months. May or June—an eternity.

When they woke in the midmorning, Keene didn't feel at all rested. He knew he could not again hold her through the night, or half of a night, without succumbing to the need to make her his.

Later that morning all the baggage was stowed on top of the carriage, and Sophie's horse tied onto the back. Keene's and George's were saddled and ready to ride. Victor had been notified of their pending departure.

After he handed Sophie and her maid into the carriage, Keene turned to find his new mother-in-law waiting for him.

"I did wish to warn you to take a care of her." Jane grabbed his arm and leaned close. "I suspect she is in a delicate way. I know it is unseemly of me to speak of it, but as you are her husband now, I felt I must caution you. She is a lively girl and I fear she will not go gently with herself and will take on too much. Do be sure she gets plenty of rest."

Keene felt cold wash from his heart to his stomach. "Yes, of course."

"I know that you had to know it could be possible. I for one am glad that she will not have the difficulty that I had conceiving. Of course, although I shall hate to leave Mr. Farthing, you must summon me when Sophie's time is near."

Keene fought the chill inside him. The hope that her father had mistaken her condition curled up in a corner of his heart and died, leaving a black hole. The idea that she wouldn't be capable of deception had to be cast aside, too. Apparently, she had given her mother the impression that he had fathered the brat she bore.

Jane gave him an odd look. "Oh, dear, perhaps I should not have told you as Sophie would want to bring you the news herself; but as a mother I cannot help but be concerned about the journey. I shall miss her dearly."

"I shall encourage her to write often, and of course we shall send for you. Be assured I shall take good care of Sophie and her child."

Jane cast a doubtful look in his direction. Had his anger radiated into his voice? He leaned over and brushed a kiss on his mother-in-law's cheek. She had, at least, made his course clear.

She stepped back and Keene looked up to see Victor, his eyes a compassionate shade of brown. He wanted to punch him for his pity. "Are you quite ready, sir?"

"Quite at the ready, sir."

"Don't even think about it, sir."

"Of course not. I should not wish to have George feel it necessary to defend your honor."

Jane looked back and forth between them. There was no way Keene would explain Victor's sick sense of humor.

NINE

Sophie crumpled the paper and threw it on the floor. She knew she was behaving tempestuously, but she couldn't think what to write. The only thing that kept coming to her was to ask, *Why have you left me behind?* She had already scratched those words from the paper twice.

Even if she asked the question, she would only get some watered-down response from Keene. He had said she wasn't ready for London, all the while his eyes searching hers for something more. Then there had been that kiss and hug following a night where she'd slept alone in the four-poster bed that had once been her husband's. He slept in a connecting room, the door shut between them.

She didn't understand.

He had shown her through the house, pointed out the nursery and secured his father's permission that she might redecorate the rooms as she saw fit. All of that was well and good, but she rather suspected more would have to happen between them before there would be any need to modernize quarters for an infant.

What had happened out in the snow hadn't felt complete. She moved to stand in front of the cheval glass. Her hair was already falling from its arrangement, largely because she had tugged on it while trying to pen an epistle to her new husband. Her gown was frumpy, the waist too low, the skirt too full, too many petticoats.

She raised it up and shed the petticoats underneath. The dress hung limply, the style simply not flattered by the lack of undergarments.

Was she an embarrassment to Keene? Was that what he meant when he said she was not ready for London? Was her ignorance of card games and dancing all too easily confessed? Her lamentable lack of fashion too glaringly obvious? Should she have withheld from him the things she wanted to learn?

Certainly his friend George had frowned at her more than once, but his friend Victor had given her encouragement. But now that she thought about it, he had given her advice as though she were the merest of imbeciles.

She whipped around and headed for the door, her petticoats a froth on the floor. Her new father-in-law sat in his study poring over papers. She trounced into the room, wanting an answer. "What have I done to displease him?"

Lord Whitley raised his silver-laced blond head and looked her up and down. "Very likely nothing. What have you done with your skirts?"

"Do you mean to leave her long?" Victor stared at the man seated on the opposite side of the carriage.

Keene shrugged.

"An odd business to be sure. I'm certain Victor and I could have made it to London without assassinating each other," said George.

Keene turned and stared out the window where rain streamed down.

"With no ill purpose in mind, I think Sophie is delightful, and she seemed quite disappointed to be left behind."

Disappointed was putting it mildly. She appeared crushed. Her blue eyes had grown bright, and Victor noticed she had donned her traveling cloak as if her husband hadn't warned her that she would be staying with his father rather than accompanying them to London.

"She's not ready for the ton," said Keene.

Victor knew why Keene thought she was not ready for polite society. He didn't want the evidence of her pregnancy springing to life before the ever-watchful and scandal-hungry eyes of the season attendees. Still, if she had confessed her sin, all should be well.

"No, she is not. She is a rather rambunctious young lady, is she not?" commented George.

"Well, we cannot all have the privilege of marrying a perfect gentlewoman and lady, like you, sir," said Victor.

George glared in Victor's direction.

Keene put a hand on George's shoulder as if to stop him from lunging forward. Turning the conversation back to a less objectionable subject, he commented, "My wife is rather impetuous."

"I say. She scrambled over a footstool like a monkey and had her skirts raised to her knees when she ran into me in the hall."

"Ah, raising skirts seems to be a fault of both your wives."

"Shut up!" said Keene at the same time George made an offer to blacken Victor's other eye.

"I cannot think you explained to her why you left her behind," said Victor, instead.

George gave him an angry look and turned in Keene's direction. To Victor's surprise he echoed his sentiments. "I do say that it is rather odd that you have left your bride in your father's keeping."

"I daresay I shall return to her soon enough."

The odd thing of it was that Keene looked as miserable as his wife had appeared when he left her. There had been a passionate embrace as though the choice to leave his wife behind was not his. But of course, it had been his option.

The carriage rattled and pain lanced through Victor's wound. He grimaced. The way of it now, he should stay alive so he might have the wedded bliss promised by the dueling pistols, because clearly Keene was the real loser in their battle.

Although a part of him wished that one of his friends would take enough offense to permanently put him out of his misery. Lord knew, he had not the courage to do it himself, and he was damn tired of pain and poverty.

"If you leave her in the country, the gossips will say you have only married her for her money," said George.

"Is she so rich an heiress? You should have introduced me sooner, for you have no need to add to your largesse." Victor tried to settle more comfortably against the squabs.

"Of course he has need of money. His father neglects his pecuniary needs."

"He does not," objected Keene. "I had no interest in Sophie's inheritance."

"Indeed, I am sure he did not," echoed Victor, remembering the refused annuity.

Keene grimaced.

There was more at stake here.

"I had it straight from Richard. It must have been painful to apply to one's younger brother for funds," said George.

Keene's mouth flattened. He looked out the window again. Victor stared at the sour expression on Keene's face. Was it true that Keene's father knotted the purse strings tight with his heir? Victor knew George to be honest. Why should he make up something like that?

"I cannot fathom why your father found your exploits so distasteful when often Richard was along," said George.

"No one found Richard's affairs worth mentioning," Victor observed. As a second son, Richard's deeds were hardly a concern to the gossips. Of course, the real reason Keene's father withheld funds was not Keene's peccadilloes.

"We are a scandalous bunch, are we not? I think I shall divorce my wife and top both of you in providing grist for the mill."

Stunned silence greeted George's statement.

"You cannot," whispered Victor.

"I can. I have thought much about this these last few days."

"You have been drunk these last few days."

"That does not mean one cannot think."

"Clearly, perhaps. Surely, George, you do not wish to drag your situation before Parliament. Do think on this. Amelia loves you dearly. She should be ruined. Even if you do not love her, do not regard her devotion so cheaply," said Keene.

"Good God, man. What would she do? She has not much in the way of family or fortune to defend her." Victor leaned forward. George couldn't divorce his wife.

"What need of family has she, when my best friends will plead her case? Although I should not consider anything *he* says upon the subject." George nodded toward Victor.

"Go slowly. Do not make this into everyone's business. As it is, only the three of us know," said Keene calmly.

"Tell him you would not do such a thing," said Victor. "Tell him." Panic rose in him. What would happen to his daughter? She would be ostracized by polite society. What would happen to Amelia? She would have to set up as some man's mistress, or hope that George settled enough on her to live in genteel poverty abroad.

Keene shook his head. "Tell him to banish his wife to his estate?"

No, that was not what he meant. Keene should tell George about Sophie's condition and end this talk of divorce. "Why not?" demanded Victor.

"Now is not the time. I will not have a loose tongue."

"Tell him."

"Tell me what?" demanded George.

"That Victor has offered to set up your wife in a cottage should you discard her."

"I did not mean it." He couldn't set up a mistress when he was on the verge of seeking a marriage. Yet how could he fail to take care of Amelia when her predicament was his fault?

"I care not." George took refuge in a bottle.

Victor silently pleaded with Keene to tell his own situation. But at the same time he understood that George spilled secrets he should not divulge. At some time in the future he should have to reevaluate what he knew of Keene's financial situation, which was damn little. But right now he was more concerned with what would happen with his daughter and her mother, the woman he couldn't marry.

"Nothing is done yet. There is time," soothed Keene.

"I never would have touched her if I had known it would come to this." Victor squirmed in his seat. "She always loved you best, even when she despaired of you ever making an offer. If you remember, you escorted a Miss Thorton to several events around the same time."

George ignored what had been a terribly hard thing for Victor to admit. Keene's gaze was far too penetrating. Victor covered his face with his hands. How had their lives gotten so tangled? Last year he hardly cared beyond the next moment's pleasure; this year he had seen the crumbling façade of his house and realized it clearly mirrored his life. Should he not look to the future, everything would disintegrate around him. The problem was, the actions of the past cast piles of stones in front of every step.

"I wish the rain would stop," said George plaintively.

"I daresay it has just started," said Keene.

Victor muttered an expletive echo, and he wondered if his ancestral home had sprung any new leaks in his absence.

"I should like to see how the current fashions look on me," answered Sophie, undaunted by the disapproving look Lord Whitley offered. She'd suffered too many more-terrifying, disapproving looks from her own father to be fazed by one from her new papa-in-law.

"That is not it."

"Yes, I quite realize." She should have put her petticoats back on, but she'd quite forgotten she'd removed them until he cast a frown in her direction. Well, it wasn't as if she had entered a London drawing room naked.

She sat in a chair across from Lord Whitley. "Keene is quite up on fashion, is he not? At first I thought he dressed rather plainly in sober colors, but on reflection, he is never flamboyant to the point of ridiculousness, is he?"

"If you came in here to talk of my son, please leave."

"Why?"

Lord Whitley's faded blue eyes opened wide as he raised his head to meet her gaze.

She guessed Lord Whitley was rather taken aback by her directness.

"I have work to be done."

"Oh, pish. I shall do it for you. Are you keeping the accounts? I have a very neat hand and a good head for figures." She stood and leaned across his desk.

Lord Whitley closed the ledger.

She sat back down. Had she offended him? Keene had seemed interested in her ability to manage her father's accounts. "I often check over my father's figures. You could ask him, but only if you should wish assistance. For I confess it is not my favorite occupation."

"What is, miss?"

"Well, I do prefer pursuits which require exertion. I imagine I should greatly enjoy dancing. I like to ride, and of course go for long walks, but it is raining, which cancels the last two, and I cannot dance without a partner, let alone that Papa—my real papa, not you—did not see fit to allow me to learn. Although Mama says one must be able to dance in London. Do you think that is why Keene didn't take me with him?"

"You shall have to put your question to him."

"Should I? I mean I already did, and he said I was not ready for London. Mama gave me a bank draft to use to furnish my trousseau. We knew Papa would not allow me to purchase gowns in the latest fashion, and Mama says one must buy in London or be hopelessly provincial-looking."

Lord Whitley rubbed his forehead with his sausage-like fingers. Sophie couldn't help but compare his square hands to

Keene's elegant long fingers that could touch so devastatingly and leave her aching.

"I mean, do you think that is what he meant? I am not dressed properly and cannot dance. Actually, I cannot play cards, either. I understand I should do that."

"Since he specifically requested permission to allow you to refurnish the nursery, I would presume he has plans to make me a grandfather."

Sophie blushed and looked down at the ring on her finger. In a hesitant voice she said, "Then I imagine I should be in London with him, rather than sitting here alone. I would wish your advice. He is your son, and I am afraid I displease him with my unfashionable appearance."

Lord Whitley leaned back in his chair. "I do not think your looks displease him, but your pert manner, miss."

Sophie pushed back the chair and headed for the door. She hadn't come into the room to be insulted.

"You say you are good with figures?"

She paused, her back to him. "Yes, sir."

"There is a deck of cards in the dining room sideboard. Fetch them and the housekeeper and come back here."

Sophie did as she was bade. The housekeeper stood in the doorway as Lord Whitley took the cards from Sophie's outstretched hand.

"Mrs. K., is there not a dancing master residing in the village?"

"Yes, sir. Him used to teach for that young ladies' academy up in Perth. He is old now and only takes occasional students."

"Send around an inquiry to see if he would consent to teach our Sophie here."

Sophie leaned forward and threw her arms around Lord Whitley's neck. "Oh, thank you, Papa."

Lord Whitley gave her an awkward pat on the back before clearing his throat, indicating that her exuberant hug had gone on long enough.

Sophie spent the next few days learning as much as she

could. She pored over the copy of the *Times* that Lord Whitley received each day. She forced herself to wade through the political news, understanding little. Lord Whitley found her a quick study at cards, and her old dancing master, whose bones creaked with every knee bend, pronounced her a highly adequate student.

Keene paced through the house like a caged tiger. He couldn't tame his restlessness. Partly it was because the house was empty. Without Richard, silence hung like a pall over the rooms. Yet, it wasn't entirely Richard's absence that provoked his agitation. There had been plenty of times when Richard had not been in residence.

When he had combed through every room and found nothing to soothe his spirit, he called for his horse. What he wanted was to ride to his father's estate and see if Sophie was willing to talk to him yet. He had given her every opportunity, held out hope until the last minute before leaving that she would divulge her secret. He'd told her nothing in the past mattered. She'd dipped her head and stared at the floor, while he waited in vain.

Keene rubbed his face. It was not in the least like Sophie to act reticent. What reason would she suddenly start now? What reason other than her pregnancy?

He pulled on his gloves and walked down the front steps to his horse. It had only been a few weeks, not long enough, yet. He had only a few months to wait. Yet waiting drove him to distraction. He needed to be doing something, anything. He rode to George's house.

The butler stood implacably at the door and said the Keetings were not at home. Keene could hear the shouts that belied their servant's statement. George, at least, was home, and his tirade could only be directed at Amelia.

"Let me in, man, before he does something he should regret."

The servant's reserved exterior crumbled before Keene's eyes. "It's an awful row, it is."

The butler refused to announce him. Keene turned the door handle of the morning salon and stepped inside. Amelia sat on the edge of a sofa, her hands gripping the cushions at her side, her face white. George stopped mid shout, his face red.

"Are you all right, Amelia?" asked Keene.

She nodded. "I am fine."

"He hasn't hurt you, has he?"

Amelia gave a fractional shake of her head. "He would raise nothing stronger than words against me."

Keene glanced at his friend. Did George realize how painful words could be?

"You interfere, sir."

"Your shouts can be heard in the street."

Silence greeted his quiet observation. Only the silence was incomplete. In the distance a small cry signaled a baby's distress.

"Oh, my." Amelia rose from the sofa. "I hadn't heard her."

"Take care of your brat," said George.

"I'll get her," offered Keene.

He paused outside the room, drawing a deep breath. Was this how his father had responded to him as an infant? His hands shook as he contemplated the anger he shared with George and the anger he felt toward George. He thought of Victor and the shoulder that was taking so long to heal. As he climbed the staircase his body felt heavy. He had shot the wrong man.

Victor pulled on his shirt and gingerly slid his right arm into the sleeve. Finally the wound was beginning to heal. His arm felt weak and useless, although for the most part he could control its movement. He lifted it to shoulder height, both fearing to use it and terrified that if he never used it, the limb would wither to nothing.

A knock on his door brought his man from the wardrobe, a cravat in hand. Victor moved to his bedroom door while his valet opened the door to his apartments.

"Sir, there is a young woman to see you."

Victor raised his eyebrows in a silent question, *who?*

His man shook his head slightly, indicating he did not know.

Victor crossed to the door. "Sophie!"

"Oh, good, it is your place. I wasn't quite sure. I found this address among some of Keene's correspondence. I didn't wish to read the letter to be sure it was current."

"What are you doing here?" Victor reached to pull her inside, thought better of it and stepped out onto the outside stair, then changed his mind again and pulled her inside. Standing outside was more likely to draw attention than pulling her inside. Just showing up at his door was bad enough.

His manservant discreetly disappeared into the back rooms. Keene would kill him if he knew his wife had called on him in his bachelor quarters. No decent woman was ever seen calling on a gentleman living alone.

"I came up to London to have some dresses made. I wish to appear more fashionable. I am sure I am quite dowdy. Papa—Keene's father—gave me his address, but I decided I should just stay in a hotel. I do not have any acquaintances here, and I hoped you could recommend a proper place to stay."

"Keene doesn't know you're in London?"

"No. He did wish for me to stay at his country home, and I do not wish to be disobedient—although it is ever my nature to be so—but I did wish to furnish my trousseau, and the draft that Mama gave me is to be deposited in an account"—Sophie reached into her reticule and pulled out a folded paper—"at One Pall Mall East. I believe it would be wise to have a gentleman accompany me, and I hoped you would consider assisting me."

"You should apply to Keene."

"I suppose I might do it myself. I do understand how banking works. I have helped my father for some years, although all of it was done by the mail."

"Sophie, Mrs. Davies, it is terribly improper for you to be here." Not to mention that Keene might shoot him again.

"I did not come alone. My maid is outside in the hackney. I wished to bring her in with me, but I was afraid the driver would not wait. And it is not as if you do not know me. I thought you must be a good friend of my husband, since he brought you to the wedding. I was not sure I shouldn't apply to his other friend for assistance, but I did think he did not like me overmuch. Since you were so kind as to offer advice, I thought . . ."

Sophie raised her blue eyes to his, and Victor wondered how Keene could resist the appeal in them. "You are his friend, are you not?"

"Something like that."

She crinkled her pert nose and Victor thought how long it had been since he'd had a woman in his apartments, so very near his bed. But she was Keene's wife, and he didn't think she understood in the slightest that a woman calling on a man implied a great deal. Her excuse of coming up to London for clothes seemed flimsy in light of the fact that in a few months new clothes wouldn't fit.

On the other hand, she had made no overt moves to suggest she had come with the intention of seducing him. Her red cloak remained tied at her neck, the hood draped over her head. Victor floundered, confused.

Was it an excuse to come to his apartments? She seemed so very innocent and sincere. She was a pretty thing, perhaps not in his first taste of women, but not the sort he'd kick out of bed for lack of appeal. How could Keene stand the delay, knowing she was his for the taking? Victor reached out and touched her shoulder. "Sophie, you do understand what people would think if they knew you were here alone with me?"

She blinked rapidly several times. "What should they think besides I am calling on a friend of my husband's?" She paused as if waiting for him to explain further. Then, in a more hesitant voice, she asked, "If I am not safe with you, who should I be safe with?"

"It's just not done."

She stepped back and turned. "I did not realize. I should go, then."

Victor wanted to toss her over his shoulder and carry her straight to Keene, except he feared his reception. "Yes, you should go."

"Very well. I guess I shall try staying at the Limmer Hotel. Is that a good place? Because I did find this letter from a friend of Keene's who had stayed there."

"No, you do not want to stay there." It was a good place for gentlemen to stay, especially those inclined to follow the fancy, but not for a single lady or a married lady on her own. What would everyone think if they caught whiff of her presence in a hotel, while Keene resided in his town house? "You should go straight to your husband's home."

"Please, I should not wish him to know I am here. I wish to surprise him, when I have improved my appearance."

She didn't need to improve her appearance, although now that Victor thought about it, her cape was rather outdated and very similar to one his grandmother wore.

"I mean, he did not expressly forbid my leaving the country, but he did not bring me with him, either." Her eyes glistened in a way that made all the rational thoughts in Victor's head melt into pools at his feet.

He knew she had been disappointed when Keene left her. Her bravado in coming to town on her own touched something in him. Why couldn't Keene have explained it to her? "He did not wish you here because of your condition."

She frowned. "My mother must have spoken with him."

"Yes, she did."

"I do seem to be getting better. I have had much less trouble of late."

It was Victor's turn to frown. In his opinion, pregnancies

didn't get better, just bigger. Although he supposed she might be referring to her fainting on her wedding day. "Have you fainted again?"

"No, I have not."

"You did explain to Keene why it happened, did you not?"

"Well, yes, but he seemed quite angry with me." She bit her lip.

"You did not expect him to be pleased."

"No-o," she said.

A knock thudded. Victor frantically grabbed her arm and pressed her into the bedroom, shutting her in before edging back the outside door.

TEN

Amelia slipped into the nursery behind Keene. She stood in the doorway while he retrieved Regina from her crib.

"George let her nurse have the afternoon off. She had a death in her family."

Keene hitched the baby against his shoulder. "Does she need to be fed?"

"I don't know."

Fortunately, the baby's cries turned to sniffs and whimpers. But if her own mother didn't know what to do for her, who did?

Amelia pleated her fingers in her plain, white muslin gown. "He means to have me sent away."

Keene looked at the pinched expression on her face. Amelia looked bewildered. She didn't cross the floor to retrieve her child from his arms. Did she lack maternal instinct? Was she too fastidious for the muss and fuss of a baby? Her expression twisted in a grimace.

"I would go, but he will not let me take Regina with me. When I hold her he becomes furious. I offered to go to the country to his estate, but he bade me leave her. What should he do with her? He will not see her himself." Amelia's soft delivery was offset by the note of panic in her voice.

Was she shying away from caring for her daughter for wanting to please George? If so, he was being totally unreasonable. "We'll talk with him."

"I cannot. I have tried. I don't know what to do. He speaks to me of divorce, but he will not let me take her with me. I try to stay and endure his hate."

"He is hurt, Amelia."

"I know. I do not think he would harm her, but I don't understand why he would separate me from her."

"Because it would hurt you. Because he is jealous of your affection for your daughter."

Her eyes searched his.

Keene supposed he should admire her calm tone, her reserved demeanor when she was so obviously distressed. He had found her demure approach fascinating before now.

Her gaze dropped to the floor. "I see."

"Let me talk to him."

Amelia crossed the floor and held out her arms for the baby.

Keene held onto the girl. "No, I want to talk to him about his daughter."

"He will not like it. I keep her from crying around him."

"Let me try it my way."

Relief flooded through Victor when he only found Sophie's maid at the door. The woman stood nervously in front of him.

"The cabbie says he ain't waiting no longer."

"Tell him he shall not receive his fare, then—Sophie didn't already pay him, did she?"

Letty shook her head.

Sophie cracked the door behind him. "Letty?"

"Go back and tell him she shall be with him momentarily."

Letty pressed her lips together in a frown and turned to do as she was bade.

"Sophie, you need to leave now. Your cabbie is growing impatient."

She slipped out of his bedroom and headed for the door. "Very well."

He stepped onto the landing after her. The least he could

do was make sure she made it to her hack safely. As she put the envelope she carried back into her reticule, Victor noticed a crony of his standing on the street below.

He couldn't risk Sophie being seen leaving his apartments by someone who later might learn she was Keene's wife. He grabbed her arm and jerked her back inside. Her eyebrows arched in question. He put a finger to his lips.

As surreptitiously as possible he peered over the railing. He didn't want his friend to see him and come up.

Unfortunately, his friend seemed to be engaged in a lengthy conversation with another person whose back was to Victor. His palms grew damp. He probably knew the other man, as well. She'd taken a horrible risk in coming here.

"What is it?"

"There are men I know out there."

"So, they don't know me."

He shut the door rather than risk her stepping out while his acquaintances were still on the street.

Victor stared into Sophie's startled blue eyes and realized she was too innocent to know how much trouble she could get into wandering about London alone. "Is there no one you could apply to who could guide you about the city?"

She shook her head.

"I implore you, madam, please go to your husband's home."

"No, I will not. If he wanted me there, he would have brought me with him."

Victor suspected it wasn't as simple as that. Much as he hated the idea of guiding her about, he couldn't let Sophie stumble around London unescorted. He prayed that Keene wouldn't kill him when he learned she'd come to his place.

"As soon as they leave, I'll escort you to Grillion's Hotel. I can't let you wander about town alone."

"It's all right. I'm sure I shall manage quite well on my own."

Victor peeked out the window several times. The men lingered an extraordinarily long time. What could they be discussing?

Sophie protested, but he refused to move from in front of the door until it was safe.

He saw Sophie's maid return, her face a mask of impatience.

He opened the door for her.

"Where is she?"

Victor winced. At the same time, he heard the steady thump of feet on the outside stairs of his apartments. He grabbed the maid, shoved her behind him and forced both of them into his bedroom. "Do not come out until I call you."

He called for his man to dismiss the cabbie as he looked out to see who was climbing the stairs now.

Keene rubbed his face. How could he make George understand? He couldn't even get George to take the baby in his arms. What hope was there for the child? His stomach clenched in rage and hopelessness.

He'd lost his brother, nearly killed Victor and despaired of salvaging his friendship with George. Each day eroded his respect for him. He wanted to fly home to the country and find comfort in Sophie's arms. Yet, her charade tore at him.

The trouble was, he understood her fear. He understood George's rage. He understood his father better than he ever had before in his life, but he couldn't condone their behavior.

Now, Victor he didn't understand, but at least there were no secrets between them, or very few. After the tension-filled atmosphere of George and Amelia's house and the silence of his own, Victor's company would be soothing.

The only problem was Victor already had company. Keene glimpsed a woman on the stairs ahead of him. He hesitated. He hadn't see the woman's face from his vantage point on the lower stairs, but he thought she looked vaguely familiar.

In the street a hansom cab waited. How odd. Did she mean to stay only a moment? Victor's valet emerged and passed him on the stair as he made his way down. "Excuse me, sir."

Keene waited until the man came back up after dismissing the hack. He followed the man through the door.

Victor greeted him with an expression of near panic on his face.

"Is something wrong?" asked Keene.

"I'm entertaining. Go away."

"I shouldn't keep you from your liaison. Perhaps we could meet later?"

Victor crossed the room, pushed on Keene's shoulder as if he would forcibly push him out of his home. "I'll call on you."

The valet disappeared into his quarters.

Sweat beaded Victor's brow. Keene watched the furious pulse at the base of his friend's bare neck. Victor's nervousness intrigued him.

Keene cocked his head sideways. Teasing his friend seemed infinitely preferable to the heavy burdens he carried around with him. "Who exactly are you entertaining?"

"A lady," said Victor.

Keene crossed his arms. It wasn't like Victor to be so secretive. And who could he be entertaining in private? At his own apartments? With the exception of a few of the eligible young misses available this season, Victor's name hadn't been coupled with anyone else's of late. "Come, now, I shan't tell anyone."

"Leave."

"So very rude, sir. You know my deepest, darkest secrets."

Keene knew many of Victor's secrets, too. There had been Amelia, although at the time Keene hadn't harbored the slightest suspicion of the extent of events that occurred between them.

Victor's nervousness made Keene want to pry.

"I'm not telling you her name."

Keene took a step toward Victor's bedroom where the "lady" no doubt hid.

Victor grabbed him. "No!"

The extreme response startled Keene. Up until now he was teasing, expecting that sooner or later Victor would tell him or at least hint at who was concealed in the other room. But suddenly it didn't seem amusing anymore.

"Why not? Are you ruining some young lady's life again?"

"No! I'm not ruining her. Please, I beg of you, do not open that door."

"Who is she?"

"She's married. Please leave."

"You should not have her in your apartments then."

"I did not ask her here. She came on her own. I should not wish to risk being shot again."

"I would never tell anyone."

Victor didn't look reassured. Instead, he looked green about the gills. "Yes, I know, sir."

"Promise me you shall give me details later."

"Of course I shall. Later," whispered Victor.

Keene made to leave. He stopped halfway to the door. An inexplicable reluctance held him back. "Are you sure you are up to this, Victor? You look ill. Perhaps you are not healed enough for the exertion of making love to your mysterious guest."

Victor paled even more. "No, I'm not."

The response was not what Keene expected. "Good God, man, you act as if Princess Caroline has taken a fancy to you." Which was within the outer realms of possibility. Being caught with the prince regent's estranged wife could be a treasonous offense. Not that he would expect Victor to encourage the princess if she did take a fancy to him. Besides, her taste in men was much less refined.

"Worse," muttered Victor.

Who the hell was in there?

"I promise I shall tell you all about it," whispered Victor, his finger in front of his lips. In a louder voice he added, "I shall see you later."

It couldn't be Amelia. He'd just left her. At least he thought she had been there still when he left George. Was she seeking out her former lover?

Keene shook his head. It was possible. And why wouldn't she? With the way George was treating her and his hardening resolution toward divorce, what did she have to lose? "Tell me it's not Amelia."

"It's not Amelia," repeated Victor dutifully.

Keene shook his head, suddenly unsure whether Victor was lying to him or not. He headed for the door, not wanting to stay any longer. The woman arrived only slightly before him. It could be Amelia. The snatch of skirts and cloak he saw wasn't enough to persuade him that it was her, but then, Amelia was probably smart enough to disguise her appearance.

She could have left George's house before he did. He had been alone with George for a quarter hour or more before taking his leave.

Keene sank down on the steps outside Victor's apartment. He wanted Sophie. But with the weakness of his resolve around her, he needed to wait.

"Is Keene gone now?" Sophie peeked her head around the bedroom door.

Victor's knees buckled, and he bent over rather than fall.

"He's mounting his horse now." Victor's valet stood at the window.

"Are you all right?" asked Sophie.

"No. I'm near expiration from fright. Dear God, do you realize he would kill me if he found you here?" He'd been afraid that she would emerge from the room when she heard her husband's voice, and he would have to explain why she was in his bedroom. With the way he turned flippant in the face of anger, clearing up any confusion was bound to turn into a deadly proposition. "I feared you'd come out."

"Why would I do that? I don't want him to know I'm in London."

Not that she cared if her husband knew she was in his bedroom, just that she wasn't in London. Victor's heart continued to pound in a mad cadence. This jolt of complete terror was not his idea of fun. He suspected he'd enjoy watching his ancestral home burn to the ground better, not that he wanted that, but at least it would free him from another of his anxieties.

"He wouldn't kill you, anyway."

"No, he might kill you instead." Then Victor would have another guilty burden to bear.

"Who is Amelia?" Sophie asked in an overly casual tone of voice.

Victor straightened. "George's wife."

Sophie drew on her hood and moved toward the door.

Victor grabbed her arm. "Let my man check to make sure the coast is clear."

Sophie rolled her eyes.

Victor wondered not for the first time if there wasn't more to Keene's relationship with Amelia than either of them were letting on.

A few days later, Sophie stood in front of the dressmaker shop's cheval glass. A seamstress pinned the new morning gown hem to the correct length, while Sophie studied her reflection. Her blonde hair curled around her head in close-cropped curls. She liked the ease of care, but wasn't sure the change hadn't made her look a little too boyish. It was too late in any case, and the little Frenchman who had cut it insisted it was both fashionable and flattering.

Letty had cried.

Since then, Sophie had seen several young ladies sporting similar styles. Victor assured her the change was pleasing, but her inquiries about whether or not Keene should like it were met with consternation, and a renewal of Victor's suggestion that she should inform her husband of her presence in town.

The seamstress begged Sophie to excuse her a moment.

Sophie looked critically at the new gown in a flattering shade of lemon. The soft drape of the material hugged her breasts and moved against her body in a revealing way when she walked. When she stood still the gown appeared deceptively demure. The style was simple and liberating. Her father would hate it. A twinge of guilt slipped through her consciousness.

"Oh, I love that gown. I want one just like it."

Sophie turned to see a young woman standing with her hands buried in a heavy, velvet-lined fur muff. "You like my dress?"

"Well, I daresay it is quite flattering to you. I do not suppose it would do the same for me."

Sophie studied the young woman's dark hair and long-lashed sable eyes. "I should imagine you need a richer color, a burgundy perhaps."

The other girl smiled and removed one hand from her muff and extended it. "I'm Mary Frances Chandler."

"Sophie Far—Davies."

Mary walked around her, looking at Sophie's gown. "It does flatter you, and the color complements your complexion."

"Thank you."

"Well, Madame is the best dressmaker in London. I should know, I've tried them all."

Sophie didn't doubt her new acquaintance's claim. Her pelisse was caped and frogged like a fashion plate Sophie had studied in the latest issue of *La Belle Assemblee* just this morning.

"One must employ great tactics to distract the gentlemen from the study of their fobs and seals, mustn't one?"

"Is that what distracts them?"

Mary shrugged and watched intently as she replied, "Their pretty pieces, whatever their shape."

Sophie wasn't quite sure what her companion meant. In fact, she had a sickening feeling that the comment was the sort that would prompt Victor to tug her away and say she must pretend not to have heard. She didn't answer.

The dressmaker and the seamstress returned carrying a gown. "Miss Chandler, if you would step into the changing room. We'll have you done in a trice."

The seamstress knelt and resumed her pinning of Sophie's hem, but when Mary emerged from the dressing booth, both the dressmaker and the seamstress moved toward her. Obviously they considered her a more important client than Sophie.

"Is that gentleman waiting outside with you?" asked Mary as she pivoted for the women pinning her hem.

"Yes."

Mary gave her a speculative look out of the corner of her eye. "I recognize him. Lord Wedmont, isn't it?"

"Yes. He is a good friend of my husband's."

"Who is your husband?"

Sophie was aware of the glances exchanged between the dressmaker and the seamstress. "Keene Whitmore Davies."

"Lord Whitley's son?"

"Yes."

The dressmaker moved over to finish pinning Sophie's gown.

A slight frown moved across Mary's face. "You are newly married, then."

"Three weeks ago." Sophie wondered if she was being indiscreet in giving her husband's name, but it was too late now. Victor would have an apoplexy and insist if she was to announce to the world she was about town, then she might as well leave the hotel and go to Keene's house.

Mary leaned her head sideways and narrowed her eyes. "We

ought to stroll together in the park. We should supply each other with an excellent foil, don't you think?"

Sophie smiled back. "I should like that."

"Perhaps your husband and Lord Wedmont would like to join us."

"I don't know." Sophie wondered how she could dodge the obvious problem of inviting her husband to do anything when he didn't even know she was in town—let alone whether he would want to do anything with her, anyway.

Besides, Victor was none too eager to escort her anywhere beyond the bank, the dressmaker, and the sundry other shops she needed to visit to furnish her wardrobe. He'd firmly dug in his heels when she suggested a simple walk to burn off energy. Instead, she dragged Letty around each morning as she explored the city at what apparently was too unfashionably early an hour for the ton to be about.

"Ah, I see you do not wish to share," said Mary with a tinkle of a laugh.

"No, it is not that. I thought we should enjoy ourselves better with just our maids."

"Of course we would, but you must understand I have a goal. You have already landed a husband, and I must, of course, concentrate my lures. But then, perhaps you could see your way to giving me pointers for convincing a fish once landed to let me go my own way."

"I should do better at teaching you how to take a fence."

"Could you, for I am a terrible horsewoman."

"Perhaps I should not, for I took an awful fall from Grace not so very long ago."

Mary laughed out loud and then covered her mouth with her hand. Sophie wasn't quite sure what was so funny about admitting a fall from a horse.

"She was not well trained, and I was prepared for her to rear when she bucked instead."

"Oh, Mrs. Davies, you do amuse me. Are you to tell me Grace is a horse?"

The dressmaker finished pinning the hem and invited Sophie to return to the dressing room to remove the gown so it could be completed and delivered.

"Of course, Grace is a horse," answered Sophie. "Although her real name is Salamanca, but I prefer to call her Grace. I mean, to name a mare after a battle seemed rather silly to me. Although given her penchant for tossing riders, perhaps she is a battle horse. Please, I would like it if you called me Sophie."

"By all means, you must call me Mary Frances. I hope we meet again."

Sophie was disappointed the walk in the park wouldn't materialize. "I do hope so, too."

But when her dresses were delivered she would have no need to remain in London. The thought was sobering. Yet, how was she to know if her new appearance would have any effect on Keene if he never saw the changes she had made?

Keene leaned against a chair and watched the animated discussion taking place around him. For once he was not inclined to participate in the exchange. When he had received this invitation to one of Lady Burress's salons, he had thought he couldn't afford to miss the engagement. Normally the highly charged political exchange invigorated him, but tonight he found himself distracted.

A couple of young men passed by him. "Have you seen Wedmont's latest?" one asked the other. "Pretty little blonde."

"I hear he's been outfitting her in the best."

"I've never seen her before. Do you know who she is?"

"I heard—"

Keene swiveled to listen.

The young man speaking caught his interest and blanched. He tugged on the other man's arm and backed away.

Keene had tried to run Victor down a few times since that day he found his friend concealing his new paramour in his bedroom, but Victor's valet would turn him away with a stony, "He's not at home, sir."

Who the hell was this mysterious woman of Victor's? How could he possibly afford to clothe his high-flier in fine feathers? And if she was married as Victor stated, why were other people privy to her identity? If he didn't know better, he would suspect Victor was trying to keep her identity secret from him.

Lady Burress stopped in front of Keene. "Are you enjoying yourself, sir?"

"Of course I am."

"I hoped you might bring your wife." Lady Burress studied him with the quiet curiosity he had learned to expect.

"She isn't on the town yet."

Keene expected to run through the usual platitudes and false statements. *Yes, he was hiding her away in the country to keep her to himself. She was engaged in remodeling his home. No, it wasn't sudden, they had known each other all their lives.*

Instead, Lady Burress took a slight step back. "Oh! I thought I heard she was in town."

Keene pushed away from the chair back and stood straight. "Where did you hear that?"

"I was talking to a young lady—what was her name?—oh, that heiress, Miss Chandler. The girl has a sharp tongue."

Keene shifted, impatient with her chatter. "I don't know Miss Chandler."

"Anyway, she said she met your wife in a dressmaker's shop."

Keene shook his head. Some niggling feeling kept him from saying it was impossible.

"Said she was in the company of your friend." Lady Burress snapped her fingers as if the name eluded her.

Keene didn't believe it for a minute. He waited until she supplied the name, even though alarm bells rang in his head.

"Lord Wedmont."

Keene managed to take a slow drink from his glass and offered a negligent shrug. All the while a murderous rage poured like melted lead through his veins. This time he was really going to kill him.

ELEVEN

"Sophie, you cannot."

"Why not? If you won't escort me, I'll take Letty with me."

"It just isn't done."

"One little trip to Covent Garden. It can't be so very terrible." She stopped at the side of the street, glancing across the busy thoroughfare at a violet seller. The pretty girl wore a raggedy gown with a rip across her shoulder, and her too-short frayed skirts exposed her bare legs to the cold and damp London weather.

"I have all these beautiful new gowns, and I want the chance to wear one for an evening." She wished she could give the little violet seller one of them. The girl probably needed it worse and would at least be seen wearing it. "I promise I won't get into any mischief. It is a perfectly respectable place."

Victor caught her arm as she started to cross the street. "Not for a woman alone, it isn't. I won't escort you."

"Fine."

Victor let go of her arm.

Sophie darted across the street, weaving between a dray wagon and a hansom cab. She heard his call behind her. She knew she could do little to alleviate the wretched condition of some Londoners, but she could buy a posy and help the violet seller in her day-to-day toils. Not that Sophie found London as squalid and poor as her mother had portrayed it. Just an occasional situation tugged at her heartstrings.

For the most part, the city was so full of life. London abounded with noises, the hawkers and peddlers shouting their wares, the continual clip-clop and rolling rumble of traffic, the greetings of friends, the play of children, the odd cockney turns of phrase that drifted to her. She only had to take in the sounds to feel invigorated. It was all so wonderful, and she would have to leave soon.

Victor reappeared at her side. "For heaven's sake, Sophie, have a care of yourself. You could get run over, darting between traffic like that."

"Oh, pish."

He grabbed her arm, leaned close and muttered under his breath, "Have a care of your condition. Or if you cannot think of yourself and yours, think of how bad it should go for me trying to explain what happened to Keene. What if you fainted and fell beneath a dray horse? He should run me through."

Hardly. "I assure you, my health is fine. You are just being a wet hen today."

Victor gave her a sidelong glance. "You're not going to the theater, right?"

"I can't very well go without an escort, can I?" Sophie pursed her mouth, hoping he might change his mind. She wanted to do one thing exciting before taking herself and her new clothes back to obscurity in the country. She swallowed down her disappointment that Keene had not found her. She had hoped that he might have seen her on the street, been swept away by her new, improved appearance, sworn everlasting devotion and offered eternal pledges to think of only her happiness. Not that the dream was anything more than a silly young girl dream.

That he hadn't seen her wasn't surprising. Victor behaved as a vigilant watchdog, steering her away from people who might recognize him, and avoiding fashionable places during fashionable hours. Sophie had dutifully followed his strictures to dine in her hotel room and remain unseen each evening.

"What would be so wrong? I'll be leaving in the next day or two."

Sophie approached the violet seller. She reached into her reticule for a coin. Victor glanced at the girl and blanched. He tugged Sophie's arm.

"I'm just going to buy a posy."

"No!" Victor backed up, leading Sophie away. "No, her flowers are all wilted."

The violet seller looked up at Victor. Her torn dress slipped down in front, and she slowly righted it.

"I don't care about the violets. She looks like she could use the money," whispered Sophie. "Look at her dress."

"A posy, sir?" The girl sauntered toward them, her gaze focused on Victor. "For your lady friend?" Her voice took on a low purr. "You could use it later this ev'ning, gov."

"No." Victor turned away.

Sophie pulled back, her fingers in her reticule. "I'll buy a bouquet."

Her pretty face crinkled in a puzzled frown, the violet seller at last turned to look at Sophie. As she took the sprig of wilted violets, Sophie realized the girl didn't have a basket of additional flowers. Sophie had bought the last of her wares. The violet seller cast one last inquiring gaze at Victor, which he steadfastly ignored, before she backed away.

"It was her last one." Sophie put the flowers to her nose and several small purple petals fluttered to the ground.

"It was her only one. Good Lord, Sophie, don't you realize she was not selling flowers?"

"She wasn't?"

"For heaven's sake, you are married. You do understand what she was hawking." Victor's ears grew red.

Sophie looked at the retreating girl and her scanty clothes. "What was she selling?"

"That is why you have no business at the theater alone. There are far too many of her kind there and men who lie in wait for them."

She was a *prostitute?* Was that what Victor meant? Why would she demand payment for something that promised to be so pleasing? But she should know, would know, if her marriage had followed a normal path. "Well, you could escort me."

"I will not." Victor drew up stiff.

Sophie looked for signs of weakening. She suspected that Victor was fond of her in spite of himself. After all, she had not imposed on him to continue to escort her around town once she had her bearings and her account in the bank, but he had shown up regularly as if she was a duty he must discharge.

"You're not going, are you?"

"I can't very well go alone, now can I?" She walked toward Victor's carriage. She couldn't go alone, and she couldn't keep hiding from her husband.

Keene mounted the steps to his town home. He had looked high and low for Victor, searching clubs and inns. He'd even burst past Victor's valet and combed his rented rooms.

He'd decided to let Victor live long enough to tell him where Sophie was. Then, he would strangle him. Shooting was too good for him. The more Keene thought about it, the more he was convinced Victor was hiding Sophie in his room that day. Why else would Victor have been so nervous? If he had been concealing Amelia, he would have been more likely to face Keene with bravado and a disgusting disregard of the possible damage.

As he stepped through the front door, his butler announced, "You have a visitor, sir. I have put him in the library. He insisted he would wait for your return."

The last thing Keene wanted to deal with was one of his regular cronies. He moved toward the library with the thought of getting rid of his unexpected guest as soon as possible.

His butler moved to announce him. Keene waved him off.

"Very good, sir." Blythe bowed and moved off.

Keene opened the library door. "You!"

Victor swung around from where he was perusing the titles of books on the shelf.

"Where the hell have you been?" Keene demanded.

Victor backed into the bookcase and then looked startled when he had no further retreating space. "I could ask the same of you. I have been waiting hours."

"What have you done with my wife?"

Victor looked far too relieved. "Well, that is what I have come to discuss."

Keene wondered if he should summon Blythe to alert the cook to set a pot of oil over the fire: strangling was too good for Victor. "Tell me, now. Then I shall kill you."

"Yes, quite. Should I summon a second?"

"I won't wait that long."

"Yes, that would be the way of it." Victor moved to a chair with maddening deliberation. "But then you might need me to find her."

Keene's heart pounded in his chest. Until this very minute he hadn't quite accepted that Sophie could be in town, could be running around with his sometimes friend, and that he had absolutely no control over his wayward wife.

He crossed the room, leaned over Victor's chair, placing both hands on the armrests and demanded, "Where is she?"

"Well, I am not sure. She is not in her hotel room even though I told her to stay there."

Keene's anger leaked out of him. "Hotel room? What is she doing with a hotel room?" What was she doing in London?

"Obviously she doesn't listen to me any better than she did you. Sit down, man, you look done in."

Keene had always known that Sophie went her own way, regardless of the strictures placed on her. He backed away and found a chair.

"She wanted me to escort her to the theater at Covent Gardens. I refused. In spite of what you must think, I have tried to look after her. She wouldn't come to you, no matter how hard I urged her."

Keene felt the blood drain from his face. "You would have done better to dissuade her."

"Egad, I bet you are right."

Keene had a sickening suspicion. "Did she say she wouldn't go to the theater?"

Victor's eyes widened. "No. She said she couldn't very well go without an escort. I assumed—Oh, Lord."

"How much trouble would she have had finding someone to offer to escort her?"

"None. Bloody hell. Your wife is rather fetching." Victor leaned forward in his chair and looked nearly as distressed as Keene felt. "Would she?"

"Yes, she damn well would."

Sophie had the feeling she had erred in accepting the invitation to attend the theater. When she'd seen Sir Gresham in the lobby of the hotel she couldn't do anything but greet him. To pretend to not know him when he and his three children had spent a fortnight in her father's home just prior to Keene's arrival might be especially hurtful to a man whose proposal she'd recently spurned. She had no special animosity toward Sir Gresham. She just hadn't wanted to be his wife.

He'd introduced her to his companion, a Lord Algany, and one thing had led to another. The next thing she knew she had accepted Lord Algany's invitation to the theater and dinner afterward and did some fast maneuvering to be sure that Sir Gresham would be included in the party.

Now the play was in intermission and Sir Gresham and the woman he'd brought with him had left the box to fetch refreshments. There was a juggler on the stage, but no one was paying him much mind, and Sophie's rapt attention on the three circling balls wasn't justified by the mediocre skills exhibited.

Lord Algany had moved his chair so close that she could

hear him breathe. His gloved hand brushed a strand of hair from her neck. "You have such lovely golden curls, puts me in mind of sunshine."

"I'm sure you flatter me too much," replied Sophie. "Oh, look"—she pointed with her fan—"he has dropped all his balls."

"Not the best of entertainment. Come, love, we should go to supper."

"Oh, no, I couldn't leave without knowing what happens to the"—Sophie couldn't for the life of her remember a single name of a character in the play they'd been watching—"the young woman with the soldier."

His hand at her elbow exerted pressure. Why was it that things that sounded like everything she'd ever wanted proved to be much less in reality? And how was she going to simply enjoy the play and the theater experience *and* extract herself from the blatant attentions of Lord Algany? Why hadn't she thought beyond the opportunity to wear one of her new gowns and get a glimpse of the stage?

"Surely, we need to wait for Sir Gresham and Mrs. Simms."

Lord Algany leaned so close, his alcohol-tinged breath stirred her hair. "We don't need them."

Sophie swallowed hard and turned to face her escort. He leaned closer, and she shied back. "You are too close, sir." She snapped her fan open between their faces.

"Your beauty is hard to resist."

Sophie rolled her eyes. Lord Algany's compliments were a shade oily and made her feel unclean. His fingers continued to toy with a strand of her hair. He grinned as if he realized his approach was making her uncomfortable, but he didn't mind her aversion as long as it was temporary.

Sophie wanted to yank away. The door to the box opened and Sir Gresham and his lady friend entered, just in time to stop Sophie from snapping Lord Algany's straying fingers with her fan.

Lord Algany stood as Mrs. Simms moved forward and

handed Sophie a glass, "There you go, love. Thought you might want to wet your whistle."

Mrs. Simms took her seat and the two gentlemen sat back down. Sophie took a sip and nearly choked. The punch could have been to pugilist school, it packed such a wallop. She looked up to catch Mrs. Simms direct a wink at Lord Algany.

Lord Algany slid an arm around Sophie's waist. "The third act is about to begin. Are you sure you wouldn't rather leave? Sir Gresham and Mrs. Simms would forgive our departure."

Sophie whispered, "I am married."

"Yes, my dear, that was clear. It's also clear that you are not staying with your husband."

"Really, I'm *happily* married," insisted Sophie.

"No such thing, love, but I'll make you happy." His squeeze didn't do the trick.

"Lud, you certainly could make me happy by letting go of me."

"More one for caresses, are you?" Her companion slid his hand up her back.

Lord Algany's practiced touch sent a cold chill down her spine. His gaze dropped to the neckline of her gown. Sophie shivered.

Her evening gown exposed a powerful lot of skin. While she felt reasonably covered when wearing her wrap, Lord Algany had insisted on draping it over the back of her chair. And now one of her hands was tied holding the glass of punch she didn't want. She jerked to her feet and reached for her wrapper.

Lord Algany was too quick. He smoothed her wrap over her shoulders. His hands lingered much longer than necessary and pressed her toward the door. She had no idea how she would get out of this situation. But between Mrs. Simms, who didn't seem to be all that she should be, and Sir Gresham, who had met her father's standards for respectability a few months ago but must have been unduly influenced by the evils of London, and the cooing between them, help from that quarter wasn't likely.

"I should like for you to take me home, now."

"I would be most pleased to take you to my home," Lord Algany whispered in her ear as he whisked her out into the nearly empty hallway.

She supposed she should have listened to Victor's advice, but she had been in plenty of ticklish situations and made her way out of them before.

Her normal predicaments were usually bouts with getting stranded—such as parting company from her saddle in the woods, clinging to the side of a house or losing a dogcart wheel—but she had no doubt she would manage to untangle herself from this situation.

She almost stomped her foot in frustration. "Look, my husband shot his man in the last duel he fought."

"Makes it all the more exciting, does it not? Here, love, I assure you he shall not catch me." The man put both his arms around her and pulled her against him. "We could remove to your hotel room, should you prefer."

Sophie bent backward to escape his grasp. "I should not prefer. I can see I shall have to ask one of the footmen to fetch me a hackney, for you, sir, are no gentleman."

He let her go. "I should not force myself upon you. Let me take you to supper."

The few people in the hall were watching them. She didn't want to make a scene, but she did not trust Lord Algany. Although if worse came to worse, she wouldn't hesitate to toss the contents of her glass in his face and then kick him in the shin. She was fairly sure she could outrun him if he had to hobble along. "If I have your word that you shall behave as a gentleman for the duration of the evening, I should very much like to see the rest of the play."

Just when she thought she had regained control of the situation, he slammed her in the stomach with a smooth look of concern on his handsome face and a low disquiet radiating from his voice. "You must tell me why your husband neglects you so."

"He doesn't neglect me." Only by chomping down on her tongue was she able to refrain from saying he didn't even know she was in town—which went exactly to Lord Algany's point.

Without her being aware of it, he backed her against the wall. "If you were my wife, I shouldn't allow you to wander about London alone."

"I haven't been about London alone. He doesn't neglect me." Her protest sounded puny. Keene simply . . . forgot she was alive. She blinked.

"Never mind, I've seen you about town, anyway." Algany leaned closer.

"No, you haven't, not alone." She could feel the heat of his body shrouding the welter of emotions his observation provoked.

"Yes, with Wedmont. Are you tired of him already? I assure you I could better supply you with gewgaws and fribbles."

"I don't . . . he doesn't supply me with anything."

"Doesn't he? I seem to recall Lord Wedmont recently took a bullet. Was it for you, pet?" Lord Algany placed a long index finger alongside his nose. "Here I had dismissed the rumors of a woman being the cause of your husband's and his fight."

Keene had shot Victor over a woman? Sophie's heart took an unexpected jolt.

"I've heard that they have often played cards since then. Odd to duel one day and be bosom buddies the next. Could it be that Wedmont won the rights to you?"

His eyes caressed her face, while he was careful not to touch her. All the while, he made her feel as if he was. How had she allowed him to encroach so? "Quit, you beast." Sophie smacked the man on the shoulder with her closed fan. "Lord Wedmont is a good friend of my husband, and he has been nothing but circumspect."

"Feisty little thing, aren't you." He smiled and gripped her wrist. "Be assured that you might dance a pretty dalliance, but in the end you will be mine."

Nothing had prepared her for these cat and mouse seduction

games. Neither Keene's nor Lord Algany's. Perhaps her father hadn't been so wrong about the evils of the city influencing the behavior of its residents. What was worse, in a depraved way she yearned for personal knowledge of the sins she was trying to ward off, but not from Algany. Sophie shoved him with all her might.

He stumbled away. An expression of shock faded into a smug grin. "Too fast for you, Sophie? You have only to say what you want." He traced a finger down her jaw. His touch made her uncomfortable. He lifted her gloved hand and kissed the back.

She didn't want to be alone with him. "I want to go back to watching the play."

"And we shall have a midnight supper afterward?"

"We shall do nothing afterward, sir."

"Mustn't tease, pet. You could do much worse than me."

Sophie shook her head and walked back into the box. She leaned over Sir Gresham's shoulder and asked if he would be sure to escort her home after the play. She suffered an agony of a wait as Mrs. Simms appeared affronted and Sir Gresham looked torn. "Mrs. Simms, you won't mind the delay if he should see me home first, will you?"

Lord Algany smiled as if secretly amused. Sophie couldn't help but think his teeth resembled a ferret's. "Have a seat, Sophie. The play is resumed."

Not knowing what else to do, Sophie reclaimed her seat. Would she have to make a scene? Cry for help? She leaned over the edge of the box. Jump to safety in the pit?

Lord Algany's whisper tickled her ear. "Forgive me, my angel, if my eagerness has put you off. You are temptation incarnate to this mere mortal man. If you should gift me with nothing more than a kiss this evening, I should consider myself blessed by all the heavens."

"Oh, bother," muttered Sophie.

"Are you enjoying your drink, Mrs. Davies?" asked Mrs. Simms, leaning forward.

"Quite. Thank you," answered Sophie as she raised the glass to her mouth and let the liquid lap against her lip. She didn't swallow and lowered the glass quickly. Where could she pour out the remainder?

"What do you say, sweetness?" whispered Algany.

"If you deliver me safely to my hotel, I might consider giving you a small gesture of my regard." A slap sprang to mind as an appropriate response, not that Sophie had ever slapped anyone ever before. Not that she had anyone to blame but herself for being in this predicament. No one other than Keene had ever pressed her for kisses, and truth to tell, he hadn't pressured her hardly at all, at least not until that moment in the snow, after their marriage.

She had been warned that gentlemen weren't always gentlemanly, but in her limited experience they had always been. But her circumstances had changed. She was no longer thought to be a naive miss who deserved shielding, but a married woman on her own without her husband's protection.

She stared at the stage without really seeing the players. She had a whole act to think of a way out of this situation. Problem was, she was much better at just doing than at planning. And without being on her home ground, she would have to rely on someone else's assistance.

Instead of planning an escape, her mind kept returning to the fact that Keene and Victor had fought a duel over a woman and it wasn't her.

"Drink your punch, my dearest," urged Lord Algany.

She took another fake sip. She suspected she would need all her wits about her when she made her bid for freedom.

Keene and Victor had circled the pit three times now with no success in spotting Sophie.

"Perhaps she didn't come here after all," suggested Victor.

"Letty said Covent Garden theater," said Keene grimly.

"Maybe her maid misunderstood. Who is Sir Gresham anyway?"

Keene shrugged. That he didn't know, bothered him. Letty's assurance that the man had spent time in the Farthing household didn't particularly ease Keene's mind. This Gresham fellow could very well be the father of Sophie's baby. A cold sweat rolled down Keene's back. Sophie was *his wife* now. He wouldn't tolerate her continuing an illicit affair.

What if she had left already? What if he was too late to prevent her indiscretion?

"There she is!"

"Where?"

A smattering of applause marked the end of the play and Victor grabbed his elbow and yanked him toward the doors.

Keene searched the boxes for his wife. On the third tier a young woman stood with her back to the stage. A man beside her was draping her wrap around her creamy-white shoulders. The heat of attraction singed him. Who was she?

He felt oddly divorced from the scene as he realized the young woman had stirred him in a way no one but Sophie had since he proposed. But it couldn't be Sophie. A halo of short golden curls covered her head. Sophie's hair was long, and everything she wore was completely closed to the throat.

"We've got to hurry. I swear they weren't there a moment ago."

The man in black left his hands on the woman's shoulders far too long, and leaned in close to her ear, his suave good looks striking a deep resentment in Keene. Algany was a rake of the worst sort, the kind who always persuaded a woman to grace his bed, once he set his sights on her. Who was this latest victim?

"Come on," urged Victor as he tugged on Keene's arm.

Algany moved even closer and pressed his lips against the creamy column of the young woman's neck. Her gloved hand landed on Algany's shoulder.

No, it couldn't be Sophie. Yet the scene playing out above

him riveted his attention. The tense urgency of Algany's seduction radiated across the crowded theater.

Keene tried to shake off his fascination with the drama playing out before him. He had a missing, pregnant wife. His situation clawed at him. For a moment he hoped he wouldn't find her, at least not in the way he feared he would find her.

"Come on." Victor tugged on the dark sleeve of his jacket.

Keene dismissed the familiarity of the young lady from his mind as Victor led him through the maze of hallways and up the stairs. He hadn't spotted Sophie, but he trusted that Victor wasn't leading him on a wild goose chase.

Victor muttered curses under his breath and tugged Keene along with increased urgency. They wove their way through the exiting patrons.

In his disjointed thoughts, Keene noticed the way his jacket fit Victor's shoulders like a second skin. He hadn't allowed Victor time to return home to change, just loaned him another jacket and proper evening breeches. He might as well furnish the man with a complete wardrobe, he had loaned him so many clothes of late.

They drew to a halt near the crowded doorway. Just ahead, Algany guided the young woman with his arm around her waist.

"Stop!" shouted Victor.

She turned around slowly.

Her shorn curls gleamed in the gaslights, but Keene knew without a doubt who she was.

Victor thrust him forward, the coward. Sophie blinked, her blue eyes mirrored by the satin of her wrapper. Algany stepped between Keene and his wife. Keene hardly saw him. He leaned to the side.

Keene sensed more than saw Victor drawing Lord Algany away. People shouldered their way around them to the exit, but Keene felt rooted to the spot.

Sophie turned her head. Keene watched the arch of her neck, the profile of her obstinate chin. He sensed her shifting emotions almost better than his own. Her surprise filtered over him as she said tentatively, “Keene?”

Victor stared. Algany wore a look of supercilious amusement. Keene didn’t know which was worse, the audience for the retrieval of his truculent wife, the place he found her in or that Algany was in the process of seducing her. Where the hell was this Sir Gresham?

How had she come from attending the theater in the company of a man who had convinced her father he had enough moral fiber to be a guest in their family home to being in Algany’s company? Not even a familial relationship obliging tolerance would have induced Daniel Farthing to condone Algany’s presence within ten feet of his daughter. And how well did she know him? She didn’t look like the innocent he’d left behind at his father’s house.

Anger frothed in his gut. He leaned forward to demand to know what she was about, but a different question left his lips. “What the hell have you done to your hair?”

TWELVE

Sophie swallowed hard. "Hello, Keene."

"What are you doing here?" Keene's angry question assassinated Sophie's hopes.

"Seeing the play." Her dreams of admiration and appreciation for her new look writhed on the ground about her fashionably slippered feet. She refused to look down at them. Dashed hopes didn't deserve notice.

Keene crossed his arms in front of his chest. She knew that posture. Oh, lud, here they went.

She stared at her husband who was not really a husband. Why had he married her?

"What have you done to your hair?" he thundered, and gripped his arms harder as if to hold himself back from beating her to a pulp.

He hated her hair. Her expectations shriveled into a tight knot inside her gut. She lifted her jaw ever so slightly and said, "I rather think it suits me."

Victor had stepped back and watched their exchange with an avid interest. "I should like to go back to my hotel. Victor, if I could impose upon you for a ride—"

"No!" Keene looked startled at the vehemence of his protest.

"Sophie, we should leave for our supper now." Lord Algany leaned over her shoulder.

"Don't touch my wife," said Keene in a low growl, anger radiating in waves from him.

Victor leaned forward. "We need to get out of here."

"Odd place to find one's wife," said Algany negligently, removing a snuff case from his pocket. "Come, Sophie, my pet, you may still leave with me."

Sophie turned. "Victor, would you be so kind as to see me home?"

Keene grabbed her upper arm and propelled her down the stairs and out the door. Algany's laugh followed her.

"Don't you mean to do something?" Victor trotted along behind them.

Keene stopped and spun around. "What am I to do? Kill him for escorting my wayward wife to the theater? She doesn't look like a woman forced to dress in fine feathers to see a play. I should kill you for concealing her presence in town."

Victor drew up stiff.

"For heaven's sake. All you men speak of is shedding blood. It quite sickens me. Victor only did as I asked him." Sophie tugged her arm out of Keene's hand and marched forward toward the street. "All I wanted to do was see a play."

Keene grabbed her shoulder. Sophie extended the glass of punch from under her wrapper rather than let the slopping liquid spill on her new gown.

His grip softened and then slid away. He circled around her. "Do you understand what could have happened? Algany wouldn't have taken a no from you." Keene's gaze dropped to the glass she held. "Bloody hell, are you drunk?"

"No, I'm not *drunk.*"

Keene took the glass from her. "What are you doing with this, then?"

"I had thought to pour it on the gentleman if he became boorish."

"Then, what?" asked Keene.

Sophie shrugged. "Do tip it on yourself, and we'll see." She moved around Keene and once again headed for the street.

She had no particular plan once she reached it, but she didn't care for Keene's anger. Her chest hurt to think her efforts to improve her image hadn't brought her one step closer to his esteem. He hadn't even noticed, other than to criticize her hair. The changes had had about as much effect as a bird's breath against a gale.

"You're coming home with me, Sophie." His tone brooked no argument.

Hope wafted up from the ashes. She pounded it down. "I will go back to the country tomorrow. I need to return to my hotel and pack my things."

"You're coming with me tonight, if I have to throw you over my shoulder and carry you kicking and screaming all the way."

She spun around and stood toe to toe with Keene. "Why? You don't want me there or you should have brought me to London in the first place."

Keene's response was grim. "I have no choice now. I am your husband."

"Is that what you are? I had quite forgotten. It certainly does not feel as if I have a husband, just a change in fathers and prisons."

Keene stood stock still. Had she pushed him too far? They stared at each other. The night whispered around them. The darkness cast shadows and made his expression impenetrable. Slowly he reached out and traced his index finger down her nose, across her lips and down her chin.

Her breath caught in her throat. A gleam in his dark eyes held her mesmerized. He slid his hand around the back of her neck. The warm touch of his fingers shredded her defiance. Her pulse pounded and her breath spilled out in a torrent.

He pushed her chin back with his thumb and leaned toward her. His lips moved over hers with a deliberateness that had her gasping and fighting her inclination to throw her arms around his neck and return his kiss with every fiber of her being.

He drew back and said softly, "Did that help you remember?"

Fury sparked the eager kindling of her emotions, then his slow smile turned her bones to powder. She didn't understand and couldn't fight his influence over her. His smile faded as he leaned close once more.

"Don't bite," he whispered. After a deliberate pause, he kissed her again.

Emotions rolled through her like a tidal wave. This was the greeting she'd yearned for, the welcome she dreamed about. Her hurt and anger faded as his kiss went on and on.

Her legs turned limp. She had no choice but to hang on to him. Her resistance turned to mush.

"Good God, man, do you mean to seduce your wife in the street?" whispered Victor.

Keene ended the kiss with gentle nibbles at her swollen lips. He pulled her head into the crook of his neck. "Is Algany still watching?"

"No, just every coachman from here to Newgate and half the crowd from the theater."

"Should not be a shocking sight to them. Where is my carriage?"

Had he kissed her just to impress upon Lord Algany that she was married? Sophie reared back from Keene. He released her.

Victor moved away, presumably to locate Keene's carriage.

Keene reached for her hand. "Come home with me, Sophie." His voice was low and urgent, no longer commanding, but compelling.

She fought to retain the independence she had discovered in the last two weeks. Hell, she struggled to regain her equilibrium when she felt like nothing more than a bundle of raw emotions. "You won't lecture me?"

He studied her a long time before he said, "Not tonight, but Algany—"

"I know. I don't ever want to be alone with him ever again." Heat flooded her cheeks. "He . . . he wasn't a gentleman."

Victor returned. "I'll get myself a hackney," he muttered.

Keene stepped back from Sophie. His gaze shifted to his friend. "You're wearing my clothes."

"I shall return them on the morrow, sir." Victor gave a polite leg.

"If they fit you less well, I should agree. But I will have their return tonight." Keene wrapped his hand around her elbow, and without sparing her another glance, led her to his carriage.

In his borrowed finery Victor waited in the library to return to the bedchamber he had used earlier to change his clothes. A servant knelt before the grate and with a rattle of fire irons and wheeze of a bellows coaxed the coals back to life.

He half feared that Keene meant to return and blow his brains out rather than let him retrieve his pale lemon pantaloons, Hessians and bottle-green day jacket. Victor hoped that if Keene meant to stain his hands with more blood he wouldn't want to ruin his own clothes in the process.

As Victor contemplated his possible pending demise, Keene stood outside the library door, his fingers wrapped around the door frame. His knuckles turned white from the tightness of his grasp. Victor swallowed hard, imagining that iron grip turned on him. Strangling would likely make less mess than shooting, and wearing Keene's clothes was no protection at all against that end.

Better him than Sophie. He couldn't quite fathom why she had thought it appropriate to attend the theater with Algany. Although she couldn't know him the way someone familiar with ton life would. Nor could he understand why, when Keene quite obviously wanted to exercise his conjugal duties, he had insisted on Victor's presence in the carriage and in his home.

Would Keene find it more comfortable to execute him with the room heated to a bearable temperature?

The servant slipped out. Victor swallowed hard.

Keene entered the room, shut the door and leaned against it. "On no account let me go upstairs."

"For heaven's sake, your wife is waiting and, by my observation, willing."

Keene looked wild-eyed. "I know. She would be, of course."

Arrogant bastard. But then, Keene had always had easy luck seducing women. His wife didn't look to be an exception. Although Victor wondered how much was luck and how much was skill. "Why insist on my attendance? I thought I was here to change into my own clothes and leave you to your duties."

"You are here to protect me from myself. I cannot let her foist her bas . . ." Keene moved to a chair and buried his face in his hands. "Bloody hell!"

Victor moved to stand beside him. "I thought she made a clean breast of it. When I asked if she had explained to you why she fainted, she said she had." Victor took a hard swallow and realized he'd just admitted he had interfered in Keene's affairs. "You said she had."

"She spun a Banbury tale. Said she fell from a horse."

"She could have. She seems an honest girl."

Keene gave him a hard look. "That's doing it much too brown. I've seen that girl take a six-foot fence. She can outride most men I know. Even if she did take a fall, how does that explain fainting and tossing her breakfast the day of our marriage?"

Victor sat down. "It wouldn't explain a belly either."

Keene popped out of his chair and paced the length of the library. "I shouldn't have touched her. I just gave her more fuel to believe she can persuade me to her bed in time to carry her charade."

"Why did you?"

Keene stopped his pacing.

"Touch her, that is."

"She meant to return to her hotel. Algany might have followed her. I . . . I . . . and I suppose because I know I can't have her."

Victor would beg to disagree. Keene could have her the minute he snapped his fingers or got over this disagreeable need for complete honesty. Some things were just better left unsaid, unheard, unthought.

Why was Keene having such a difficult time resisting the lures of his wife? Sophie was not in Keene's usual taste. Admittedly, Sophie was a pretty girl, but Victor wasn't overwhelmed by her charms.

Keene resumed his pacing, a frown marring his features.

"Why was she with Algany?"

"I don't know. When I started to warn her about him, she said she never wanted to be alone with him ever again."

A tap on the door made Keene shoot toward it. A maid handed him a bundle of blue satin. "Begging your pardon, sir. The mistress asked for something for which to sleep in."

"Stoke up the fire in my room this night. She shall have to sleep in her undergarments. Tell her we'll retrieve her trunk tomorrow."

The maid bobbed a curtsy.

"Oh, and ask her if she has eaten. If she is hungry have Cook prepare her a supper tray, and be sure she has hot chocolate and fresh rolls when she wakes in the morning."

The maid cocked her head sideways and gave a puzzled look to her master. "Hot chocolate, sir?"

"Yes, and eggs and kippers or whatever she expresses a desire for." Keene waved his hand in the direction of the stairs.

The maid bobbed a second curtsy, wide-eyed. "Yes, sir."

"Quite considerate of you," observed Victor.

"She is breeding." Keene took the bundle across the room to his desk.

Victor trailed after him.

Keene opened a locked drawer, removed the contents and stuffed the wrapper and Sophie's dress inside.

"What are you doing, man?"

"Making sure she has no clothes to wear for an escape."

"I'm not sure she had a lot on under that." Victor pointed to the evening gown on top.

"Do not remind me." Keene shoved the drawer shut, then turned the key. He pulled it from the lock and deposited it in his waistcoat pocket.

"If she doesn't want to be with Algany . . ." Victor let the question trail off.

"It's not Algany I'm worried about."

"You put her in your room?"

"None of the others are prepared. Which is why we must go out." Keene grabbed Victor's arm and steered him toward the door. "Shall we try the Cocoa Tree?"

Victor spotted a contract lying on top of the papers Keene removed from the desk. Without his really meaning to read the document, Victor's attention was drawn by a passage. The words jumped out at him as serious as if they had been written in blood. "You mean to let Sophie retain control of everything she inherits?"

Keene grimaced. "Yes."

"Her father drove a hard bargain. Does he know of your father's threat?"

"No, this was my idea." Keene stashed the contract in another drawer.

Underneath the contract was a draft for three thousand pounds. Victor studied the signature. Daniel Farthing. Why had Keene failed to cash his wife's dowry draft? Did he still entertain ideas of an annulment? For that matter, what kind of man allowed his wife total control of property she inherited? A man who intended to end his marriage before it mattered?

* * *

Amelia held the baby tight to her breast. The half light of the dawn stole in through the windows. She had crept up to the nursery to snatch a few minutes with her daughter before the household woke. After that, the orders barring her from the third floor prompted her to confine her activities to the floors below rather than requiring any servant the unpleasantness of enforcement.

Hairs along the back of her neck raised. She was being watched. She turned slowly. George stood in the doorway, his face puffy and his eyes bloodshot. For once he might actually be sober.

"I'm sorry. I should not have disobeyed you. I'll go downstairs." Amelia placed the sleeping infant back in her crib and settled the blankets around her daughter.

"How is it I am the one who was wronged, but you manage to make me feel deuced guilty."

"Because it is not in your nature to be unkind."

"There you go again."

"I am sorry. I'm weak and foolish, and I never wished to hurt you."

"And if you had it to do all over again?"

Amelia looked at the tiny girl sleeping so peacefully in the crib. The swell of love for her daughter and the urge to shield George from the worst of her own nature vied for honors. The helplessness of knowing she could not follow either path successfully tore her in a thousand ways.

She whispered, "I cannot wish for something that would take her away. I would give my soul that you were in the carriage that night. I closed my eyes and pretended you were."

"It wasn't me. It wouldn't have been me."

Yes, George was so good and honorable that he never would have let himself succumb to a passion not sanctified by church and state. In fact, it had taken some prompting before he believed her assurances that she wanted his lovemaking, and that she trusted him implicitly. She had known he would never hurt her . . . physically. She almost wished he would beat her or slap her instead of throwing knifelike words that gouged at her soul. "I know."

George growled. He stalked into the room.

Amelia splayed herself in front of the crib as if to block him, her arms extended.

He stared at her. "I cannot understand how you think I would hurt your child. You know me better than that."

"I do not know you anymore. You are not the man I thought I married."

"Nor are you the woman I thought I loved."

"So both of us were deluded."

"Then we are at point nonplus."

"No. We can move on from here." She shifted her gaze to the weak light filtering in the window. "There is hope for us if you have come to see the baby. We can be a family."

"I did not come up here to see the baby."

Why else would he have come up to the nursery? Nothing else was here. If he had an order for the nursemaid, she would have been summoned to him.

Desperation clawed at Amelia. "I still love you, and I knew you could not love me when you knew the worst, but I hoped."

"Damn you, for these games." George retreated to the door.

She blinked the tears from her eyes. "I would be a perfect wife. I promise, I won't come up here again without your blessing. I want nothing more than to love you again."

He paused in the doorway, his back to her. "I have decided there is no course of action open but a divorce. I came to inform you of that, madam."

"No!" She clapped a hand over her mouth, hardly believing the shriek came from her.

The baby let out a wail to rival the trumpets of Jericho.

"You will leave the child here and be gone from my house by noon. I have given orders for your bags to be packed."

* * *

The pips on the cards blurred before Keene's eyes. His luck had run foul or his concentration had been destroyed by the thought of Sophie in his bed, clad in scanty underclothes. Of course, the rather liberal drinking he had been doing hadn't helped. It certainly hadn't curbed his imagination when it came to Sophie. He needed to send her back to his father's house as soon as possible.

"I'm hungry. Let's go," said Victor.

Victor looked as tired as Keene felt. He shouldn't have kept Victor out all night with his shoulder still on the mend.

Keene played out his losing hand, scooped up his remaining markers and pushed back from the table. A maudlin rush of appreciation for his recovered friendship prompted him to throw his arm around Victor's shoulder. "I'm glad for you. I don't know how I should have kept myself from her."

Victor rolled his eyes. "I'm glad your clothes fit me so well."

"I hope your luck was better than mine."

"Not much. I need to find an heiress soon." Victor steered Keene out to the street.

The sun burned Keene's eyes. He shut them and relied on Victor's guidance. "Only heiress I've heard about lately is a Miss Chandler with a sharp tongue. She should be bang up on the mark for you."

"Haven't met her."

Keene stumbled, his legs nearly useless after hours of sitting in deep play. "She knows you."

"Does she?"

"She saw you with Sophie buying clothes. What on earth were you thinking?"

"Sophie wanted to impress you."

Keene drew to a stop. The bright sunlight cut through his dulled senses.

"She thinks you are ashamed of her," Victor said.

Keene's shoulders stiffened. "You know she is not ready for London."

"She doesn't understand why you don't want her here."

It ought to be perfectly clear to her, now that he had refused to sleep with her several times. Why wouldn't she just spill the bag on her pregnancy? "She'll bloody well figure it out soon, won't she?"

"She is green to town life. She needs guidance." Victor's damn calm words came equipped with barbs.

"You can't guide Sophie. She's like a runaway freight wagon on a steep hill. All you can do is clear the path or get out of the way."

"Rather out of your taste, isn't she? You usually like your women biddable."

"I like them modest and restrained, not stupid."

"Sophie's not the least bit addlepated."

"She's a complete pea goose. Why'd you let her cut her hair?"

"That was her idea."

"My point exactly." Keene felt regrettably sober far too fast. "I liked her hair long. And up. I liked it up. If she wanted to please me she should have left it long."

Victor shook his head.

"When your nose is clean, you can wipe mine."

"No, thank you," answered Victor with more calm than was normal for him. Which was a good thing, because most of Keene's appreciation for his rediscovered friendship was evaporating in a black haze.

"She called marriage to me an exchange of prisons."

They walked in silence a few minutes before Victor spoke. "My aunt had a cat once. She kept it in a wicker cage. Had to have a new one nearly every week. The cat kept clawing his way out, you see. Then she went and had a cage made of metal. Damn cat nearly chewed its leg off trying to get out."

"What does that have to do with me?"

"Damned silly to keep a cat in a cage if you ask me."

"I'm not keeping her in prison," Keene shouted.

"I was just talking about my aunt's cat. Died, you know."

Keene couldn't help himself. "How?"

Sophie stared at the yellow pantaloons and green jacket draped over the back of the chair. She shrugged and dropped the dressing gown. She had been through the wardrobes and found nothing to wear except her husband's clothing. These might very well be his, too. Although why they would be in another bedchamber as if laid out for her use, Sophie hadn't a clue.

She'd looked long enough for female clothes; these would have to do. Fortunately there was a pair of tasseled boots on the floor beside the chair. Her feet would probably fit like twigs in the fire grate, but they would do to get her to the hotel. Good thing she had cut her hair. Otherwise, she would really garner stares as she walked through town in men's clothing. Now she could just hope people mistook her for a boy and none of the people who "counted" would see her.

It was one thing to have her clothes taken away, but to be told the master had them when she asked for them was really too much. She'd been sent to her room on bread and water many times, but never, ever, had her clothes been held hostage.

If she was honest with herself, that might have stopped her from sneaking out a time or two, but, really, to leave a female with nothing to wear besides her drawers was beyond the pale.

Later, as she made her way down the front stairs—no point in trying to sneak out a back entrance, she didn't know the lay of the house—the knocker sounded. She paused, gripping the rail to avoid pitching down with the overlong boots. The socks stuffed inside only kept the boots from sliding off if she held her toes up with each step. Her shins already burned from her practice steps in the hallway.

The butler opened the front door, and Sophie peered down, trying to see.

“Is Mr. Davies home?” The tense female voice drifted up to Sophie.

She bent down and caught a glimpse of dark hair.

The butler replied with a large dose of starch, “Mr. Davies is not at home.”

“Please, would you tell him I need to speak with him? It’s urgent.”

There was a pregnant pause. “Madam, he has not returned home this morning. Would you care to wait in the drawing room?”

“Oh.” There was another drawn out pause. “I’ll wait in my carriage.”

“Would you like me to see if Mrs. Davies is at home?”

The question seemed to surprise the visitor. “I . . . yes.”

Sophie could either hope they didn’t notice her and make a break for it when the butler led the caller to the drawing room, or she could just go forward and learn who sought out her husband at such an unfashionable hour.

“This way, Mrs. Keeting,” said the butler.

Mrs. Keeting? George’s wife? The woman Victor implied bore her husband’s child. Curiosity got the better of Sophie. Instead of retreating while she had a chance, she watched the woman step inside the entry hall.

Her sable hair was piled on top of her head in a sleek, smooth, loose swirl, the kind of soft demure style that Sophie’s hair would never tolerate. The visitor shed her green pelisse and gloves and gave them to the butler.

Her simple white morning gown adorned with a green ribbon covered a slim figure. Amelia glided across the floor and only paused as her blue eyes met Sophie’s. Her elegant hand rose to her throat. Her dark eyebrows lifted in a delicate arch of surprise while her cherry lips moved into a soft “O” of surprise. Even the expression of shock on her porcelain perfect features was elegantly understated.

This woman was everything Sophie was not: strikingly lovely, delicate, dainty and disgustingly demure.

A rush of pure hatred flowed through Sophie and shocked her with its intensity. She wanted to turn and climb the stairs, but with the boots felt like a clod. The moment stretched to an eon before they heard the scrape of a key in the lock.

Keene stumbled in, his evening clothes wrinkled, his cravat flat. His hair was mussed, his dark eyes glazed, and he was in dire need of his razor. A wide-eyed anticipation replaced his tired expression when he noticed the visitor in the hall. "Amelia."

"Oh, Keene, he . . ." She moved toward him, her hands outstretched. She bit her lip rather than continue the sentence she started.

Keene took Amelia's hands in his. "Blythe, would you have coffee brought to the drawing room."

The butler bowed and disappeared into the back of the house.

Keene didn't even close the front door before he stepped forward to take her hands in his. Was he so enamored of her that he forgot the gaping door and the cold air rushing inside?

"He has banished me. I'm sorry. I did not know where else to turn." Amelia's words caught on a sob. "He insisted I leave her with him. I don't know where to go or what to do."

"Come, we'll talk about it."

Victor entered, then shut the door.

A turbulent sea of impressions washed over Sophie.

Amelia's head turned in Victor's direction. After a glance at his friend, Keene tightened his grip on Amelia's hands as if to keep her to himself. Sophie saw a hint of yearning on Victor's face before his expression closed off.

"Go home, Victor." Keene tugged Amelia toward the library.

Victor stepped toward the stairs. "My clothes—"

"—will be here tomorrow," Keene said.

"My clothes!" Victor stared up at Sophie.

No hope for it now. Sophie stepped down, the boots clumping like leaden buckets on her feet.

Keene glanced up at her and then clenched his eyes shut as if removing her from his sight could banish her from his life.

Sophie turned to run back up the stairs, but the empty toe of the boot caught on a riser, and she pitched forward.

THIRTEEN

Victor, being closer to the staircase, reached Sophie first. Not that she had slid down more than a couple of steps, but Keene's heart jolted with each thump. He pushed Victor out of the way and reached for Sophie. He guided her shoulders as she moved to sit on the stairs.

She shrugged away from him. "I'm all right."

"This is your *wife?"* asked Amelia with not quite an air of condescension in her tone, but a mix of shock and disbelief.

"Hard to believe, is it not?" Keene rose to his feet.

Sophie sat on a stair by his knee. "Well, I shouldn't be wearing these clothes if Keene had left me anything to wear last night, but he took my dress off to heaven knows where, and none of my other clothes are here."

Keene winced.

Victor coughed politely and turned slightly.

Amelia looked at Keene, Sophie's clothes, and then at Victor. Two tiny lines formed between her flyaway eyebrows, while a flush crept up from her neck.

The last thing Keene wanted was to leave Victor and Amelia alone together, but a private moment with Sophie would require leaving the two former lovers together.

When he entered the house and saw Amelia standing in the entry hall he'd been tempted to shut and lock the door before Victor entered the house, or pull Amelia into the drawing room out of sight, but he hadn't had time to do either.

"Go upstairs, Sophie. I'll send your dress up to you," Keene whispered.

"It's an evening gown."

"She has you there. She is at least wearing morning clothes. Although I have to say we are getting shockingly loose with our apparel," said Victor. "Perhaps Amelia would care to contribute."

"You don't have any dresses to wear?" Amelia half turned toward the door, her hand raised in an uncertain gesture. "I do have my bags in my carriage."

"I'm leaving," said Sophie with a mulish cast to her expression.

Keene closed his eyes and wished them all to perdition. He reached under Sophie's arm and lifted her to her feet. "You're not leaving. Don't make me restrain you. Now go upstairs and get out of Victor's clothes."

"They're your clothes? I am sorry." She gave Victor a sheepish smile. "They were lying over the chair, and I didn't know."

Hounds of fury nipped at Keene's feet. His wife couldn't spare him more than a surly line, while Victor got a pretty apology and smile. Keene begrudged that smile more than anything.

Amelia was doing her best not to stare, and Victor had developed a fascination with Sophie's display of his breeches.

Keene jostled Victor's shoulder. "Do you mind, sir?"

Victor's gaze fastened on the pantaloons stretched across Sophie's flat belly, accommodating the soft flair of her hips. They fit her far differently than when he wore them. "Not at all. She doesn't look a bit—"

"Don't say it."

Victor looked him square in the eye and finished, "—like a chap."

"I don't? I thought with the short hair and everything I might pass for a youth." She tugged the bottle-green jacket down. She turned her head up toward Victor with a plea in her expression.

Keene felt a mixture of rage and relief . . . and frustration. There wasn't the slightest hint of a protruding belly. "No, she doesn't. I hate your hair short."

"Well, I shall be about my way, and you shan't have to see it."

"Upstairs, Sophie, or I shall carry you."

She flashed him a defiant look and started down the stairs.

"Damn it, Sophie." Keene caught her arm, looked directly at Victor and pointed toward the morning room, while nodding in Amelia's direction.

Victor placed his hand on the small of Amelia's back and led her into the front room. The heat of her skin reached him through her muslin gown. Victor wanted to both hold her and run away as fast as he could.

He glanced back in time to see Keene tip Sophie over his shoulder and carry her up the stairs.

Victor shut the door on Sophie's protest. He wanted to issue his own protest to have a care for Sophie's condition. Which reminded him of the shared child he had with Amelia. "How are you?"

She ducked her head and stepped away from his hand. "I am well."

"And the baby?"

She drew a swift breath, and looked away. Victor noticed the sheen of moisture in her eyes.

"She is healthy, isn't she?"

"Yes, she is fine."

There were a dozen questions that begged to be asked. *Does she look like me? Is she really mine? Why didn't you tell me?* Instead, Victor gestured toward a chair. "I'm sure Keene won't be long."

"Oh."

There was a wealth of confusion and speculation in Amelia's soft response. And the truth of the matter was, if

Keene had an ounce of sense in his head, he should stay abovestairs a long time and let the waters be as murky as possible.

In Victor's opinion, knowing Amelia's child was his made the situation more awkward. If he hadn't known, if George had been a candidate for fatherhood, there would have been only the occasional twinge of uncertainty.

"I should leave. I think Keene has enough on his hands." Amelia swiveled away from Victor.

Why had she turned to Keene instead of him? After all, it was his actions that got her into this brouhaha. "No, sit, Amelia. 'Tis well and good that Keene has a glimpse of the other side."

"What?"

"Never mind." Victor shifted restlessly from one foot to the other. "The child is well?"

"Yes." A hint of impatience colored Amelia's tone. She gingerly sat on the edge of a chair.

"What do you plan to do?"

Amelia's head tipped down. "I don't know. I suppose I might stay with my mother, but she is newly settled in the gatehouse as there wasn't a dower house on my father's property and the estate now belongs to my uncle." Amelia raised her head. "I shouldn't wish to be so far from my daughter, and I had hoped that my mother might stay at our house."

The only thing that occurred to Victor as Amelia spoke was that he didn't even know his daughter's name. "Things have reached a pretty pass, have they not?"

A single tear trickled down Amelia's alabaster cheek. Pain welled up under Victor's breastbone. He stepped toward Amelia's chair. He had held her once, comforted her once when she despaired of her situation—and brought her to this catastrophe.

She flew out of her chair, and in an uncharacteristically determined stride, avoided him. She steered toward the drawing room door. Her voice trembled, "I shouldn't have come here. I just thought Keene . . ."

"What did you think?" That Keene would protect her? Shelter her? House her as his mistress? Jealousy tore at Victor.

She shook her head as she reached for the knob. The door opened. Keene stood in the doorway, confronted by Amelia. Both of them froze. She drew a deep, shaky breath as if she meant to halt the tears freely running down her cheeks.

Keene stepped forward and placed his hands on Amelia's upper arms. "Everything will be all right," he soothed.

"Nothing will ever be right," sobbed Amelia, and she stepped straight into Keene's embrace.

A pit of black yawned before Victor. He folded his arms across his chest to keep himself from punching something. Irony laced through him. That night in the carriage, he had wondered if he was a substitute for Keene, a role he knew well. "Very touching."

Amelia backed out of Keene's arms, the graceful downward slope of her neck calling out her own swan song.

"I suppose you should just move in here." Victor heard the words leave his mouth without making a stop in his brain first. "You will stay close to your baby and won't be imposing on your mother. What do you say, Keene? Amelia could stay here, couldn't she?"

Keene looked startled by the notion. He frowned.

"I mean with your *wife* in residence, there is no impropriety, is there?"

Amelia cast her doe-like expression in Keene's direction. Hope glistened through her tears.

Keene looked back and forth between them, crossed his arms and leaned against the door. Victor couldn't fathom what was happening behind Keene's closed expression.

"I daresay it is a good answer for the time being. What do you say, Amelia? Should you prefer to stay in London with my wife and me?"

How she restrained herself from nodding in glee was beyond Victor. But she managed a mild response with that innate grace that was all her own. Her outstretched hand was the only sign of her nervous tension. "Would your wife be upset?"

Victor had learned a few things about Amelia that night in the carriage, more than he wanted to know. Unless he missed his guess, she was desperate to stay here. Why, though? Did she trust Keene to avoid taking advantage of her situation? Or did she hope he would?

Keene didn't bat an eye. "Sophie should be delighted to have a guest."

Victor wasn't so sure.

Keene turned to him with a look as sharp as shards of glass. "We shall have to fetch her trunk from the . . . post inn."

"You let your wife come in on the stage?"

"I don't think *let* had much to do with it," said Victor.

Amelia glanced back and forth between the two men and then ducked her head in the ultimate gesture of humbleness. And why not, thought Victor. She had achieved everything she wanted, hadn't she?

Sophie rubbed her stomach where it had rested across Keene's shoulder on the trip up the stairs. Not that it hurt, just tingled.

The silent maid held Keene's dressing gown. Sophie slid her arms into the sleeves.

The back of her legs where his hand had rested tingled, too. All of it was for naught. He'd left the room quickly, but not so quickly he hadn't managed to say he was sending her back to the country as soon as possible. He didn't want her here in his home.

That suited her just fine. She wanted nothing more than to leave behind her husband's smoldering looks that led to insubstantial ashes of nothing. She would go back to his father's house with all her fine new clothes and impress the cattle.

She'd done what she'd set out to do, see London. So, why did she feel so unhappy?

No time to stew, she thought. The play had been fun until Algany got out of hand. But she needed to leave. Now that she was married and capable of moving about with a little independence, she wouldn't stay where she wasn't welcome.

The first order of business was to find clothing to wear. She wouldn't be held back by Keene's refusal to return her dress. Her decision made, she was impatient to be on her way.

"I need a pair of scissors, a needle, and a spool of white thread, pins, lots of pins. And a ribbon, preferably red," she said to the maid. She dropped the dressing gown on the floor.

The girl bobbed a lopsided curtsy and nearly stumbled into the door.

Sophie ripped back the covers on the bed where she'd spent a long, lonely night, and wrestled the sheet from the mattress.

A short time later a knock on the door startled her. Was the maid back already? "Enter."

Keene stepped into the room, took one look at her and his step faltered. "What are you doing?"

"Amusing myself."

He took a look at the pile of brocade and silk on the floor and back at her. Leaning against the door his eyes traveled over her scantily clad form. "You object to my dressing gown?"

"Not if you're wearing it."

He picked it up and held it out to her. "Humor me."

She snorted and crossed the room to retrieve it from his grasp. His nostrils flared and his eyes glittered as she drew close, but she didn't miss his fully extended arm and the way he pressed back against the door as if she had some dreadfully contagious disease.

"Sit down, Sophie."

"Shouldn't you be downstairs with your guests?"

Keene rubbed a hand across his face. "Devil take it, yes. But we need to talk."

"I can't see that there is any need."

"Put the dressing gown on and sit down, Sophie."

"I'm not a leper, you know. I assure you I shan't infect you with my nature. It is not contagious."

The knave grinned. "I assure you, that is the least of my concerns. Now, sit, before I have to force you."

"You could at least ask." She flounced toward the bed and perched on the edge of it.

He winced as if she had not followed his directions as he liked. "Please, Sophie, drape my dressing gown around you."

He had at least tacked please onto this command, so she complied, leaning forward and stuffing her arms into the sleeves. Keene closed his eyes and set his jaw.

Sophie sighed. Talk must be Keene's word for a lecture. She supposed one's father's strictures were simply preparation for the rebukes of a husband. Impatient to be done, she turned to the window and stared out at the gray London sky.

"Why did you come to London?"

It was an odd way to start a lecture. She turned her attention back to her husband. In many ways he felt more like her cousin than a husband . . . except for the few kisses they'd shared. Heat crept up her chest. Her dreams of impressing him with stunning gowns and winning his heart were too raw to share.

He remained silent while her hopes for a loving marriage collided with his determination to send her back to the country.

"I needed new clothes," she finally answered.

"Whatever for?"

To make you notice me, want me, love me. She shifted her eyes away, all too aware of the heat in her face. "For my trousseau. Mama gave me money to buy what I needed in London. You are very fashionable, and I thought you would want me to be so, too."

Keene folded his arms across his chest, his dark gaze spearing her. "What did attending the theater have to do with furnishing your wardrobe?"

"I just thought it should be fun."

"Why would you choose to attend in the company of one of the most notorious rakehells in London? A man known to ruin women for the sheer joy of it."

Each word he added stabbed her. "I thought since Sir Gresham introduced me to him and would be there, it would be acceptable. I didn't ever plan to be alone with either of them."

"Not with Gresham, either?"

She shook her head.

"You're lying."

Had he thought she was seeking a lover? Was that why he was so angry with her?

She wouldn't even know the first thing about how to seek a lover. Besides, she wanted *him* to continue her education in that regard, not some stranger. She shivered. "I thought it was a respectable event. I thought that with two gentlemen in the party it was perfectly proper. I thought Victor wouldn't take me alone because that wasn't all right, but with two . . ."

"Never again."

"I am not allowed to attend the theater, or attend a ball or . . ."

"Not in Algany's company, not alone with any man, and especially not in Gresham's company."

"Would you have taken me if I asked?"

"You should not have gone."

It was an evasion of the first sort. But he caught her off guard with his next question.

"Do you want to stay in London?"

To allow him to see how very much she wanted to stay would be like handing him an executioner's ax. "You made it clear you were sending me back to the country."

"Yes, well, I was angry. Now, do you want to stay here with me? For I would like you to."

She stepped toward him, her heart singing with hope. "You would?"

He reached for the edges of the dressing gown and pulled

them closed, at the same time pulling her closer. His eyes drifted to the bed and back down to her face. "Our guests are waiting for me. Now, are you willing to stay?"

Her heart pounded and the heat of his hands seared her skin through his dressing gown. "I thought I embarrassed you."

His eyes crinkled. "You do. When you are at a theater in bad company, or wearing Victor's clothes." He drew her closer with every complaint. His voice dropped lower. "Or staying at a hotel."

"Cutting my hair." Her voice was breathless.

"What were you thinking?" His eyes searched her face.

"I was told it was fashionable."

He twirled a strand around his finger. His warm breath brushed across her face. "I suppose it suits you."

"But you don't like it?"

"No." The light in his eyes softened the word.

Her heart pounded in her breast.

He stroked a finger down her temple. "Sophie, I have to go back downstairs. If you stay, have Amelia guide your choices on what entertainments are appropriate for you to attend."

"Amelia?" Her insides dropped like a stone.

"She'll be staying with us. I believe you said you were looking forward to the diversions of London. I have no desire to keep you imprisoned. You may attend as many balls and amusements as you wish. I only beg you to allow yourself to be guided in your choices."

Sophie wavered. Temptation warred with dismay. "By Amelia?"

"If I pick and choose your entertainments, how shall I ever escape the moniker of jailer? No, I want you to be free to make your own choices."

He didn't look like he wanted her to be free. He looked like he'd eaten rotten meat.

"I would, anyway."

He leaned closer. His grip tightened on the dressing gown. "I know."

She searched his face. She didn't doubt that he wanted her to stay. His earnest offer to give her complete freedom spoke volumes. But why? How much of his change in heart correlated with Amelia's arrival on his doorstep?

She drew a deep breath. She didn't want complete autonomy from Keene, but she did want to stay in London.

"It is the normal way of things, to have a more experienced woman show you around during your first season. And Amelia is available to help."

His gaze intensified, and he leaned fractionally closer.

Sophie melted into his dark gaze. How could she refuse him anything when he looked at her like that? "I'll stay."

His grip loosened. He looked over her head. "I'll have the servants prepare you a room."

Dread filtered down her spine in an icy wave. If she had delayed answering any longer would he have swayed her with kisses? She flushed. It would have been ample persuasion.

He stepped to the side, crossed the room and opened a door. "This used to be my mother's room. It will be yours now."

Holland covers shrouded the furniture. Did Keene really want her here, or was she just to cloak Amelia's presence? And why was the mother of his child staying with them?

Keene stood alone in George's library. Tension tightened the cords of his neck into knots. He picked up an empty crystal decanter from the sideboard and lifted it to the light. A few drops of brown liquid dribbled across the bottom of the glass, while the sunlight shone through, refracting blue on the wall across the room.

Keene knew beyond a shadow of a doubt his handling of Sophie stank. He'd found it hard to resist the lure of an already mussed bed and his wife wearing only a shift under his dressing gown. The iron grip he held on his desire threatened to disintegrate to rusty dust.

He hadn't thought he could kiss her and walk away, and he had wanted to kiss her so badly it hurt. He didn't trust himself to stay in the house, knowing that in his room Sophie waited for her clothes to arrive.

So he'd headed for the one place sure to remind him of the necessity of avoiding Sophie's bed until her deception became impossible to carry.

George's butler entered the room. Concern knitted the old man's brow. "I'm sorry, sir. We can't seem to locate him. I don't believe he stepped out. Would you care to wait?"

"I might look in on the baby."

"Very good, sir."

Keene climbed the stairs to the third floor with wary trepidation. On one hand he greeted the news that George couldn't be found as a temporary reprieve. On the other hand, George's disappearance worried him. Given that the man was suicidal not so very long ago and that his servants had lost him in his own house, could despair have overruled his will to live?

Keene doubted he would be of any help in alleviating George's mind. Although he intended to leave out Victor's part in the impromptu plan, Keene would have to say that he had invited Amelia to stay with him. But George's refusal to let Amelia take her daughter didn't make sense to Keene. Why keep a child fathered by another man?

What purpose could be had by holding the baby here?

How would a man ready to off himself care for a helpless infant?

The only comforting piece of information was that Amelia claimed her husband never looked in on the child, had rarely been within a stone's throw of the nursery. Nor had he so much as glanced at Regina the few times Keene had brought the baby down and urged George to hold her.

An unnatural quiet pervaded the house. Of course, with

Amelia gone, George couldn't yell at her. Even the baby was silent.

Keene walked down the stark hallway of the third floor, his boots clicking against the polished wood floor. The nursery door stood ajar.

He understood George's resentment of the child, understood his own father's favoritism of his flesh and blood son. But more than that, his heart ached for the misery of a child without a choice in fathers.

He pushed the door all the way open and drew to an abrupt halt.

George leaned over the crib, both his hands over the rail.

Good Lord, what was he doing? Surely he hadn't banished Amelia so he could . . . Keene could barely finish the thought. His legs threatened to buckle beneath him. George wouldn't, would he?

"What do you mean to do, Amelia?" Victor asked.

"Whatever are you talking about?" She glided across Keene's drawing room, skirting around furniture.

Victor gave her a hard look. She had absolutely no reason to treat him like a pariah. "I mean, what are you about, coming here? To Keene's house?"

"I only thought that he should have a care of George. He has stood by him through this."

"I doubt your husband would have welcomed my presence in his home." Guilt covered Victor like a mantle. "By the hounds, I did not know you would marry him. I did not know you carried a child. I took a bullet for this. . . . What do you want of me?"

She paled and turned away. "I want nothing of you."

He knew that. She made that obvious by giving him a wide berth, dipping her eyes, avoiding him in polite company. She had turned to Keene in her most desperate moment, this time. Had Victor failed her when she had turned to him before?

"Bloody hell, Amelia, I have enough affection for you that I should not misuse you."

"Not set me up in a cottage?" The words came out as if each one choked her.

Victor's anger ebbed like a low tide leaving behind the refuse of his life. He sank down on a sofa, his face in his hands. "I was mad at Keene. I meant it for him."

"Why?" whispered Amelia. "Why slander me? Have you not done enough?"

"You wouldn't understand." Victor wasn't sure he understood it himself. Standing across from Keene that dawn, the weight of the Spanish tooled pistol in his hand, watching him wrestle with his conscience, anger and envy spurted through Victor like a malicious poison. He'd egged on Keene enough to shoot.

Amelia's skirts rustled. When the white muslin of her gown entered his sight, he tilted his head back to look up at her.

Frown lines marred the smooth skin of her brow. "I am sorry. You did nothing wrong. It was my fault. I was weak and foolish." She turned and sank down beside him.

Her apology sat like a sour lump in his stomach. He had seduced her, or she had seduced him. It didn't matter. As a gentleman he was responsible for protecting a lady, sheltering her from himself if need be and taking care of her if he failed in the first two.

"You are right. I have turned to Keene for my own selfish reasons. I think he above all others has the best chance of convincing George to allow me to have my child."

Our child. But she wasn't really his and never would be.

"I will do whatever it takes to get my daughter."

"That's the part that scares me, love."

Amelia rose to her feet and sidestepped away from him. "If George could get past the circumstances of her birth, I think she would be better left with him."

Victor jerked.

Amelia hovered near an armchair, her expression once again smooth, faraway, as untouchable as marble.

Victor studied her for the longest time. Heat and fire hid under that cool mask, and Amelia didn't trust him with it. Did she trust Keene? Or George? Herself?

As if aware of his studied interest she turned toward him, a winged eyebrow lifted ever so slightly in inquiry.

"You realize that if the baby shows any sign of his paternal lineage"—Victor heard the opening door, but didn't turn his gaze away from Amelia—"everyone shall suspect it is Keene's."

Amelia blinked at him as if the idea had never occurred to her. Perhaps it hadn't.

Victor turned his head slowly, knowing he had said too much.

Sophie stared at him from the doorway, her blue eyes large in her pale face.

FOURTEEN

Each beat of Keene's heart pounded like a stone against his ribs. His gaze was riveted on George leaning over the crib. Bursting rockets couldn't have turned his attention. Dread oozed from his every pore in a feverish sweat. He hesitated to step forward, yet fear spurred him on. He dashed into the room, his footsteps loud against the polished wood floor.

"Quiet, man, I just got her to sleep," said George.

Keene stopped, one foot held in the air. "What?"

"I am following your advice. The least you can do is not make me regret it." George turned around. He slowly assessed Keene. "Surely it is a little beforehand for evening clothes?"

Keene set his foot down gingerly. "What advice?"

George returned his attention to the crib. "To make my peace with the child. To hold her. She seems a spirited little imp. She must get it from Victor. She certainly doesn't get it from her mother."

Anxious energy rocketed around inside Keene until he didn't know what to do with himself. He tiptoed over to the crib, feeling awkward and slovenly.

The baby lay on her stomach. The rise and fall of her back marked her steady breathing. Her little rosebud lips were pursed as if she suckled even in sleep. Downy wisps of dark hair poked out of her cap. She looked perfectly healthy and unharmed.

"You look done in," said George.

As if his words had inspired it, exhaustion descended over Keene like a cloud. He knew the comment could be attributed to his wearing last night's clothes. He couldn't have changed from his evening clothes with Sophie in his room and escaped unscathed. Keene straightened. He had not come to consider his own problems.

Keene looked at his friend, taking in George's clear eyes, the lucid expression. "You kicked Amelia out."

"I suggested she leave for a while."

"Do you still mean to divorce her?"

"I don't know. I thought I needed some time to think this through."

"I daresay."

"Clearly."

"You have stopped drinking, then?"

"I think the servants have contrived to hide all the spirits, if there are any left." George stroked the baby's back. "I gather I am a mean drunk."

"I don't recall that."

"Perhaps I am just mean to Amelia. It would help if she would say something in her own defense, but she just sits there and takes my abuse. I feel worse and worse and yell all the more."

"Some would think a submissive wife a godsend."

George flashed him a look. "I trust I should not wish for a wife as troublesome as yours, but I should wish she would not look upon me as if she were a slaughtered doe that I just brought down."

"Bloody hell, George. You've exiled her from her home, withheld her child."

"Why doesn't she fight for anything?"

"Why must you punish her so?"

"I don't know. I can hardly stand the sight of her. I can barely stand that she married me as a last resort."

"That's not what she said to me."

George moved to a straight chair beside the crib. "You know

it's true. She should have married you first, but then both Victor and I told her you would not marry as long as Richard held his spot as your heir. Then she cast out her lures for Victor, but he could not marry her for his pockets are to let. Amelia only has her breeding to recommend her, as much good as that has done."

"If you married your first choice, you would be with that toothless orange seller in Windsor." A thirteen-year-old George had been crushed when he finally worked up enough courage to purchase an orange from the pretty little peddler and her smile revealed unsavory gaps. "Besides, I think Amelia respects you more than she respects either of us."

George rubbed his face. "I'm sure she does not now."

Keene put his arm around George's shoulders.

"I keep thinking, if the baby was Victor's—I mean through a wife of his—I should be very fond of the child, perhaps even a godfather."

"It happened before you asked Amelia to marry you, and I gather only the once."

"I know, but I cannot accept her as my child. I can't."

A crushing weight settled on Keene's heart. He shook his head and pulled his arm away from George's shoulders. "Amelia is staying with me. Let her have her child."

George studied him. "You just don't understand."

"I understand better than you know." But doubts bubbled in his mind. How would he fare with Sophie's child? Would he feel as strongly about the firstborn as he would feel about his own children?

"I'll do the right thing. I'll raise her as my daughter. She'll never know the difference."

"Yes, she will."

Was he was wrong to think foreknowledge was better? Perhaps Victor was right in thinking a suspicion was easier to ignore, that a doubt was better than a surety. But it was too late for that. Keene already knew his wife bore another man's child.

* * *

Sophie sat in her hastily stitched sheet, a draft creeping through the opening in the back. Victor had long since departed. Amelia sat in a corner of the drawing room, looking demure and sophisticated, everything that Sophie was not. And yet, Amelia was a woman who had appealed to her husband at one time, perhaps still did.

Keene looked done in, but he flashed Amelia a compassionate smile as he crossed the room. His glance at Sophie had been more along the lines of a shaken head.

"We shall put it about that you are staying with us to guide Sophie through the labyrinth of society." Keene watched Sophie as he spoke.

Amelia nodded. "I understand."

Sophie was glad someone did. "Why?"

Amelia blushed and looked down.

"Amelia and George's estrangement isn't anyone's concern."

"Lud! Is it anything like our estrangement?"

Keene scowled at her. "Sophie, we haven't been estranged."

"Separated then?"

"No, it isn't at all similar." Amelia's quiet statement broke through the illusion of being alone with Keene. She turned toward him. "Perhaps it is not the best of ideas. If George means to divorce me"—her breath caught, as if speaking the word out loud was painful—"then I shall not do your wife's reputation well."

"You couldn't damage it more than she is bent on doing. I found her in Algany's company last night. I trust it is her ignorance that led her there. She was very sheltered in the country." Keene winced. "She needs a wiser woman to guide her past the pitfalls of London."

Sophie hated the way Amelia's eyes widened and then she lowered her gaze as if that tiny break in her composure was unacceptable. How could Sophie ever emulate the poise that Keene so admired?

He knelt down in front of her chair. "Sophie, Amelia will guide you. She will help you pick and choose what invitations to accept and escort you about."

Sophie didn't want to look at Keene's earnest expression. She glanced at the other woman. Amelia bit the corner of her lip. She stopped almost immediately, straightened her spine and erased the hint of apprehension from her porcelain features. She crossed her hands in her lap and glanced down at them.

Sophie suspected the woman rarely lost control. The unexpected cracks in her demeanor led Sophie to the conclusion that she no more wanted to act as a guide than Sophie wanted to be led by her.

Sophie narrowed her eyes, her focus on Keene. "May I speak with you privately?"

Amelia rose from her chair. "I'll just have the servants show me my room, if that is all right."

Keene stood and led her to the door. After the door clicked shut, he turned around.

Nervous energy spilled over, and Sophie stood and crossed to the window. "You are very fond of her, are you not?"

"Yes, I'm fond of her. I'm fond of George. I want them to work out their problems. They won't, if she is too far away."

"She doesn't want to lead me around London." Sophie crossed her arms and turned to look out the window. Did Keene really want to help salvage his friends' marriage or did he just want to keep Amelia accessible?

"Whatever are you wearing? Bloody hell, you need her guidance if you are buying clothes like that. Or am I buying it? Where have you instructed the dressmakers to send the bills?"

Sophie squeezed her eyes shut. She had forgotten the irregular closure of the sheet gown. "You will be relieved to know that you shan't have to pay my mantua maker bills. Remember, Mama gave me money for my trousseau."

"I daresay I'd be relieved if no one paid for that dress."

"Perhaps you had better tell me why she is staying with us."

"Because Victor suggested it, and what could I do but extend an invitation."

Sophie clenched the drapery in her hand. "Do you wish me to be like her?"

"No one could fault Amelia's behavior in polite company. If you could be more like her . . ." His voice fell off.

What? Would Keene love her if she was more like Amelia? Did she want him to?

Keene moved to stand behind her. He settled his hand at her waist. "She is always perfectly behaved in public."

His touch warmed her skin, but she was still sorting through her disappointment at learning another woman would be staying with them, that he had seen the opportunity to pass off his wife's introduction to London to another person and stolen it. That the mother of his child would be living with them. "But not so in private? I understand she had a baby that is not her husband's."

Sophie held her breath waiting for Keene's response. Would he tell her he'd fathered the child?

His response was slow. The "Yes," drawn out. His expression grew enigmatic. "So you know about it?"

Her heart pounded. "Not everything."

Keene moved away from her. His distance pulled warmth from her. "The crux of the problem is that she lied to George. She let him believe he was the father."

Sophie wasn't convinced. Keene paced the room. She turned to watch him. "Is that what George says?"

"No, but I think if she had been honest—"

Sophie snorted.

Keene rolled his eyes.

She supposed snorting was one behavioral faux pas of

which he wished to break her. If he thought her so unmannerly, why had he married her? Why, indeed, other than a mixture of misplaced family honor and obligation? Certainly not to get an heir through her.

He folded his arms across his chest as if he would launch into a homily. Perhaps all men expected a woman to be modest, meek and mindless. Did he think she was too featherheaded to understand the connection between him and Amelia?

She started to suggest he just tell her the whole story, but her throat felt raw. She'd never believed that Keene held her in any great affection before his proposal, certainly he didn't now. Her hope that he might come to love her needed to be thrown to the wolves. She should be content that he allowed her the lifestyle she'd always wanted, the freedom, the gaiety, the clothes. His former mistress living with them shouldn't be so bad.

Questions and half-baked inferences swirled into a muddy mix in Sophie's brain. She turned to stare out the window.

She put a stop to her runaway thoughts. All of the mysteries surrounding Amelia and her ill-conceived child really had nothing to do with anything Sophie wanted. She supposed if she didn't go chasing after things that were not likely to be, she could be content with her marriage. She presumed she and Keene would rub along tolerably well. Her behavior was more likely to upset him. And her mother had warned her that Keene would not be content with one woman's company. Her hand closed around the curtain, and she gripped it as if it were a lifeline.

Keene's voice startled her out of her thoughts. "You may tell me anything."

She pivoted to return his words. "Odd, I was about to say the same thing to you."

Two lines furrowed between Keene's eyebrows, and he tilted his head sideways. "But you do understand, you should not speak of Amelia's situation to anyone."

How simpleminded did he think she was? "Of course, I

understand that. But I still do not think she wishes to be my teacher."

"She will, though. Sophie, you must let her lead you. She knows everyone who is anyone. She'll steer you around trouble. You don't know what you're about. The gossips here can destroy you."

"I have never been afraid of what people think of me."

"You need to have a care what people think and how your actions would reflect on me. You could destroy me politically."

He had political aspirations? "You aren't a member of Parliament . . . are you?"

"I can't be. I don't own property. I can't run for a seat in the House of Commons without an estate, but I do plan to take my seat in the House of Lords when I inherit the title from my father. For now, I do what I can to influence the lawmakers."

Why hadn't she known? For an awful moment she felt dim-witted and all at sea. But then, how could she have known? She hadn't been around him enough to form any opinion of what he did in London beyond staying out all night. Anger spurted through her. "Were you perhaps campaigning for something special last night?"

"Of course not."

"Shooting one's friend in a duel doesn't adversely affect one's influence?"

"Sophie, we are not discussing my behavior. Fighting a duel may be a regrettable lapse on my part, but being seen unescorted in Algany's company is a much less forgivable offense."

"For a woman."

"For you."

How did housing his former mistress sit with the ton? Or was their former liaison a well-guarded secret? It must be, if George accepted Keene's company. How could Keene have been any more honest about the situation than Amelia was?

"I still don't think you have consulted Amelia about this. She doesn't seem the least bit enthused by your proposition."

"She'll do it, though. And if you aren't willing to let her help you, I'll send you back to my father's house."

"I have no choice, then?"

"You have a choice. You may return to the countryside for the time being."

What kind of a marriage was that? What had she gained by marrying him?

Keene crossed to her side. His voice dropped to a soft murmur. "Sophie, this is not just about me. I am concerned about your welfare. Last night you could have been badly abused. I don't want you in situations where you could come to harm. You are reckless beyond consideration."

A protest rose to her lips. His fingers stopped it with a gentle touch that shot sparks rocketing through her.

"Any misstep you make now could have long-lasting repercussions. Not only for me, but for you and for our . . . uh . . . for any children."

Her breath did a stutter step. The corner of his mouth curled as his fingers slid across her cheek. He gave a small shake of his head.

"What?" she whispered.

He didn't answer. Instead, he leaned down and brushed his lips across hers. Her heart began a footrace. He pulled back. "No more hotels, Sophie."

She nodded like a deaf-mute.

"No more travel without my escort."

Her head continued to bob up and down as if independent of her control. Why didn't he just kiss her again?

He wound a strand of her hair around his finger. "I can't protect you if I don't know where you are."

Did he want to protect her? She wanted to melt at his feet. Not that she needed his protection.

"Have Amelia guide you in fashion, too."

Sophie stopped the snort before it escaped her. Keene grinned. She wasn't sure if she wanted to smack him or beg him to kiss her again. The only thing she knew was he muddled her thoughts, jumbled her senses and made her blood dance.

A knock on the door prompted Keene to turn. "Yes?"

The butler entered and stood uneasily in front of the doorway.

"What is it, Blythe?"

"Begging your pardon, sir. But it seems the upstairs maid reports that your bed linens have gone missing. The housekeeper is concerned we may have a thief among the servants."

Keene looked at Sophie, then shook his head. "Not among the servants. I believe my wife is the culprit. No need to concern yourself with their removal."

"Very good, sir. I'll have the maid put on fresh sheets." Blythe bowed and left, discreetly closing the drawing room doors as he exited.

Keene cocked an eyebrow at her. "First, Victor's clothing, now, a sheet, Sophie?"

She shrugged. "My clothes aren't here, and you stole my evening gown. I suppose I should wear nothing."

"As enchanting as that sounds, love, I should not think it quite the thing." His dark eyes held hers. "At least not in anyone's company but my own."

He had to be kidding if he thought she would share his favors with Amelia.

Later, as the three of them rode to an "at home," Sophie plied them with questions. "Will there be dancing?"

"No dancing. We shall just make our way through the room and introduce you to as many people as possible," Amelia answered.

No dancing, no refreshments, a lot of names she would never remember, still, her eyes glittered with excitement. Keene almost regretted picking the bland soiree for Sophie's first exposure to the ton.

Their carriage inched forward, caught in the crush of people to arrive. "Is it always like this?"

"Usually." Amelia cast an inquiring look in Keene's direction.

He leaned back against the squabs, holding his silence. His voice might reflect the feeble grip on his control. He wanted nothing more than to stare into his wife's luminous eyes and make her his. Her enthusiasm infected him with desire.

Sophie leaned forward and looked out the window. Her décolletage dipped dangerously low. He wanted to feast on the sight. He shut his eyes. How was he to make it through the next few months with her so near?

He should have sent her back to his father's house, out of temptation's reach.

Finally, they stopped in front of the house's steps. Keene slid out and reached back to hand out the women. Sophie didn't wait. With her skirts gathered around her knees, she leaped off the stair. The sight of her sheer pink stockings and the glimpse of bare skin above her garters made his blood fire.

He swallowed hard. "Lower your skirts."

She raised her startled face. "I didn't want to rip them."

He could drown in the blue pools of her eyes.

Keene appealed to Amelia. How could he explain what the sight of Sophie's legs did to him? He folded his arms across his chest to prevent himself from reaching out and lifting her back into the carriage to spirit away home to bed.

Amelia looked between them. "Keene would have assisted you. Any gentleman would."

Keene leaped forward, realizing he'd been remiss in assisting Amelia. He held out a hand. She placed her fingers in his and gracefully descended the carriage stairs.

Sophie chewed her lip.

Keene wanted to give her mouth a very different sort of attention. What was wrong with him that he was acting like a green boy on the verge of losing his virginity?

He held out his elbows to both women. Underneath his

superfine jacket perspiration dampened his shirt. He couldn't spend the evening circulating in such an aroused state.

Once they had made it up the stairs and into the congested salon, Keene bowed and said, "I'll leave you ladies to your own devices. I shall return in an hour."

"He's leaving?" His withdrawal made Sophie's question moot.

Amelia leaned close. "Don't worry about it. This crush isn't Keene's favorite pastime, but it is a good place for you to get your bearings." She turned to greet a gentleman in clocked socks.

Amelia gently steered Sophie to meet person after person. Many were curious, and she managed to lightheartedly say she had no idea what Keene was about. Amelia nodded encouragingly until Sophie could paste a smile on her face and convince others that husbands were mysterious, contrary beasts, and that his absence meant nothing.

Inside, as she absorbed the animated style of talk, she wished he were here. But then, when had Keene ever done anything other than ignore her and leave her to her own devices?

She grew cross that her thoughts revolved around her absent husband when she should be enjoying the high life she had so yearned to experience. His disapproval was far too overblown and hurt much worse than any reproach her father had ever laid at her door. And considering the source, it made her angry.

She laughed harder and spoke faster. Amelia gave her a gentle smile and hung back, only stepping into the conversations when Sophie grew too animated.

Sophie vowed she would enjoy this evening, if it killed her. To perdition and back with Keene.

Amelia led her across the room to a woman surrounded by a crowd. "This is Lady Jersey, one of the patronesses of Almack's. She's very important," Amelia whispered.

The crowd parted at Amelia's light gesture. "Lady Jersey, allow me to introduce you to the new Mrs. Davies."

Sophie doubted if she could ever emulate the easy grace Amelia used. She would have tugged on a man's jacket or shoved through the throngs of people. Sophie felt like a gauche country bumpkin compared to Amelia.

Lady Jersey nodded, unmasked curiosity lighting her countenance. "So you are the young lady who absconded with one of our most eligible bachelors."

Amelia watched her out of the corner of her eye. Sophie wondered if she should act like a cat who swallowed a canary or one that lapped up sour milk.

"I'm not so sure that Davies didn't steal her from all the hopeful gentlemen." Amelia gave a soft smile.

Sophie finally found her voice. "I'm quite sure I've done a service to all the other young ladies who might have considered him a prize."

"You do not?" Lady Jersey's voice had an edge, and Amelia sucked in a startled breath.

Like a cat dropped upside down, Sophie needed to scramble fast to get her feet underneath her. She thought of her wedding day when they had embraced in the snow and of the interrupted kiss yesterday. "When he is not cross with me, I am quite fond of him."

"Our Keene is cross? I can't imagine."

"Quite. I daresay we know each other too well."

Lady Jersey smiled. "How long have you known him?"

"Since I was born. We are distant cousins. He stayed with us every summer. I remember when he used to hitch horses to the dogcart and take the corner of our drive at full gallop until he could do it without landing in the ditch or scraping the pillars." She was rattling like a spook with a chain.

"I can't imagine Keene in a ditch."

"I don't think he liked it much. He liked that I saw it even less." He'd probably be totally disgusted that she had compounded her transgression on his privacy by blabbing it to the world.

"You must be the cousin he nearly drowned," said Lady Jersey.

"No, he saved me once when I fell into the river."

Lady Jersey shook her head. "I am quite sure he claimed to have pushed you in. I imagine you both have amusing anecdotes to share about each other. Funny, he is such a dark horse that none of us thought he should ever marry. I shall be at home tomorrow afternoon, do stop by, ladies."

"We should love to," answered Amelia.

"I do so hope I will see you at the Wednesday assemblies. I am sure you will want to speak with Countess Lieven. She is just over there. Good evening, Mrs. Davies, Mrs. Keeting." Lady Jersey turned to greet another eager aspirant.

Amelia turned to Sophie, a rare, full-blown smile on her face. "You did it!"

"I did what?"

"Secured vouchers for Almack's. By the stars, it took me weeks. I was so afraid to speak to the patronesses that I could hardly do more than mumble when they were around."

"I was speaking off the top of my head."

Amelia patted her hand. "You did a grand job. Keene will be thrilled."

"Not if he learns I have been telling tales about him." He'd probably strangle her. It was a good thing she hadn't told about the time she convinced him to jump his horse over the paddock gate and he'd parted ways with his mount and landed in a pile of offal.

"We shall have to call on her, of course, but it is truly wonderful. Let us go talk to the countess before she leaves."

"Of course." Sophie stared across the crowded room, her mind wandering back to the day many years ago when Keene had pulled her from the water. He claimed to have pushed her? Better yet, had he actually remembered her existence when he wasn't rescuing her?

A young woman caught her eye. Sophie eagerly waved,

before she remembered she should have consulted with Amelia about the acceptability of doing so.

Amelia frowned ever so slightly, but by the time the dark-haired woman shouldered her way across the room, Amelia's face was a pleasant mask of serenity.

"We meet again," said Sophie's acquaintance from the dressmaker's.

"I would like to introduce you to my friend"—Sophie copied Amelia's style of introduction—"Mrs. Keeting, this is Miss Chandler."

Mary Frances extended her hand. Amelia slowly leaned forward to return the gesture. Her words dripped with reserve although Sophie couldn't find fault with her manner. "Charmed, I'm sure."

Mary Frances beamed. "I am so delighted to see you again. We must get together. Are you perchance attending the coming-out ball of Miss Cecilia Covens, Friday next? We were at school together."

"I believe I might know her older sister," said Amelia.

Sophie could almost feel her escort relax. After they had spoken a few minutes and Mary moved away to speak with someone else, Sophie turned to Amelia and said, "I should have asked before I hailed her, but I was so eager to see someone I met on my own. Did I make a mistake introducing you to Miss Chandler?"

"No, Miss Chandler is apparently accepted in polite company, but I shouldn't make fast friends with her. She comes from trade." Amelia's eyes widened, "Oh, no!"

"What?" asked Sophie.

"How are you, my angel?" asked a familiar voice just behind her left ear.

Sophie swiveled around and encountered the urbane good looks of Lord Algany.

"I'm well enough, and you?" Sophie answered politely.

Algany smiled in a way that might be considered charming; Amelia squeezed her elbow.

"Where is your keeper?"

"Keene? He's not a keeper, he's my husband." And not much good at either.

Amelia's hand tightened, and she tried to pull Sophie back. Only, in the crush, there was nowhere to go.

Algany flicked his gaze over Amelia. "And where is your husband, my dear Mrs. Keeting?"

Sophie stepped forward. "They'll be along soon enough. One does need to part company now and then."

Algany's gaze transferred back to Sophie. "I quite agree. A diet should always be full of variety. As the same food time after time grows boring."

Sophie blinked and wondered if she should just disagree on principle. "I would imagine you have enough experience to know . . ."

Algany smiled a wolfish smile.

". . . what is pleasing to you, of course. But I fear there are those of us who would dine on the same fare night after night and never grow tired of it."

"Oh, you shall grow tired of the same meal. And I shall be happy to be your guide in exploring new tastes when you do." He leaned his head sideways and his heavy-lidded gaze assessed Amelia again. "Whenever you should like a supper companion, I'm ready to aid." He bowed slightly and moved away.

"Oh, Lord," whispered Amelia. Her hand against her chest, her eyes followed Algany's movements across the room.

"What?" asked Sophie.

"You shouldn't encourage him." Amelia's attention remained riveted on him.

"I was trying to discourage him." Sophie rather thought that her dissuasion was compelling Algany to look for greener pastures in Amelia.

"He's ruined more than one young lady. How could you have allowed him to take you to the theater?"

"I didn't know."

Amelia's rapt fascination with Lord Algany's retreating figure ended. Her soft gaze landed on Sophie's face, and after a second of studying her, she said, "How could you? Even those who are warned off, fall prey to his magnetism. They say he will resort to foul means if he can't get what he wants by fair."

"I really don't find him all that charming."

"You don't? He's very good-looking."

Sophie shrugged. She thought he was rather full of himself and pushy. Although, truth to tell, on this evening in the polite company, he hadn't pushed particularly hard.

"Yes, really, why would you want the attentions of Lord Algany when you are married to Keene?"

Yes, why indeed? Except her marriage to Keene left her feeling unfulfilled. She didn't think Algany would make her feel any better, not when, like Keene, he seemed equally interested in Amelia.

FIFTEEN

Later that week, Sophie skipped down the stairs, her rose-pink ball gown layered with silver netting caught in her hand. Keene stood near the door, dressed in black evening clothes. His gaze raked over her and stopped on her legs. Her heart tripped harder in her chest. Would that he didn't affect her so.

After a second, he closed his eyes. "Lower your skirt, madam."

Sophie let the material fall and continued down the stairs in a sedate walk.

Keene looked past her to the stairs. "Shall we go?"

Amelia's gloved hand trailed lightly down the railing as she descended.

Sophie bit back a wave of consternation. How would Keene ever forget her boisterousness when confronted by Amelia's complete decorum at every turn?

"Do you know who else might be attending?" Amelia asked.

"Victor might. You don't know?"

"I haven't been out much since the baby."

Keene led them out to the waiting carriage and handed them up. As before, he sat across from Sophie. She watched the quiet exchange between Amelia and Keene.

Amelia turned to Sophie. "Is there anything you wish to know?"

Sophie shrugged and shook her head.

"Have Amelia instruct you in manners."

"I wasn't raised in a barn, Keene. I have a fair idea of how to address people. I should imagine it is the same in the country as at a ball."

"I mean that you can't run around a ballroom with your skirts hitched to your knees."

"I rarely run in ballrooms."

Amelia followed the exchange without speaking.

Sophie's excitement over attending a ball was being sucked out of her. When they finally reached the house and exited the carriage, Amelia drew her aside.

Sophie wanted to brush off the hand around her arm.

"Don't let him perturb you. I think Keene is quite nervous for you."

"He is quite nervous I shall embarrass him."

Amelia shook her head. "Your exuberance will be regarded as refreshing; don't feel you must follow my manner."

"But you are held out as my example."

"I . . ." Amelia stared into Sophie's eyes and then dipped her head. "I am always quite certain I shall be a social outcast if I slip."

"What are you two whispering?" Keene interrupted.

"Last-minute advice," answered Amelia smoothly.

Once they had passed the reception line where they were introduced to the debutante whose sparkling eyes restored Sophie's excitement, they stepped into a room filled with ladies dressed in all colors of the rainbow. Musicians played at the far end of the room on a raised dais. Dancing hadn't begun yet. Sophie glanced around, eager to test her memory of names and faces of people with the complete confidence of knowing Amelia would supply her with the information if she failed.

A young man dressed in blue superfine approached and greeted Amelia. He turned expectantly toward Sophie.

Amelia made the introduction.

"May I beg a dance of you later?"

Keene surged forward, then hovered over her shoulder. Was he afraid she couldn't correctly accept an invitation to dance?

"I should enjoy that." Sophie hoped that her response had enough graciousness to please her husband.

"I shall return later to claim it," said the man with a bow.

Keene scowled at her. Had she done something wrong?

"You do want her to fit in, don't you?" Amelia asked.

He stalked away.

"Where is he going, now?" asked Sophie.

"I should imagine he's seeking the refreshments. He looked in need of something cooling." A soft smile danced across Amelia's lips as she watched Keene walk away.

Sophie shut her eyes and forced her concerns about her husband and Amelia out of her head. She was here to have a good time, and *she would enjoy* the dancing.

She opened her eyes and spotted her friend Mary Frances across the room. She smiled and waved eagerly.

Mary Frances looked up from where she assisted an elderly man into a chair. She gave a discreet wave and took the chair beside the man, leaning close to speak into his ear.

Sophie asked, "Do you know, is that gentleman Miss Chandler's father?"

Amelia shook her head. "That is the recently widowed earl of Brumley. I suppose he is on the lookout for a new wife."

Victor joined them. "Brumley? Out of the card rooms is he?"

Amelia nodded.

"Is that his latest prey?" He nodded toward Mary Frances.

"Possibly. Perhaps we should warn her."

If Mary Frances was in any danger, of course they should warn her. Only Sophie hadn't the slightest idea what hazard the two of them were discussing.

"Rather too pretty to be his victim," Amelia said.

Victor shook his head. "Far too young."

Sophie frowned. She imagined that Mary Frances would be able to outwalk the elderly man, should he attempt anything untoward. "You sound as if he plans to slaughter her and eat her for breakfast."

Victor took pity on Sophie. "Brumley marries rich women and then gambles away all their money."

"Oh."

"No need to worry. He prefers widows," Amelia said.

"With an impeccable pedigree and not likely to outlive the depths of their pockets."

"The last one was quite a bit older than he."

Sophie was taken aback. How could anyone have been older? "She must have been quite stricken in years."

"Rather. Still, if Miss Chandler's pockets are very deep, he might consider her a fair catch." Victor made a leg. "Excuse me. I believe duty calls upon me to rescue the fair maiden."

Miss Cecilia Covens took the floor with her father. Other couples joined them. The young man who had asked for a dance earlier approached. Sophie allowed him to guide her into the set. Across the room Victor led Miss Chandler onto the floor. Thrilled to see her friends together, she smiled at her partner, but the smile froze on her face as she noticed Keene leading Amelia into another group.

But then Keene couldn't dance with her if she was dancing with someone else, could he? Undoubtedly he would ask her to dance later. Besides, it wasn't as if she wanted him hanging on her sleeve every minute.

She turned her attention to her partner. With the music and the accompanying dance movements, she couldn't stay cross. Before long, she was laughing at the nonsensical ramblings of her companion and adding her own. She caught Keene's dark eyes and flashed him a smile.

Keene didn't feel like smiling, not as long as Sophie was enjoying herself too freely with her dancing partner. He wanted to take the man and pound his face into the floor. The bloodthirsty urge came from nowhere and shocked Keene. He attributed his violent reaction to not knowing who fathered

Sophie's child and his suspicion of every man she graced with her smile.

"I think she's having a good time."

Keene swiveled back to look at Amelia's averted face. "But you're not?"

She shrugged. "Of course, I'm having a wonderful time."

"George will come around."

Amelia turned hopeful blue eyes in his direction. "Did you see Regina today?"

Her concern about her daughter softened his temper. He gave her news that a year ago he would have considered absurd: how many times Regina had nursed, had her nappies changed, how long she'd slept. Amelia hung on his discourse as if he were reciting the secret recipe for ambrosia.

"How our conversations have digressed," said Keene.

Amelia smiled softly.

Across the room, Sophie's infectious laughter pealed. That he could hear her from this distance made him wonder if everyone would turn and stare. When he glanced around, no one seemed to be taking any notice. Nevertheless, he wished she would restrain herself. Her lack of decorum made him queasy.

He wanted to snatch her out of the ballroom and pull her into a dark corner and. . . . The image that popped into his head wasn't of a lecture. No, the sight of her sheer pink stockings as she descended the stairs early in the evening fostered fantasies of untying her garters. The idea of removing them tormented him.

Amelia said something he hadn't heard. "What?"

"I asked if you mean to dance with Sophie?"

Dance with her? How could he dance with her and not be crazy to make love to her? Yet, he couldn't make her his wife. He couldn't give her the fuel to perpetuate her charade. "No, I believe I shall ask Victor to escort the two of you home."

Only when he was outside on the street, the cool night air soothing his heated skin, did it occur to him that asking Victor to escort Amelia in a closed carriage was possibly not the smartest of choices.

Sophie watched her husband exit from the ballroom. Her throat grew tight. She swallowed hard around a barrier that hadn't been there a minute ago.

"Might I have the next dance?"

Sophie swiveled around and caught the too-knowing expression of Lord Algany. "By all means."

Her voice trembled as she spoke, and she wished she could be more discreet with her emotions. Across the room, Amelia appeared totally serene as she spoke with a young woman. Had she and Keene disagreed over something? Was that why he left with such a scowl on his face?

"Perhaps I should fetch you a drink instead."

"I should enjoy a dance, better."

Algany held out his arm and Sophie placed her gloved hand on his sleeve. He leaned close to her ear, his breath stirring her hair. "Your husband is a fool to leave you alone."

"I'm not alone," she whispered.

"No, you have me at your disposal, my dearest."

But she was alone, and as charming as Lord Algany could be, she couldn't forget the pressure he'd put on her at the theater, so when the dance ended, she claimed a prior obligation to dance with Lord Wedmont.

Algany insisted on handing her over himself. Victor looked as though he was headed in Miss Coven's direction when Sophie rapped him with her fan. "Have you forgotten you promised this dance to me?"

"Sophie, I did not!" He turned and saw Lord Algany and added, ". . . realize it was this one. I thought you promised me a waltz." Victor extended his arm. He stalked out into the set. "I promised this one to the guest of honor."

"I'm sorry. I'll tell her it was my fault for mistaking the dance, and you were too gentlemanly to point it out."

"I daresay she'll find a replacement." Victor shrugged.

Sophie watched as Algany approached Amelia. Her prior dance partner was not suffering the loss of her company. Victor wasn't happy about dancing with her, and Keene hadn't even bothered. "I should have enjoyed myself better in Algany's company."

The man at least *wanted* to dance with her.

"I couldn't very well leave you with him. Keene would kill me."

"More like to send me back to the country."

"He can't with Amelia staying there."

That Keene only wanted her to stay in London as a cover for Amelia's stay was exactly what Sophie feared.

Keene stared across the dimly lit room as his wife laughed. The candlelight danced on her short blonde curls. Soon she would take the floor with one of the men crowding around her. In just a couple of weeks, she had blossomed into, if not the toast of the season, at least one of the young matrons favored by several regular admirers. Amelia would be sure she did not dance more than twice with any one man. Although, to give his wife her due, Keene had never seen her exhibit favoritism toward any man other than Victor.

"Amelia looks tired," Victor commented.

Keene glanced around to be sure no one could overhear. "I think she is worn out waiting for George to make a decision."

"Has she tried talking to him?"

Keene shook his head.

"Sophie looks quite animated."

"Her natural state."

Sophie laughed and skipped up to her friend Mary Frances.

Keene shook his head. Amelia cast a strained glance in their direction. Her mouth suddenly rounded in an "O," and she swiveled around, presenting her back to them. Keene looked to see what horror Sophie had committed, but she was simply talking to the heiress.

Victor looked over his shoulder toward the door. "George."

Keene turned around.

"Excuse me," said Victor, making a polite bow.

Coward.

When George reached his side, Keene said, "It's good to see you here."

"I thought I should make an appearance. Have you seen my wife?"

"Yes." Keene once again glanced around to make sure no one hovered close.

"That bastard!"

Keene glanced over his shoulder to see Victor leading Amelia to the dance floor. He grabbed George's arm. "Get a grip, man."

Her uncertain glance in their direction tore at Keene's heart.

"Let's go to the Cocoa Tree. The company here bores me," said George.

Keene nodded. He didn't want to stay and watch Sophie. The more he watched her, the more he wanted her, and the harder it became to sleep at night, knowing she was in the next room, the next bed, her pregnancy still concealed, still imperceptible. There were moments, too many moments, when he didn't care any longer.

His brother's friend and Keene's one-time second, John, entered the assembly hall as they approached the exit.

"Hello, Davies. Keeting, how's the baby?"

George smiled. "She holds her head up a bit now."

Keene could have wept with relief at the signs of acceptance, even joy, on George's face. After they exchanged pleasantries with the young man, George and Keene climbed into George's carriage.

"Are you feeling better about her?"

George scowled. "I cannot forget that she is not mine."

Keene rubbed his forehead. "You needn't forget, if you can forgive."

"You don't understand."

Impatience burst through Keene. He understood. Why was it so hard for everyone to be honest? Why did Sophie persist in pretending she didn't understand his hints to spill the soup? For that matter, why hadn't he told George his own circumstances? Not that he'd ever lied except by omission. "I understand what it will be like for your daughter. God forbid there is ever another child."

"What do you mean?" asked George sharply.

"I mean I am not my father's son. Richard was his, but I was not."

He turned to the window. The gas lamps lining the street cast pale globes of light in a futile attempt to ward off darkness.

George's shocked gaze weighed on Keene.

"I'm sorry, I shan't make the Cocoa Tree tonight. If you'll put me down, I'll catch a hackney home."

George tapped on the speak-through panel to the coachman's box and directed his coachman to Keene's square. He slid the window shut. "I'm sorry, I didn't realize."

The carriage swayed on the cobbled streets. George slumped in his seat. After some time, he said, "I don't know how your father did it. He must be a better man than I to accept a child by another man and continue on with his wife."

"I don't know. He cared for me, raised me. Perhaps he knew before I was born. He never spoke to me about it directly, but I always knew I was a burden, not a blessing."

"The devil, you say."

"I don't think he should have minded so much if I were not his heir."

George reached across the open space and squeezed his arm. "Yes, it makes sense. I thought he disliked your way of life, but Richard was no better. And you two never looked alike."

A wave of sadness crept over Keene. "No, we didn't."

Sophie looked more like his half brother than he did. George stepped down from the carriage at Keene's house and walked with him to the door. "Are things well with Sophie and you?"

Keene shrugged. "Well enough, I suppose."

"I hope so. You deserve happiness."

"It doesn't come because one is entitled. I fear it must be worked upon."

At one time Keene had thought that regular funds would keep him happy, but the dowry draft still sat locked in his drawer. His father had carried through on his promise to support him and Sophie, but the money burdened Keene. When he had supported himself through gambling, there had been a certain freedom.

He climbed the stairs to his room. He opened the door to Sophie's bedroom and stood looking in. There were more and more nights when he peeked in to see her sleeping, her voluminous nightgown shrouding her too-perfect figure.

He hungered for her sweet smiles, her eager touch, her innocent blushes. But the blushes couldn't be so innocent. He longed for the days when she had followed him around like an eager puppy. All grown up, she was finding her niche in society. She was never restrained, but oddly enough, no one seemed to mind.

Keene leaned his head onto the back of the chair and stared at the trompe l'oeil paintings on the ceiling. If he squinted he could believe the ceiling was laid in recessed panels, rather than a flat expanse. He put the bottom of his fresh-from-the-cellar wine-cooled glass on his forehead.

It didn't help.

He'd taken to arriving home in the wee hours of the morning and waiting until Sophie woke before crawling into his own bed. The thin door between their rooms provided scant deterrent. Better to avoid the temptation altogether.

Fortunately, she was an early riser, even though she was out quite late at balls. She also possessed that enviable talent of falling asleep the minute her fluffy blonde curls hit the pillow. He knew: he'd peeked in on her too many times.

That took care of the mornings; then he urged the women to drive out to the park in the phaeton, which only seated two comfortably. Then dinner to muddle through before they were off to one entertainment or another. Keene would escape to a gentlemen's club as soon as his control started slipping.

If he avoided being alone with Sophie, he could make it through the waiting period. He did the math in his head again. Sometime before his proposal in early January plus four months. If he could make it until May, perhaps the end of April, concealing her pregnancy would be impossible.

He didn't know if he could make it through the next twelve hours. He hated this collapse of his restraint.

Until recently he'd prided himself on his superb self-discipline, but his wife's reckless disregard of consequences must be catching.

Last night he'd drawn her into an anteroom and kissed her.

A huge mistake.

Noise on the stairs outside the library drew his attention. He'd left the door open so he could hear Sophie enter the breakfast room.

He set his glass on the table beside him and rose from his chair. Sophie paused outside the library door and adjusted her feathered cap in the looking glass opposite the door. She wheeled around, the train of her navy velvet riding gown twisting around her legs. "Keene."

"Going riding?"

"Yes." She backed away from him as if she expected him to deter her. "I know it is quite an unfashionably early hour, but this way I can give the horse his head."

"Give me a moment to change, and I'll accompany you."

She backed toward the front door. "That won't be necessary. I have a groom to go with me."

Why didn't she want him to go with her? Was she meeting

someone? Her early morning ride was a stealthy thing. She hadn't even eaten breakfast. She'd been eager enough for his company last night, eager for his kisses. "Why not?"

"You haven't been to bed. I'm sure you're tired."

He folded his arms across his chest rather than grab her and shake the truth out of her.

Her shoulders drooped in front of him. "I know I should not ride early in the morning, but no one is about to see me."

"You might be thrown," said Keene sarcastically. How had she expected him to believe she was thrown in the first place?

"Oh, no." She opened the front door. "Brutus is too well-trained." She clapped a hand over her mouth.

"You're riding my horse?" His seventeen-hand horse? She'd look like a child perched on his Brutus's back.

A groom walked his gelding down the street. A second horse stood docilely by.

"Well, Daisy is still at your father's. Oh, please, Keene, I don't ride him hard, and I am quite light, hardly a chore for him at all."

"I'll send for your horse."

"Does that mean you don't want me to ride Brutus?"

If she didn't go riding he would remain all alone with her, and that was dangerous. "No, you may go."

She hesitated a minute, then crossed to him and kissed his cheek. He clenched his arms tighter. "Go on, then."

He followed her to the curb and lifted her to the saddle. He cast a sharp glance at his groom. "Don't let her out of your sight."

"No, sir. I wouldn't, sir."

Keene watched the horses walk down the street. His hands itched to hold her waist again, his cheek tingled from the press of her lips and his blood was on fire. Sleep would elude him for a long time. Perhaps he should fetch her horse himself. It would give him a few days away to cool his fevered blood.

* * *

Sophie couldn't believe he'd left without so much as a by-your-leave. She hadn't even known until she and Amelia sat down to dinner four days ago, and Keene was absent. She wished she could forget he was gone and enjoy the parties. But almost unconsciously she scanned the other guests, looking for her husband.

Perhaps when the hour struck eleven and no further admittance could be gained to the exclusive assembly rooms, she could stop hoping he would show up.

"Might I have the next waltz?"

Sophie didn't need to swing around to know that Lord Algany was standing behind her. He had a habit of approaching from the back.

"But of course," said Sophie smoothly. He was a bit of a salve to her ego. Not that she wanted to be around him long. Too much salve left her feeling greasy.

"I hear your husband has left you all alone and retreated to the country."

Did everyone besides her know that Keene had left London? "He'll be back soon."

"Not too soon, I hope." Algany's gaze traveled over her face and held her eyes. "Might I say you are looking especially delicious tonight."

"You might say it, but I doubt I should believe it." Not that Algany wasn't sincere, but his lingering gazes, while similar to Keene's, did nothing for her. Keene had only to flick a sidelong glance in her direction and she was all aflutter. It wasn't fair.

"Of course you should, angel. You are the most refreshing woman I've encountered in a long time. How you maintain such an air of innocence quite intrigues me."

"I fear you are too jaded, sir."

"You are right, of course. It is why I am drawn back to you again and again, even though you do not offer this poor man any encouragement."

Sophie shrugged. "I am warned you are a very bad sort to

encourage." Her smile probably softened the blow. Perhaps she should try the same tactics with Keene. Her refusals with Lord Algany only seemed to encourage him more.

"Folly. I should bring you nothing but pleasure. Who is this maligner of my character?" His ferret smile said he really had no interest in learning who slandered him. He extended his arm as the opening bars of a waltz began.

One thing that could be said was that Algany was an excellent dancer. They sailed about the floor in a way that made Sophie's heart lighten. It was hard to stay heavy of heart when one was light on one's feet.

She hardly noticed that the hour of eleven passed and only those members of Parliament who had been detained by late business or those whose carriages were already in the line outside on the street would be admitted. She smiled wider at Algany.

He pulled her closer, every now and then their bodies would touch on a turn.

"I shall step on your feet if we don't have a care," she warned.

"A small price to pay for the pleasure. Sophie, let me take you to supper. I know a lovely place that serves the most delectable fare. Quite discreet, too."

She shook her head. She should protest his using her Christian name, but he would only switch to an endearment. She glanced toward the entrance.

"He is out of town, isn't he?"

Her eyes shot back to Lord Algany's. She didn't answer.

"You know, jealousy can be a wonderful tool for a wife to bring a husband to heel." He lifted his hand from her waist and brushed his fingers across her cheek.

Sophie swallowed hard and wished again for the reserve to hide her true feelings. She shook her head.

"Of course, you must bring your dear Mrs. Keeting along. I should be happy to escort both of you to supper."

Sophie hesitated, looking at Algany. She glanced across the

room to where Amelia stood near a wall, looking about as listless as Sophie felt.

Victor watched Amelia from across the room.

Algany's fingers traveled down her neck and he languidly placed his hand back on her waist. "Perhaps Lord Wedmont should like to make a fourth."

Algany spun her through a turn.

"While Keeting is still about town, he doesn't seem to have a care for what his wife is about."

Sophie hoped her expression didn't betray her knowledge of Amelia's situation. Algany's gaze was too sharp. But if he thought he could wheedle a secret like that out of her, he was mistaken. She pressed her lips together.

"And then there is the hapless watchdog, Wedmont. Although he looks rather hangdog tonight. I am never quite sure who he is to be watching."

"Lud, you do have an imagination. He is not a watchdog."

Algany raised an eyebrow.

Sophie began to feel she was out of her depth. Her heart was beating too fast. Keeping secrets had never been her strong point.

Algany had noticed the quick cadence of her breathing. His eyes dropped to her décolletage several times. "He is not doing a good job of watching you this evening, that is sure."

"Even if was to look after me—and he is not—what trouble could I get into here in Almack's hallowed grounds?"

"Why, none, of course." Algany's attempt at an innocent expression wasn't entirely successful. "But one could make plans, of course." He grinned, but didn't wait for her refusal. "Come, angel, you are rather flushed. Join your guardian, and I shall bring you ladies a glass of some of the sumptuous orgeat served here and you might discuss my offer of real refreshment afterward."

He led her to Amelia and bowed.

"Did you dance with Lord Algany again?" asked Amelia.

"Once tonight. Don't worry, I shan't do it again this evening."

What was the point? Keene wasn't here to scowl at her, then drag her away into an anteroom and make her crazy with his kisses. She'd had to push him away last time. Jealousy might be good for a show of possessiveness on Keene's part, but it hadn't lasted until they made it home. He hadn't even come in the house, just driven off to a club.

No, if she danced with Algany again, he would just pressure her to join him for a private or semiprivate meal.

Amelia's blue eyes followed Algany as he walked across the floor.

"Don't worry, he shall be back. He wants us to go to supper with him."

Amelia paled.

"Oh, Victor is invited too."

"What did you say?"

"I couldn't very well speak for all us," said Sophie as she smiled at a young man coming to claim a country dance with her.

She tried very hard not to notice the thin trickle of guests still making their way through the door. One more dance and the latecomers would be turned away.

Keene stuck his watch back in his pocket and cursed the time. He likely wouldn't make it before the doors were shut for the night. He'd just made it back into town when he realized it was Wednesday. He'd driven his valet crazy with jumping into evening clothes and insisting on a simple Napoleon style for his cravat. He'd had two long days of travel to think about his marriage to Sophie and her deception.

When he reached his father's house, Keene had discovered the nursery remained untouched. Instead, his wife had taken dance lessons so as to not embarrass him when she arrived in London.

She hadn't pressed her advantage the other night when he'd kissed her in the anteroom. If she'd suggested they go home then, he'd have consummated their marriage that night. Instead, she pushed him away, reminding him they were in a public place. She'd said they better go back into the ballroom, knowing his carriage was just outside. She'd withdrawn from him the morning after their marriage. If she meant to foist some other man's brat on him, would she have let those opportunities pass?

Maybe she met all his pleas for confessions with blank stares because she had nothing to confess. Could her parents both be wrong?

Lately, he hadn't seen any signs of pregnancy. She wasn't sick in the mornings. Her waist hadn't thickened. She hadn't fainted since their wedding day when she claimed nerves. She didn't look any different from the day he proposed, except for the short hair. Pregnant women looked different, softer, rounder. What if he'd waited all this time and she wasn't even with child?

Keene pressed his fingers to his temples. What if he was deluding himself because he wanted her in his bed? Her kisses left him breathless, aching, hungry for her.

The rooms were overwarm, and when Sophie returned to Amelia's side she took the glass Lord Algany held out with relief. She had swallowed half of it before she held it away from her with a wrinkled nose. She would have preferred water.

"The best I can offer here." Lord Algany gave her a wry look.

Amelia laughed.

Sophie stared at her houseguest. She couldn't remember ever hearing Amelia laugh.

Algany tucked Amelia's hand into the crook of his arm and offered to take them on a turn about the floor. Sophie looked at his smug expression and decided he would feel quite too full of himself with both of them on his arms. "I'll just wait for you here."

"Are you sure?" Algany didn't look happy with her answer.

"Very sure. I'll just sit and wait." She fanned herself with her hand.

Algany hesitated a moment before walking away with Amelia.

Sophie found a chair. Out on the dance floor Victor danced with a rather horse-faced young woman. As Sophie stared, the woman threw back her head and brayed. Victor winced. Sophie glanced around to see if others had noticed. No one else was staring, but she couldn't focus on anyone else. Everyone seemed farther away than they had before.

She blinked hard. She hadn't fainted in weeks. The swimming uncertainty that had overtaken her several times in the week following her fall on her head hadn't happened in quite some time, not since the day of her wedding. Moisture beaded her upper lip, and the glass slid from her fingers.

SIXTEEN

Keene's carriage fell into line after the deadline. He held his breath until he made it through the door, fearing that at any moment some overzealous footman would point out that he wasn't in the queue in good order.

He searched the room, his eyes lit on his nemesis Lord Algany. Only for once he wasn't dancing court on Sophie. Amelia clung to his arm. Keene continued searching for his wife, but the oddness of Amelia clinging to anyone brought his puzzled gaze back to her.

The pair was making their way about the room. They stopped and Algany bent over and assisted a woman to her feet. She swayed. Sophie?

What the devil was wrong with her?

Algany wrapped an arm around her waist and steered her toward the entrance. Keene started for them and was waylaid by a greeting from Lady Jersey.

He held out his elbow and asked her to walk with him.

She followed the line of his sight. "You are anxious to see your wife."

He started to protest, but ended with a lame, "Quite."

Sophie crumbled. Keene nearly ran to her side. Algany held her up, while Amelia stood back, her eyes wide in her face, her hands over her mouth.

"Come, we must get her some fresh air," Algany said as Keene approached.

"Give her here."

Algany blanched as he looked up. "I thought you were out of town."

"I'm back, now." He scooped Sophie into his arms.

"Is she all right?" asked Lady Jersey.

"Probably, she's just overheated," said Algany. "It's very warm in here." He backed up, pulling Amelia with him.

Lady Jersey looked directly at Keene. "Is she . . . ?" her question trailed off.

"It's likely she is."

Lady Jersey put her hand on her lips, her eyes growing speculative. "It would be too early to know for sure. I shall send around the name of a physician who specializes in these things."

Amelia stood back while Algany whispered to her.

"Where's Victor?" Keene asked her.

She shrugged, her eyes wide.

"I'll see to it Lord Wedmont escorts Mrs. Keeting home." Lady Jersey put a hand on Keene's shoulder. "We should find your wife some feathers to burn."

"Keene, you're back!"

He looked down into Sophie's wide blue eyes. She looked a little unfocused. He set her on her feet, and she swayed against him. She looked around and turned her face into his shoulder. "Why is everyone staring at me?" she whispered.

Keene wrapped his arms around her and stroked her back. "You fainted, pet."

"I did? I dropped my glass." She bounced up on her toes and looked over his shoulder.

"Come, I'm taking you home to bed."

"You are? I don't know if you should, I don't feel so well."

Keene felt his ears grow warm, although he wouldn't have removed Sophie's head from his shoulder to save his life. She seemed to have forgotten their audience.

Lady Jersey herded the onlookers away.

"Can you walk outside?"

Sophie nodded her head, moving against his shoulder. "I'm sorry."

He whispered in her ear, "Want to tell me why you fainted?"

They stood locked together for a time until he finally felt her head shift side to side against his shoulder.

He swallowed hard. "Let's go home, Sophie."

They could hash out the truth of the matter when they arrived home. Only, Sophie was so wan and pale he took pity on her and had her maid help her to bed. He knew the truth of it, anyway. It didn't take Amelia's confirmation that they hadn't drunk any spirits and that Sophie had been fine earlier in the evening. It didn't take hearing the sounds of Sophie being sick in the morning to know that she was suffering the symptoms of her condition.

He sent for the physician Lady Jersey recommended. When the man arrived Sophie was sleeping. After feeling her brow for fever, the physician and Keene returned to the drawing room where Keene told him of Sophie's fainting and of being ill the two mornings. The man confirmed Sophie's symptoms were those of a woman with child. He recommended very moderate exercise and fresh air, and avoiding crowds and excessive dancing, a bit of peppermint to aid her digestion and plenty of undisturbed rest.

Yes, she would have plenty of undisturbed rest.

Later in the morning, Sophie skipped down the steps. Keene came out of the library and stood at the bottom of the stairs.

"Oh, you're back."

"I brought you home from Almack's last night."

Sophie frowned. Last night was such a muddle she wasn't sure what had happened. "I thought I dreamed it."

"Are you feeling all right, now?"

Her enthusiastic bouncing down the stairs should have been answer enough. "I'm just fine."

His grimace was fleeting. “I brought your horse. I thought she might as well stay here in town. There is a hunter I have that you might prefer when we are home.”

Was he giving her a horse?

He looked over her head. Had he already lost interest in her? “There was a letter for you.”

He handed her a missive with her mother’s spidery scrawl on it. Sophie popped the seal and eagerly read. All was well back home, if a little quiet. Her mother said she looked forward to receiving news of any coming additions to the family, and Sophie felt the burn of tears at the back of her eyelids. She was doomed to disappoint her parents in that there was no news to announce and none likely in the future if Keene didn’t make her his wife in more than name.

“Your parents are well?” He leaned close to her. His dark eyes watched her with concern.

“They are fine.”

He reached for the letter, but she folded it in tiny squares and tucked it in her palm. The moment stretched out and Sophie grasped for something to fill it. “So, you came back last night?”

“I missed you.”

“By my reckoning, you’ve only lost the fifteen minutes a day we spend in the same room. Just a little over an hour. Why, we can make it up in a day.”

He grinned. “Feeling neglected, Sophie?”

Yes, she felt neglected, abandoned, ignored. “I don’t know what you’re about.”

He wound a finger into her curls and watched her with a steady gaze. “It doesn’t have to be this way. Just tell me all your secrets.” His breath caressed her cheek.

“I knocked a wheel off the dogcart trying to drive like you.” There, that was a confidence that she hadn’t wanted to share.

“Anything else?”

She shook her head. He was in a mood to tease, and she didn’t want to play.

His eyes bored into hers for the longest time before his lips twisted in a wry grimace. She could hear the ticking of a clock contrasting with the irregular thump of her heart, the shallow cadence of her breathing. His finger stroked the side of her face, under her chin, down her neck.

Sparks shimmered under her skin where he touched her. They shot in fiery bursts through her, igniting a slow burn low in her body. He bent toward her. His kiss melted through her, turning her insides to fuel for the fires he started.

She wanted so much more than his slow sensual kiss. For a time he complied, his arms pulling her to him. Then he pushed her away and bent over, gulping air into his lungs.

"You're leaving." It wasn't even a question.

"Yes."

She shook her head and walked into the morning room. She didn't want to be there, but where else could she go? Keene didn't offer the option of leaving with him.

She was tired of the games, tired of having her hopes dashed. Her parents' quiet home in the country suddenly seemed appealing. At least there she knew where she stood.

"Where are the women off to tonight?" Victor asked Keene.

"Opera." Keene slouched in his chair in the poorly lit library.

"You're not going?"

"I haven't been since I . . . proposed to Sophie."

Victor studied Keene. "Since you pulled your protection from your little canary."

"There is that."

"Who is escorting them?"

"John."

"He hates the opera."

Keene shrugged and stared into his glass, now empty. "I said I should relieve him of the need to see them home."

"So you are going?"

"I wouldn't be able to stay away."

"And you shall be by my place later, then."

The corners of Keene's mouth curled in a sneer. "Unless my wife decides to spill the soup about her baby." He glared at Victor. "Don't worry. It can't be too much longer before her belly swells."

Victor shook his head. "Your box?"

Keene nodded.

"Should you prefer, I can see them home."

Keene didn't answer. Victor left him to wallow in his self-inflicted misery. He'd be sharing it with him later anyway.

Lord Algany sidled up beside Sophie and held out his arm. "Come with me, my angel, I have something to show you."

"Where?"

"In my box."

Sophie hesitated. She had just walked with their escort John Milholland about King's Theater during the intermission between the opera and the ballet to follow. He had taken his leave, assuring her that Keene would be along to see them home. She was returning to the box where they had left Amelia recovering from the vapors induced by the moving opera.

"Won't take but a minute," Algany urged.

She put her hand on his sleeve. She didn't trust him. She suspected he had something to do with what had happened to her at Almack's.

He led her to his box and opened the door, a smile on his face. "Since you won't consent to go out to supper with me, I have brought it here to share."

Sophie hesitated at the door of the box. Inside Algany's box, four of the chairs had been removed and in their place sat a sofa and folding table covered with shaved ham, pickled salmon, pears steeped in brandy, scones, clotted cream, enough food to fell Wellington's army by gluttony. Two bottles of wine sat on the end of the table alongside a stack of china plates, silver, napkins, and glasses. A footman stood in the corner with a towel draped over his arm. "Do have a seat, and we'll send for the lovely Mrs. Keeting to join us. I can see her just over there alone in your box."

Algany's hand at the small of her back pressed her inside. "To convince you my offer of supper was sincere."

While the back of the box was as readily visible as the two front chairs, the drape was open. Algany turned one of the chairs around and gestured for her to sit on the sofa.

Sophie sank down onto the cushions.

He nodded to his footman.

The man set the towel on the table and moved to the door. Her back was to it, but she could have sworn she heard the click of tumblers before the door was shut.

"He has gone to invite Mrs. Keeting to join us."

From her vantage point, Sophie couldn't see Amelia once she sat. She couldn't see much at all since the sofa was lower than the chairs. Algany picked up a plate. "What may I serve you?"

"There are so many choices, I can't decide." The hairs on the back of her neck stood on end. "What are you having?"

Algany sat in his chair and scooted it forward. Almost as if on cue, one side of the curtain, shielding the back of the box, fell closed. "Dratted thing," muttered Algany. "Never wants to stay back."

Her senses on full alert, Sophie stared at him. He put the plate down and moved to pull the curtain back open. It fell shut again as soon as he sat back down. Sophie scooted down on the sofa to be on the inside half of the box that was still open. "I don't want to miss the ballet," she said.

"Of course not." Lord Algany smiled his ferret smile.

The one side of the curtain hanging closed blocked some of the light in the box. Algany handed her a plate with far more food on it than she could eat, and opened a bottle of wine. He poured her a glass and himself one, too.

"We should wait for Amelia."

"We should, but I know you don't want to miss the performance, so we shall be rude. There is more than enough food that she shouldn't feel slighted."

Algany handed her the glass. "It is a bit heavy, but I think you'll like it."

He couldn't hide the gleam in his eye as she raised the glass to her lips.

"Where is Sophie?" Victor asked Amelia as he slid into a seat behind her in the box.

"She sent this note saying she started feeling unwell and Mr. Milholland was going to escort her home."

Victor stared at the note. Had Sophie started feeling lightheaded the way she had at Almack's?

Keene joined them just before the end of the performance. His question was the same as Victor's.

When Amelia handed Keene the note, he turned white. "This isn't Sophie's writing."

"Are you sure?"

"Not positive, no, but she should have been home before I left if John brought her home."

"He wouldn't have . . . would he?" Victor asked.

"No, John is trustworthy. Other than picking weapons."

"Good thing," muttered Victor.

Keene stared at the note. "Mayhap it is her writing," he whispered.

Victor scanned the boxes for Sophie. He had an odd sense of déjà vu. He noticed the box with the drawn curtains. He pointed across the crowded theater. "Whose box is that?"

Keene knocked over his chair standing up. "Algany's!"

Other patrons of the theater stared in their direction.

Keene was through the door in a flash. Victor was right on his heels.

Sophie stepped out into the hallway and closed the door behind her. "Oh, good, you are here. I'm quite ready to leave."

Keene's rage ebbed slightly. Sophie appeared unscathed, unaffected and totally uninterested.

Of course, it was possible that she had already gotten what she came for. He glanced her over. She looked cool and unruffled—well, as cool and unruffled as Sophie ever looked. She didn't look like a woman who had just concluded an illicit meeting with a man.

Keene's attention was solely on Sophie. "Whatever were you doing?"

"Well, I have been waiting the longest time to get some ink to leave a note."

"Isn't he in there?" Keene stared at the closed door. Victor had a hand on his arm as if to restrain him from charging in and killing Algany, which Keene was wont to do if it wasn't for the baffling calm demeanor of his wife. When he kissed her, her eyes would grow bright, her lovely fair skin would flush and her expression would grow bemused. She looked . . . tired and world-weary.

"Well, yes, the note wasn't exactly for him. Besides, he is indisposed. So I thought I should leave a note." She turned and walked down the empty hallway.

He was sick? Exasperation churned Keene's thoughts. He hated talking to her back as she walked away. He caught her arm. "Sophie."

She turned and stared him in the eye.

"You must have a better care for yourself. You should avoid any sickness, now. Think of your own health." *Think of the baby's health.*

"My health is fine. If you are afraid I might pass some infection to you, I shall endeavor to give you as wide a berth as you give me." She flipped the train of her evening gown behind her and started away again.

He didn't like it. The sight of her moving away from him turned his stomach. The thought that he couldn't stop her from being alone with other men, men like Algany, made him seethe with frustration. He turned and rammed his fist against a wall.

"That will undoubtedly stop Algany from pursuing your wife," commented Victor.

"I'm going to kill him."

Victor stood between him and the door and gripped his shoulders.

Sophie returned to his side. "I'm sure you needn't bother. Lord Algany will undoubtedly be leaving London."

"Did he say so?"

"No, well, he didn't know he would have to before now."

"Sophie, start at the beginning."

She rolled her eyes and snorted. "I'm quite cross, and I should like to leave. And I *don't* need *you* to rescue me."

Keene folded his arms and stared at her. Algany opened the door of his box and stood with his hand held across his forehead.

Keene lunged toward the man and Algany dropped his hand for a second as he stepped back. Across his forehead in thick black letters was the warning, "Women Beware."

Algany slapped his hand back across his forehead and bowed. "Good evening, gentlemen. Your servant, Mrs. Davies." He scurried off down the hall. His manservant, loaded down with hampers, followed behind him.

Sophie watched him with a gimlet eye. "Well, I don't expect he shall insist I have any more private suppers with him again."

Keene was too stunned to answer.

"I quite agree," answered Victor.

Sophie took off again.

"You'd better go after her. She'll wait in the street." Victor pushed Keene in his wife's direction. "I'll see to it Amelia gets home."

Victor retrieved a distraught Amelia and led her to his carriage.

"Is she all right? I should have realized something was amiss."

"She's fine. I gather Algany waylaid her and she rather took care of him."

"I should have known something was wrong. I felt so strange at Almack's the night Sophie fainted. Keene will be so disappointed in me."

Amelia's worried glance was similar to the one that prompted his kisses a year before. Victor resisted the urge to put his arm around her.

"I should have gone with her. She is so innocent sometimes."

Victor couldn't help himself. He put his arm around Amelia's shoulders. She turned into his embrace.

The slow heat of desire crept up his body. "Remember who I am. I'm not Keene."

Amelia's hands slid across his shoulders. "I only know that you are not George."

Victor pushed her away.

Amelia looked down, her head shifting from side to side. "I'm sorry."

"Me too."

"Did I see you on Brutus this morning?" Victor tilted a glass of punch to his lips.

"Yes."

"Really, I thought Keene brought your horse."

"I put Miss Chandler on Daisy," said Sophie.

"Sophie is teaching me to ride." Mary Frances leaned forward.

"Where's your doddering old fool?" asked Victor.

Mary Frances winced. "He's quite a kind gentleman." A flash in her dark eyes betrayed her.

"We need some punch." Sophie ignored the two almost-full glasses sitting on a nearby table.

Victor rolled his eyes. "Your servant, madam. Should you like four or five more glasses, be sure to let me know." He stalked off to do as he was bade.

Sophie wrapped her arm in Mary Frances's and tugged her along in a brisk walk. "Tell me what has happened."

"Lord Brumley tried to kiss me."

"Well, he should kiss you if you are to marry him."

"He hasn't proposed, and it was quite disgusting." Mary Frances's shudder of revulsion spoke volumes.

"Well, it is not so disgusting when it is someone under eighty. Well, not that I should know, but when a man is under forty, perhaps."

"I'll put up with it when I have to, but no sooner."

"Brumley isn't the only available bachelor."

"He's the only shot I have at becoming a countess."

"Well, yes, but there are other gentlemen, *younger* gentlemen."

"If I seek a man my own age, I will have to tolerate him for years; besides, a title would be out of the question."

"It's not everything. I should much prefer a husband who cared about me." If only she had one. Instead, she had a husband who could hardly stand to be alone with her.

"Yes, but my dearest, my most lovable quality is my father's fortune." Mary Frances smiled wryly. "I'd like marriage to a doddering old fool who has more interest in cards than in my affections. I would hope that my appeal would be short-lived."

Victor stood like an imbecile holding the two glasses of punch. He knew he'd been sent on a fool's errand, but the least Sophie could do was wait for him to return instead of leaving him looking addlepated. He spied a new entrant to the salon.

He watched as Keene's eyes circled the room and then stopped. Victor measured the hungry line of Keene's sight and turned. Sophie and Mary Frances strolled together. Victor approached them, eager to discharge his errand.

He studied the heiress. He'd made inquiries and found her appeal stretched to several thousand a year. Beyond that, she was not unattractive, but she'd set her cap for Brumley.

Brumley might be on the lookout for a new wife. Then again, he hadn't completely depleted his cash reserve from his last wife. He might be simply toying with Miss Chandler, enjoying her fawning over him and measuring how far she might be willing to pursue him.

Amelia joined them at the same time as Keene did.

"Have a drink, Amelia." Victor handed her a glass.

"I suppose I aspire too high," Mary Frances said as they approached.

"Not necessarily." Victor handed her the remaining glass of punch. "You might try broadening your horizons, though."

"You don't know what we were speaking of."

"I might hazard a guess it concerned the nasty old coot."

"I've never called him that," protested Mary Frances.

"No? I rather think you should. In which case you should take a turn about the floor with me."

Sophie watched Victor extend his arm and Mary Frances placed her hand in the crook of his elbow and they walked off. "Do you think Victor is setting his cap for Miss Chandler?"

"Mmm," answered Amelia.

Sophie cast a sharp glance at her companion. Amelia sighed. In the few short weeks they had been making the rounds of entertainments, Amelia had gone from listless to as animated as a cobblestone. "What's wrong?"

Amelia shook her head.

Sophie frowned. She knew what was wrong. Amelia was estranged from her husband and infant daughter, yet pretended to everyone that all was well. Better acquainted with the ways of society, Sophie understood the pretense.

She wrapped her arm in Amelia's and strode forward. "If you could be anywhere, where would you be right now?"

Amelia's eyes glistened. She dipped her head.

Sophie pulled her forward. She didn't mean to make Amelia cry, even though it might do her good to get it out. There was something to be said for a good fit of the vapors when things didn't seem right.

"I'm sorry," whispered Amelia.

"Would you like to go home?"

"Oh, yes!" The sudden spark of life in Amelia surprised Sophie. Just as quickly, Amelia snuffed it out. "But I can't."

"Sure you can. We don't need to stay."

Amelia gave a soft shake of her head.

Sophie steered them out into an empty passageway and swung around to face Amelia. "You mean *your* home?"

Amelia tugged her arm away, looking in every direction but at Sophie.

"You miss your baby?"

Amelia clutched at Sophie. "Oh, yes, and George. I just want to see them and be sure they are well. I know it is quite goosish of me, but I haven't seen them in so long."

The breaks in Amelia's composure were so few and far between that Sophie suspected worries and fears had been preying on her mind for some time. "Let's go, then."

Amelia closed her eyes, gave a tiny shake of her head and reopened her eyes. "What?"

"We'll call on your husband and take a peek in on the baby."

Amelia blanched and looked around. "I can't go there."

Sophie headed toward the front door. "Why not?"

Amelia lagged behind. She finally fell in step beside Sophie. Her voice dropped to a shaky whisper. "George evicted me."

Sophie pivoted. "Did he say you couldn't visit?"

"No, but—"

"Pish. Keene visits. I don't see why we may not. Besides, if you wish, you may simply tell your husband that I expressed a desire to see the baby, and you didn't know how to tell me no." From what Sophie could see, Amelia had a hard time telling anyone no.

"Oh, we can't. Keene said he might come here tonight."

Sophie stopped. Why had he told Amelia and not her? "He did?"

"Well, yes, he asked where we should be tonight and said he might attend, too."

Might wasn't a surety. Besides, when Keene showed up at the same functions he rarely did more than offer a greeting before being on his way. She knew he was involved in political dealings, and the rumors of Lord Palmerston being made an English peer and moving from the House of Commons to the Lords had caused a flurry of speculation about a by-election.

Beyond that, Sophie's hopes for her husband's attention had been raised and dashed too many times. As long as he didn't think she needed rescue, he didn't pay her any mind. And the truth was, she resented his belief that she needed rescuing on a regular basis.

"Bother. If he wanted our company, he should have come with us." Sophie started forward. "I'll call for the carriage, and we'll just pop by your house. I know it is late to be calling, but surely one is allowed latitude with one's own family."

"I'm not sure this is a good idea. I don't think he wants me there."

"Has he forbidden you to see your baby?"

Amelia winced. "He said I must leave her, and he doesn't want me there."

Sophie heaved in a deep breath. "Yes, but what do *you* want?"

Amelia blinked.

"Come on. We shouldn't have even gone out if you are so miserable."

"But—"

"I know, you shall tell me that you aren't any less miserable at home, and that we might as well let me enjoy myself, but you need to fight for what you want, and I think you want to see your daughter. There is no earthly reason that Keene, or for that matter, your George, should find a brief visit to your house unacceptable."

Amelia didn't look convinced, but she followed Sophie. One thing Sophie knew was that her companion found it very difficult to say no in the face of a strong will.

* * *

"He did what?" Keene asked Victor.

"Lost twenty thousand pounds at the Cocoa Tree last night. You have to go get him. He is in deep again tonight. I would have stopped him, but I fear my influence would cause him to entrench deeper."

"Twenty thousand?" While George's finances were healthier than his friends', even he couldn't afford to play that deep.

"Yes, give or take a few thousand. Come on, Keene. Frankly, I shouldn't mind seeing him sink, but Amelia and the baby shall drown in his stupidity, too."

Keene moved toward the door. He would have to go see to George. He greeted the problem with relief and disappointment. His plans for the evening had included attending the ball where Sophie and Amelia went. Staying away from Sophie grew more difficult by the day. "Is he drinking?"

"No, he is managing this folly without the aid of being properly shot in the neck."

"Well, at least he does not mix his vices."

"Apparently the man cannot live without his wife, but is too full of spleen to live with her."

"He's hurt."

"Well, yes, but both of you are too damn caught up in what is past. The only thing you can control is what happens from this day forward. You are going to lose Sophie if you don't start treating her as your wife."

"What do you mean?" demanded Keene.

"What do you think of Miss Chandler? She is often in your wife's company."

Keene shook his head. He didn't have any interest in his wife's young friend, who seemed a little brittle about the edges. Not that he could quite put a finger on what it was that bothered him about her. He wanted to know what Victor knew about his wife, but Victor exhibited a mawkish disinclination to elaborate.

* * *

If Sophie had ever thought Amelia's beauty was cold, the current expression on the young mother's face erased that thought. She jiggled the little baby in her lap, nuzzled and cooed at the wee one. The baby responded in happy gurgles and toothless grins, and even the drool that fell on Amelia's evening gown didn't dampen her enchantment.

Sophie couldn't decide if Amelia was relieved or disappointed that George wasn't home. A little of both, perhaps.

The sound of the door and strident male voices interrupted the mother and child. Amelia raised stricken eyes. Yet she leaned toward the opening door.

"You!" George reared back. "What are you doing here?"

Color drained from Amelia's face, and the hint of hope in her expression withered.

Silence hung like a noxious cloud over the room, invading all the corners and settling into the nooks and crannies.

Amelia broke the pall, speaking in a perfectly modulated voice. "Hello, George, how are you?"

"We came to see the baby," Sophie said.

Amelia stood up and tucked the infant in her arms. "We were just about to leave. I'll ring for her nursemaid."

Exiting seemed like a good idea, except George blocked the doorway, and Sophie didn't particularly feel like challenging him. She liked to think of herself as brave, but not foolhardy.

Keene and Victor peered around George's shoulders.

"You don't belong here." George's voice was tight with anger.

Amelia nodded. "I understand."

Sophie swiveled to look at her. "You do?"

George spurted into action, striding across the floor and adopting a menacing posture, towering over Amelia. "What do you mean to do? Steal the baby away?"

Amelia shook her head. "No."

"You come when I am not here. What meaning could you have?"

"I didn't know that you were gone."

He pushed closer and tighter. "I can't believe you would do this."

Amelia seemed to shrink in on herself. "I'm sorry."

Sophie stared. Was she the only one appalled by George's aggression and Amelia's cowed reaction? Victor averted his face and moved to the far side of the room. Keene stepped behind George as if ready to intercede.

"You're a lying—"

Amelia laid her hand against George's chest. "Please, I'll leave."

George seemed to crumble. "Damn you."

Amelia moved to skirt around her husband. She faltered. Sophie traced the line of her vision to Victor.

Victor leaned his palms against the wall, one knee cocked as if he would push through the plaster. He suddenly stalked out of the room. The slam of the front door made Amelia wince.

The baby began to fuss. Amelia bounced the tiny tot, whispering in her ear.

Keene stepped forward and held out his hands. "I'll take her upstairs to bed."

Amelia passed Regina into his hands, her eyes on George.

The image of Keene holding the baby zinged through Sophie. He looked natural and comfortable with the baby tucked in the crook of his arm, in a totally different manner than a woman would hold a child. Still, the baby looked secure. And she was his.

SEVENTEEN

Keene tilted his head, indicating she was to follow him. Sophie hesitated, not sure she should leave Amelia alone with her irate husband.

Keene called from the stairs. "Come with me, Sophie."

She hesitated.

"Leave us," said George.

Still, Sophie waited until Amelia gave a tiny smile and nod.

Keene stood on the stairs waiting for her. Sophie glanced back at the drawing room. She moved forward. Keene continued up the stairs.

Sophie trotted after him. "Are you sure we should leave them alone together. He . . ."

"Won't hurt her."

Sophie craned her neck, trying to see down into the drawing room. "Are you very sure?"

"More danger he could harm himself."

"Do you think so, for I think he looked quite angry at her."

"Sophie, he needs to tell her what he's been about."

She lingered behind. "Will he divorce her or not?"

"I don't think he could afford to now. Will you come along?"

She lifted the hem of her skirt and darted up the stairs.

Keene stood on the landing at the top and frowned at her.

She let go of her gown. Keene's frowns made her feel like a misbehaving puppy.

That he stood waiting for her with a baby nestled in his arm made an ache and yearning start under her breastbone. He was her husband, but only in name.

His dark eyes moved over her. There was something in the set of his mouth that made her want to glide like Amelia did, and then, of course, because she wouldn't be able to sustain the pose, she'd melt at his feet.

"You look rather fetching tonight."

His compliment startled her. "I do?" She crinkled her nose, regretting the question as soon as it popped out of her mouth.

Keene simply watched her. He slowly raised his arm and held out his hand to her.

Sophie wanted to run forward and thrust herself into his embrace, but would he even remember she was alive tomorrow? She gathered her skirts and sedately walked up the remainder of the steps. His dark gaze burned through her every step of the way. When she reached the top, he wrapped his free arm around her waist, the baby cradled in his other arm.

"I see Amelia is teaching you some decorum."

"She is a saint."

"A miracle worker, perhaps."

Sophie turned her face aside. He was pleased she hadn't run into his arms. She wanted to be his wife, the mother of his children, but he didn't want her. He wanted some mild, meek, Madonna type. Not that she wouldn't love children, but she suspected she would romp with them on the floor more than cuddle them in her lap.

The baby whimpered in his arms.

"Would you like to hold her?" asked Keene.

Sophie was startled by the notion. Earlier she had thought to gather the infant in her arms, but Amelia was so starved for contact with her baby, Sophie held back. Keene had been here almost daily, and obviously from the easy way he held the child, the chore was familiar.

The lump forming in Sophie's throat might make her croak if she spoke, so she held out her arms.

Keene put Regina in her hold, positioning her hands and murmuring light encouraging words. His fingers were warm against her skin. He stroked her arms.

The warm wiggling body against her chest provoked protective instincts Sophie hadn't known were there. She looked up at Keene. Why had he put his baby in her arms? Did he realize she knew?

He stroked a curl back from the edge of her face. "Don't look so scared, Sophie."

"I'm not scared," she whispered.

"I love this child, even though I am only her godfather."

Anguish broke through her. She could love the baby, too, precisely because he was the father.

"I could love any child not my own," he said.

Why the lies? "And if it was your own?" she asked.

He shook his head as if she didn't understand. She understood all right. She wasn't the naive country girl that she once was.

He leaned closer. His lips brushed hers. The kiss shattered her scant reserve. She strained for the power and passion she'd tasted before. Her heart ached with the need. Yet, she couldn't stand the strain of deceit. She couldn't play polite games. She was too honest and forthright for that.

She wanted Keene with every fiber of her being, but somewhere along the line she knew she would no longer be satisfied with less than his full attention. She wanted a marriage in every sense of the word. Yet, he hid himself from her. She couldn't make him give of himself.

She looked down into the little face.

Dark wisps of hair peeked out from under the cap. Her features were still unformed, but Sophie followed the shape of her rosebud mouth, the tiny button nose and the line of her eyebrows . . . the line of her eyebrows. Sophie shifted her gaze up to Keene's face and noticed the same arch, thicker, more masculine. "She looks a bit like you."

She held her breath, watching the transformation in Keene's

face. The slip of his self-assurance. She thrust Regina back into his arms. Sophie scurried down the stairs, hearing the baby's startled cry.

Keene was sure Sophie had verged on confessing her guilty secret before she'd run away. He would have gone after her and pressed the issue, but he had an upset child screaming in his ear. Not to mention several distressed friends floating about. He bounced the baby, trying to soothe both their ragged spirits.

He hoped that George and Amelia were making progress in resolving their difficulties. But more than anything he wanted to get Sophie home, to pursue her odd statement that Amelia's baby looked like him.

Although now that he peered closely into the unformed face, he thought perhaps there was a hint of Victor's features overlaid by Amelia's. He sighed. Would life have been easier for him if he resembled his mother?

Keene counted the time in his head. Sophie must be three months along. Surely, she couldn't hide her pregnancy much longer. Perhaps even now the signs were hidden under her high-waisted gowns. Was a baby born six months after marriage enough of an anomaly that he could safely make her his wife? For he didn't think he could stand to avoid her any longer.

He craved her touch, her zest for life. He wanted her easy laughter, her pleasure in simple things. He wanted her bright smile in his heart. Yet, as he knew he wanted her, he felt her sliding away.

He could simply slip into her bed or he could seduce her into his. And he'd never had much of a problem persuading a woman to share her body with him.

He handed the baby to her nursemaid and descended the stairs. Amelia stood in the foyer, her eyes bright with unshed tears.

"No progress?" he asked.

She shook her head. "He doesn't want me here. Doesn't want me to see the baby."

Keene looked at the closed door. "I'll talk to him."

"No, Keene, leave him alone."

Keene swiveled around. "What did you do when he told you he doesn't want you here?"

"What could I do? I said I should stay away."

George's words echoed in his head. *Why doesn't she fight for anything?* "I don't believe he truly wants you to stay away."

"I pledged my obedience."

Keene stalked toward the library. He flung back the door. "If you want your wife back, you shall have to stop sending her—what are you doing?"

George straightened from behind his desk where he had yanked open all the drawers, their contents a jumble. Doors on a cabinet hung open. "What did you do with my pistols?"

"I took them. You have no need of them now." More than that Keene had made sure all the powder and shot were removed. "Did you tell Amelia of your losses?"

George turned, his nose red and his eyes puffy. "So I can look like even less of a man in her eyes?"

"If you don't want her here with you, then what need do you have of her good opinion?"

George dropped down into the chair behind the desk.

Amelia stood in the doorway. "What losses?"

"George lost over thirty thousand pounds gambling. Twenty last night and another ten tonight."

"Oh, George." Amelia glided across the room and reached for her husband.

He held out a hand to ward her off.

She drew to a halt, her spine ramrod stiff. Her head dropped forward. She stared at the floor as if she'd become a connoisseur of fine rugs and was determining the exact weaver by the pattern in the Turkish carpet.

Keene watched George's expression turn from belligerence to a plea for comfort, but Amelia couldn't see it with her gaze downward. She lingered for a moment before turning around. "Shall we go, Keene?"

George reached for Amelia's hand, but she was gone.

Victor would have shared an analysis of George's actions, or perhaps another cat dying of a broken heart story, but the only thing Keene could think to say before he shut the door was, "You're a fool."

As Sophie stood outside, the breeze ruffled her short curls. She didn't understand why she'd run away from Keene. It wasn't in her nature to flee from a challenge. But the way she had been trying, subjugating her reckless nature to become some demure, correct, boring lady tugged down her spirits.

If she won Keene's affection under the guise of being something she was not, what good should that be? What good was Amelia's perfect obedience when her one slip was wielded like an ax?

Sophie had no idea why Keene had married her. He would do a lot of the things his father asked out of loyalty, but she knew him too well to believe that he would shackle himself to a woman he disliked. It was only that thought that kept her hanging on to the hope that their marriage could be real in all senses of the word.

Yet, she was tired of banging into his displeasure at every turn. She couldn't make Keene love her, but she could be who she was. She would no longer pursue his good opinion.

She paced down the street, impatient to be on the way. At the end of the block she turned and walked back toward George's house. She didn't want to stray out of the coachman's earshot. She should, of course, wait in the carriage, but she was not the most patient of creatures.

As she drew up alongside the carriage she noticed him leaning against the boot. His dark hair stirred in the breeze. Had he been waiting for her to return? Or waiting to see if she needed rescue?

He stepped away from the carriage. A street lamp behind him silhouetted his broad shoulders and slim build. Now was her chance. Her heart thundered in her ears. She sucked in her breath and stepped forward, her hand landing on his upper arm. When he didn't move forward, she hastily revised her plan to throw her arms around him. Nervously she said, "This seems a perfect place for a kiss, don't you think?"

"I daresay so, if your husband wouldn't shoot me for it later."

She snatched back her hand. "Victor?"

"At your service." He bowed.

Mortification danced a jig in her stomach. "I thought . . ."

"That I was Keene. Yes, I know. Happens all the time."

Sophie giggled. Perhaps her impulsive plan for seduction was meant to be thwarted.

"We do share certain characteristics."

"Just as well. He probably should have found my suggestion quite untoward."

"He does exhibit a regrettable steak of stupidity every now and again. Of course, most often it is laid at my door."

She giggled harder thinking of how it should have been if she had just thrown herself upon him as she'd intended. Perhaps her behavior had been modified by Amelia's teachings.

"Sophie."

She tried to restrain the laughter bubbling inside her. Instead, tears dripped from her eyes. She let loose a hearty peal, and clapped a hand over her mouth.

"It's not funny."

"No, I know." She couldn't stop.

Victor stepped forward. "Your laughter is enchanting."

Was he about to throw caution to the wind and take up her invitation?

Just then the door of the house opened. Keene and Amelia descended the steps.

When they reached the coach, Keene handed Amelia up. He turned to Sophie. "What is so amusing?"

Sophie bit the insides of her lips. "Nothing."

Keene cast a glance toward Victor, who shrugged. Sophie's shoulders shook with her effort to restrain herself. Amelia's martyred silence and Keene's sharp gaze stifled her unmerited mirth soon enough. Although when she looked at Victor and his amused half smile caught her off guard, she suffered a mild relapse.

All the way home, Keene's dark gaze alternated between her and Amelia. Frankly, if he found Amelia's perfectly composed mask more to his liking then more the fool he.

"Would you like to return to the ball?" asked Keene.

"I should," answered Victor.

Sophie looked at Amelia. "I believe Amelia wishes to retire for the night, isn't that so?"

Amelia nodded.

"Yes, but the three of us might return."

And so they did. Keene's dark eyes followed her around the room when he wasn't sweeping her into a waltz, claiming more of them than was appropriate even for a husband. She could hardly take her eyes off him. She barely noticed her friend Mary Frances and Victor sliding off to a dimly lit corner and engaging in a terse discussion.

"What do you think they are talking about?" Sophie asked Keene as he swept her through a turn in the dance.

"Who?"

"Victor and Mary Frances."

"The heiress? Marriage I should imagine."

Sophie stopped mid step and clapped her hands together. "Really?"

"I daresay. I wish you wouldn't stop like that." But his eyes smiled down on her nonetheless.

Another couple swept by them, the woman's skirts brushing their legs. Keene curled his arm around Sophie's waist and pulled her to the edge of the dance floor.

"Oh, she does so hope, but she didn't think she might aspire so high. He is an earl, after all."

"His pockets are to let and hers are rather full."

The bounce in Sophie's step flattened. "That is what he cares about?"

"I daresay he postponed caring about it until he had no choice, but most marriages are based on power alliances or needs of the pocket."

Sophie stared up at Keene. Not hers.

Keene wouldn't have had any need of her modest inheritance, not with being his father's heir. His brother Richard might have been a different story. And certainly she didn't bring any political clout to the union.

Keene propelled her into a curtained alcove. His intense look cast shivers down her spine. He leaned close, his breath warm in her ear. "Sophie, I want you."

Her knees wobbled, threatening to dump her to the floor, but his arm around her waist was a solid bar of support. He swung her around to face him. Her sensitive breasts met the solid wall of his chest, startling a surprised squeak from her.

"Ah, my pet, you do make the most enchanting sounds."

Her ears burned, but her humiliation was short-lived. His lips nibbled hers and warmth swept down her spine, flooding her body. He held her with an easy embrace, while his lips worked magic on hers. Her jaw loosened and he took full advantage, his tongue touching hers, engaging it in a swirling dance.

She clutched his shoulders, fearing her legs wouldn't support her. The kiss went on and on. He threaded his hand through her short curls, holding her head steady for his onslaught, while his other hand rubbed against the small of her back.

An ache started between her legs. She wanted to press that part of herself against him and whimpered when she couldn't figure out how to assuage the pressure.

He slid his hands down, cupping her and pulling her against a hard ridge that met her belly. He lifted her to her toes, tilting her hips to cradle against him.

So close, so close to what she wanted.

His low moan resounded in her ears. Could it be that he felt the same need for pressure, the same frustration at not being able to get it exactly as he wanted? His mouth broke away from hers. His breath rasped against her neck. Each hot moist burst made sensations race along her body, always returning to the low ache in her womanly parts.

He began a new onslaught, his mouth moving against her neck, finding places that cried out for his attention. She shivered in delight and smoothed her hands across his shoulders, wanting to touch every part of him and clutch him closer to her pounding heart.

Memories of moments like these kept her tossing in her big lonely bed at night. Her throat caught with desperation. "Please, I don't want this to end," she whispered.

"Tell me, Sophie."

She floundered with his request.

He pulled his head back, his dark eyes searching her face. His lower body pressed against hers. The ridge of hardness drew her curiosity. "I want you."

She reached inside for the words to pull him to her, to cleave his heart onto hers, to make him love her the way she adored him. "I need . . . I need . . . I need . . ." She couldn't find the words to describe what she thought she wanted. She needed that hard instrument pressing against her lower abdomen, lower yet. She needed it tucked between her legs. How that would help she didn't know, but it felt right.

"No secrets, Sophie, not now."

Her thoughts swirled in confusion. She didn't have any secrets, but he did.

He spoke slowly. "Earlier when we were at George's—"

"Amelia's baby."

"Yes." His eyes held hers, the look so intense she wanted to melt at his feet. She tore her gaze away. His honesty ripped through her, but at the same time a wave of peaceful acceptance followed in its wake.

She put her hand on his waist. His sharp intake of breath sent a starburst of passion coursing through her. She didn't care if he had fathered Amelia's baby. She moved her palm closer to his center, her eyes dropping to the bulge in his breeches. Did she dare to touch him there? "I'm glad you told me. I've suspected for some time, and of course Victor all but told me, and it doesn't matter."

Keene's narrowed eyes and cocked head weren't the response she expected.

"You are the father of Amelia's baby?"

"Good God, no! Victor is."

"He is?"

"There you are."

"Speak of the devil," muttered Keene, discreetly sliding his hands up to Sophie's waist.

"I need to borrow your carriage to see Miss Chandler home." Victor's brown eyes coursed over their intimate embrace. His expression turned wry.

Keene's eyes, dark with passion, held hers. "Get a hackney."

Victor rolled his eyes and stepped forward. "You don't understand," he whispered in Keene's ear. "I need a *closed* carriage."

Keene's head snapped around, his look sharp and accusatory. "Haven't you learned anything?"

Victor heaved a deep sigh. "We shouldn't speak of it before I address Mary's father, but Miss Chandler has done me the honor of agreeing to be my wife, pending her father's acceptance of my suit."

"I shall hold you to that. Your witnesses, ma'am." Keene bowed to her. "Didn't Miss Chandler arrive in her own carriage?"

"A word with you, sir," Victor said.

"I did, but Lord Wedmont has sent my companion home without me." Mary Frances frowned. "Without my leave."

"Not an auspicious beginning, Victor," commented Keene. "Must consult the ladies, especially your future wife."

Sophie was incredulous. "Good advice. Pity you don't hear the words of your own song."

"Hush, pet." Keene chucked her under the chin.

Victor shifted impatiently, silently begging Keene. Although since Keene could barely look away from his flushed wife, perhaps he wasn't quite catching the unspoken plea.

"Very well. Ladies, if you would care to take a turn about the floor, we shall meet you at the door in just a moment."

Sophie tucked her arm in Mary Frances's and leaned her tousled blonde curls close to Mary's smooth dark hair. Mary appeared wide-eyed as Sophie led her away. Perhaps the girl was a little awed at the easy success of her pursuit of a gentleman.

Keene turned his back and leaned his forehead against the wall. "Damn lucky you came along just then. I should have been sneaking along the corridors in a few moments to find a bed."

"Pretty havey-cavey business if you ask me. Let me borrow your carriage to take Miss Chandler home. Just take Sophie home in a hackney."

"Where's your carriage?"

Keene was mighty forgetful or distracted. Definitely distracted. Victor bit back the sarcastic retort hanging on his tongue and settled for a gentle reminder. "I came with you."

"Ah, yes." Keene pulled his forehead away from the wall. He swiveled around and headed for the opening of the alcove. "Well, no hope for it. We shall have to drop Miss Chandler on our way home."

Victor grabbed his arm. "No. Just drop us at your house, and I shall take her in my carriage from there. Although I do think yours is better appointed."

Keene swiveled around and stared him in the eye. "I fear you are about to do Miss Chandler some evil."

"I shall endeavor to be sure she enjoys it quite well."

Keene shook his head, disappointment obvious on his face.

"Oh, give over. I have every intention of making her my

wife. Sooner rather than later. My businessman tells me that Mr. Chandler drives a hard bargain. I should not wish to be in negotiations with him for months on end. And if I do not have my hands in his pockets by the end of a fortnight I shall be cast in the clink."

"I have some money, three thousand pounds I could give you this night."

Sophie's dowry money. No doubt some sense of honor kept Keene from cashing the draft before the marriage was real in all ways.

"It won't be enough. If I can persuade her father there is some urgency to the marriage, I shall procure a special license and then we'll honeymoon in Portugal or Spain. Perhaps I, too, shall have an early stork delivery. Although I fear my luck has not extended to someone else performing the misdeed. No doubt my future bride is a virgin."

"I cannot allow you to misuse my wife's friend."

"Don't draw up stiff on me now. I shan't mistreat her, but I do require a private carriage so I might be assured of enough time to persuade her to my way of thinking."

"Do you love her?"

Victor thought his eyes might pop out of his head. "I cannot fathom that question from you."

Keene paced back and forth in the short alcove, frustration coloring his face at the two steps in, pivot, two steps out.

Victor decided that lying might be the better part of valor in that moment. "I do swear that I hold Miss Chandler in the highest esteem. I believe my emotions have . . ." All right, lying to Keene didn't sit well with him. "I am fond of her and believe I shall easily come to love her. I don't know her that well yet."

"Nor do I, but Victor are you sure? I know she is Sophie's friend, but I am not entirely . . . she . . . something about her troubles me."

Was Keene actually concerned about him? Victor had

thought it was an unmarried woman's seduction Keene objected to. "Her father's pockets should ease your mind."

"I should have seduced Sophie when she came to my room the night I proposed." Keene raked his hand through his hair.

"You do not mean to wait any longer, do you?"

"I don't know that I can." Keene grabbed his arm and propelled him out of the alcove toward the ballroom entrance. "Very well, you may take her in my carriage after we are home."

"Take her I shall." Victor grinned.

"God help me. I have no idea why I am helping you."

"You shouldn't wish to see me in debtor's prison," replied Victor. He glanced toward the entryway where Sophie stood, her eyes bright with anticipation, obviously primed and ready. Beside her Mary Frances stood, her hands nervously clenched together under her chin. He might have a tough row to hoe convincing his bride-to-be that she wanted to be seduced. "Care to give me any pointers?"

"Go slowly, tense women can be deadly. They bite."

Keene stalked toward the door before Victor could wrest an explanation from him.

An hour later, Victor stared at his future bride as she shrank farther and farther into the squabs. "Miss Chandler—may I call you, Mary?—Mary, I thought we should spend this time getting to know each other better."

"My name is Mary Frances, milord."

He took her hand in his. "My name is Victor. Of course, you may call me anything you want. Victor, Vicky, darling, or, of course, you arrogant bastard."

The words startled a slight smile from her.

"Ah, there, you do have a lovely smile, my countess." The night was cool, but sweat streamed down his sides. Never had he had so much at stake. He stroked her hand, his thumb finding the edge of her glove and a patch of bare skin. "You do have the softest skin of any lady I ever knew." She might have had crocodile skin for all he noticed.

"Knew in what way, milord?"

Ah, there was the hint of the bold brassy woman he'd met in the ballrooms and salons. He flashed her a smile he hoped was charming. "Ah, do you want to hear tales of my past exploits? I fear I do not kiss and tell, Mary Frances."

He ran his bare fingers along her cheekbone. "You do have lovely eyes, my dearest."

Victor scooted closer on the seat. He looked at the carriage blanket folded on the opposite seat. "Are you cold, darling?"

She shook her head.

He paused in reaching for the blanket. "Are you very sure, for I want nothing more than your comfort."

"Perhaps then you should sit across from me so I don't have to tweak my head sideways to see you."

In for a penny, in for a pound. "Then how shall I kiss you?"

"You shouldn't."

"All engagements should be sealed with a kiss. You did say yes, did you not?"

She nodded. If her eyes opened any wider he didn't think her eyeballs should stay in her head.

"Don't be frightened, Mary Frances. I swear I shall never do anything to hurt you, now or when you are my wife."

She nodded crookedly.

"But I should ever so much hope that you would allow your betrothed a kiss." He raised her hand to his lips and pressed a kiss against the back of her hand.

Her eyes followed his every move with a wary trepidation.

"Just a taste of your sweet cherry lips should send me to my grave a happy man."

Her brown eyes nearly crossed. Perhaps too much flattery for a city girl. He turned her hand over and sought the tiny expanse of skin between her glove and the sleeve of her pelisse. Her fur muff lay in her lap, her other hand buried inside it.

He stared deep into the warm depths of her eyes. They were really quite fine. She couldn't help it that he preferred blue to brown. He could learn to like her eyes, especially when they flashed with high spirits. He leaned closer to her.

She shrank away.

"Come, my lady, you shall have me believing you find my countenance distasteful."

"Oh, no, I'm sure you are quite handsome." She shook her head, though. Either she didn't think so, or she objected to his fast and loose use of titles.

But he knew his main attraction for her. "And a peer."

"Oh, yes."

"And do you wish to be my countess?"

She nodded, the gleam that he enjoyed entered her eyes.

"Then do let me kiss you."

She squinted her eyes shut and leaned forward, her mouth pursed for a peck.

"Ah, I am pleased that you are not well versed in kissing, my love, but you shall have to learn."

Her eyes popped open. The carriage rounded a corner, and she was thrown toward him. Fortune was smiling on him. He wrapped his arm around her shoulder to steady her. She struggled against him.

"Easy, my countess."

She stopped instantly.

That was the trick, then, to remind her that she would be gaining a title when she married him. He tilted her chin up and feathered the lightest of kisses against her throat just behind her ear. Her startled intake of breath was no assurance that she liked his caress.

Her stare was not quite settled as he pulled back. He held her eyes as long as he could stand to before leaning in and brushing his lips across hers. At this rate seducing her would take an eternity, but the coachman was instructed to drive around Mayfair until hearing a knock on the pass-through. Then he was to feign being unable to find her street.

Her eyes fluttered open as he waited for her response.

"See there, not so bad, was it?"

She touched her hand to her lips with such a bemused expression. His groin tightened in response. He lifted her hand, placed it on his shoulder and repositioned her for another kiss, a real kiss this time.

Her participation was delayed, but the uncertainty made his heart pound with tenderness and desire. He whispered encouragement against her lips, before plunging in for another kiss. She welcomed him this time, straining toward him. He pushed her muff to the floor and stroked her back.

He reminded himself again and again to go slowly, but his bride-to-be displayed her own enthusiasm. He lowered her to the seat and kissed her deeply, her body softly pliant beneath his chest. He twisted to lie on top of her, framing her face with his hands. Her hair had pulled loose from the topknot. As he settled over her, he found the top button of her pelisse.

She screamed and pushed all in one motion. Suddenly her willingness and compliance was a flurry of thrashing legs and shoving arms and twisting skirts. Her hands raked out, her fingers curled into claws.

A knee nearly caught him in the groin and his cheek stung from a blow or scrape. Victor's first thought was to protect himself. He curled his legs up on either side of her twisting body and sat on her, catching an arm in either hand and pinning them against the side of the carriage over her head. "Shhhhh!"

The carriage stopped.

Her eyes flashed white in the dim interior, too much white, like a frenzied horse. "Hush, Mary Frances, I'll stop. Shhhhh, hush. Don't hit me."

He reared back, dodging her snapping teeth.

EIGHTEEN

Sophie handed her wrap to the butler while Keene stood in the doorway looking out after the carriage he'd sent away with Victor and Mary Frances in it.

"Would you like a tea tray sent to the drawing room, sir?"

"No, Blythe, we are retiring for the evening. Would you have Letty sent to Mrs. Davies's room."

"Very good, sir. Your valet?"

"I won't be needing him."

Sophie didn't wait for her husband to close the door. No doubt he intended to go out again. Otherwise, why would he refuse his servant? So many times he'd brought her to the brink of desperate yearning, then left her all alone. She flew up the stairs, her slippers pounding the steps beneath her feet. She heard his voice behind her, but didn't stop to listen.

She didn't think she could stand another time of watching him slip back out the door as if he couldn't stand to remain in the same house with her.

Keene watched Sophie's headlong flight up the stairs with amused interest. She was either very eager, or very energetic. Both, he hoped. They still hadn't resolved the pregnancy issue, but he no longer cared. He would coax a confession from her in the aftermath, but he could barely stand the delay to let her maid help her undress.

He should have volunteered to play lady's maid but he felt too impatient to deal with the tapes, ties and pins of her clothing. Better to maintain the proprieties and only contend with her nightgown. Because he was quite sure he would very likely rip her evening gown from her lovely body.

He crossed into the library and poured himself a brandy. Not because he needed it, but because he feared he would sprint up the stairs himself. His hand shook as he raised the glass to his lips. How could he go slowly enough for her, if he felt this desperate for her touch?

Each tick of the clock sounded loud to his ears, and echoed in the taunt tenseness of his body. One second closer, one second closer, but the minutes were like eons. The quarter hour he forced himself to wait grew to an eternity.

His brandy sat on the desk in the library. He left it after one sip. He ascended the stairs, forcing himself to take each tread and not bound over a single riser. Anticipation pounded in his gut. Desire and need made him hard as stone and would have made his valet's help to undress a rather embarrassing proposition.

He forced himself to remove each article of clothing slowly and methodically. He stood naked in his cool room, praying for control, before he pulled his dressing gown around him and headed for the connecting door to Sophie's room.

There was no response to his soft knock, but he knew she couldn't be asleep yet. He cracked open the door and peered around. Lamplight filtered over the turned-down empty bed. He stepped into the unoccupied room, desire crashing into disappointment. Where was she?

"Stop it, Mary Frances." Victor grabbed for the fist she managed to jerk free while he avoided her bite.

Her name was too damn long. She cuffed him in the head before he managed to get it out. "I'm not hurting you. And I'm not letting you go until you calm down."

"You're trying to ravish me."

"I'm not trying to ravish you. I was trying to seduce you."

" 'Tis a fate worse than death."

"It is not. It's a rather enjoyable thing we'll do together when we're married."

She didn't look convinced, but at least she was listening, although her hair covered half her face like a wild woman from the Amazon.

"Now will you stop kicking and biting?"

She gave him a mean stare. Bloody hell, did he really want to marry this vixen? Did he have any choice? He needed her father's money. Damn it, one minute she'd been enjoying his kisses, the next she was thrashing around like a trapped wildcat.

"Now stop this, for I need to see why the coachman has stopped."

The fight went out of her in a whoosh. "We must be at my home."

No chance of that. The coachman had been given explicit instructions to keep driving until he had Victor's signal. Still, there must be some impediment to the carriage's progress. He tentatively let go of her wrists.

She covered her face with her hands. He pulled her to a sitting position, backing off of her in the same motion.

"Why?" she whispered. "Why would you seduce me? I don't have the lineage or powerful relatives to protect me. My only recommendation is my fortune. I am only a daughter of a wealthy tradesman. Without my virtue I have little value."

A wave of tenderness swept over Victor, in spite of the sting in his cheek. "That's not true. You have beauty to recommend you. I should desire you if you were penniless."

"But you shouldn't marry me."

"But we are to marry. We've settled that, haven't we?"

"I don't know. I don't understand. I know that more than anything it must be my fortune that draws you."

He pulled her hands away from her face. "It is, and I need it quickly, love. But I do think that we can find a way to love each other in spite of my title being what draws you."

A knock sounded on the carriage door. *What the devil was his coachman about?*

"Mary Frances, I should be glad to approach your father the minute we reach your house. I do mean to make you my countess, but I should like it done quickly."

He could be making the biggest mistake of his life in being candid with her, but he sure as hell thought Keene and George were going about marital honesty all wrong.

"Why quickly?"

The knock sounded on the door again. *What the devil was up?* "I have quite a few outstanding debts, love. I'm rather in the suds and cursed close to being tossed in debtor's prison. I don't want a devilish long delay in marrying you, and your father is known to drive a hard bargain. A certain urgency in needing to marry might give me an edge in negotiations. Plus, I did think we might have a bit of pleasure in creating a pressing need to marry quickly."

He leaned over and opened the door. "Why the devil aren't we moving?"

"Begging your pardon, sir. We do seem to be in front of your friend Keeting's house and there does seem to be a bit of a to-do."

Mary Frances pulled her long sable hair back from her face. "So I am just a commodity to you?"

"You are much more than that. You are to be my wife. I don't take that lightly." He turned to his coachman. "What kind of a to-do?"

Sophie eased around the door into Amelia's room. The light peeping through the threshold indicated she was still awake. And Sophie was far too keyed up to fall asleep alone in her bed.

"How are you doing?"

Amelia put her finger in the book she held in her lap and

closed it. She patted the bed beside her. "As well as can be expected, I suppose."

The puffy redness around her eyes spoke of tears.

Sophie stepped closer to the bed and folded her arms behind her back. "Are you upset that I suggested we see your daughter? It went worse than I thought it would."

Amelia raised her knees under the bedcovers and leaned forward. "I was glad to see her. And how should I ever know how it would go if I never tried?"

"Well, waiting hasn't changed much." Sophie took another step closer to the bed. "I do think I owe you an apology."

"Not for suggesting I visit my child. I am so glad I saw her and held her again. Besides, I am sure you are right. It is better to do something rather than wait endlessly for someone else to do something."

Sophie folded a leg underneath her and sat beside Amelia. "You mean your husband?"

She nodded. "It doesn't appear that my absence has made his heart grow fonder."

"I don't know, gambling to excess does not sound like the move of a contented man." Of course, her father would lament gambling in any form. "Perhaps he doesn't like you being away from him any better."

Amelia shrugged and the sheet slipped down a bit.

"But I do owe you an apology, for I mistook the situation. I thought that the father of your baby—"

"You mean Victor?" Amelia plucked at the sheet.

"Well, yes, but that wasn't what I thought. I thought Keene—well that you and he—I thought he'd fathered your baby. And I do believe I was rather cool to you."

"Oh, no, not Keene, and you have never been cool."

"Have you and he . . . ?"

"Never." Amelia's expression was incredulous. "I can't believe you have said this to me."

"I'm sorry."

Amelia's blue eyes sparkled. "No, it is wonderful. Even if

I thought such a thing, I shouldn't say it, ever. I do so admire your forthright manner."

"Rather leads me to trouble more often than not."

Amelia reached out and tapped Sophie's shoulder. "We all have our weaknesses. I should say that if Keene had been interested, I would have. . . . But he has eyes for no one but you." She wrapped her arms around her knees. "I am quite jealous, if you must know."

Sophie studied her houseguest, wondering if Amelia was being honest, but there was something so intimate and open about sitting together in their nightclothes discussing things. "I fear there is little of which to be jealous. Keene is quite oblivious to my presence."

"No, he is not. I have seen how he looks at you."

"How does he look at me?"

"Like he wants to . . . you know, bed you again and again." Amelia blushed. "Heavens, how I miss that part of my marriage. I could take George's distaste for me if he would just welcome me back into his bed."

Midnight confidences and all that, Sophie felt she had to confess. "Keene's never . . . I, he has never shared his bed with me. What is it like?"

"He what?"

"We've never—at least I don't think we have. We've kissed, but he always stops before it feels as if we're through."

"Sometimes it takes a while. Gentlemen tend to finish first."

"How long? For I should like to . . ." Sophie thought of that curiously hard part of his anatomy that had been pressed against her abdomen earlier and faltered when she didn't know the words to use to describe it. ". . . have more. I mean, he kissed me earlier at the ball. But always when we come home, he goes to his room and I mine, and there we stay. I wait for him in my bedroom, but he never comes to me. He often leaves the house."

Amelia stared at her in disbelief. "Fustian!"

Sophie shook her head and to her dismay a big fat tear rolled down her nose and dripped on the bedspread.

"Oh, my poor Sophie." Amelia leaned over and wrapped her arms around her shoulders. "Perhaps he is being cautious with your inexperience. Did you give him the impression his urges scared you?"

"Well, after the wedding when Victor told me Keene had shot him, I did flinch a couple of times, but I was never scared of the . . ."

"Making love," supplied Amelia.

"I was never scared of that." With her head dipped down, Sophie noticed that Amelia's night clothing was very different from the long flannel gown she slept in. She leaned back and examined the revealing lace-edged scoop neck of the nearly sheer gown. "What are you wearing?"

"A nightgown. George did so like my nightgowns." Amelia pushed back the covers and slid her legs out of bed. "I had one made up for after I recovered from having the baby. Although why, I shouldn't know. Because it always ended up on the floor far too quickly to be worth the effort of tying all the ties."

Sophie's face flamed. "On the floor?"

Amelia swiveled around and stared at her. "Stars above, Keene really hasn't made you his wife yet, has he?"

Sophie shook her head.

"You want him to, don't you?"

"More than anything."

"Then you shall have to show him you are ready. George was rather shy at first, but I wouldn't have thought . . ." Her voice trailed off. Amelia opened a drawer and pulled out a frothy concoction of lace and ribbons. "Here, wear this and go to him. He'll understand."

Sophie clutched Amelia's nightgown to her and stared at Amelia. "What is it like? Is it as wonderful as when he kisses me?"

"Better."

"I can't take your nightgown."

"I'm not using it. It's not the sort one wears when sleeping alone. Here, I'll help you put it on, and there's a wrapper, too." Amelia's gaze swept over Sophie's nightgown. "Besides, you look like a nun in that. Is it any wonder Keene stays away?"

Keene paced around her room like a caged tiger. Finally, he conceded defeat with a growl. He couldn't prowl the house looking for her while wearing only his silk dressing gown. He slammed into his room and grabbed his breeches from the neatly folded stack, shoved his legs into them and then sank down to a chair and fisted his hands in his hair.

Where was she? Still in the house? Did he want to know if she wasn't? The seconds ticked by as he hovered in uncharacteristic indecision.

He turned his head as the whisper of the connecting door drew his attention.

Sophie stepped into his bedroom, her feet bare, her body sheathed in a frilly insubstantial gown of nothing, covered by a sheer wrapper. She stood still in the doorway, her body clearly silhouetted by the light behind her.

He sat stock still, desire building in his body, throbbing in his loins, pounding in his soul. He wanted her so badly he couldn't move.

"I couldn't sleep. I thought perhaps we could talk."

"By all means. Come in." His voice was hoarse.

She stepped forward and shrugged out of the insubstantial wrapper, leaving her arms bare. She leaned forward just a bit to drape the wrapper on the doorknob.

He could see the smooth globes of her breasts, the merest half moons of pale pink nipples teased him, before she straightened. He swallowed hard, forcing himself to look in her face.

"It is a bit warm in here, isn't it?" she said.

No, it wasn't. Goose bumps stood out on her bare arms.

His gaze was drawn to the beaded tips of her breasts. Cold or desire? "Nearly an inferno. Perhaps your nightgown is too warm."

She took another step in the room, and folded her arms behind her back. The movement thrust her pert breasts forward and exposed the cleft between them through the now gaping ribbons down her front. Her nipples were barely concealed by the gown, playing a hide-and-seek game with his libido.

Her boldness amused him, but at the same time there was a piece of him that dreaded what it meant. Inexperienced innocents didn't have the confidence to stage all-out seductions. What had happened to her tentlike high-necked night wear?

Yet, the sight of her flirtatious removal of her wrapper had his blood thundering. He folded his arms across his chest. How far would she go?

"Do you like it, Keene? Do you think it is too fussy? All these ribbons." She tugged at the ribbon threaded through the scooped neckline of gown. "Perhaps I should remove some of them."

"By all means, if you feel they are unnecessary."

Removal of the ribbon she had her fingers on would loosen the low neckline even more. His heart danced with anticipation. Ribbons held the edges together down her front. Would she be daring enough to untie all those?

She toyed with the ribbon. He wanted nothing more than to sit and wait out her play, but he couldn't stand it anymore. "Let me help."

He had the ribbons untied in seconds. Her hands hovered shoulder high as if she would assist him if he stumbled or knotted the ties, but he was too sure of what he wanted to risk a delay caused by impatience. He drank in the creamy white skin, the soft swell of her breasts. He touched a finger to the material's edge, ready to peel back the gown, when her startled breath drew his gaze to her face.

Her eyes were wide and bright, too bright. Her expression tense and uncertain. Was she scared? "Sophie?"

She stared at him. His body pounded in a demand for release. Yet, this was the first time he'd ever made love to his wife. She deserved a slow seduction, kisses, caresses, soft words, and his control was like a thrown glass speeding toward the hearthstones.

"Do you know what you do to me?" he whispered.

She gave a tiny uncertain shake of her head.

Waves of desire crashed through him. He couldn't do it. He couldn't go slowly with her, not nearly as slowly as she deserved. Never had he felt so desperate for a woman. "Touch me, love. I'm dying for you."

Her hands inched forward, landing tentatively on his shoulders. His breath rasped in and out. The coolness of her fingers clashed with the heat of his skin and shot ragged sensations ripping through his veins. He couldn't take her while she was so tense, but desperate longing bade him ignore her nervousness.

Yet, some place in his brain kept reminding him her pleasure in this meant more than his, which was an odd twist on his belief that seeing to a woman's pleasure would heighten his, but he was too far gone to sort out nuances.

He traced his finger along the edge of the open material, his eyes drinking in her every response. When her lips parted he leaned forward, diving into the welcome warmth of her mouth, tasting and teasing her.

Her welcome return of his kiss brought a hitch to his breathing. He wanted to kiss her forever, all the way through. Yet, he wanted to press his lips to every square inch of her flesh. He shoved his dressing gown off, letting the silk pile on the floor around his feet. Her hands against his bare flesh were nearly enough to send him over the edge. Her tiny caresses spun webs of enchantment.

He pulled her against him, molding every inch of her pliant body against his harder frame. Shudder after shudder ripped through him. He continued the kiss until in his head he was begging her to push forward, to take the next step, to give him a sign that she was ready to be stripped of the insubstantial nightgown and tossed on his bed, the secrets of her body ready to be plundered.

No longer able to get air to his lungs, he broke away from her mouth, his breath rasping in and out. He stroked his shaking hands down her back, molding her curves and pressing her closer and closer.

Her breath was coming harder, heavier, but not nearly as labored as his. "Sophie, I can't hold back. I need you too badly."

He sought her face, her lovely blue eyes. She stared at him. He pushed her hand down to feel the pulsing hard length of him and nearly lost his mind as her fingers closed around him, and her gaze dropped down. The movement of her hand might be tacit permission to push forward, but he wasn't sure. After all, he'd placed her hand there. He groaned and pushed her hand away, fearing he wouldn't last through her ministrations.

He kissed her neck. "Tell me what you want, what you need. I swear to you I'll please you. We'll make love all night long if that is what it takes." He kissed lower, down the open neckline of the nightgown. He traced his finger down, blazing the path for his mouth.

Her stiff intake of breath mirrored his own wonder as he edged back the sides of the nightgown and her lovely breasts filled his vision. He circled one rosy tip with his finger, watching it pucker and tighten.

"Tell me what you like, love," he murmured just before he took the perked nipple in his mouth.

"Oh, that," she whispered. "Th-that feels good."

He pushed the nightgown from her shoulders with only the fleeting thought that in the future he might use it to tease her with. Not tonight, though. His need was too urgent. He'd waited far too long.

He sought her mouth, mimicking the moves he wanted to make with their lower bodies. Swirling, dipping, rubbing against her playful tongue. His hands remained at her breasts, engaging in the play and tease of her flesh. He stroked his fingers along the curves, nipped at the pink tips, and lifted the weight of them in his hands.

He was so hard, each throb was painful. His skin was on fire. He could no longer deny himself the release he craved. He needed to be inside her, her softness around him, and the sensation of spilling his seed into her warm wet flesh. Every restraint he had stretched to the breaking point. He shook under the strain of holding back.

"Sophie, I can't wait any longer. I need you. I promise I'll see to your pleasure in any way you want, but I need you now."

"I only want to please you," she whispered.

It was enough for him. He forced out the thought that the love play time was too short and stripped her nightgown down past her hips, leaving it to froth on the floor. He shed his unfastened breeches as he backed her to the bed. Her eyes were wide as he lifted her to the mattress, the blue only a slim rim around the black of her irises.

Her face was flushed, the skin of her chest pink. Her eyes dipped and darted back up to his as if she didn't dare look upon his body. He had no such qualms about looking his fill as he knelt on the bed and positioned her with her head on the pillow. He pushed her legs apart, the glimpse of her glistening woman's flesh sending a new agony of desire crashing through his already overloaded system.

She raised partway up, and he pushed her down, settling between her legs, his rod nudging the tender folds of her center. He bit back the urge to thrust forward. His body quaked in response to his demand for self-control.

"You're trembling," she whispered.

"Quite unusual, love. I don't usually. Are you ready for me?" He searched her eyes, regretting his haste, but helpless before his raging desire.

He'd wanted her too long. Long before she was his wife, long before she was even a grown woman. He'd wanted her that day he pulled her from the river. The knowledge was a revelation to him, yet not a surprise. On some level he must have always known he wanted her. He threaded his fingers through her short blonde curls and held her eyes with his.

Her face had gone from pink to fiery red and her embarrassment charmed him, amused him and frustrated him as he waited for her consent.

"Please, I think so." She bit her lip.

He kissed her tortured lip with his eyes wide open. Hers fluttered shut.

"No, Sophie, open your eyes."

He pushed his hips forward as she met his stare.

"Oh," she whispered. "Please."

Oh, was right. He slid into her flesh and met—

"Ow!"

—resistance. *Ow?* He shifted, wondering if he had the angle wrong like the greenest of boys and pushed forward again.

She dug with her heels, trying to get away from him.

"Sophie, I need you. Don't fight me."

His plea stopped her struggles. He stared into her eyes and his heart melted. "Ow" wasn't the most romantic sweet nothing he'd ever heard whispered in the heat of the moment, but coming from her it poured another layer of desire on his already befuddled wits. His pregnant wife was really a virgin?

NINETEEN

Sophie fought to contain her panic. She wanted to please Keene, but he seemed to be asking her to contribute in ways she didn't know how.

Sensations so new and powerful rode through her on wave after wave, and she didn't know quite how to respond or channel the stormy sea of passions. Everything had gone so fast to this point. Her reactions tossed her around like a small ship at the mercy of titanic swells.

His gaze was so dark and penetrating she feared she would melt into him, yet it anchored her to him. He was her beacon in these uncharted waters.

But the hard push of his male part against her wasn't working. Yet he pressed into her with a relentless pressure, and she thought she might cry out again. Amelia had said there might be some pain, but that it was nothing, over in a trice.

"Sophie, darling, relax. Trust me, it will only hurt worse if you fight me."

The pressure against her eased, and she drew a deep breath. "It won't work. You're much too large to fit."

Keene grinned. "It will work."

He thrust his hips forward, this time he held her shoulders so she couldn't move away. The resistance of her body broke. He slid his shaft inside her, stretching and filling her to completion. The brief pain disintegrated to nothing. His groan resounded in her ears as he dipped his head down to her shoulder.

She marveled at the intimacy of his body within hers, his skin against hers, the beat of his heart so near her own, his breath caressing her face. This was as close to heaven as she'd ever been. This was love.

He lay perfectly still, except he quivered low like a bow stretched taut. She smoothed a hand over the tight muscles of his back and was surprised to find a light sheen of perspiration. In spite of what she'd said earlier to excuse removing her wrapper, the room was chilly. She wasn't cold with him lying over her, covering and warming her skin with his, but he didn't have her body blanketing him.

She turned and kissed his cheek where it lay so near her own. "You're trembling."

"I'm a dolt. I have gone much too fast for you, and I can't hold back." He propped himself on his elbows and stroked her face. His eyes so darkly disturbing to her before were full of tenderness and concern. "I don't want to hurt you, didn't want to hurt you."

"It doesn't hurt now."

His hips rocked, and she heaved in a startled breath at the coiling tight sensation that built where his body joined hers.

"You're certain?"

She nodded. His mouth found hers and began anew with the pleasure of kissing, while he slowly drew in and out of her, layering passion on top of pleasure. His movements grew more urgent, more desperate. Sophie writhed beneath him, seeking a harbor in the storm of her emotions and this new swelling tide of sensations. Yet, she knew the journey would end where it should, because she loved him with all her soul, and he must love her to share this so intimate and private pleasure with her.

He shuddered and groaned and thrust into her. A torrent of warm heat flooded her body as he slumped against her, his manhood pulsing within her, his breath coming in heavy gasps. She wasn't quite sure what had happened, but she knew he had burst through some dam and released himself into her.

A flood of tenderness and love swept over her.

She wanted nothing more than to embrace Keene, to tell him how she had always loved him, from when she was a little child following him around.

Surely, now that he had made her his wife, he wouldn't leave her alone all the time. Perhaps he had waited so long to bed her to allow his own feelings to grow.

He stirred, turning his lips to her shoulder and pressing damp kisses on her skin. He stroked her hair and shifted to his elbows. He rained tender kisses on her face.

Sophie wiggled, the heaviness of her lower body impatient with the ceased movements. "Is that all?"

Keene grinned. "No, not for you, but give me a minute. I'm spent." Yet, his hands began a slow roaming journey over her skin, leaving trails of starbursts in his wake.

Sophie couldn't imagine feeling more content, more loved, in spite of the tenseness of her body. His full attention filled her with satisfaction and a hunger for more. The only thing she could imagine intruding on this sense of well-being was if he began ignoring her again. And surely he wouldn't do that.

"What sort of a to-do?" Impatience threatened to get the better of Victor. Would he have been able to persuade Mary Frances to continue her seduction without the fisticuffs if his coachman had continued driving as instructed?

"Well, it seems the servants have dragged several mattresses out into the street, my lord."

"Perhaps they intend to beat the bugs out."

The coachman frowned. "I hardly think so, sir. It appears that they think they might cushion his landing."

Mary Frances whispered, "What is the problem?"

Victor leaned through the door to follow the line of his coachman's outstretched arm and pointed finger. "Bloody hell!"

* * *

"Oh, well if you are tired, you needn't—oh!" Sophie curled her fingers into the sheets at the long sweep of Keene's hand over her curves.

A smile of satisfaction tugged on his lips, even as he pressed them to the graceful column of her neck. He should have taken more time teaching her the wonders of making love, spent more time to be sure she was more than receptive. He should have had her hungering for his touch the way he had for hers. Except he hadn't realized it was the first time for her.

He was a complete and utter idiot. She was no more pregnant than he was. How her parents had reached that conclusion he didn't know, but he could shoot them for making him delay this moment of wonder for three months. Well, he could shoot them if he felt the least bit of anger with the world, but he only felt foolish.

He rolled to his back, taking her with him. She sprawled on top of him, and he rubbed his hands down her back, loving the feel of her. Concerned she might grow cold, he gathered the covers to pull over them.

"We are done, then?"

His wife was lovely and oh so damnably innocent. Even though he wanted nothing more than to fall asleep with her in his arms, he fought the replete languor that followed his explosive climax. He couldn't remember the last time he had felt this wonderful. Perhaps he never had, but Sophie was not by any stretch of the imagination satisfied, and what was worse, she had no idea what was wrong, but her chaotic breathing and her wriggles told their own story.

"Not in the least. We are just moving to the next entertainment." The lady's pleasure.

He might have to go for a long cooling walk later if he thought too long upon slaking his needs upon her again tonight. He didn't want her sore. Her body's tensile resistance had surprised him, but then, virgins were not his usual fare.

With her surprise and dismay at the delay, she was no doubt caught as unaware as he was by her body's fragile barrier.

Slowly he roamed his hands over her body, while he pressed kisses anywhere he could reach. She grew expectantly still on him. "Are we doing it again?"

Not exactly. "Would you rather talk?"

She shrugged.

He shifted her body to rest beside him, where he could touch her more freely. "I'd rather kiss you."

Her lips were pliant under his. Her taste swirled on his tongue, sweeter than nectar. Her eager whimper and heartfelt sigh when he ended the kiss charmed him to the bottom of his feet where her toes tangled with his.

He stared into her blue eyes and grinned. The smiles kept coming even though he was trying damnably hard to complete the serious business of training his wife, a business he hoped to take a lifetime with.

She stared back. "Why did we wait so long?"

Because he was a stark raving lunatic. That was one way to erase his amusement. The last thing he wanted was to tell her he had doubted her virtue. The reason hardly made sense in light of the evidence and would only misdirect her pleasure. "Someday I'll explain."

Her forehead crinkled. "Not now?"

"Not now." He kissed the tip of her nose, feeling a wave of love sweep over him. He resisted it for a moment, but then it seeped through him like a gentle flood. He did love her, more than he realized before now. In this moment, loving her felt like the only right thing.

He circled her breast with his fingertips. She edged her chin down and her gaze dipped. Her shift away from his touch startled him. Right now he simply wanted to show her the world and return to her the gift of complete fulfillment.

Perhaps he had spent too long regaining his equilibrium. He knew a woman's desire left untended could flicker out. He would spend all night rekindling it if he had to, but perhaps Sophie wanted to talk.

He scooted her closer to his body and tugged her legs over his. "That was one hell of a nightgown, Sophie. Will you wear it again for me?"

"Amelia said it should end up on the floor so fast as to make its wearing pointless."

Did Amelia have something to do with his wife's presence in his bedroom? "Not pointless, love. But I shall endeavor to leave it on longer next time, if that should please you."

Her blue eyes held questions.

He swallowed harder. Did he have the answers for her? Never had it mattered so much. He feared saying the wrong thing, doing the wrong thing. "What, Sophie?"

"Why did you marry me?"

He could lie and say he loved her, which he suspected he did at the time but hadn't known it. He searched for a reasonable explanation. The truth was he hadn't wanted to marry her and had only done so because he'd had his hand forced, and he was damnably glad his father had greased his path to give him what he really wanted. "Does it matter?"

Her eyes glistened in the dim light, and she shifted her gaze away to stare up at the canopy of the bed. He doubted she found the draperies fascinating all the sudden.

He took a deep breath and dug in. "Sophie, my father made you his heir."

"I can't inherit." Her gaze shot to his. "His estate is entailed."

"Only a small part. Before, Richard was to have most of the estate and the farms. I would only have the title and the old estate house with the ten acres it sits on."

"The dower house? Oh, Keene, why?"

Her face scrunched in both concern and confusion. True, she couldn't inherit the title, but was she ready for explanations that his father hadn't sired him, that he had no idea who his natural father was? And did it matter to the point he wanted to make?

"Why would he do that?"

The words tumbled out of his lips before he could stop them. "I'm not his son."

He held his breath, waiting for her reaction. Not many people knew. Victor knew, and he'd just told George, and now Sophie knew. Of everyone, her opinion mattered most. His real father could be a stable hand for all he knew.

"You married me to get your father's estate?"

No. She would have control over her inheritances and the ability to decide to pass them on to their children. "No! I'll never get it."

Her blue eyes filled with moisture.

"It doesn't matter, Sophie." What mattered was he could have walked away from his father's blackmail. In anything else he would have refused. He would have refused any other woman. But it was her, handed to him, and even when he thought she carried another man's child, he'd wanted her. He'd been ridiculously blind.

Many times in his life he'd considered leaving England and making his fortune elsewhere, but once marriage to Sophie was an option, the idea of leaving deserted him. Oh, he suspected he'd wanted her all along.

"It *does* matter." Her voice trembled.

He framed her face with his hands. "What matters is that you are my wife and I—"

A pounding on the door made them both jump.

"Keene, are you in there? You have to come, now." The door crashed open, and Victor charged into the room.

"Bloody hell!" Keene flattened his body over Sophie's. "Get out!"

Victor scooped up Keene's clothing off the chair and tossed it toward him. "You have to come, *now.* George is about to kill himself. You have to stop him."

Keene's heart froze. He twisted to look at Victor. The horror and dread on Victor's face spoke to Keene like nothing else could. Victor hadn't looked this alarmed when they faced each other with pistols at dawn. He didn't think his friend even realized Sophie was in the bed with him.

"We'll finish this when I get back." He slid out from under the sheet and grabbed his breeches.

Victor must have belatedly realized how intrusive his interruption was, but instead of a characteristic sarcastic remark he jerked around and paced away. "He's about to leap from his roof. Mary Frances is talking to him, but, God, Keene, you have to save him. Your carriage is outside."

"Did you tell Amelia?" Sophie sat up, the sheet clutched to her chest.

Victor swung around, his face pale. "Good God, no!"

"I'll come with you." She swung her legs to the side of the bed.

"Sophie, just stay here. I'll handle this. I don't want you there." He didn't want her parading around naked in front of Victor, either. Keene grabbed his boots and a shirt and headed out the door.

Victor was right on his heels. "Your pardon, ma'am." He paused long enough to pull the door shut.

The silence of the room chilled Sophie. She put her head in her hands. Keene had married her because she was his father's heir. And he'd left her again. She'd never felt more alone in her life.

She threw her head back and kept the tears from spilling out. Admittedly, Keene had a good reason to leave her this time, but it hurt nonetheless. He didn't want her with him while he dealt with a crisis. Perhaps the only place he wanted her was in his bed, and even that had only followed her throwing herself at him.

Her heart bled. Was this how George felt? He shouldn't, because Amelia did love her husband. But Sophie had no such assurance. Keene married her because she was his father's heir.

It was almost too much to absorb. But beyond her own

problems, Amelia deserved to know that her husband was about to leap to his death. Sophie pushed back the covers, ignored the stain on the sheets and scurried into her own room to get dressed. She slammed the connecting door, even though the point was moot.

"There is only the phaeton, madam. The master has the carriage. And the coachman is gone with them," Blythe said.

"I'll drive."

"Are you sure?" asked Amelia, clutching her arm. Then, "Hurry, please," she whispered.

"Very good, ma'am. I'll have it brought around." Blythe left them to carry out her request. An open phaeton at night might not be the best choice, but it was the only one.

Less than fifteen minutes later they pulled up in front of Amelia and George's home. Servants bobbed around the front carrying lamps, maids sobbed with aprons thrown over their heads.

Keene stood on the roof of his carriage, his white shirt only half buttoned. The cool night breeze rippled his dark hair and the edges of his shirt, exposing the chest that Sophie had so recently laid her head upon. A lump formed in her throat, and a wash of heat swept through her.

His effect on her had always been devastating, now it was earth-shattering. She tore her gaze away from him.

"Oh, God," whispered Amelia beside her. She had her hands over her mouth. She was so pale Sophie was afraid she might swoon.

Sophie followed the line of Amelia's vision. George sat near the edge of the steep slate roof, his feet propped against the gutter, his head buried in his hands.

"George, come down, man. We'll talk this out," Keene shouted.

A gentle rain misted Sophie's face as she stared up at the solitary man.

"No, you don't understand. I can't do it. I can't be what you think I should. I miss Amelia, but I can't pretend that child is mine." The barely audible words drifted down from the man on the roof.

"I'm here," whispered Amelia.

Sophie twisted around, assessing the situation. A pile of bedding littered the street in front of the house. The drop from the roof might not be fatal anyway, unless George chose to dive off head first. She didn't understand why Keene was trying to reason with a crazed man.

A dormer window stood open behind George. The rain picked up, while the habitual London fog stirred by the stiff breeze drifted around in ghostly wisps.

Keene must be freezing in just his shirt. Sophie didn't think he even had socks on. She reached beside her and came up with Keene's jacket and a waistcoat that she'd grabbed at the last moment before leaving.

She signaled to one of the footmen who accompanied them to hold the horses. She handed the garments to Amelia. "Give these to Keene."

She felt the weight of Keene's gaze as she leaped from the side of the phaeton without unfolding the step. She didn't look back at him as she moved toward the house. In the doorway Mary Frances and Victor stood together. She looked disheveled, and he looked distraught.

The distant keen of a baby's cry caused Victor to jerk his head toward the sound.

"Do you know where I might find some rope?" asked Sophie.

Victor stared up the stairs, his face full of yearning. "The baby."

Sophie wasn't even sure he'd heard her. Perhaps Mary Frances would be more assistance. "Good idea, go fetch the little darling and take her to her mother." Amelia would need to be occupied.

Victor met her eyes briefly before bounding up the stairs.

Sophie followed him into the house. Mary Frances trailed behind her.

"We need to find a length of cord or something we can use to rescue George."

"My father is going to kill me." Mary Frances's eyes glazed. "I can't believe this is happening to me."

As far as Sophie could see there wasn't that much happening to Mary Frances. Surely, she hadn't had her heart broken this night. Or wasn't about to watch her husband destroy himself. No, she'd had a proposal earlier this evening. Had it been just this night? "Help me, and you'll be home sooner."

"I fear I shouldn't bother to go home, now." Mary Frances turned toward the drawing room and bumped into a pedestal with a vase on it.

The vase rocked and Mary Frances grabbed it before it fell. She set it back on the pedestal with a slow deliberation that set Sophie's teeth on edge.

"Stars above. I believe that is a genuine Ming vase." Her voice was filled with awe. "I very nearly broke it."

Sophie didn't care if it was a solid gold vase. She crossed the room to a writing desk near the front window. She opened the drawers of the desk and rummaged through the contents.

Mary Frances backed away from the vase, her hands outstretched as if she would take a flying leap to save the pottery if it decided to plunge to the ground.

The vase didn't matter. George deciding to plunge to meet his maker was the issue at hand. Sophie's hand closed around a ball of twine, no doubt used to wrap packages for mailing. She pulled it from the drawer and flew toward the doorway.

Mary Frances grabbed her arm and steered her a ten-foot-wide berth around the vase. "It has to be worth twenty thousand pounds at the very least."

Sophie shook her off and raced up the stairs. If she could secure George so he couldn't leap, then they could move to the next order of business, getting him in from the roof. She found the open window by the draft spilling down the hallway.

She secured one end of the twine to a bedpost in the room. She stepped over an empty bottle of blue ruin to reach the open window. Lifting her skirts, she climbed out on the rain-slicked slate shingles.

The mist had turned to a steady drone of rain. She inched carefully down to where George sat huddled near the edge of the roof. Now that she was close to him, she could see he was crying, his shoulders shaking.

"I can't live like this," George said repeatedly. He didn't seem aware of her presence.

Sophie could hear Keene, his voice persuasive, but she wasn't sure George was listening. She looped the twine into a circle wide enough to slide over George's head and shoulders.

"Sophie, what the devil are you doing?"

Keene's shout startled George at the same time Sophie slid the loop over his head. He reared back, his flaying hand allowing her to get the loop around his torso, but as she yanked on the end of the half hitch knot she'd tied, her feet slid out from under her.

George shoved her away, and she lost what was left of her balance. She heard Keene's anguished shout as she careened off the edge of the roof.

TWENTY

Keene's heart jolted with a vicious thump as Sophie rolled over the edge of the roof. He lurched forward as her body swung down and came to a swaying halt when she caught the guttering. One of her slippers fell slowly to the ground, turning end over end as it fell to the mound of bedding in the street. His stomach flopped.

Keene hit the cobblestones of the street with a jarring thud, falling to his knees. He belatedly realized he'd jumped from the carriage roof. Beside him Amelia clutched some dark clothing to her chest.

He was up and running before he could think, before he could accept help to rise. He had to stop Sophie from falling. He burst through the door and took the stairs three at a time, cursing every step. What if she fell before he made it? *Please, God, don't let her fall.*

He ran down the hall, his boots clumping on the floor. Victor leaned out of the nursery. "I heard your shout. What happened?"

"Sophie." Her name barely croaked out of his mouth. Keene couldn't get any more words past the block in his throat.

Victor followed him into the room with the open window. Keene dove out the window, his hands slipping on the slick slate. He slid and scrabbled to the edge where he could still see her fingers clasping the rim of the rain trough.

"I tried to reach her. I can't." George struggled against the twine wrapped around him. His every movement tightened the knot holding him in place. "I didn't mean to knock her off. God, I didn't mean to."

Keene didn't pay him any attention. He couldn't lose Sophie, not now. Not when he'd finally found her. He reached her and wrapped his hands around her wrist, holding her, but he had no leverage. He braced a foot against the gutter and tried pulling on her, but he slid toward her instead of hauling her up.

For an eternal second he thought he would slide off, too. George wrapped his arms around Keene and held him, providing him with the resistance he needed.

"I'm going to pull you up."

Sophie raised herself up a couple of inches so she could peer over the edge of the roof. "No, Keene, you can't. There's a window just below me. If you open it, I can get in there."

Keene tugged on her arm. George behind him braced him.

Sophie blanched. "Stop!"

"Help me!" Keene shouted. Her fingers were bleeding, yet she continued to hang onto the gutter rather than release her hold on it. Why didn't she let him have her weight?

"The twine won't hold the weight of the three of us. Please, Keene, let me go."

"No."

"Even if I fall, I should likely just break a leg."

Small comfort. "I can't let you go."

"You can't pull her up, either," commented Victor from the open window. "Hang on, Sophie. I'll get the window open." His voice grew distant. Keene heard him yell for Mary Frances.

Keene pulled on her. He wanted her safe in his arms.

"Let me go, Keene."

"I can't."

"You have to trust me. I don't need you to rescue me."

"Why didn't you stay home?" He couldn't let go of her wrist, yet he slowly realized his hold was futile. But he could no more let go than he could bring the man in the moon close enough to catch her.

He heard sounds below him.

"I've got her legs, let go, Keene." Victor's voice was close, but distorted and disembodied.

George spoke behind him. "Let her go, man."

"If she falls, so help me God, I'll strangle both of you."

"I'll swing toward the window and release," said Sophie. "Don't hold on if I'm not going to make it. Landing on my feet should be better than falling on my head."

"I'll guide you," answered Victor.

"No!" shouted Keene in blind frustration.

"Let me go, Keene. You're hurting me."

"You can't control everything." George tightened his hold around Keene's waist.

Keene released his grip on his wife. His stomach knotted and cramped. He watched her inch along the gutter and then loosen her hold, and he died inside with each movement away from him.

Sophie endured the sickening drop to the window below her. Victor had his hands against her legs. He guided her fall, catching her around her thighs when she was low enough. She feared he might pitch out the window with her if her weight overset them, but he managed to guide her through the casement, and probably saved her some nasty bruises.

Her hands hurt, and her heart pounded in delayed realization that she could have fallen to her death. Victor let her slide to the floor. Sophie held on to him, her arms around his neck. A sob escaped her throat.

He was so similar in body type to Keene that she could close her eyes and pretend it was him, except Keene wouldn't work with her, wouldn't hold her in the aftermath of danger.

Sophie knew in that moment, as Victor held her and rocked her in his arms, that she had to leave. Keene would have chosen the moment to lecture her. Even when he had assisted her off the window ledge at her home, he hadn't offered her comfort, and Lord knew she needed it now. The last thing she needed was a lecture.

Keene charged into the room. Thunderclouds darkened his eyes. He streaked across the room and grabbed Victor's jacket with both hands and yanked him away from Sophie. "Stay away from my wife."

Keene swung Victor into a wall. A small table fell over. Mary Frances took a step toward it and then drew up short.

Victor swiveled around, anger marring his features. "Damn it, man, would you have preferred I let her fall?"

Keene turned toward Sophie, his face twisted in fury. "What the hell were you thinking? Don't you have a brain in your head?"

Sophie swallowed hard and lifted her chin a notch. "What I did made more sense than trying to talk a despondent man out of a desperate act."

Victor stepped forward and put his arm around her shoulders. "Good God, Sophie needs comfort, not a scold."

Keene stepped forward and shoved Victor back toward the open window. "Don't touch my wife again."

He shoved again, and Victor stumbled backward. He gripped the casement on either side of the gaping opening.

For a moment Sophie wasn't sure if Keene meant to push Victor out the window. Keene reached out, his hand fisting around Victor's lapel.

"Don't—"

"Would you try to kill your own brother, again?" Victor's face mottled as darkly as Keene's.

"What?" Keene reeled back almost as if he'd been slapped.

Victor shook his head, straightened his jacket and stepped away from the window. They stood facing each other, as alike as two peas in a pod. Oh, Victor's hair was a shade lighter and longer, but their features twisted in rage were so similar as to defy coincidence.

Victor stood implacably straight and looked at Keene with

an expression of total disdain. Keene's expression was harder to read. Shock and uncertainty surfaced through the anger.

"That's enough, Keene," said Sophie.

"I meant to pull you back," Keene whispered.

Victor smoothed the rumpled material of his jacket. He joined Mary Frances on the far side of the room and wrapped his arm around her waist. She held Amelia's baby in her arms.

"What about George?" asked Sophie. She stared at the picture Mary Frances and Victor made.

"Oh, God, are you all right? I didn't mean to make you fall." George and Amelia entered the room. He trailed the twine behind him, and she hung on to him as if afraid to let him go. He sank down on a chair and buried his face in his hands. "I'm so sorry."

"No harm done." Victor sidestepped Keene.

Keene's face twisted. Sophie resisted the urge to go to him, to offer him comfort. He moved behind Victor and closed the window. When he turned around, a stony mask sat on his face.

Amelia sank down beside George. She took his hands in hers. "I want to come home, George, but you can't keep treating me like I'm the worst person in the world. You've done thoughtless, insensitive things that have hurt other people, too."

"I want you home. I can't live without you, but I've lost all that money and have no way to repay it. We shall be in debt for the rest of our lives. I have made a much worse mess than you."

"You might sell that vase downstairs. Mary Frances says it is worth twenty thousand pounds," said Sophie.

"You have other art around the house. I saw a painting I believe might be a Holbein," offered Mary Frances.

A light of hope crossed George's face, and then he obliterated it. "I can't do it. I can't forget that the baby is not mine."

Victor stepped forward. "You don't have to. Just do the best you can. It won't matter. Or Mary Frances and I can take her and raise her as our own."

Mary Frances jumped. Did she know the baby was Victor's?

"Keene says—"

"Keene doesn't know how good he had it." Victor's voice was laced with venom. "He could have been raised by the man who sired him, but hardly knew his son existed, who forgot to see that there was food on the table or decent clothes to wear. He could have watched his mother languish and rot from neglect, knowing that her husband had fathered a half dozen by-blows among her friends. Some not so willing to participate in the conception."

Keene folded his arms across his chest and looked down.

Victor swiveled and faced him. "No, he has no idea what it is like to envy a half brother who has a parent who sees to his needs. He may have felt the lack of love, but he never curbed his behavior to meet the expectations of the man who raised him. He never had to doubt that his basic needs would be met, that his inheritance would be more than a pile of moldering rocks and nothing left of the estate to maintain it, no farms to raise food, nothing but a mass of ruinous debts."

Sophie's gaze darted to Keene. He could set Victor straight and explain that he wasn't to inherit the bulk of his father's estate, but he remained silent. He watched Victor steadily.

"No, our father was an unforgivable bastard, and you don't know how lucky you had it. Would that I could as easily give my wife total control of her assets and inheritances."

Total control? What was he talking about? Victor's gaze swept over her.

Victor slumped as if the wind had dropped from his sails. He covered his face with his hand. "Now that I have made a complete fool of myself, perhaps we should go, Mary Frances."

But Mary Frances didn't step forward. Instead, Victor crossed to her and bent down and kissed the child's forehead. He turned toward George. "You will do as good a job as anyone can, perhaps a better job than I could. I don't even know her name."

"Regina Victoria Kendra Keeting," supplied Amelia.

Victor's countenance crumbled.

Sophie placed her hand on his shoulder. He patted her hand and whispered to Mary Frances.

She shook her head. "I can't go home. It is too late."

"Then it is off to Gretna Green, and I shall have to rely on your father's reasonableness."

Mary Frances bit her lip.

"He can be reasonable, can't he?"

"Occasionally."

"For a countess, perhaps."

Victor raised Sophie's hand to his lips. He leaned forward and whispered, "I hope you are all right, and we have done no harm to your baby."

What baby?

"There isn't any baby." Keene stepped forward.

Sophie stared at him and cast a questioning glance in Victor's direction.

Victor seemed incredulous. "There isn't?"

"Not unless she has just conceived my child."

"How do you know?" Victor frowned at Keene.

Keene's lips curled in a wry half smile. His eyes held Sophie's. "I believe there was only one immaculate conception."

Sophie took a step back. "You thought I was with child?"

Keene stepped toward her. "Your parents told me you were."

"How could they have thought that?" Disbelief stunned her. She shook her head. "They didn't say that."

"Something about seeing you in a man's bedroom, and of course the fainting," supplied Victor. "Your father did say it. I overheard."

Keene gave him a nasty look.

Sophie thought back to when she had gone to Sir Gresham's room to calm him in the midst of his nightmares. "Oh, there was that time I—"

"It hardly matters," interrupted Keene.

"Oh, good grief, Sophie, your fall from Grace—the horse

named Grace," supplied Mary Frances. "She had a concussion. You did say you landed on your head."

Sophie nodded. How could he have thought she was pregnant?

"Algany drugged us both at Almack's, didn't he?" Amelia added.

"He tried to do it again at the opera, but I switched the glasses, and just to be sure, I accidentally on purpose dumped mine out. When he refilled it, I slipped most of it into his glass."

Mary Frances giggled. "When I first met you I thought you were Victor's mistress."

"Quite a few people thought you were Victor's mistress," said Keene.

"But I never . . . except that one time I thought he was you."

Keene drew in a stiff breath, his nostrils flaring. He turned toward Victor.

Victor threw up his hands and backed away. "I never laid a hand on her. Family loyalty and all that."

Keene winced. "Are you sure of it? Your father . . . ?

"No, I am not sure, but all my life I have been mistaken for you. Even at Eton, they would see me and call out your name, the students, the instructors, the mistresses. I'd say it is rather likely."

"You do look alike," said Sophie.

Keene's attention riveted on her. "I want to speak to you alone."

"I'm leaving." Sophie took a step toward the door. "Amelia, are you staying here?"

"That's up to George."

"Lud, he isn't the one to make any decisions right now. I'm sure he's three sheets to the wind." Impatience tempered Sophie's voice. She didn't want to speak with Keene alone, yet she owed him a private account of her decision to leave him.

"I have been drinking," said George solemnly. "I believe I

should never touch the stuff again. I'm not quite in my right mind when I have imbibed too freely."

"You're right. I'm staying here, George. This is my home and my daughter's home, and I won't be parted from her again."

"Ah, but how else could George insure your return?" asked Victor facetiously.

"You held Regina hostage for my return?" She pressed her lips together and lowered her head. "I wanted nothing more than to come home to you, but I won't tolerate such use of my child ever again."

George stood. "She should be abed. If she is kept up too long she will be quite out of sorts tomorrow, poor tyke."

Amelia gathered the infant from Mary Frances's arms, and they walked to the door as a family, George's arm around his wife.

Victor turned toward Mary Frances. "If we're going to Gretna Green we should be off, but we need a bit of blunt to see us there."

Mary Frances opened the reticule she had dangling from her wrist. She pulled out a wad of banknotes. "Will this be enough? I do have this brooch we might sell, and of course some of your fobs might fetch a pretty penny."

Victor's eyes nearly popped out of his sockets. "Lord, I had no idea you were wearing such enchanting stuff." He bowed to Keene. "I trust you shall look in on George a time or two."

"Perhaps I shouldn't. I am very near to killing him for putting Sophie at risk."

Victor shook his head and led Mary Frances to the door.

Keene pushed the door shut behind them. Sophie stood in front of the window with her back to him. When he had crashed into the small salon earlier he had wanted nothing more than to hold her and comfort her, but she was in Victor's arms and a jealous rage overtook his reason.

He moved across the floor to stand behind her. He leaned

forward to kiss her shoulder. "I believe we were interrupted at a most inopportune moment before."

She stepped away. "I don't believe the servants will be able to get everything inside before it is saturated. Did Amelia give you your jacket?"

His damp shirt suddenly chilled him. He reached out and wrapped his arms around Sophie. He wanted to continue what he started to say before Victor burst in on them, to tell her that he loved her. He found her hands and turned them over so he could see her palms. The red abrasions across her fingers and palms made his heart race from remembered fear. "I've never been more frightened in my life."

She pulled out of his embrace. "Don't lecture me, Keene."

His hands dropped uselessly to his sides. "I'm not lecturing you. I'm telling you how very scared I was." Didn't she understand how hard it was for him to admit to fear—no, terror? "I should have died if you fell."

She shook her head and walked across the floor toward the table that had been knocked over earlier and leaned over to right it. She stood, folded her arms across her chest and looked at him, her head cocked sideways. "I've decided to go home."

His world dropped out from under him. "You can't."

"I thought you told me when I asked about the marriage settlement that I could go home anytime I wanted."

"Why? You like London, the dancing, the amusements . . ." The expression on her face made his voice trail off.

"I do like the dancing and the company, but Amelia hates every minute she is away from her daughter. Mary Frances sees the parties as a means to an end." Sophie shrugged. "It's all so empty and meaningless without sharing the pleasures with those you love. I want to go home to my parents."

Was she simply homesick? "For a visit?"

She shook her head.

With each turn of her head another shard of stunned dismay sliced through him. Facing losing her twice in the space of an hour tore him to shreds. "I can't let you go."

"Didn't we just go through this?" She gestured toward the ceiling.

He was still reeling from Victor's revelation; this was too much for him to handle. He dropped to a settee and stared at her. Half a second later he sprang to his feet and crossed the room. He grabbed her shoulders. "You can't leave me."

"You don't want me here, and I'm not happy."

The protest that rose to his lips died at her statement of unhappiness. He stared into her blue eyes and wondered where he had gone so wrong. "Is it because I am not my father's son?"

She snorted in impatience. "As if that should change who you are."

"What, then, Sophie? Forgive me for being so selfish earlier this evening, for I shall make it up to you. I want nothing more than to finish making love to you."

A softness washed over her face and her voice grew husky. "What more was there?"

"There was this." He kissed her.

She shook him off. He could see the resolution in her squared shoulders. "I believe we did that already."

"Ah, but there is more I have to show you." The heightened cadence of her breathing gave him hope. She wasn't adverse to him. "Sophie, my pet, I want to hold you and touch you and make you feel as wonderful as you made me feel."

She pulled away, and he stared at her as she crossed the room, one hand holding her other elbow. "I still think I should return home."

He swallowed hard. "If you should be happier at your parents' house, then we shall both go there."

She swiveled around. "But your political designs."

He stepped toward her. "I daresay the world shall survive without my machinations."

Her lip quivered. "Why should you torture us both with your presence? You should be happier here."

"I shall be happier with you."

"You avoid me like the plague."

"And more the fool I, because there is no place I'd rather be than in your arms." He took a step toward her. Would she keep running from him?

"I would rather leave alone."

She walked to the door and his soul ripped out as she reached for the doorknob.

"Don't leave me, Sophie. Everyone I have ever loved has left me."

She hesitated with her back to him. "That's not true."

He stepped closer to her. What did he have to lose? If she left, he would be nothing. "My mother, my brother."

"They didn't leave you. They died."

"And you throw yourself into danger at every turn. I dread your reckless disregard of your person. I would have no reason to live if you had fallen to the street."

"Keene, you avoid me at every turn."

His stupid belief that she was pregnant. "Because I could hardly bear to see you and not make you my wife. Bloody hell, Sophie, I waited as long as I could, only to learn it was for naught. There was never a reason to wait."

Her hand dropped off the doorknob, and she slowly turned around. "Why the wait?"

"Because I thought you carried another man's child."

He could see her protest before it left her lips. He held up his hand.

"I didn't care that you carried another man's child. I only wanted you to tell me, to not deceive me. I didn't want to give you the ammunition to pretend your unborn babe was mine. I love you. I've always loved you."

She stared at him, her lovely blue eyes filling with tears. "But I came to you."

He took a step forward, holding out his arms. "Not a moment too soon. I had been to your room earlier, but you weren't there."

She looked less than half convinced.

His arms remained empty, a gaping chasm between them. "I think my father must have realized how I felt about you. He forced my hand, but marriage wasn't my only option. I've managed to get by all of my adult life without his assistance. I'd often thought I could go to India and make my own way in the world, but it was marriage to you he offered me." His voice broke. "I wanted that more than I—"

She crashed into his chest, and he wrapped his arms around her, holding her tight. He'd never let her go.

"I love you, Sophie, and I shall spend the rest of my life trying to make you happy. I don't think I could have avoided you any longer, even if your kisses had meant my death."

She pressed her lips to the underside of his chin. "My unruliness is not contagious."

He tilted her head back to drink in her face. "You are a bit wild."

She yanked his head down and kissed him on the mouth. She pulled back and stared at him. He felt measured and found wanting. If he could just have another chance, he would find a way to bring her the moon and the stars if he had to rip them from the sky.

"I suppose that was rather too bold of me, and I should not have run across the room to you."

"I love that you run to me. I love your enthusiasm for life. I'm so sorry my distance has hurt you. Wounding you was never my intention. I just wanted to protect myself." He stroked his fingers down her neck.

Her lips parted as she tilted her head back. He couldn't resist the invitation. He ended the kiss only after she eagerly clung to him with a magic that threatened his control. "Ah, love, I know I've made a hash of our marriage, but if you give me another chance, I shall endeavor to make you love me."

"Oh, Keene, I already do. I always have."

With her fevered avowal his world righted itself. His grin threatened to split his face in two.

"I thought you hated me. You always lecture me so."

"I do so wish you would try to stay on the inside of the upper stories. Your safety means everything to me."

She frowned.

"Ah, and Sophie, when you raise your skirts and run down the hall it requires every ounce of my willpower to resist scooping you up and carrying you to my bed. You have the most delectable ankles and knees and—"

"There is no need to resist any longer. I am quite happy in your bed."

"Well, then, there is only one thing left to do."

"That is?"

"Find a bed and complete your instruction in making love."

Sophie cast a glance around the room. "A sofa won't do?"

"I'm afraid it will have to." He released the few buttons fastened on his shirt. "For I don't think I could wait long enough to get you home."

She pushed his shirt from his shoulders. And he bit back his groan of enthusiasm. His need was nearly as overpowering as before, but this time, if it killed him, he was doing it right—for her, for their future, forever.